Table of Contents

The Hunter's

Book One

By Tommika Larkin

Dedication

To the little girl who was too frightened....... I forgive you. Stay in Veyloris as long as you need.

Prologue

"He who fights with monsters should be careful lest he thereby become a monster."

— Friedrich Nietzsche

The Huntstone

I was not silent.

I was waiting.

Waiting is not ignorance. It is discipline.

I have endured centuries of stillness, not blindness. I have watched crowns rise and fracture. I have watched councils rot beneath words like *balance* and *neutrality*. I have recorded every oath sworn to ideals and broken the moment power felt heavy.

The prophecy does not awaken for noise.

It awakens for alignment.

The first stirring came with a birth.

No ritual marked it. No god claimed it aloud. Only a fracture in pattern; a life born carrying too much weight for one soul. Fire where there should have been caution. Shadow where there should have been fear.

I noted her.

Then I slept again.

Not because the moment had passed but because the world was not yet ready to be judged.

The Academy continued like it always had. Hunters were trained. Directors were chosen. Loyalty was spoken of as virtue rather than necessity. I allowed the illusion to persist.

But illusion requires enforcement.

Each third year, they are brought to me.

Not to be tested for strength. Not for obedience.

For alignment.

I bind those who kneel before me not to the Academy's rules, but to its purpose. I measure what they will become under pressure, not what they believe themselves to be. Those who align rise as Hunters, oath-bound beyond court, council, and crown.

Those who do not... leave.

Their memories of me are stripped away. Cleanly. Thoroughly. Without cruelty.

Knowledge of prophecy is not a right.

It is a burden.

The same judgment is rendered upon every Director.

Titles mean nothing to me. Intent does.

Those who align are permitted to rule in stewardship. Those who do not are unmade — not in body, but in knowing.

For that task, another was bound.

The Warlock of Secrets.

His bargain was struck long before the current courts remember how to fear properly. Immortality, in exchange for silence. Precision. Restraint. He erases only what must never be carried beyond these walls the Huntstone, the archive, the architecture of prophecy.

He does not punish.

He preserves.

I do not wake fully for births.

I do not wake fully for wars.

But when she crossed the threshold of my grounds, the wards tightened.

Stone remembered.

Ley-lines drew breath.

Awareness became attention.

One thread anchored.

One thread observed.

One thread carried memory older than his own name.

Three.

Not chosen.

Not summoned.

Aligned.

They believe this is about power.

They believe this is about loyalty.

They believe this is about love.

They are not entirely wrong.

Love is the most destabilizing variable of all.

It forges.

Or it fractures.

And prophecy does not distinguish between the two.

The God Trials are not vengeance. They are assessment. They have come before — when realms mistook survival for worthiness, when unity fractured into prideful dominions too divided to stand.

This realm was spared once.

It will not be spared again without proof.

I am not the architect of prophecy.

I am its witness.

I do not choose rulers.

I prepare them.

What rises now is not a crown.

It is convergence.

And this time, I am awake.

Chapter One: Arrival

"Man is nothing else but what he makes of himself."

—Jean-Paul Sartre

Allyssa POV

I'm in cuffs. Again.

Not just cuffs; enchanted ones. Ironwood and Fae-forged, locked tight around my wrists, humming like a damned lie detector. Designed to suppress magic. I heap sarcasm into every word as I remember what the Hunters told me as they secured me into them. Appear weaker than you are. Let them underestimate you. It keeps them sloppy. I let them think they have me leashed. It's adorable, really; like chaining a hurricane with twine. They think the cuffs will hold me. But they're a symbol of a world that would rather leash me than see me rule.

The Hunters flanking me are tall, silent, dressed in regulation black, a sigil seal printed on their sleeves in bronze, the tree of life surrounded by runes that translate to "all things in balance", and a wolf his head bowed in front. They hold my arms like I'm a rabid animal. Probably because I *am*. Or maybe it's because I broke one's nose and bruised another's rib on the way here. I didn't even mean to. Reflex. Still healing, poor bastards. I learned early: control is an illusion. Power is the only real currency.

Winter cycle had claimed Veyloris early this year. Snow blanketed the mountain roads, muffling sound and sharpening the world into clean edges. I preferred it this way. Winter cycle stripped things down to what mattered. Cold was honest. We're tearing through Iseryth Dominion (Seelie territory), almost missing its capital Aureslong in the distance, on a glass-bottom hovercraft thing that slices through the silver forest like a blade. Open sides, air cold and electric, smelling of ozone and crushed pine. The driver, some Fae-blood with a jawline that could cut glass spins a glowing globe between his fingers like it's a toy. I watch it, trying not to roll my eyes. Show-offs. I thought they were taking me to the Seelie courts for what I did to that Mac soithigh of a foster father. The road carved through the northern spine of Veyloris, the jagged mountains rising like the ribs of some ancient beast. To my left, the forests of the Lyrravene Wilds shuddered with their own intelligence. To my right, the distant shimmer of Calyxion, the Tribunal's glass citadel, mocked the horizon.

They weren't. They're bringing me to The Academy, The Verdant Athenaeum as the elders call it, no one calls it that anymore. The Academy rose from the valley like a cathedral grown rather than built. Mother Nature's mark was unmistakable. Vines that glowed faintly with magic wound along stone older than any kingdom in Veyloris. We screech to a halt at the gates, magic pulsing through the wrought-iron symbols of a wolf and the tree of life. The Academy looms behind them, sprawling and gothic like some medieval fortress ripped from a fever dream. Ivy strangling stone like it's holding a personal grudge. Towers stretching for the blood-orange sky like they're trying to claw their way out. It's beautiful in that tragic way; like a corpse dressed for a ball. This place reeks of power. Old power. I can *taste* it. The Seelie and Unseelie courts are a kingdom of masks. The Academy is a kingdom of hunters. And I? I am the wolf they all fear.

The cold sharpened everything. The air. The stone. The silence. Something old and quiet stirred inside me, counting distances. Doors. Lines of sight. *No corners. Don't turn your back, it whispered to me like it always did.* I breathed through it until the pressure eased, filing the instincts away where they belonged. They had kept me alive once. Now it advises and I keep it in its cage. Somewhere deeper inside, something smaller wondered what it might be like to belong. The feeling cut off just as fast, feeling the vulnerability like the threat it was.

Students entered the Academy willingly now, most between eighteen and twenty-five, and left as Hunters three years later if they survived the training. Loyalty was not optional. Once sworn, it bound tighter than blood. No Hunter ever truly left the Academy. They were deployed. Never dismissed.

The forest surrounding the Academy is like nothing in the mortal realm. The trees here are vivid, some ancient hybrid between pine and predator snapping shut if you get too close. Like nature's version of a bitchy door policy. Gorgeous, dangerous, my type of place, I belong here already. They're bringing me in like this I look over myself; leashed, filthy, smiling. I make sure I'm smiling. Let them see the monster. Let them stare. Their judgment amuses me. Let them gather around for the show; hopefully they brought snacks.

The guards march me up a polished rune etched stone path toward the Administration building. Protection and safety runes I realised. I'm hyperaware of how tightly their fingers dig into my arms; like I might explode at any moment. They're not wrong. I look left. The blond one pretty sure one of the other called him *Matthews* catches my eye. "So," I purr in my most saccharine English accent, "do I wave now? Or sign autographs?" He bites back a grin and almost flinches in the process, I like him. The lead female fae doesn't even glance back. Well that is a little rude, now I have to keep up my bitchy wit.

"I bet she's just *riveting* in bed," I murmur. "All that anger. Pillow-biting levels of fun." Matthews laughs. Then leans in close.

Mistake.

My breath stops.

Flesh memory sears across my brain like a cattle brand; hands too rough, breath too close, trust always betrayed. My instincts scream violence, but I freeze instead. I *hate* that I freeze, the self-loathing coming off me is stifling. "I shouldn't laugh,"

Matthews whispers, his tone low and unexpectedly soft. "But you're making it difficult." I force the smirk back onto my face, while that part of me that demands I stand tall, snaps the mask into place. He saw it, the raw, and that cannot be allowed. I shove the panic down. Deeper, lifting my chin, feeling the strength from within settle me.

"Gods," one whispered, "a Black Wolf hasn't crossed the borders of the Verdfall since the fall of Stormglen Pack.

"They say she's marked," one of the guards muttered under his breath, not quite quiet enough.

"What, like the others?"

"Worse. Heard the Warlock's watching her."

"You mean *him*? The one who walks between lifetimes?"

"The one who remembers," the first said, voice low. "They call him the Warlock of Secrets. Makes your soul forget itself, if he wants. Burned the name of the last Tribunal out of the stone."

I didn't flinch. But inside, something pulled taut.

Warlock of Secrets.

I didn't know why, but the name tasted familiar. Like a warning. Like home. Something pulled at me across Veyloris, through ley lines, through shadow paths, a whisper older than the Seelie courts of Aurelsong, older even than the Unseelie abyss of Umbrakyn. There's something about this place... It's in the air. Like a song I almost remember. My blood starts to buzz, hot and twitching beneath my skin. Then it hits me. A Heartbeat, Fast. Frantic. Not mine.

It drums in my head like war, overlaying the pounding in my veins. My nostrils flare as the scent slams into me; vanilla and rain. Comfort and clean violence. It instantly calms the beast within and anchors me to the here and now. It also sends a sliver of arousal up my spine. Diabhal é. The scent of him is a claim I didn't ask for. But now it's mine. And I'll tear the world apart to keep it.

All I can think is: Mine, mine, mine. The possessiveness hits me like a sledgehammer. Why the fuck do I feel so possessive over this natural's scent?

My wolf *shreds* through the surface. I growl, low and primal, as my skin starts to burn. My bones itch to snap and twist into my other form. Looking down at my half-transformed hands, I realize these cuffs may block my magic, a satisfied smirk crosses my lips, but these Na leathcheanna forgot one thing. They didn't use silver. Their mistake. And one I'm going to use to my advantage.

"Matthews," the brunette mutters, A warning? Or fear? I don't really care. I need to get to find that intoxicatingly amazing scent.

"Cooper," Matthews yells, seeing my body trembling from the force of holding my shift and my claws pushing through. "She's shifting!" Cooper turns her expression annoyed then she sees me and finally registers what is happening. Her face goes pale, her eyes widen in fear, sweet, delicious fear, she opens her mouth to shout a command. A sinister smile engulfs my face "too A chailleach". With a feral snarl, I *snap* the cuffs and transform. My wolf explodes out of me; fur black as void, eyes glowing a blinding aqua. Gasps erupt, screams of fear surround me like music to my ears and I growl low and fierce. Students scatter. I don't wait. I *run*.

The smell of blood pulls me, tugging my instincts like a leash. Past trees that seem to breathe, past Wisteria blossoms that sway and whisper in a wind that doesn't exist. For a heartbeat, they seem to know me. Then I find him. Caspian. His name barrels through my head, a voice I've never heard before. He's bleeding, vanilla and rain turned copper and iron.

Three males tower over him two blondes and a brunette all over six foot, all muscle and malice obviously bred for combat. The two blondes look like they have had one too many broken noses turning their noses permanently crooked, the brunette has a bad case of Colliflower ear on his left a sneer that says he's used to getting away with this and getting in Caspian's face laughing and calling him names like half breed and bastard. It looks like they have been hitting him, Caspian's lip is split and there are deep bruises all over his arms and face. They've shredded his shirt and humiliated him. Three on one fucking pathetic excuse for hunters, if they could ever be called such a thing, not if I have my way. I don't get the chance to marvel and take in Caspian's beauty.

Something in me *answers to my bloodlust roaring*. Familiar. The red haze descends. I want to tear their throats out. I want to *drown* in their screams. But then... his eyes meet mine. Ocean-blue. Fae-wolf hybrid. Fragile. *Mine*. And all that bloodlust? It reorients. Refocuses. Not gone, just... redirected. I shift back; naked, bare, unapologetic. Their eyes rove over me with hunger and awe and fear. Predators, but they've forgotten who the apex is here. Amadáin.

They forget what I am when I'm not fur and fang. I drop into a crouch, naked, unashamed. They stare mouths agape like prey caught in headlights. That's all they are. The first one rushes me; blond, overconfident. I don't even flinch. I spin, low and sharp, my leg sweeping his out from under him with a sickening *crack*. He yelps. Hits the ground. My fist finds his jaw twice before he blacks out. One down. The second grabs my shoulder. Mistake. I pivot, grip his wrist, and twist until I hear the satisfying *pop* of dislocation. He screams. I smile cruelly, satisfaction overtaking my features. Then drive my knee into his face. His nose collapses like a rotted peach. He falls sobbing, blood gurgling from his mouth. Two down. The third one, the one with the dark hair and trembling hands, lifts them in surrender. Smart. But not smart enough. Because I can smell his fear; rich and sweet, like burnt caramel. It drips off him like sweat. My pupils dilate. The wolf in me howls with approval. I stalk toward him slowly. His lips tremble. He tries to say something, plead, maybe, but I don't care. His terror makes my veins sing.

He thinks he's safe. He's *not.* I punch him anyway. Once. Twice. Blood sprays. My knuckles split, but I don't feel it. His face has a myriad of beautiful splits from my blows, eyebrow, cheek, lip, all bleeding, I love seeing the colour red run over their faces, a masterpiece of rage. I grab his collar and yank him close, letting him see it; the madness just under my skin, the darkness licking at my bones like wildfire. His wrist snaps under my grip. The crack echoes. He screams. Gods, I love that sound. I lean close. "You don't get to look at him like that," I whisper, voice thick with something ancient and unhinged. "You don't get to exist near him." I raise my fist again.

"Allyssa," His voice. Caspian. The bond pulls like a tide. My arm freezes mid-air.

He's behind me. He's standing there; shaking, bleeding, but his eyes... they're soft. Like he sees past the blood, the dirt, the monster I am. Like he's not afraid of the darkness licking at my bones. He sees everything. The ruin and the rage. And somehow, he stays. Gods help me, I want him to keep staying. Something inside me leaned toward the warmth he offered.

The rest of me closed ranks and crushed it before it could show. I lower my fist. My breath is ragged, and I'm shaking from the inside out. Not from exhaustion. From need. The fight, the blood, the dominance, it feeds me. But Caspian is stronger than all of it. And then it happens. We lock eyes. Everything stops. The world falls away. The trees, the air, the males crawling in the dirt. There's only him. The bond ignites. Like a circuit; sparking, locking, sealing. We're caught in a storm of light and agony.

The bond doesn't just snap. It devours. His soul fills every crack in mine, searing away the rot and ruin until all that's left is him; soft and bright and mine. I have been through too much for my walls to crumble, but Caspian lets me in without reservation, I see *everything*, his fears, his hopes, his gentleness. I offer nothing back. Just protection. It's all I have, it's all I know.

The mark sears into my shoulder blade, luminous atomic rings spun like halos. In the centre, suspended like a moon inside an atom, were his initials: C.A, burning like molten obsidian, his white wolf seared in, a broken crown that makes no sense on the other side. He is mine and I am his. Forever. When time resumes, I'm still on my knees in the dirt, trembling; not from weakness. From restraint. Because I could have killed that male. And part of me wanted to. That part is still whispering. And it sounds an awful lot like me again. This isn't just a test of my strength. It's a test of who I'll become. And I already know the answer. Let them try to break me. Let them try to cage the Black Wolf. He should be running. He should be repulsed. But he's still here, still watching me like I'm worth saving. I hate that he sees it, the raw, the unguarded. I want to snarl, to bite, to drive him away... but he's the only thing that feels like calm in the chaos. He should fear me. He doesn't. And that terrifies me more than the darkness ever could.

Chapter Two: Claimed

"Light thinks it travels faster... the darkness has always got there first, and is waiting for it."

— *Terry Pratchett*

Caspian POV

She stopped. I don't know how, but she did. I expected her to finish him off, to snap his neck like a twig and smile while doing it. She wanted to. I should hate that she smiled when she broke him. Should hate that it made me want her even more. But gods, I'd let her devour the world if she promised to keep me whole. She looked like something beautiful and terrible made flesh. But then I said her name, and everything shifted.

"Allyssa." She didn't respond. Her head tilted slightly, too far to the side to be natural. Not curious. Measuring. Like something inside her was recalculating her surroundings. Her eyes had gone dark. Not fully black. Not yet. But the turquoise I'd noticed earlier had been swallowed from the edges inward, shadow bleeding through like ink dropped into water. She wasn't looking at me. She was looking *through* me.

My instincts flared, sharp and sudden. Not fear exactly. Awareness. The kind you get when you realise you're standing too close to something that doesn't need to prove it's dangerous. I had turned twenty-one in June. Old enough to be dangerous. A year here was enough to sharpen my senses and take notice when in the presence of a predator. Her gaze flicked over my throat. My hands. My stance. Calculating distance. Angle. Outcome. *Safe or not safe, she seemed to be trying to determine.* The same lessons I was taught from my father back in Frostpine.

The air around her felt... compressed. As if she were holding herself together by force alone.

"Allyssa," I said again, quieter this time. Something shifted. The tension snapped, not outward, but inward, like a leash pulled tight. The darkness receded from her eyes in stages. First the black. Then a flash of something feral, silver-bright and ancient. A wolf.

And then, turquoise. She blinked once. Twice. Her posture softened by a fraction, shoulders lowering as though she'd only just realised how tightly they'd been drawn. *Black Wolf,* I told myself. Power. Instinct. Alpha reflexes. That explanation fit well enough. It didn't explain the way my pulse was still racing. Or why I had the distinct, unsettling sense that something inside her had *noticed* me... and decided to let me live.

She turned to me fully then like I was the only solid thing in a world made of glass. Eyes wild. Hair tangled from her shift. Blood dripping down her knuckles. Naked, furious, perfect.

I held out my jacket, she took it. The moment her fingers brushed mine, it was like being struck by lightning in a downpour; shocking and alive and terrifying. Heat coiled up my spine. Not just attraction, or lust. Bond. I knew it in my bones. She's mine. But more terrifying; I'm hers. Her scent washes over me again sweet caramel and crisp mountain air and something darker. I try not to shudder at the way it grounds me. The way it makes me want to fall to my knees and worship her as much as protect her.

She slid the jacket over her shoulders like it belonged to her; which, I guess, it does now. She wrapped the jacket around herself, every movement casual, a faint blush on her cheeks and a hint of want in her eyes, that quickly left as soon as it came to the surface. The way my jacket clung to her felt almost obscene. It hid everything and somehow revealed more. My brain short-circuited, and I had to force myself to look away before I started ogling like I have never seen a female before. Never have I ever been jealous of an item of clothing before and holy fuck those long sexy as sin legs on display... "*Keep it together*" my wolf berates me even though his tongue is lolling out and he is panting like he ran a marathon and I snicker at him internally. I can't keep the fierce blush coating my cheeks from where my thoughts took me however. The bond snapped taut between us like a drawn bowstring, electric and unbreakable.

I couldn't stop staring. Her wolf was like nothing I've ever seen; jet black, eyes glowing aquamarine. But it was her fae form that stole my breath. She's all edges and elegance, scars and strength. Her body is a map of violence and survival. Her power is coiled under her skin like a predator waiting to pounce, and fuck me if that isn't the hottest thing I have ever felt. Damn it, there goes my thoughts again, seriously I know I usually have way more self control than this. Then I look back up and when she looked at me, there was something else. Fear, not of me, of herself. And that, somehow, made me love her more. The way she could break the world but hesitated to break me.

The bond opened. Suddenly, I was falling into her. I saw her the moment I did. Not her memories, not her thoughts. Just... the walls. Towering obsidian spires. Locked doors. Barred windows. Endless corridors, each one colder than the last. It wasn't absence of light. It was structure. Like something built from night itself. The pain of her silence screamed louder than words ever could. Every time I touched a door, it shocked me. Rejected me. Hurt. She didn't mean to, I don't think. But it still broke something inside me. She saw that. I felt it; the flicker of guilt. The soft ache of her apology. She wrapped it in protectiveness, sent it through the bond like a balm. But it wasn't enough. I didn't want her protection. I wanted her to choose me. And she didn't.

The pain of that felt worse than any physical wound. And then came the branding. The Bond Tattoo; Ceangal doscartha. It carved itself into me, white-hot pain down to the marrow. Across my shoulder blade, two luminous atomic rings spun like halos overlapping each other. In the centre, suspended like a moon inside an atom, were her initials: A.M. Glowing. Permanent. Sacred. To the left was her beautiful black wolf and, on the right, a delicate white rose; the symbol of the seelie court where my bloodline hails. Intertwining itself around those halos was mother nature's vines, alive and endless. I collapsed the moment it finished. I barely registered the blur of motion, her foot catching one male, her fist knocking another out cold. She fought like she was born for it, and maybe she was. Maybe we both were. I wanted to help her. But I couldn't move. I was too stunned. Too full of her. She looked like death incarnate, but she was mine. And I was hers, I'm already obsessed

The third male raised his hands, begging. She didn't stop. And I; gods help me; I didn't want her to. I wanted her to show them what she was. I wanted them to fear her. To see the way her rage moved like wildfire. To know what it was like to stand in front of a goddess and feel small. But then... she went too far. Her knuckles cracked into his cheek again and again. His blood painted the dirt. And the look in her eyes; it was rapture. A dark, intoxicating joy that made my wolf inside me curl its tail and watch, reverent and enthralled.

She wasn't just punishing him. She was enjoying it. That's when I called to her again, this time through the bond. Not a command. Not even a plea. Just a whisper: Allyssa. She froze. Turned. And the wild thing behind her eyes... quieted. She pulled away from the male. Her breath ragged. Her body trembling. Not from weakness. From restraint. Her darkness curled around her like smoke. She was holding back. For me. She didn't even know how much that meant. She could end the world with those hands, and I'd still stand beside her, begging to be burned by her fire. I stepped forward, just as three guards burst from the trees, my head whipped in their direction; Matthews among them. Weapons drawn, panic in their eyes. They looked at me like I was her victim.

"Did the wolf do this?" a fae guard asked.

They were ready to blame her. I wasn't going to let that happen. "She saved me," I said. "That's all she did." They didn't believe me I roll my eyes, you could feel the skepticism rolling off the rigid set of their shoulders, the pity in their eyes for what I am sure they think is my naivety. Mr. Lakemond seemed to be no different when he arrived. "Stay away from her," he warned me. "You don't know what she is." But he was wrong. I do. She's the dark half of my soul. The part of me that will burn down the world to keep me alive. And I'm the light she refuses to admit she wants. She didn't let me in today. But I felt it. That flicker. That pull. She wants me. She just doesn't trust herself with me. Not yet. But I'll wait. Even if it kills me. Because even in that moment, even with the blood still warm on her knuckles, I knew: I didn't fear her, much, okay maybe a little. I wanted her even still. All of her; teeth, claws, and the soft places she hides.

I didn't understand it then, but even in that moment, it felt like fate was watching. Like she was always meant to stand above us all.

It wasn't long before I'd learn what Matthews saw that day; and what he chose to keep to himself.

Matthews POV

She ran. Not like a wolf. Like something wounded that refused to bleed in front of witnesses.

Caspian stood in the clearing, still catching his breath, still glowing faintly with bond-magic like it didn't know how to stop. The others were scattering now. The fight was over. The males who thought it smart to provoke a Black Wolf were unconscious; or worse. Serves them right. And Allyssa, after that final blow, after Caspian stopped her with nothing more than a voice and a hand she had disappeared into the trees like smoke. I noticed her shadows though not quite staying in line with her, taking note of that and letting Lakemond know, it's important. But Caspian stayed looking longingly at her retreating wolf, fingers curled into fists in obvious war on if he should follow or give her space. He bends down and winces in discomfort while picking up the discarded jacket and smelling it as if no one was watching, sighing in comfort at what I assume is Allyssa's scent.

I don't know why I waited. Maybe because I'd seen him before. Once, during a fire drill; he shielded two younger students with a failing ward and refused to move until they were safe. Another time, giving his own rations to a starving dryad refugee while pretending he'd "already eaten." The male was too soft for this world. But there was steel under all that sweetness. And he'd just commanded the Black Wolf with nothing more than a word.

That... unsettled me. Then the other Hunters arrived with Lakemond and they all burst through the tree line in a panic, I just stood out with them. Caspian pointed them in the wrong direction but Lakemond saw the tracks and found her scent before taking off, I stayed. Caspian turned, cautious but not afraid. "She's something, isn't she?" I said. He gave a half-smile, his eyes holding a little extra shine, and replied. "Something." There was no accusation in it. No pride either. Just awe. And worry. I sighed, crossing the few steps to him and offering my waterskin. He took it. Drank. Nodded his thanks.

"She isn't always like this," I said. He glanced at me, eyebrows raised. "I was there when they pulled her from her stepfather's house." "They didn't assign just anyone to find her," I added, lowering my voice. "They put him on her case. The Warlock of Secrets. The one who walks between lifetimes." Caspian blinked. "He's real?" "Very," I said. "He's bonded to five Black Wolves before her. They say he remembers every soul he's ever served. Some say he *remakes* the ones he chooses."

"Is he dangerous?" "He's a paradox," I said. "He burns memories into you, from you, finds your deepest secrets as payment, conjures that you most desire. And when he's done? You'll thank him for it. His reach is terrifying" I went back to recounting the experience to him "Last night. Almost eighteen. We thought we were picking up a student. Not a massacre." Caspian flinched. "She had no mercy. Not like a warrior. Like something that enjoyed it. We found her covered in blood, straddling her stepfather on the basement floor, he had precise cuts to his lower arms and legs, deep gashes along his chest, she had sliced in his abdomen where she had reached through and pulled his lower intestines through, not all the way, only enough to cause pain but keep him alive by packing the sides with rags to keep him from bleeding out. He had burns all over his neck and back while she had carved her initials into his upper arms over and over. She had castrated him, the most terrifying... her stepfather's face peeled half off in her hands like she'd been... studying it. Not rage. Not panic. Curiosity."

Caspian paled, his eyes growing wider throughout my recounting.

"And when we pulled her off, she looked at me like I'd interrupted a private moment. Not embarrassed. Just... annoyed." He opened his mouth. Closed it again.

"She didn't cry," I said. "Didn't panic. Just sat there, like we were late. And I swear to the gods... she wasn't angry. She was calm."

"She was hurting," he whispered.

"Yes. But not just from what he did. From being ignored. From being unheard. She spent nearly twelve years under that monster's roof. Physically abused. Emotionally gutted. And... from what Lakemond uncovered... sexually abused. From age six to twelve. Then he moved on. Waited. Until the day she snapped."

"What made her snap?" he asked.

"No one knows," I said. "Not for sure. Only the Director has that piece. Whatever it was, it broke her silence. And she made damn sure he wouldn't hurt anyone else ever again." Caspian's hands curled into fists. His breathing had gone shallow. "You know her file went missing, right?" I said quietly. He blinked. "What?"

"Her entire case was buried. Surveillance orbs never reported in. The old Director? Complicit or negligent. Her intake records were forged. Trauma scans edited. They pretended she was just another feral. Another half breed with an attitude. The Tribunal let it happen." I let the weight of it settle. "Lakemond found it all. Dug through the lies. Matched timelines. Interviewed healers. Found bones that shouldn't have healed. Found scars that didn't belong on a child. At least that is the gossip mill says in the fully pledged circle anyways" The forest was silent. "She didn't survive it," I said. "She outlived it." I leaned back against a tree. "She will protect you. From everything. From herself. That matters. But don't think that means she's safe. Or that you are."

His voice was soft. "I don't want her to be alone in it." That caught me. I studied his face depper to see his emotions as if they would give me insight into the future but there was no pity, just respect.

"Then don't try to fix her," I said. "Just don't flinch when she shows you the worst parts." I stood, communication orb buzzing; Lakemond. I was being recalled. Meetings. Strategy. Allyssa. Adjusting my blades, I hesitated. "If you're not careful, she won't break you. She'll make you watch as you break yourself for her." I turned toward the shadows. "She's not just dangerous," I added. "She's necessary. But that means the world will always want to leash her.

"And the warlock? He's not here to leash her," I said quietly. "He's here because she's the one soul he can never forget. That's what makes him dangerous." Caspian looked at me like he'd just been handed a blade with no instructions. "Be careful with your heart," I warned. "Because the moment she accepts his... it will change everything." But you... you're the only one she might let close enough to hold the line."

Caspian didn't speak. But I saw the answer in his eyes. He already had. What they don't know is that the Tribunal is watching. They're waiting for the Black Wolf to slip; to either leash her or destroy her. And they'll use Caspian to do it. But I, along with the Director and the rest of the active Hunters, we're working in the shadows. We're biding our time. Helping her; helping Allyssa; in any way we can. Because we see what they don't. We know she's not just another wild half-breed to be put down. She's the future leader. The future queen.

Chapter Three: The Fall and the Flame

"What matters most is how well you walk through the fire." — Charles Bukowski

Allyssa POV

I ran. Fast and hard, like the fucking world was nipping at my heels. Running isn't just survival. It's control. And control is the only thing that keeps me from becoming something worse than a monster. Like if I slowed down, the truth would catch me. And that; *that;* I couldn't survive. Trees whipped past in a blur of green and blood memory. Wisteria limbs reached out like old gods trying to claim me. I didn't stop. I couldn't. I'd just bonded with someone, Caspian, his name in my mind forcing me to gasp at how much I love his name and how unwelcomed those thoughts are, traitorous mind. This is permanent, that clawing sensation of being trapped comes over me, my skin feeling itchy and tight. Irrevocably, this can't be undone, there is no way back, those thoughts spur my legs to move even faster, avoidance always the best strategy... right..... "What the actual fuck was the goddess mother nature smoking? I want a hit." My inner bitch helpfully supplies the answer. Because she hasn't fucked with my head enough, obviously. She had to give me a bond to someone who not only wants to see the softest parts of me but one that I could so easily break, she either has gone insane or she has more faith in my self-control than I do.

My heart roared in my chest, not from fear; don't be stupid; I don't get scared. Not really. It was rage. Confusion. Desperation. The raw ache of not being in control. That's the thing, isn't it? I *choose* who gets close. I *choose* who sees me bleed. And now this naive youngling; this beautiful, soft-eyed male with loyalty stitched into his soul, I scoff at my thoughts calling Caspian a youngling is ridiculous with the muscles that were bulging, the expanse of his chest, and the three day old scruff he was wearing, but there was this air of naivety those eyes that held so much compassion for a world so cruel, that youngling, seemed like the right fit but he saw too much. And worse? He didn't *flinch*. Not when I broke bones. Not when I smiled through blood. He *wanted* me. Fucking idiot gave me his jacket and the look he was giving me, like I was his every dream and fantasy, I wasn't sure why I didn't respond violently to him looking at my body like that. Especially since the damage I did to the males that looked at my body but his gaze was different, it didn't make my skin crawl.

The bond didn't just snap. It devoured. His soul poured into mine like molten gold, too bright, too soft, too much. My heart stuttered, my breath caught, and I wanted to tear it all away. But I didn't. His feelings rushed through the bond like a freight train I didn't ask for, warmth, worry, *want*. I could feel his yearning for me like a hand curling around my throat. It felt like a crown, like a leash. And I don't let anyone leash me. Not even him. So I did the only thing I could. I shoved the bond behind a wall. Thick. Brutal. Untouchable. Like everything else inside me. He didn't need to feel what I was feeling right now; this need to devour and protect in equal measure. It's not safe. *I'm not safe.* Especially not for him.

Behind me, I heard the snap of branches, the slicing of air and the scent of another wolf. Someone was following. I grinned; this is what I needed. *Good let them try*. Let them see what it means to come up against the Black Wolf. I twisted through the trees, breath steady, body electric with speed and the thrill of the challenge. The forest thickened, growing wilder the deeper I went. Vines slithered beneath my feet like they recognized me. But then; the weight hit me, hard. A second wolf, bigger, heavier, trained came at me from the side, caught off guard by my split attention. We tumbled down an embankment in a tangle of fur and rage, growling, clawing. Every nerve in me howled for dominance.

He pinned me. *Pinned me.* The fucker was pressing me to the dirt, growling low, demanding I submit, fucking laughable thinking the release of an alpha aura would do the job. Compared to mine his is child's play. He is expecting me to submit to his alpha aura but I just chuckle in wolf form. For a split second, I considered killing him, I could feel his power radiating from him, my own magic roiling across my skin trying to get out, lash out. I am still yet to figure out what element I have control of. I know I am half fae, but what kind of fae, I have no idea.

Then I freeze. Not from fear. Curiosity. Does he see me for what I am? Something to be controlled. Something to be weaponised. Something to be worshipped, if that druid male was to be believed. The questions are old. Older than this realm. Older than the night the portal tore open in front of me in the mortal world and my body moved before my mind could argue. I hadn't chosen to run.

I had obeyed something deeper. Something under my skin. Something that had already begun to coil. There had been blood before that night. A lot of it. Purpose carved from violence.

Structure built from instinct. A place where my hunger had not been questioned — only rewarded. It had been all consuming, but it was starting to feel like it wasn't enough.

Until the portal. Until this realm. And now here he stands. Another wolf. Another man with answers. I need to know what he sees when he looks at me. Because if he sees a weapon—

He won't live long enough to use me.

My hackles rise. The fur at the back of my neck prickles. Not fear. Warning. His answers now will determine if I stay in this makeshift prison or not. He shifted first, a tall male, maybe in his thirties. Brown hair, soft brown eyes, puppy dog eyes, which meant I immediately didn't trust him. Noone with that look is to be trusted, they look all trustworthy, but they are the most dangerous, no one suspects them.

"Allyssa," he said, backing off, hands raised in peace. "I'd prefer if we could talk in your fae form." I stayed in my wolf form and snarled, fuck your comfort. He sighed like a male used to resistance and expected nothing less from me. "I'm Director Lakemond," he offered, digging into a bag for clothes, is that why I feel like I know him, have I smelt his scent somewhere before. "Not that you'll give a shit. But I'm not your enemy." That made me bark out a laugh; dark and sharp. That's rich, everyone is my enemy because no one can really be trusted thus an enemy. The clothes he pulls out just a pair of sweatpants for himself and a crop top and boyleg booty shorts for me. He puts the sweatpants on with practice moves not taking his eyes off me, smart, and lays the clothes for me in front of himself.

"The Tribunal wouldn't send just anyone to find your kind of storm," he added, voice softer now. "They sent someone who's done it before. The Warlock of Secrets he's been watching from the day I looked into your file my predecessor left." I stilled. That name. It wasn't just rumour, he is real. As if he could read my mind "Very real," Lakemond confirmed. "Bonded to five Black Wolves before you. They say he remembers everything. Even the things you wish he wouldn't." "Not that he works for the tribunal, pretty sure he just informed them of his plan to be involved so they wouldn't send anyone else" Lakemond said under his breath.

I circled him, slow and deliberate, the way a queen walks among her court; dangerous, coiled, and untouchable. I could feel the fae and wolf hunters closing in, their panic practically vibrating through the trees. I give a wolfish grin as the threat of a fight pulsates in the air, good, let them fear me. Let them know exactly what I am, I'm not here to make friends. I'm here to command that voice within helpfully provides. Because one day, I will be more than just the Black Wolf. And they will all kneel. "I know what you did to your foster father," Lakemond said, voice quiet but even. "And I don't blame you."

I stopped, mid-circle cocking my head to the side analysing his face to see if he is fucking with me. I turned back into fae, slow and proud, not bothering with shame or modesty as I pulled the clothes over my skin, the clothes tight and still showing the tiny white scars that score my abdomen and thighs. I keep studying him, seeing if I can catch a chink in the façade. He didn't look away but kept eye contact out of respect. Good. I wouldn't respect him if he did look away. "You're not here to punish me," I said, stepping forward, voice calm, eyes burning. "So why the fuck *are* you here?" The queen in me recognised the game immediately.

His smile was sad. Like he knew exactly how fucked I was and still hoped I'd figure it out. "Because if you don't find a way to control what's inside you, you'll destroy everything, and everyone, who tries to love you." I don't flinch. I don't break. He said it like he was handing me a lifeline. But we both knew it was just a leash with better marketing. He's not wrong, and that pisses me off even more. "You sound like you've rehearsed that little monologue," I sneered. "Did you write it on your way here? Or is that just what you tell all the psychopaths you collect?" His smile widened. "Only the ones destined to lead."

That stopped me, scrunching up my face to show my annoyance at his statement. "What?" "You think people fear you because of your power?" he said, stepping closer. He doesn't flinch. Smart man. But there's something in his eyes. Like he sees the crown I've never worn and already knows it's mine. "They fear you because you were born to wear a crown. And no one knows how to bow anymore." "Veyloris has not seen a Triskillian alignment in over a few thousand years," Lakemond said, voice hushed as if the stones themselves remembered. "Not even in the reign of the

High Wolves of Frostpine." I hated how much I liked hearing that, I hated how true it felt. His words coiled inside me like a prophecy I'd always known but never dared speak. My wolf is preening like the compliment unlocked a praise kink that I was sure we didn't possess previously. I'm not sure what he was offering in that moment, loyalty? Respect? Something more? What I did see however, is the fear behind his eyes, smart. His gaze held conviction along with that fear, they all fear me, and I like it that way. If they fear me, they won't try to own me, they won't try to fix me, they won't be able to fucking hurt me or catch me off guard ever. And yet... somewhere in the haze of bond-static and bloodlust, I felt it again. That flicker. Like a finger trailing through the edge of my thoughts. Not Caspian. No, this one felt older. More dangerous. A presence I'd forgotten I remembered. Cold magic and warm hands. *He* was watching. Or worse waiting. His magic slid through the air like a shadow peeled from the old Warlock enclaves of Draethen, volatile, hungry, and devastatingly patient.

Lakemond watches me like I'm going to snap his neck any second. Perhaps I would, Im a little unpredictable when the bloodlust is still waring for control. I cross my arms and lean against a twisted tree trunk, letting the silence stretch like a loaded gun. Let him sweat, I want to see how long it takes before he squirms a sick analysing smirk lifts the side of my mouth, I do love a bit of psychological mind fucks. To my disappointment however, he doesn't move or squirm under my silence and my smirk falls into indifference, not bad teach. "Alright, Director Puppy Eyes," I say finally, voice dripping with venom-laced amusement. "You've had your heartfelt TED Talk. Now tell me; where's the male?"

Lakemond raises an eyebrow. "Caspian?" "No," I deadpan. "The other male I bonded with in the woods while covered in someone else's blood. Yes, Caspian." A twitch at the corner of his mouth gives away his stoic mask. Oh? Amused, are we? "Well?" I press, the casual tone in my voice doing a piss-poor job of hiding the sharp fucking need underneath. "Is he alright? Or did your Hunters freak out and toss him in a cell for public indecency and getting his face punched in?"

"He's resting," Lakemond says. "No punishment. He defended you, in fact, quite adamantly." I blink, once, then snort. "Defended *me*?"

"Yes." He says with a straight face. He better not be serious, I do not need to owe anyone anything here.

"Like... verbally?" I push further, just to be sure I have the extent he went to.

"Yes." He replies eyebrows raised in challenge to his statement.

I blink again, Fuck sakes "I didn't ask for his protection. I didn't ask for anything. Except maybe a stiff drink and a map out of my own head." and is that a glimmer of pride I'm feeling. I look away, lips twitching. "Fucking idiot," I mutter, not appreciating this new development of feelings, eww.

Lakemond doesn't ask if I mean it, he heard me clearly choosing not to acknowledge it. "He said you saved him," he adds gently. "That you only hurt those who deserved it." I stare at the forest, my expression flat. "Yeah," I murmur, voice colder now. "Because we *all* know that the people or naturals who deserve it always get what's coming, right?" Obvious sarcasm and a hint of a challenge director puppy eyes. Lakemond's silence sharpens. "You want to know why I beat those little bastards?" I say, turning back to him, teeth bared in a smile that isn't a smile. "It wasn't just about Caspian. It was about *me*. Because I know; Know! that fuckers like that, they always walk away. They get community service and a fucking therapy pamphlet, or rewarded for strength."

My voice lowers. "And then they do it again." I take a step closer, close enough for him to see the storm behind my eyes. "So I made sure," I whisper. "I made sure they'll remember *me* the next time they even think about touching someone smaller than them. They will be praying to the goddess Lilith herself to come for them, so they are not left with me." I lean back, grin flashing "Consider it a public service."

"Allyssa..." He starts. "No, no," I cut him off with mock sweetness. "This is the part where you say I shouldn't have done it. That there are *rules*. That *justice* will prevail. Go on, say it so I can laugh in your fucking face." Lakemond is quiet. Then he voices a little more firmly "I was going to say... thank you." That pulls me up short. "What?" "For stepping in," he says. "And for not killing them. That's progress." "Selene give me strength," I mutter invoking the moon goddess herself . "Set the bar any lower and I'll trip over it." I say to him. He laughs softly, I hate that it warms me. "You know," I say, aiming to derail whatever soft feelings might be trying to grow claws in my ribs, "for someone in a position of power, you're surprisingly chill about one of your students attempting *felony battery.*" "I'm pragmatic and not entirely sure what that means," he replies, amusement and curiosity in his face. "And I'm not blind. Those males were predators." "Were?" His jaw tightens.

Ah. So we're not going to play 'they *were just kids*' card. Probably wise, to let it go before my anger can gain another foothold on me. "And Caspian?" I ask again, quieter this time. "He... didn't get in trouble?" "No," Lakemond says. "But he did look like he was carrying the weight of the world when I left him." My mouth tightens. Of course he did. That male radiates guilt like a fucking halo. I shouldn't care. I *don't* care. ...I care. *Goddamn martyr types.*

I roll my neck, exhaling through gritted teeth. "Fine," I mutter making my exasperation clear. "So we're not expelling him. Or me? Subtle power play in the use of "we're" in my response." "No, technically that isn't how it works anyway, it will be up to the alignment testing at the end of the third year" Lakemond says, either not catching on or ignoring it my power move. "You're both staying, though I do expect you to attend an entry assessment." He continues with a smirk. "Do I get a crown?" I reply smirking back. "Not yet." He is grinning now, the easy banter is nice. I smirk again. "Figures, always the bridesmaid."

He steps forward, slowly. "I know you don't trust me or this place, you've had no reason to but give it time, Allyssa, give me time to prove I'm not the enemy you think I am. Let people see the *real* you." "If the prophecy stirs," Lakemond murmured, "then every faction in Veyloris, from the Druidic groves to the Vampire empire of Sangreal, will feel the tremor." I laugh. And laugh harder, until it hurts. "Director," I breathe through my laughter, "the real me makes people piss themselves and beg for mercy. I don't think that's gonna win me the fucking popularity contest." And I don't want it to. Because fear... Fear is *control.* And I know exactly what to do with that. "Besides, popularity contests are for the kind of females who bake cookies. I'm more of a death-by-chocolate kind of female." I wink.

Chapter Four: Entrance Assessment

"Things are not always what they seem..."

-Phaedrus

Lance Lakemond POV

I did not conduct entrance assessments personally.

Not anymore.

I had professors for that. Departments. Protocols.

But when the Black Wolf walked through my gates one month into the Winter Cycle, stirring the Huntstone.

I made an exception.

The assessment chamber was circular and warded, stone etched with measurement glyphs that responded to breath, pulse, and magic draw. Professor Vyn stood to my left, hands clasped behind her back, expression clinical. His opinion matters, carries weight with me, I need her input here.

Allyssa stood in the centre of the circular warding floor, hands loose at her sides. Still. Watching. Not defensive. Not relaxed.

Evaluating.

That was what unnerved me.

I had seen that stillness before.

On battlefields.

On rulers.

On beings who survived by calculating cost before committing to violence.

Professor Vyn stood at the periphery, silent for once. Even she understood this required precision.

"Miss Black," I began evenly. "This is a standard entrance assessment."

Lie. It was not.

"You arrived one month into the Winter Cycle. Before placement, we determine aptitude, stability, and compatibility."

Her gaze did not waver.

"Proceed," she said.

Not nervous. Not eager.

Command given as though she granted permission.

Interesting.

"Describe the territories of Veyloris," I asked, wanting to know how much she has been told about the realm she was hidden from.

Her answer was immediate.

"Seven sovereign dominions. An eighth miniature territory governed by the Tribunal. Verdfall Enclave sits centra, fortified and magically neutral. Not to forget the Ocean Kingdom in the Saphire Coast of course."

"Neutral?" Vyn prompted.

Her gaze flicked to the professor briefly. Assessing.

"Supposedly." Her voice held a hint amused suspicion.

I did not react outwardly, but as the Director of this Academy I have so many questions about this young female that needed answers not only politically but for the future that has yet to come to pass. One that she is going to be the focal point of.

"Continue." Vyn said.

"Unseelie Dominion governs Umbrakyn and its shadow lattice, they cover the land that stretches between Verdfall and Sangreal. Seelie Court presides over Aurenslong and the upper ley-lines of the North East Territory. Frostpine territories hold North West forests the largest werewolf community of the realm. Druvenwald maintains druidic enclaves next to Frostpine. Calyxion holds the Eastern Saphire coast ports. Draethen Neighbour's Sangreal along the Southern edges. Shutter bay holds the largest stretch along the western coast that has numerous smaller villages held by committee for all naturals to live together no matter their ancestral dominion, it also has control over the largest port to the Saphire ocean which is the only way in or out of the ocean dominion. Verdant territories rotate stewardship, right in the centre of the land-dwelling realm."

"And portal gates?" I asked, heavily impressed by what she has learnt about the realm in the last three years, I can see the intelligence in her eyes as she speaks, it lights up her entire face.

Her jaw tightened almost imperceptibly.

"Reopened three years ago. Unclear why Selene, Lilith and the Mother withdrew protection. New races crossed, but were quickly pushed back to where they came from. Balance destabilised." I leaned forward before I realised I had moved. Putting the scholar away for the time being, there is too much she still needs to know, and not enough time before we will need her to be what we need to survive.

She did not mention loss. She did not mention blood. Good. She compartmentalised. Terrifyingly well. She seems to be containing herself better than any previous reports about the black wolf, this is positive, this means my plans need to be moved forward at a faster pace.

The chamber shifted. Illusion wards flared to life. Forest. Dusk. Three opponents.

"Engage," Vyn instructed.

She didn't.

Most candidates attacked too quickly. Fear or ego driving them into the obvious trap. Allyssa stood at the centre of the warding circle and stretched her shoulders once, like she had just stepped into a sparring match she fully intended to enjoy.

The first opponent lunged. She sidestepped lazily. Not fast. Not urgent. Lazy. The blade missed her throat by an inch. Vyn stiffened beside me. The second opponent circled. The third feigned injury, limping convincingly toward cover.

She glanced at the "wounded" one and smirked. "Oh, that's adorable," she muttered. She let the flanker come within striking distance. Let him believe he had surprise. Then she caught his wrist mid-swing, twisted, and dislocated his shoulder with a clean crack.

But she didn't finish him. She shoved him toward the second attacker and stepped back, folding her arms as the two illusions recalibrated.

She was playing. Not testing herself. Testing us. "Miss Black," Vyn said coolly. "This is not theatre." Her eyes flicked to her.

"I'm aware," she replied, just as coolly.

The third opponent rushed from the rear. She ducked. Rolled. Came up behind him. Instead of breaking his neck, she leaned close to his ear. "You should really commit to the limp," she said softly before shoving him forward.

Vyn exhaled sharply. I took a step closer to the circle. She was not fighting to survive. She was demonstrating that she could control the pace of the fight. The illusion shifted aggression parameters, escalating.

This time all three attacked simultaneously. She moved faster. But still not fully. Still controlled. She disarmed one. Swept the second. Kicked the third into a tree hard enough to splinter bark.

Then she stepped back again. Waiting. Mocking. "Are we assessing my restraint," she asked lightly, cocking her head to the side, "or my efficiency?"

There it was. The arrogance. The awareness that she was being measured. The deliberate refusal to give her full capacity. Vyn looked to me. I held Allyssa's gaze. "Again," I said. The illusions reset. This time I adjusted the difficulty myself. Higher reaction speed. Tighter coordination. No theatrical tells. "Engage."

She didn't stretch this time. Didn't smirk. Didn't bait. She rose to the challenge without a word. The message was clear enough. She moved the instant the first illusion twitched. Flanker down in one strike. Neck snapped before the second had completed his step.

She pivoted through the third's attack, used his momentum against him, disarmed, and drove a blade cleanly through the sternum.

Three seconds.

Then silence.

The illusions dissolved.

Snow from the simulation fell as harmless light. Vyn stared. I did not. I was watching her breathing. It was steady. Unchanged. For the first time since she entered this room, I chose my next question carefully. "Why wait the first time?" I asked quietly.

She tilted her head slightly. "Because impatience is predictable." A beat later. "And predictable enemies are boring." There was something almost amused in her tone. I needed to know more.

"Source?" I pressed. "A book," she replied with a shrug. No elaboration. No explanation. But I did not need one. Sun Tzu. The mortal war book. The same copy retrieved from her belongings when the Hunters found her in that basement. Dog-eared. Bloodstained. Read enough to reshape instinct into doctrine. I had read it out of curiosity.

"Appear weak when you are strong," she added after a moment. "Strike when the outcome is already decided." She said it like a casual thought. But it wasn't just instinct. It was philosophy. And philosophy is far more dangerous than rage.

Vyn folded her arms. "She could have ended the first engagement immediately." "Yes," I said. "And chose not to." She stated it, disbelief threading the edges of her voice. That was not arrogance alone. That was control. And control meant she was aware of her power. Which meant she was also aware of the threat she posed.

I looked back at her. "Do you enjoy combat?" I asked, trying to sound as casual as possible, not letting on how her answer would dictate the precautions I put in place around her, because of her.

Her smile was small. Sharp. "I enjoy winning." I recognised the danger in it. She did not crave violence. She craved certainty.

Vyn did not step back. She stepped aside. "Application," she said. The chamber reconfigured. No forest. No theatrics. A stone room. Iron chair bolted to the floor. A Shadowkin male bound in suppression cuffs, projection calibrated higher than standard second-year resistance.

"This one will not respond to kindness," Vyn said quietly. "Extract the coded route." Allyssa studied the construct, an actual replica of a student here who did his assessment and passed with flying colours.

Then she studied the restraints. Paying particular attention to the swirling ink that marks the shadowkin. All of them with different meanings and responding to different emotional ques. Noone but the shadowkin understand the meanings of each tattoo, its their most covenant secret. Then she clocked the door. Then us. She noticed everything. "Begin," Vyn instructed.

She approached slowly. Not softening. She pulled out the chair opposite the construct and sat. "You look tired," she said. The Shadowkin laughed. And she smiled. "Try harder." He said. Interesting. She shifted. Subtle. Shoulders slouched slightly. Gaze lowered. "I know what they do when you fail," she said quietly.

The projection didn't flinch. Too disciplined. She recalibrated. Faster than most seasoned interrogators. "You weren't trusted with the full route," she said instead. Nothing. "I would've split it too," she continued casually. "Give you just enough to die believing you were important."

The ward pulsed. Not collapse. Strain. She leaned back. Her eyes flicking down to his markings and smiled faintly. She is seeing something in the markings, intrigue has me pinned to see what happens next.

"You're disposable." He lunged against the restraints. Good. She had found ego. But then—

He went silent. Deliberately. Cutting off engagement. That was new. Most candidates would escalate there. Threaten. Taunt. Break composure. She didn't. She studied him and his markings again, I could almost see her mind switching into overdrive while she contemplated her next move. It was longer than was comfortable.

Then she stood. Walked behind him. Did not touch him. "Your handler isn't the one who scares you," she said quietly. Silence. "Your brother is." Vyn shot me a look. That detail had not been programmed. Was she improvising. Or was this calculated, how fascinating. Perhaps projecting. Or fishing.

The Shadowkin's pulse spiked. There. She heard it. Looked down to his markings along his arms again. She didn't press. She softened instead. "You failed him once already." What the hell was this. The construct's breathing changed. "Drelith-Vey," he snapped. Partial phrase. Incomplete.

The ward did not collapse. She tilted her head. Not satisfied. "You don't know the second half," she said calmly. "I do!" "Then say it." He hesitated. Just a fraction. And that was the crack. She leaned closer. "Your brother was trusted with it, wasn't he? Perhaps I should just go and ask him myself" Her voice coming in with a lethal edge to hit with just enough malice to understand her implication. Silence. The projection's ward flickered violently.

"Tell me," she whispered. As she raked a claw that she had partially shifted down his throat. I was so transfixed and a little entertained that I didn't even register her partial shift. He spat the final sequence. The ward shattered. Silence returned to the chamber. She stood slowly. No triumph. No smile. Just assessment.

Vyn's voice cut through. "You improvised psychological leverage not built into the simulation, how did you know what to say to him." Vyn clearly interested in her method. I think she may have found a favourite student.

She shrugged.

"Everyone repeats patterns and have biological weaknesses that a hidden but not undiscoverable." Then she looked at me. And I decided to test her properly. "You've done this before," I said evenly. She didn't answer. "You worked with mortal gangs," I continued. "Two reports confirm it. Three Hunters we sent to observe you returned... unsettled."

Her expression did not change. "They said you let them think they had you cornered," I went on. "Then disarmed them before restraining them. Extracted what you wanted." The Hunters that came back not only had physical bruising but psychological ones.

Silence. "They also said you smiled while doing it." Her shadow shifted. Not aggressive. Closer. Tighter. Interesting. Just as Matthews had reported.

"They were in my way," she said calmly. Not defensive. Not ashamed. "And the mercenary contracts in Veyloris?" I pressed. "You interrogated targets before killing them." A pause. "Yes." No justification. No embellishment. Vyn stepped forward. "If we remove violence as an option," she said sharply, "are you still effective?" She considered that. Actually considered it. Then:

"If the tool isn't on the table, I don't need it."

A beat.

"But if it is on the table," she continued quietly, "I'll use whatever's there."

Her eyes didn't waver. "It depends on the person in the chair."

Not bloodlust. Not cruelty. Utility. That answer was worse. Because it wasn't emotional. It was measured. Vyn folded her arms slowly. "She adapts to parameters," she said. "Yes," I replied.

But I was not looking at her hands. Or her posture. I was watching her shadow. It had not lashed out. It had not flared. It had tightened. Protective. Possessive. As if guarding something behind her ribs. Very interesting. Assessment complete. And I understood something I did not enjoy admitting. She did not prefer violence. She preferred certainty. And she would reach it by whatever means were permitted. Or not.

I stepped forward fully now. "Combat proficiency exceeds second-year requirements," I said calmly. "You will attend third-year tactical sessions on top of the third year combat class." No reaction. She had known before I said it. "Interrogation resistance and applied psychological extraction: third-year." That earned a flicker. Not pride. Recognition. Vyn's posture shifted beside me — not restrained anymore. Energised. She had found a student worth sharpening.

"Magical theory," I continued evenly, "second-year." Neutral again. I did not elaborate. I would not, without more answers. "Political history and territorial governance: first-year." Her jaw ticked once. There it is. "You lack foundational realm exposure, and even though you were able to advise the territories, you are still required to understand the history and political landscape not just the physical one" I said, voice level. "That is not an insult. It is a correction." She inclined her head slightly. Controlled. But there was tension beneath it — not resentment. Awareness. She knew exactly what she had missed.

She had left her foster home not quite fifteen. That is when I took over from the previous director, inheriting his investigation, knowing I was going to need Mazzer involved. Records confirmed her affiliation Mazzer was very thorough. Disappeared from a foster registry the same week a younger mortal girl had also gone missing from the same home. I had read the report twice. The mortal police never found Allyssa, after her foster father reported her missing three weeks after she actually went missing. Actually from what Mazzer found, they started looking and a few days later closed the case never looking for her again.

Three years later she had surfaced in Hunter intelligence threads — just shy of eighteen — slipping through reopened gates into Veyloris. No escort. No sponsorship. No faction claim. For the next two years she moved across territories on short mercenary contracts. Efficient. Surgical. Reputation spreading faster than her name. I was surprised when Mazzer said he kept loosing her.

Twenty years old. And already this composed. I did not comment on the circle's readings. The assessment ward had calibrated normally. Her magical output had not.

It had not spiked.

It had not flared.

It had not overreached under pressure the way young Naturals so often do.

It had remained steady. Too steady. The instruments did not register scarcity. They registered depth. Her Well was the largest the circle had measured in over a century. Not volatile. Not fractured. Contained. Waiting.

And that troubled me more than instability ever could. The readings did not behave like elemental affinity. There was no flare of fire, no drift of wind, no pulse of earth, no tidal undertone. Instead, there was density. A pressure. A tightening.

I knew that signature. Very few did. I was personally acquainted with the only other living being whose Well read like that —Density, pressure, tightening and I would have known if a child bearing that blood had been recorded twenty years ago.

There had been no such child. Which meant this was not inheritance in the traditional sense. And that troubled me deeply. Does she know I wonder.

Vyn cleared her throat lightly, far too pleased with herself. "She adapts to parameters," the interrogation professor said again, unable to fully suppress the note of anticipation in her tone. I glanced sideways at her. "You're volunteering," I observed. Vyn did not deny it.

"She thinks in layers," Vyn replied. "She doesn't react. She positions." I turned back to Allyssa. "Yes," I said quietly. "She does."

"Who removed you from Veyloris?" I asked. Silence. Not defensive. Not evasive. Absent. "You do not know." I continued. "No." She just simply stated, no emotion, not giving anything away.

I believed her. That was the worst part. "You were placed deliberately," I said softly, wanting to see how she reacted to being a possible political pawn. Her shadow tightened closer to her spine. Protective. "You were not discovered," he continued. "You were positioned." A flicker in her eyes. Not surprise. Recognition. "I figured," she said.

I studied her. "You joined a gang at fifteen." Her expression did not shift. "You survived all these years in mortal territory without faction or pack backing." Silence. "You crossed into Veyloris alone." Stillness. "You built a mercenary reputation before your twentieth winter." A beat. "And you think that was random?" Her lips curved faintly. "No, I know what I am Director" she said. Good. Maybe she understood the board she stood on. I dismissed Vyn with a glance. The professor left, already calculating lesson structures in her mind.

I remained. "Miss Black." Her attention sharpened instantly. "You are not a weapon to be deployed." A pause. "You are not a symbol to be paraded." Longer pause. "And you are not as alone in this realm as you were in the mortal one." That landed. Barely.

"If someone comes for me," she said quietly, "I won't wait for permission." I did not doubt it. "I would expect nothing less." She turned toward the door. I watched her shadow move with her. Not lashing. Not flaring. Following. The chamber sealed behind her. I remained still for a long moment.

Impossible readings. A Well too vast for her age. Shadow responsiveness tied to emotion — not instability, but inheritance. A twenty-year-old with strategic doctrine etched into instinct. And archival silence where there should have been record. Whatever she was—

She had not been hidden by accident. Her Well was not fractured. It was contained. Which considering what she has been through is so wildly insane. I wondered whether whoever concealed her had intended this outcome—

Or whether they believed time and distance would thin the bloodline's reach. And if someone had placed her in the mortal realm to survive—

Then the Academy had just inherited something sovereign. Something not meant to be measured. I intended to understand it. Before whoever buried her decided to retrieve what was theirs.

Chapter Five: The Academy Bleeds Stone

"You must have chaos within you to give birth to a dancing star." — Friedrich Nietzsche

Allyssa POV

The Academy was carved into the bones of a mountain and crowned with towers that scraped the breath from the sky. Stone and storm forged this place; not hands. Even the trees at its edge leaned away from it, as if the forest knew better than to question what lived here. The combat fields sprawled across terraces built into the cliffs of the Verdfall Enclave, overlooking the misted valley where Greenhollow lay tucked like a secret in the earth.

To the world, it was a school.

To Hunters, it was scripture in stone.

To me? It was another set of walls I'd learn to break. They call it a crucible. I call it a challenge.

The path wound through centuries of blood. Once a battlefield. Then a fortress. Now a crucible. The outer gates gleaming ironwood and obsidian, etched with runes that have never opened for the mundane. Only Naturals walked these halls, Vampires, Druids, Shifters, Witches, fae, Half-bloods (half fae-half wolf). Creations, born in blood, raised in command or more affectionately called half-breeds. Sent to the Academy before we were even done growing and taught to kill before we could vote. At least that was how it once was, now all the naturals in our realm get to choose to become a Hunter if they can get through the three years and get past the final trial. Most come through to the Academy between age eighteen and twenty-five to start studying and training, willingly having themselves carved into Hunters.

We were half of everything; and whole in nothing. The half-breeds. There are not many of us as there used to be. We are the individuals for whom Academy attendance is compulsory, although not as early as was once demanded of us but without the choice like the other factions receive. All the other natural councils agreed half breeds must attend the Academy and on that the Academy didn't disagree. I'm still unsure if that is because they feel we are too dangerous or wanted to get rid of us, to show the law of not allowing cross-breeding is punishable and that we would be in service to the laws of Veyloris to atone, I roll my eyes and the distain tastes foul in my mouth from their bullshit.

The wars had ended between the seelie and unseelie courts, but the hierarchy hadn't, now we were the law. The shadows between kingdoms, enforcers, guardians. The secret steel beneath every diplomatic smile, but that didn't mean we were welcome.

We weren't them.

Not just fae. Not just werewolf. Not noble-born.

Not pure.

And they made sure we remembered it.

Every Natural in Veyloris feared the Black Wolf, yet here within Mother Nature's sanctuary, the hunters watched me with awe instead. Reverence. Hunger. And I in that moment I admitted to myself quietly that maybe I didn't hate that.

I stood at the edge of the training courtyard, cold wind biting at my skin. It was my first day of classes here, even though everyone was already a month into the Academic year. The winter sun caught in the white rune ring etched into the blackstone tiles. Beyond the trees, snow hung heavy on the branches like powdered bone. In the eastern hall, politics was taught behind stained glass that glowed like molten jewels. Below, students moved in formations; shield-magic drills, illusion-casting, tactics that reeked of court politics. Some on the field and on benches laughing with each other, something small and hopeful stirred before I buried it.

Caspian stood five feet behind me, and I felt it; his presence, heavy and gentle all at once. Like he was built to be a shield I hadn't asked for. He looked so calm; like the world could break and he'd still stand there, unshaken, asking me if I was okay. Seeing him again after our first encounter last week is intense, he looks good, in his sparing gear arms bare, muscles bulging, who the fuck said I liked bulging muscles, I mentally face palmed my reaction to him. His scent hit me again and I swear I nearly moaned out loud, what the actual fuck, the bond tries to tug me into his direction but I not only ignore it, I strangle it into submission. I wouldn't have gotten far in my life if my will wasn't absolute and as stubborn as a unseelie cu-sith those adorable fae hounds and I share a lot of traits. Craving that softness, not an option. The desire for him, weakness that I can starve into silence. I didn't turn around again couldn't.... Because the bond was already whispering truths I wasn't ready to hear.

How he watched me like I was both a prayer and a promise.

How his hands wanted to touch the bruises he'd never see.

How he didn't understand what I was, what I am, but wanted to anyway.

"Move," someone sneered behind me.

I turned slowly. My wolf bristling at the disrespect, demanding I do something about it. Outwardly I school my features into that of mocking boredom.

A group of upper-year Hunters blocked the archway. "Kael" one of the others said a terrified warning coming through just that one word. Hmm Kael I took stock of him golden hair, perfect teeth, eyes that screamed pure-bred privilege. The kind of male who never had to ask twice for anything.

"You're in my line of sight," he said, He was giving me his best menacing glare, like he thought he could alpha his way past a wolf who'd already eaten bigger threats for breakfast. Cute.

I arched an eyebrow. "Maybe try closing your eyes. You'd save us both some trouble."

His lips twitched in a smirk. "Big words for a half-breed."

Caspian shifted behind me, and I flicked two fingers back an action to make him stand down, I do not need him. The bond strained at my rejection, a feeling of hurt came through but I ignored it, he needs to be tougher than that.

Kael stepped closer, that smirk still there. "I heard you broke a student's collarbone last week. Accident?" his eyes rove over me part leer, part cocky disbelief, what I took it as was a challenge of course.

"No," I said flatly. "Deliberate." Already bored. The memory of that fight, a fresh wave of satisfaction running through my blood, too bad Caspian stopped me from continuing.

Another step from Kael. "You always this mouthy? Or is it just the leash that's missing?"

I let a slow smile cut across my lips the dangerous edge clear. "You offering to put one on me, Kael? Careful. You wouldn't survive the foreplay."

Silence.

The satisfying crack of his nose sounded like music. Shame it wasn't set to a better soundtrack.

Kael was on his back before any words had left his lips. My claws pressed to his throat, the air between us electric, I let a little of my alpha aura out. His eyes went wide with panic and something that smelled like arousal. You have got to be kidding me, I roll my eyes at the scent of arousal. The queen within already saw that reaction coming.

"You forgot the first rule," I said quietly squeezing his throat a little tighter, looking at his face starting to turn a pretty shade of purple from lack of oxygen. "Don't provoke the wolf."

"You'll be expelled," he gasped with what little room he had left to move his voice box.

I leaned down, letting him see every sharp edge I'd ever bared. "You think they'll expel their Black and White? Their top bonded pair?" My voice was silk wrapped around a blade. "You're not just weak, Kael. You're expendable. Because this is my game, Kael. And you're just a piece on the board"

I stood and turned away, leaving him fighting to fill his lungs behind me.

The Battle Game courtyard was built like a gladiator's ring; sand scattered over blackstone, runes carved into every step. The air always smelled like sweat and magic, thick with the ghosts of a thousand training battles. Battle strategy lived here and I was all for it. The warrior in me was excited beyond belief and I had to tamper it down before it showed in my face.

Professor Merin perched on the edge of the stone steps like a crow eyeing fresh roadkill. His eyes were glacial blue, sharp, amused, and entirely too perceptive. He'd seen centuries of bloodshed, and he wore it like a second skin.

"Crude, but effective," he said, his voice like silk over a blade. "You do understand that sometimes intimidation alone is enough, yes?"

I smirked, I truly feel like he gets me. "Where's the fun in that, sir?"

"Ah, the artist's dilemma," he mused, tilting his head. "I can see you have a flair for the dramatic." Approval shinning from his eyes.

Around us, the other students shifted nervously. Some looked at me with fear, others with fascination. No one spoke, good, let them wonder if they were next.

Battlefield games had always felt less like a lesson and more like a rehearsal for a play I already knew by heart. They taught strategy, I taught them that nothing beats the real thing. Sun Tzu words echoing through my mind a sweet hum of calmness washing over me.

Professor Merin watched me leave, his smile thin and knowing. They think this is about power. It's not. It's about survival. And I'm very good at surviving. Chaos was in my blood. But maybe, just maybe, that was exactly what this place needed.

The next day, in Magical Ethics, I sat in the corner, half-listening while Professor Helvain droned on about the Laws of Mundane Interference.

"...as decreed by the Arcanum Tribunal," he continued, pacing slowly in front of the slate board, "who oversee cross-faction compliance and maintain the central Archive of Sovereign Record."

The Tribunal. Record-keepers. Judges. Neutral in theory. Neutrality is a convenient mask for power. Each faction ruled its own land. Frostpine had pack law. Shutter Bay had council codes. Draethen had contract governance dressed up as consent. The Seelie cloaked their rules in etiquette and virtue. The Unseelie... bent theirs until they resembled something else entirely.

But the Tribunal ruled what touched blood.

Bloodlines.

Portals.

Children.

"The Law of Sovereign Lineage," Helvain went on, voice heavy with rehearsed authority, "prohibits unsanctioned cross-species unions where such unions may destabilize magical balance."

Unions. That was a gentle word for it. In some territories, it meant exile. In others, quiet execution. Frostpine tolerated it when it suited them. The Unseelie barely blinked if the power gained outweighed the scandal.

The Tribunal called it destabilization. What a crock for what it actually is control. Caspian shifted three rows back. I didn't look, but I felt him. Warm. Steady. Watching. Cross-species. His existence was proof the law bent when it wanted to. Although from what I hear, he is here because he isn't allowed to take any real power in the pack hierarchy because of him being a half-breed. I sneak a glance over to him, he is sitting next to that red head I see around him all the time, what's her name again, Laya. His head was looking down into his lap, luckily my vantage point allowed me to see what had his attention.

A communication orb was in his hand and the name Emily was flashing on it's surface before his emotions spiked down the bond, uncertainty, worry, and then he mutes the call and his emotions steady out. I look back to the professor.

"Further," Helvain continued, chalk scratching behind him, "the Bloodline Oversight Accord mandates the registration and monitored development of all recognized cross-blood offspring within Veyloris land territories."

A murmur rippled through the room. "Originally," he added, with the careful neutrality of someone reciting revised history, "hybrid children were required to enter Academy custody at ten years of age for early stabilization."

Custody. Such a polite word. "The civil unrest that followed," Helvain continued, not looking at anyone directly, "resulted in the Maturation Amendment. Cross-blood enrolment was adjusted to occur between eighteen and twenty-five years of age, allowing for familial development and voluntary reporting."

Voluntary. If you ignored the fact that unregistered bloodlines were flagged. Monitored. Restricted from portal access. Denied faction inheritance rights. You could keep your child. You just couldn't pretend the Tribunal wasn't watching. The Archive recorded everything. Blood. Births. Bonds. Even whispers.

Frostpine had protested the original decree. I'd heard that much in passing. Pack-raised wolves didn't surrender their children easily. Shutter Bay nearly fractured its council over it. The Unseelie... complied publicly and did whatever they pleased privately. The Academy doesn't seem to try and stop anyone from being together here. I mean none of us are allowed to leave once we are over the threshold. Only those pre-approved are allowed communication orbs. So in other words, those that have proved alignment with the Academy, mostly third year students.

Helvain cleared his throat. "The purpose of the Accord is stabilization. Hybrid magic historically presents volatility risks if left untrained." History like being used and enslaved to have petty wars between factions, yeah good times.

Volatile. A word they used when something refused to be predictable. My gaze drifted, unbidden, three rows back. Caspian. Cross-blood son of an Alpha. Registered. Observed. Delayed until maturity. Still claimed. Still powerful. Still here.

Helvain turned to the board again. "Failure to register a qualifying bloodline is considered obstruction of sovereign law." Obstruction. Not rebellion. Not resistance. Just paperwork.

I wondered who had signed my name into the Archive. Or if they ever had.

Helvain pivoted smoothly. "Unauthorized portal use beyond sanctioned gates remains punishable under Tribunal decree. All inter-realm crossings must be registered through a licensed anchor or approved shadowkin. Tribunal employ." Of course. Portals meant migration. Migration meant diluted bloodlines. Diluted bloodlines meant less predictability. Less control. The Tribunal preferred predictability and control.

Warlocks required signatures. Hunters required authorization stones. Most naturals required permission stamped by someone more powerful than them. And yet. I had crossed. Through the gates. Without a licensed anchor. Slipping through the cracks, before they tightened security.

Helvain turned back toward the class. "These statutes are not restrictive. They are protective. They preserve order." Order. Order preserved by deciding who was allowed to love. Who was allowed to travel. Who was allowed to exist. Perhaps I am being overly hash due to my dislike of the tribunal.

Caspian's gaze brushed against me again, warm and insistent, like he wanted to smooth out every sharp edge and see what was left underneath. Idiot. Beautiful, sweet idiot. Male. Female. Fae. Hunter. Desire and curiosity twined together in the air, sweet and heavy. Hunger under law. Law under hunger. After class, one of them approached.

Bright eyes. Smooth voice. I wondered if he practiced that in the mirror or if it was just natural for idiots. "You ever consider dating outside your bond?" he asked, casual and cocky.

Outside the bond.

Outside species.

Outside law.

I tilted my head. "I consider a lot of things." His eyes lit up with anticipation and lust. I stepped closer, close enough for him to see the edge behind the smile. My lips brushed his ear and he shivered, the scent of arousal rising uncontrollably. "Like whether your bones would shatter faster than your pride." I like that flicker of fear. It reminds me that I'm still in control. And I snap my teeth just to fuck with him. His laugh was thin. Nervous. He didn't come back. Neither did the female who tried later, after leaving with flaming cheeks from embarrassment.

I wasn't being cruel. I was being kind. Because mercy is a luxury I've never been able to afford. And kindness? Kindness is just another blade in my arsenal. Honestly, I didn't trust myself not to devour the ones who looked at me like they could tame me. Like I could ever be tamed. I scoffed at the thought. And Caspian? Caspian looked away thinking I hadn't noticed his staring. But I felt his jealousy flare, hot and bright through the bond.

Wildfire licking at my skin. He either hadn't learned how to block me yet... Or he wanted me to feel it. If it was the latter— That was bold. And bold was interesting.

By my ninth day we finally have a free day and that night, I found myself on the rooftop of the east tower, cold air of mid-winter cycle biting through my thin training shirt. The Academy glowed behind me, an empire of secrets and ambition. In the distance, the Seelie capital shone like starlight on glass. A storm was brewing in the west, clouds bruised purple and black.

Change was coming.

And it would not ask for permission.

I had chaos inside me. And if this place was going to bleed stone for it, I would make sure it was worth the cost. Let them whisper about the Black Wolf in their polished halls of power. Let them call me mad. I would wear that madness like a crown.

For three years, I had crossed Veyloris searching for something I couldn't name. Learning where I came from. Learning what people were willing to trade for brutality when survival was on the line. I moved through territories and factions alike, taking work no one else would touch, earning coin and passage with violence I knew how to wield.

It was freedom. The kind I didn't know existed while growing up in the mortal realm. A belonging so sharp and unexpected that I never wanted to leave.

Until they moved her back to him.

I slipped through the gateway without permission, without hesitation, and dragged her out before the damage became permanent. When it was done, when she was safe again, no, I took deep breaths sealing the memories clawing their way toward the surface behind an iron door I'd forged myself.

I looked back across the landscape one last time. Beautiful. Dangerous. Alive.

She was in good hands now.

And I was done running.

A brush of cold push of air, almost like a caress drifted over my spine, faint, deliberate. Warlock magic from the southern Draethen, threaded with secrets.

Chapter Six: Snow Moon Rite

"Man is least himself... Give him a mask, and he will tell you the truth."

-Oscar Wilde

Allyssa POV

The Snow Moon Rite was not a night of silence. Right in the middle of the winter cycle.

It was a welcome. A proving. The first breath of the new year drawn beneath Selene's full gaze.

Snow blanketed the Academy grounds in luminous white, not as hush but as offering, every surface reflecting moonlight back toward the sky in quiet acknowledgment. Across Veyloris, the Rite was being observed in a thousand different ways, but its meaning was singular: Selene watched her children tonight. Measured their devotion. Their connection between all naturals. Packs, covens, creating a sense of community, connecting all naturals of Veyloris on a spiritual level. She marked who understood that the moon did not only grant power; it demanded return, a give and take, a partnership.

I felt it in my bones before I allowed myself to name it. The pull. The pressure. The sense of being weighed. An urgency to connect. In the last three years I have always hated this rite the most. I always just found a bar with random naturals all without family or friends that hosted the rite and stayed just off to the outskirts, staying enough to honour the rite and fulfill the urge the rite invoked on all naturals to connect with one another.

For some, devotion meant blood and hunt beneath her light with the pack. For others, service freely given through the long winter months to the orphaned, the forgotten, the moon-touched left without pack or protection honing in on connecting with the children. Shapeshifters ran the forests in ritual pursuit. Witches burned silver herbs in open courtyards together. Warlocks offered binding oaths to winter charities and orphan sanctuaries devoted to Selene's abandoned children together.

And when the offerings were made, when gratitude and connection had been proven rather than spoken, all factions gathered as one — to feast, to drink berry-dark spirits of Veyloris, and to celebrate survival beneath a moon that had never once stopped watching.

Tonight, she would see us.

And I did not know if I wanted to be seen.

The call to shift came like a pulse through the marrow. Wolves gathered at the forest's edge in loose formation, breath fogging the silver air. Snow crunched beneath boots and bare feet alike as fur rippled into existence, bones reforming without apology. Frostpine's pack stood closest to the tree line, disciplined, proud, their pelts reflecting the moon like polished blades. A red-wolf stood off to the side watching me, not going off with any of the other groups of wolves.

I returned to look toward the Frostpine pack, not realising I was staring after a few minutes. And they closed ranks. Not violently. Not overtly. Just enough. An elder female from Frostpine held my gaze as her fur rippled into ash-grey. Not hostile. Not welcoming. Measured.

The Black Wolf was not a part of their pack. I felt it like a wall. I shrugged, making sure my mask was firmly in place while the monster inside surged at the sharp sting of rejection I had not even asked for. Behind me, Caspian's bones broke and rebuilt with fluid grace. His white wolf rose from his skin in a clean surge of moonlight, massive and controlled, ocean blue eyes burning clear and steady.

Frostpine called to him immediately, low howls layered with expectation. His pack of course it was. His wolf is absolutely stunning though. The urge to drag my hands through his fur and bury myself there was stronger than I anticipated. The pack made space for him. He did not take it. His white wolf stepped sideways, coming to stand at my shoulder instead. The call shifted. Questioning. He ignored it. I watched him through the veil of my own transformation, black fur sliding over muscle, bones cracking into something truer. When I stood fully formed, taller than most, darker than night should allow, the Frostpine wolves had already turned toward the forest. My wolf wanted nothing more than to be with her bonded but our distrust ran deep and she understood the reluctance and respected it for now.

"You don't owe me this," I said through the bond, distrust sharpening the edges of the thought. Caspian's wolf didn't look at me. He looked ahead. "I'm not here because of you," he replied calmly. I bared my teeth slightly. "Then why?" A beat of silence. Snow drifting between us. "Because I choose where I run." Simple. Annoyingly simple. Also lie. Selene's rite doesn't allow for lone naturals of any species.

We broke from the main hunt and ran north instead, away from Frostpine's coordinated formation and into the untouched stretch of forest where the snow lay deeper and the trees grew older. Selene's light poured through the canopy, turning every movement into silver.

Curiosity slipped its leash before I could stop it.

My wolf leaned into the bond.

"You're from Frostpine?"

The eagerness in her voice had me internally groaning, we already know this I say to her. She ignores me.

Caspian's wolf flicked his gaze toward us, warmth flaring instantly through the link. He answered quickly, almost as if afraid I'd take the question back.

"Yes. Youngest son of Alpha Everette Alpenfang of Frostpine."

I tried to rein my wolf in. Too late. The little girl inside me — the one that hoarded stories like treasures — surged forward with her.

"Do you have siblings? Have you always lived with them? What would your role have been? What's your mother like? When did you shift for the first time?"

The questions spilled out faster than I could dam them.

Caspian didn't retreat.

If anything, he leaned closer through the bond, amusement and something softer warming the tether between us.

"Alright," he said, a quiet laugh threading through his thoughts. "Let me see if I can keep up, curious mate."

The word mate sent a strange ripple through me, but he continued before I could react.

"I have two half siblings. Asher and Emily. Asher's next in line for Alpha. Emily designs magical weaponry. She's terrifyingly brilliant."

Pride laced his tone. Not arrogance. Affection.

"Yes, I always lived with them," he added gently. "That's... an unusual question."

Realisation flickered through him. Foster homes. Mortal realm. No pack.

He didn't press.

"My mother wasn't in the picture," he said instead, voice steadying. "My father's first mate was Luna. She died before I was born. I had my grandmother. And stories of what a Luna and mother should be."

The longing beneath it was quiet. Controlled. But it was there.

And I had no idea what to do with it.

The little girl retreated immediately. My wolf faltered. Shared control shifted back to me with an unspoken plea.

Fix it.

I didn't know how.

Combat? Easy. Strategy? Instinctual.

Grief? Vulnerability? I might as well have been asked to recite poetry in a battlefield.

"Hey," I muttered through the bond, rougher than intended. "We should probably get back to the hunt. Before the rest of the festivities."

Smooth. Truly.

Caspian didn't mock me. Didn't push.

He sent gratitude instead.

And somehow that made it worse.

So I did what I always did when something scraped too close to the bone of feelings.

I ignored it.

"I like that you're curious," he admitted through the bond. "About me."

I ignored that too.

The hunt was clean at first.

The different magical creatures in the woods still caught my attention. Even after three years in Veyloris, some of them felt unreal in the flesh. Echo-cats darted through the trees, six-legged blurs that covered impossible ground in seconds. Then a bramble-boar crashed past, its wooden armour crunching as it ran.

Memory struck fast. My first hunt here.

I had been starving. New to the realm. Stupid enough to think a bramble-boar would fall like a mortal one. My wolf warned me. I shut her out. Pride and hunger make poor teachers.

I tracked it for hours, waiting for weakness that never came. When I finally struck, jaws snapping around bark and blood, I remember the smug satisfaction. I told my wolf I could take care of us here too.

The blood hit my throat.

"Night," she had said calmly. "We'll talk when we wake."

I didn't even make it ten steps before the soporific venom dragged me into the dirt. My last thought had been regret.

I blinked the memory away, my wolf's laughter warm in the back of my mind. We only needed an offering tonight, not a lesson.

We gave chase.

The forest narrowed to rhythm and breath. Instinct. Speed. No prophecy. No politics. Just pursuit. Caspian tried to warn me off the boar, sending the reminder through the bond — soporific blood, reckless target.

"I know," I sent back, already airborne.

This time I aimed for the throat seam beneath the bark plating, ripping clean before the toxin could settle.

We howled beneath Selene's light. Pride flared through the bond.

Then the wind shifted.

I stilled.

Vampire. Not the faint residue of city scent. Fresh. Focused. I felt her before I saw her. A flicker of shadow too deliberate. A heartbeat too controlled. The predator watching the predators.

An assassin lunged from the ridge, silvered blade aimed for my spine. She gave no warning and no words. Caspian's roar split the forest. Too late. I twisted. The blade grazed fur, slicing heat along my flank, but momentum was mine now. I collided with her midair, driving her into the snow hard enough to fracture bone. She was fast, I'll grant her that. Fangs flashing. Nails like knives.

She expected hesitation. She miscalculated. My jaws found her throat before she could pivot. Bone crunched. Blood flooded the snow, dark and obscene beneath Selene's light.

The forest went still.

Caspian landed beside me, white fur already stained red from proximity alone. His eyes scanned the tree line, searching for a second attacker.

None came.

Two figures emerged instead. Hunters. Fully pledged. At least three years in by the weight of their oath marks and the steadiness in their gaze. They did not ask questions. Did not look surprised. One inclined his head toward us. Both offered submission. Respect. My wolf surged forward, preening before I reined her back.

"We'll take it from here."

I stepped back, releasing the body. The vampire's eyes were still open, shock frozen there. The Hunters bound her in silver-threaded rope with practised efficiency.

"For Director Lakemond," the second said quietly, answering the question in my gaze and I acknowledged him and released the hold I had on them with my alpha aura I didn't even realise I had let loose.

Of course, the director had hunters following me, I would to until I was sure I wasn't going to go on a murder spree, especially with how they found me.

Snow began to fall again, light and indifferent, covering the blood almost immediately.

Caspian brushed his shoulder against mine.

"You're hurt."

"Barely."

But the assassin hadn't been random.

Selene watched.

And someone had decided the Black Wolf would not see spring.

Chapter Seven: The Sweet Male Who Wouldn't Let Go

"There is always some madness in love. But there is also always some reason in madness." — Friedrich Nietzsche

Caspian POV

Four weeks.

That's how long it's been since I met Allyssa. Since we bonded. Since she saved me from being pounded into paste by three douchebags with daddy issues.

Four weeks since she kissed the earth with bare feet, covered in blood and power and a kind of beauty that makes you question your religion. Two weeks since Snow Moon Rite and she was attacked. Two weeks since she had asked blurted questions like it was a sweet interrogation. I sighed it was the most adorable thing I have seen from her.

Two weeks of total, soul-destroying, absolutely infuriating silence. The bond I have with her festering like a wound unable to heal, like an ache that I am equally proud and resentful of. It's like that adorable time with her was a mirage and now I'm dying of thirst.

She hasn't said a single word to me. Not in person, not through the bond, not even a "Hey, remember that life-altering moment where our souls became permanently fused? Cool, right? Nope, nada, radio fucking silence. I've tried. Oh, believe me. I've tried everything. Muffins. Courtyard run-ins. Strategic shirtlessness during training, which by the way really difficult considering we are in different combat classes, luckily I have a free space between her combat class and min, so I get to watch her, that sounded way creepier than it should have. She ignored them all. Which, you know, is a perfectly normal way to treat your soul-bonded mate. Right. Sure. Perfectly normal. Like cupcakes at a funeral. The Muffin was still there an hour later, untouched. She ghosted the muffin, who ghosts a muffin? It's not like I expect her to braid friendship bracelets and plan our future wedding or whatever. I just... I want to understand.

I want to talk, n*eed* to talk, because I can feel her. Even with her bond-block up, I still get the echoes; flashes of emotion like distant thunder, rage, control, sadness wrapped in barbed wire. She's there, she's hurting, but she won't let me help, and it's driving me fucking insane.

I go to the combat arena to clear my head. The Arena of Roots sat at the heart of the Verdant Athenaeum, carved around a colossal living oak whose branches were said to touch every ley line in Veyloris. There's something comforting about the sound of blades clashing and instructors screaming insults like poetic affirmations. It's like therapy; except with more bruises. Today's a senior training session. The arena's half full, mostly older recruits showing off for anyone who'll watch. I sit up in the stands, chewing on a protein bar that tastes vaguely like ass and regret, when I see her. Allyssa. She's stretching near the obstacle wall, hair pulled back, shoulders tense, aura prickling with barely restrained violence. Every motion she makes is precision-crafted to say *don't fuck with me*; it works.

Most of the other students give her a wide berth, like she's radioactive, and honestly? She kind of is, but me? I'm staring like a dumbass, again. Gods, she's beautiful; Not the delicate kind, not the polished, magazine-cover kind, she's raw. There's a storm living in her bones and lightning behind her eyes. Because every time she moves, it's like she's writing a new kind of scripture; one made of fury and devotion and something that sounds an awful lot like worship. Watching her fight is like watching nature decide to end a bloodline. And every time I think I've seen the worst of her; I just want more.

I should've walked away. I told myself that, sitting up in the grandstand of the class arena, watching Allyssa warm up like she didn't just ruin my entire ability to think straight every time she breathed. *I would tell her she was torturing me, if I didn't think she would in fact enjoy that information a little too much"* I say to my wolf, he just sends through his desire and a sense of pride of his bonded, I just roll my eyes at his blatant favouritism. She's down in the pit, stretching like she owns the place; because, let's be honest, she does. Most of the students are five years older than her in their last year of the Academy, and every one of them keeps sneaking glances like she might unhinge her jaw and eat them whole. Honestly? She might. And I'd probably still follow her into the woods after.

Her ponytail is high and tight, her shoulders coiled with calm fury, and the entire arena smells like anticipation and subtle fear. Gods, she's stunning, and dangerous, and mine....Sort of, soon, eventually, if she accepts us. The other recruits start whispering when she moves to spar. Some blonde female witch. What's her name again. Paige, I think, murmurs a spell under her breath. I stand in disbelief and indignation, "Nope," I mutter. "Not today, Satan." I have been studying mortal realm stuff in my spare time, trying to understand her and where she comes from. They say that a lot it seems.

But before I can open my mouth to warn her, Allyssa whips around and snarls, "Paige, try that spell again and I'll introduce your face to an infestation of flesh-eating beetles like last time. Or maybe you want to see what happens when I get creative." The arena goes quiet, Paige goes pale, and I have the biggest shit eating grin on my face as I sit back down, impressed, and slightly terrified. *That's my female, w*ait. No. Not *my* female. I mean of course she's her own person and I respect that. But also; *mine.* Shut up, brain.

She's partnered with Kael; upper rank, big mouth, average skill. I've seen him train before. He's got a decent hook but zero discipline.

Allyssa doesn't even blink.

They circle each other like wolves testing the air. Kael lunges.

She doesn't step back.

She lets him come close, his breath hot and eager, his arrogance thick enough to choke on.

Then; like a blade unsheathed in the dark; she moves.

A pivot. A twist. Her elbow slams into his nose, cartilage shattering with a crack that echoes through the stone arena. He stumbles back, blood already dripping down his face.

She doesn't pause. Doesn't even blink.

Kael's eyes flare wide; panic blooming like a bruise. He charges again, desperate and clumsy.

Allyssa ducks, slides her leg behind his knee, and wrenches his arm back. A pop, a hiss of pain; his shoulder dislocates as she drives him face-first into the dirt. Every crack of bone, every gasp, it's like the bond itself is purring in my chest. My wolf likes it. Wants more. And I hate that part of me almost does too.

His muffled scream is music to her ears. You can tell by the slightly unhinged, sadistic smile that is on her lips. But she doesn't stop.

Two more recruits; one female, Half fae half witch I think, one male, pure blood seelie; rush her from behind, fury and fear mixing in their scent. Allyssa spins on them like a storm. "Really?" she calls, voice ringing clear and amused. "Three against one? Are you sure you don't want to give me a blindfold too? Maybe tie one hand behind my back?" Gods, she's enjoying this. She lets the first female get close enough to grab her hair; then snaps her head forward, slamming her forehead into the female's nose. Blood spatters the dirt. The female drops, clutching her face, sobbing. She sweeps her leg under Kael again as he charges blindly, and he eats dirt a second time. This isn't a fight. It's a lesson. And then; The temperature shifts. Like static in the air before a storm.

The male hesitates.

Mistake.

Allyssa lunges, claws slicing the air. She rakes them across his arm; just deep enough to mark him, to let him feel the price of his arrogance.

He screams.

She kicks his knee out, and he collapses like a puppet with cut strings.

I glance toward the top tier of the stands and freeze. A man I've never seen before stands there; mid-thirties, maybe older, sharp suit tailored like sin. His hair is bright blue, his eyes; gold, and his entire presence drips with magic and predator calm. He's not a student. Not a professor.. And he's staring at Allyssa like she's art he lost in another life. My wolf snarls in response a predatory claim to their mate. The smile on his face? It's admiration. Maybe more. My hackles rise. *Who the fuck is that? I say to my wolf* No one else seems to notice him; just me. And Allyssa. Because in that moment, she stops. Mid-fight. Turns slightly. And locks eyes with him. Something flickers in her expression. A twitch. A breath. Recognition?

Her brow furrows; but then it's gone. She blinks the moment away like swatting a gnat, turns back, and slams her knee into the third recruit's gut, knocking the wind out of him. He crumples. The other two groan from the floor. All down. Just like that. She stands over them, breathing steady, the absolute vision of a goddess who did *not* come here to play.

The man on the balcony bowed his head; mocking or respectful, I couldn't tell. But I wanted to punch him anyway. And then... I wanted to rip that suit off and see if he was all glitter and charm or if there was something beneath that would bleed. I hate that I want to know. The way he looked at her; it wasn't innocent. It was *familiar*. And she saw him. He's not just another pretty face in a suit. He's a question mark I can't afford. And she looked at him like he was an answer. She *felt* him. I know she did. My jaw clenches, and my wolf claws at the edge of my skin, fear starts to take hold, what if this man can unravel what is supposed to be unbreakable. Mine I growl in my head. He doesn't belong here. He doesn't belong anywhere near her. And if he thinks he can......*No*. Breathe. Not here.

Kael groans from the dirt.

She stalks over to him, eyes glowing with that eerie, turquoise light. Her mouth twitches in something like a smile; except there's no warmth in it. She plants her foot on his chest, pinning him. And then; she lets it slip. The air shivers. Magic ripples out of her like a thunderclap, that alpha aura; raw, commanding, absolute; slamming into everyone around her.

Silence. Every eye in the arena is on her. As I look around the arena another wave of her Aura slips free and I could have sworn I felt a royal fae aura of submission there. I think everyone else did as well because as my head turns taking in the crowd every other natural is in a submission stance based on their respective species stance of submission. Shifters are showing their throat, fae have bowed their heads palms facing up, witches, vampires and everyone else has bowed their heads with either their palms up or beside them palms facing outwards.

Then I see it: my own reflection in the polished blackstone beneath my knees. My throat bared. My palms open in offering. Like a supplicant at her altar. The realization hits like a fist. For a heartbeat, I want to stay there; let her take whatever she wants from me. But I can't. Not if I'm going to be her equal, at least not in front of others.

I force my eyes to break from her and flicker up; across the stands, searching. That's when I see him. The man with the blue hair, watching her with that same quiet reverence. Not bowing. Not kneeling. Just watching, like he's seen this before and he's been waiting for it.

My skin prickles with something cold. Because even as Allyssa's power demands my submission, I know that man doesn't bow to anyone. And neither should I. Not completely. Not if I'm going to stand between her and whatever the fuck he thinks he can claim.

My legs tremble with the effort, but I stand. Because no matter how much of me wants to kneel for her forever, I know that's not what she needs. She needs someone who can meet her in the darkness and not flinch. Someone who can see the monster she's been forced to become and still offer her the soft places she's never known. And gods help me, I'm going to be that someone. Even if it means letting her break me to prove it.

She hasn't noticed everyone in the crowd; keeping her eyes trained on Kael in front of her. Kael whimpers, his head turning to the side, to avert his eyes and holds his hands up palms facing up in offering. Full submission. She smiles down at him, voice as smooth as silk but sharp enough to draw blood. "Next time you want to measure your worth, Kael," she says, her tone honeyed and cruel, "pick someone who's not going to make you beg. Thanks for the warmup, pretty boy. Now run along before I decide to really play". Her Aura snaps back to her and everyone is released.

She steps off him, turns, and walks away; unhurried, untouchable, her aura still crackling in the air like a storm that refuses to fade. I look to Kael, still on the ground but staring at her, clear longing and desire shining on his face. My gut twists at the sight; I'm about to jump down and force him to stop looking at what is mine when his expression contorts in pain, eyes rolling white.

I freeze, scanning the arena, searching for the source. That's when I see him; the blue-haired male, mouth moving in a silent snarl of disgust, his eyes locked on Kael. He doesn't break that gaze, even as Kael gasps and groans, his whole body shuddering like he's caught in a vice.

And then... it's over. Kael collapses back to the dirt, gasping for breath, and the blue-haired male is gone. Just gone. As if he was never there.

I don't know how to feel about this. My wolf purrs with satisfaction at Kael's punishment; he deserved it for daring to look at her like that. But another part of me burns with loathing that the blue-haired male thought he had the right to do it. To discipline one of our own. To stake a claim in a moment that should have been between Allyssa and me.

I file it away; along with the flicker of fear that he could make someone as arrogant as Kael kneel without even touching him. Because if he can do that to Kael, what could he do to me? To Allyssa?

I don't know. But I'm going to find out. Because this is our fight. Our bond. And I'll be damned if I let anyone else decide how it ends. My communication orb notifies me of an incoming message from my sister Emily, the message flashing on its surface as I drag my thumb over the notification. "Cas, you need to answer your gods damn orb, or so help me I will come down there. I am just worried about this bond you have with the black wolf. My sweet little brother deserves better than this." My heart aches at her message. I have a few similar messages from her, I have yet to hear from the rest of the family, but Em's messages have made it even harder to contact anyone. I want them to love her, I don't think they realise just how much their opinions mean to me. So I put the orb back into my pocket and ignore Emily, just for now.

Later that day, I sit outside the mess hall, doodling circles in the dirt with a stick like some lovesick wolf with boundary issues. I'm not even hungry. I just want to see her. Even if she doesn't see me. Even if she won't. Maybe I'm crazy; maybe this bond is some cosmic joke and she's just waiting for the right moment to stab me in the chest and say "plot twist." I tell myself I'm not afraid of her darkness. But the truth? I'm terrified. Terrified of what it will demand of me. And what I'll give; without hesitation. Perhaps Emily was right to be worried about me. I shake those thoughts away as a memory surfaces.

Allyssa her face the day we bonded. Not the blood. Not the violence. The look. The way she looked at me like I was the only thing keeping her grounded. Like if she let go, she'd vanish. And I knew, right then: she wanted to be seen. She just doesn't know how.

Later that night, I'm pacing the dorm courtyard like a fool with a heartbeat too loud for his chest. I keep seeing the way she looked at him. Not shocked. Not afraid. Curious. Like something in her recognized him; and decided to say nothing. And the part that's killing me? She didn't block him out. Not like she does with me. Me; the male she bonded with. The male who bleeds for her. The male who's dying to be let back in.

All I get is silence. But him? He got a look. A flicker of something I've never seen her give to anyone else. Even if it was faint. Even if she didn't mean it. It still fucking burns. My jaw aches from how hard I'm clenching it. My wolf snarls, pacing the cage of my ribs, demanding I do something—anything—to protect what's ours. Because that's what she is. Ours. And if that male—whoever he is—thinks he can stake a claim? I swear to the moon, I'll bury him under the arena floor myself.

Tomorrow, I'll try again. Because here's the thing about me: I'm the sweet male who says please and holds the door open. The male who apologizes when he steps on someone's foot. But I'm also the male who'll burn the world down if the people I love are in danger. Those three bastards who jumped me? They're still healing. I saw the bruises. The casts. Justice came, and it didn't wear a robe. It wore teeth. And if the system hadn't made them pay, I would have. With or without Allyssa.

Because love doesn't mean being soft. Sometimes it means becoming the sharpest fucking edge in the room. Next time she looks at me, I'm not asking for answers. I'm demanding them. Because this bond? It's not just fate. It's a choice. And I'm choosing her. Even if she hasn't figured out how to choose me back yet. Maybe that's the reason in my madness of jealousy, the one thing that makes all this chaos worth it.

It's her. It's always her.

I'm done playing the sweet male she can ignore. Next time she sees me, she'll see everything. All of me. The male who bleeds for her. And the male who will break anyone who thinks they can take her from me.

Chapter Eight: A Lesson in History

"Power tends to corrupt, and absolute power corrupts absolutely."

— Lord Acton

Allyssa POV

History class was never quiet at the Academy. Too many old truths. Too many factions with opinions about who should have died and who didn't die enough.

Professor Halvaren didn't bother waiting for the room to settle. He was the type of professor that had a permanent scowl on his face, looking at the students with a clear "who hates me enough to have me teaching these idiots" type of look, it honestly brings a smile to my face every time.

"All right," he said, clapping once, sharp. "Let's start with a question. Who here can tell me why the Academy exists?"

A few hands went up. Too eager. Too rehearsed. I rolled my eyes.

"Yes," Halvaren said, pointing to a Seelie female in pale silver robes.

"To train Hunters," she said. "To protect the realm."

Halvaren nodded once. "That is what we do. Not why we exist, perhaps listen to the question properly before you answer next time hunter Bella." The female ducked into her chair, I chucked quietly, maybe this will be more entertaining than I thought.

The professor turned. "Another."

A Shadowkin male skin black as coal, shadowkin signature inky moving swirls up his arms, teeth sharp, eyes pin points of red, spoke without raising his hand. "To keep balance between factions."

"Closer, Hunter Felix, but that is only part of it, is that the type of answers I should expect from you this year?." Felix flickered his whole body turning to a shadow before becoming corporeal again, the pattern just above his elbow pulsing.

Someone else muttered, "To stop wars."

Halvaren looked to the source of the interruption and smiled thinly. "There is always one that gives that ridiculous answer. Incorrect. Wars," he continued, "are inevitable. They are the natural by-product of power, scarcity, and pride. Anyone who tells you otherwise is selling doctrine, not history." He says with such annoyance that I couldn't help but chuckle.

A ripple of discomfort passed through the hall. I leaned back, arms crossed, watching. My wolf stirred, alert now. Listening. Halvaren's gaze landed on me. "Black Wolf," he said calmly. "Why?"

A few heads snapped my way, a range of looks on all the faces from lust to envy, to distain, disgust and outright hostility, one in the front though doesn't even look, interesting. I smiled at them all, amused at all the range of emotions I was seeing.

I looked back to the professor and shrugged. "Because no one else could be trusted to do it without turning into tyrants."

A pause. Then Halvaren laughed. Once. Quiet, approving. "Yes," he said. "Exactly."

He turned back to the room. "The Academy exists because every faction failed the test of power, and the goddess's decided to intervene while allowing some autonomy for its children."

A hand lifted near the back. Werewolf. Salt-scented. Coastal pack tattoo's etched boldly into his jawline, and up his arms.

"What about the sea dominions?" he asked. "My pack borders Shatterbay. We keep hearing they refused to sign the Concord entirely."

A few heads turned. Interest sharpened.

Halvaren paused.

"Correct," he said. "The sea courts declined participation."

He gestured once, and the projection widened. Coastlines glimmered. Vast. Blue-black. Separate.

"The sea dominions unified early," he continued. "One rule. One crown. One law beneath the tides. They watched the surface fracture itself and decided restraint was not something we had earned."

A murmur rippled through the hall.

"They maintain their own kingdoms, species, and trade routes," Halvaren went on. "Contact is limited. Controlled. Intentional."

The wolf inside me huffed softly. *Smart*, she murmured.

"They have made their position clear," Halvaren said. "When the surface stops devouring itself. When balance is enforced rather than promised. Then they will come to the table."

A student scoffed. "So never."

Halvaren's gaze flicked to him. Sharp. Unimpressed.

"History is a long argument," he said. "We will revisit the land–sea accords later this year. And next. Assuming you're still enrolled."

That shut them up.

The projection wards ignited, casting light across the stone dome. A map of Veyloris unfurled above us, veins of magic glowing like a living thing. "Before borders," Halvaren continued, "before councils, before crowns, there were gods."

Halvaren waved his hand, and the ceiling dissolved into a starfield.

A collective groan rose from the students.

Halvaren's expression sharpened. "Do not groan. Gods shaped this realm. Ignorance of them is not rebellion, it's stupidity."

Symbols ignited one by one.

"Selene," he said. "Goddess of the Moon. Patron of shapeshifters. Wolves, cats, serpents, those who draw power from cycles, tides, and change."

The moon flared.

"The Mother of Nature," he continued. "Creator of aligned life. Dryads. Druids. Forest nymphs. Satyrs. Those bound to growth, decay, and renewal."

Roots spread across the projection.

"Lilith," he said next, voice neutral. "Goddess of blood and hunger. Vampires. Ghouls. Demons. She governs survival through consumption."

A crimson sigil of an open hand holding a black flame pulsed.

"Warlocks and witches," Halvaren added, "are not the creation of a single god. Nor are the fae. They are the result of overlap. Compromise. Interference."

He paused.

"It was these three goddesses who bound themselves to Veyloris," he said. "Who hid it when the portals first opened. Who kept this realm intact long after others were culled. And as we are all aware three years ago they re-opened and we had different realms come through them. Noone yet knows why the god's protection of the portals have been lifted, and I know with the new races has come battles where some in this room have lost family and or friends. We will talk more about this later in the year. For now lets get back to the foundational knowledge."

The wolf inside me lifted her head.

They stayed though, she said again.

"When the other gods threatened this realm," Halvaren said, chalk tapping once against the board, "it was not born of cruelty." A ripple of confusion passed through the class. "It was curiosity." Murmurs followed.

"All realms were experiments," he continued, voice flat as archival stone. "Forged to test possibility. To refine magic. To measure evolution. According to the oldest texts, the gods did not build worlds for worship."

He paused. "They built them for trials." The ley-lines flared, brighter now. The projection shifted above us. Images unfolded in ghostlight: battlefields, councils, forests burning, cities rising and falling. "Every few thousand years," Halvaren went on, "the realms were tested. Physical strength. Loyalty. Honor. Strategy. Intelligence. The relationship between magic and those who wielded it."

His chalk scratched across the board without him touching it. "Those deemed unstable were culled. Reset. Begun again." The word reset hit harder than destroyed. My jaw tightened. "Veyloris," he said, "was approaching its trial." The projection shifted again.

Selene's crescent burned bright. Mother Nature's glyph glowed gold-green. And Lilith's black flame pulsed in warning. "They broke rank." The crescent fractured into light. The leaf-glyph sank into stone like a secret buried too deep. The palm holding the black flame closed.

"Together, they sealed Veyloris. Hid it from divine sight. Bound the ley-lines in a way no other realm had been bound."

The projection darkened. Something rose in place of the vanished sigils. Black. Smooth. Seamless. A stone. No symbol etched into it. No divine mark. Just weight.

"The old texts disagree on why," Halvaren said carefully. "Some claim Veyloris had already proven itself. Others say it was about to be erased." Thus our seasonal rites. When they refused the Trials, they not only sealed Veyloris. They altered how the realm feeds its power.

Instead of being tested by gods, Veyloris sustains itself through the three season rites. The three seasonal transfers? They are the compromise, for as long as we can sustain it.

His gaze flicked briefly toward the central ley-line column that ran beneath the Academy.

"Only the Huntstone knows the full truth."

Silence fell thick. The ley-lines pulsed once. Not in agreement. Not in denial. Just... awareness. The Huntstone. It dominated the image the way it dominated the Academy grounds: without decoration, without explanation, without apology. A few students inhaled sharply. Halvaren let them look.

"What do you know about it?" he asked.

Silence stretched. Then, from the upper tier, a quiet voice. Unseelie. Male.

"It does not respond to magic."

Halvaren inclined his head. "Correct." Another student, bolder. "It's Umbrakyn glass."

"Perhaps."

"Volcanic obsidian," someone added. "Forged under pressure no surface forge can replicate."

"Maybe."

A pause.

"And?" Halvaren prompted.

I felt it then. A faint pressure behind my eyes. Like something listening. The wolf leaned forward in my mind, attentive. *Listen,* she urged.

A Warlock student scoffed. "It's unbreakable."

Halvaren's mouth twitched. Not quite a smile.

"Almost."

That earned him their full attention.

"Officially," he continued, pacing slowly, "the Huntstone is classified as a relic of unknown origin. Its earliest documented mention appears in pre-Exodus records, approximately nine hundred and forty years before the Academy's founding."

A ripple of surprise. "The Academy," he went on, "was not built to house the Huntstone. It was built *around* it."

The image shifted again. Architectural overlays appeared, showing walls curving, foundations bending, entire designs adjusted mid-construction to accommodate the monolith's presence.

"We adapted to it," Halvaren said evenly. "Not the other way around."

Something in my chest tightened. The wolf exhaled slowly. *It was there before the crowns,* she murmured. *Before the hunts.* The monster did not like it. *It measures,* it whispered. *And it remembers.* Halvaren stopped pacing.

"Several early factions attempted to remove the Huntstone," he said, voice calm, factual. "The first, a coalition of high warlocks, failed spectacularly. Every excavation spell collapsed. Every binding ritual unraveled."

A student raised a hand. "They were cursed, weren't they?"

Halvaren looked at him. "Define cursed."

The student swallowed. "Their bloodline died out."

A beat.

"Yes," Halvaren said. "Within three generations. No illness. No external attack. Every heir born still. Every legacy ended."

The room went very quiet.

"A second attempt," he continued, "was made two centuries later by a joint Seelie tribunal. They did not even reach the stone. The delegation vanished en route. Their descendants followed within a decade."

Someone whispered, "That's not coincidence."

"No," Halvaren agreed. "It is pattern recognition."

He tapped his cane once against the floor.

"Since then," he said, "no faction has attempted removal. Scholars who notice the pattern tend to stop asking questions."

A vampire muttered, "Cowards."

A quiet voice answered from two rows down. Unseelie. Same male as before.

"Or survivors."

Heads turned. The Unseelie student didn't look up. Halvaren let the tension breathe.

"Symbolically," he resumed, "the Huntstone represents the longstanding treaty between the Academy and the Umbrakyn Dominion. The Court provided the glass. The Academy provided sanctuary."

A Seelie student snorted. "They don't form alliances. They bargain."

The Unseelie male finally lifted his gaze.

"And you mistake the difference."

A few students shifted uncomfortably. Halvaren's eyes gleamed faintly with approval.

"There are legends," he said, voice lowering, "that the Huntstone once served as a conduit."

A murmur spread.

"For what?" someone whispered.

"For whom?"

Halvaren did not answer immediately. "No verified record confirms this," he said carefully. "But certain myth circles suggest it functioned as a *voice*. Not a weapon. Not a gate."

His gaze swept the room.

"A witness."

The wolf stirred again. A pulse of something old. *Remember,* she urged. *Not yet,* I told her. *Not here.*

"What we do know," Halvaren concluded, "is that the Huntstone responds to prophecy. Not predictively. Reactively."

Halvaren folded his hands behind his back. A pause. A Seelie student near the aisle raised a cautious hand. "Professor... is the Academy aware that the Huntstone has been... different lately?"

A ripple moved through the hall. Not panic. Curiosity sharpened by fear. Halvaren did not answer immediately. "Yes," he said at last.

His gaze lifted. It did not stop on me. It passed over me. The Monster felt it like a blade sliding between ribs. *He sees,* it hissed. *He knows where to look.* No one else noticed. Of course they didn't. To them it was just another academic pause. Another professor measuring his words. The wolf stilled, alert but calm. *Not threat,* she murmured. *Attention.*

Another student spoke quickly, pressing the opening.

"Do we know why?"

Halvaren's mouth curved faintly. Not a smile. A warning.

"The Academy is investigating," he said. "Beyond that, the matter falls under restricted historical inquiry."

A murmur of protest. Someone muttered, "That's convenient."

Halvaren's cane struck stone once. Clean. Sharp.

"Students who have not completed their alignment assessment," he said coolly, "are not entitled to speculative access to prophecy-adjacent research."

Silence. He let it sit.

"The Huntstone," he continued, "has outlived kings, courts, and gods who believed themselves permanent. Whatever it does, it does so on its own terms."

His gaze moved on. The pressure behind my eyes eased. The Monster did not relax. *He will watch you now,* it warned. *They always do.* Good, the wolf replied, unbothered. *Let them.* He gestured, and the warded air shimmered. A series of dates burned into existence above the lecture pit, etched in pale gold.

Year 0 of the Concord Era

Founding of the Verdant Athenaeum

"Let's begin properly," he said. "The Academy was founded three thousand, two hundred and fourteen years ago, at the end of the Fae Wars. Long enough," Halvaren added dryly, "that every faction in this room has rewritten their role in those wars at least three times since."

The projection shifted. Two figures appeared. One dark flames dancing along his arms. One light water swirling around his feet. I saw a figure in the back nothing focal, more of a blur of blue hair.......

"The first Black Wolf," Halvaren said, voice steady.

"Adrian Nocthyr."

Something in my chest tightened. The wolf inside me went very still.

"And the first White Wolf," he continued.

"Caelum Vale."

The names carried weight. Even spoken casually, they pressed into the room.

A hand shot up. "Weren't they weapons?"

"Yes," Halvaren replied without hesitation. "And executioners. And saviours. And the first Directors of this Academy."

He turned slightly. "Power does not come in clean shapes."

The image widened. Behind the Wolves stood two more figures. Their mates.

"Katarina of the Dravenwald, bonded to Adrian. A druid-general."

"And Seraphine of the Tides, seer and strategist, bonded to Caelum."

A murmur rippled through the students. Cross-breeding was murmured across the room, and I let out a warning growl. They all shut their mouths.

He let all that information sink in and land before adding, dryly, "Which should already complicate some of your assumptions about the Academy and, the original black wolf although there is still truth to the stories of the black wolf that should keep that healthy dose of fear present."

I felt my wolf stir, a low pulse of recognition. *They ruled together*, she said. *Not above.* Halvaren flicked his fingers. A bright blue crystal orb floated forward, spinning slowly. Inside it, memories shimmered. A stone hall under construction. Wolves pacing its perimeter. Runes being laid into the earth itself.

"These are contemporaneous records," Halvaren said. "Preserved memory-anchors. Not stories."

He gestured to another projection. A journal page appeared, its script sharp and angular. *"The land resists crowns. It accepts stewards. Almost like it whispers not yet, I wonder what it's waiting for."*

— Adrian Nocthyr, Founding Journal

Halvaren turned. "The Academy was not founded to rule the realm. It was founded to prevent any single faction from doing so."

"When a monarch grows oppressive. When a council tips toward conquest. When treaties fail quietly behind closed doors," Halvaren said, "the Academy intervenes." He did not elaborate. He didn't need to.

"After the deaths of the first black and white wolves," Halvaren continued, "the Academy refused to allow takeovers." The projection shifted again. A long list of names scrolled past. Different species. Different origins. "Directors are elected," he said. "Chosen by faculty consensus and by The Academy itself." That last part drew attention. I leaned back slightly. My wolf's ears pricked. *Careful,* she murmured. Halvaren smiled thinly. "Yes. The rumours are true. To a degree."

A student blurted, "The loyalty ritual?"

Halvaren's annoyance was immediate. "It is not a ritual. It is an alignment assessment." He tapped his cane again.

"After the vote and a consensus has been reached, the newly appointed director is taken to the Academy to be sworn in. The Hunters guide the new director to a part of the Academy that housing the alignment assessment and is classified, and yes before you ask it is the same assessment you will all do in your final year to be sworn in as Hunters of this Academy. If the new director or new final year Hunter fails, this assessment and you are not aligned........

He shrugged. "Then you are sent home. Your memories of the Academy removed. Cleanly."

The room went cold. "We do not apologise for this," Halvaren said flatly. "We take responsibility for power. That is the difference. That is why communication for students outside the Academy is forbidden." I swallowed. Somewhere deep inside, the little girl in me recoiled. Necessary, the warrior answered coldly.

The image zoomed in. Flames engulfed a forest.

"The Grove," he said. "Formerly the Heart of the Driads." A hush fell.

"A previous Black Wolf," Halvaren said, "burned the Driad lands."

The words hit like a blade. Halvaren seemed to be studying the other students with this harsh reality.

I felt it immediately. The wolf recoiled. Not in shame. In fury.

Lies without context, she growled.

A student near the front spat, "Genocide." Looks to be a witch, wait I know that witch. That is the one that hovers around Caspian, damn it, her name is on the tip of my tongue.

Halvaren nodded. "That is the charge history remembers. Ms Laya." Laya that's it. Clearly she is not a fan. Well neither am I, her heart shaped face, always staring at Caspian with adoration, makes me want to puke. But I am not threatened, I haven't seen anything more between them, when I do let myself look. At least not from Caspian. Even if the ease in which they talk and laugh together makes my imagination run wild with all the different ways to kill her.

Then the professor changed the projection. I tore myself away from my murderous thought and regained my emotions and focused.

Roots, poisoned. Rivers blackened. Dryads collapsing where they stood. "The Fae Wars ended," Halvaren continued, "in Year 12 of the Concord Era. The poisoning of Dryad lands began seventy-eight years later." The hall went very still. A student frowned. "Why the delay?"

Halvaren nodded. "Good question." He flicked his fingers. A trade ledger appeared. Names of factions. Resource tallies. "The Dryads were being harvested," he continued calmly. "Poisoned. Drained. Their resources stripped by every faction represented in this room." The murmurs started amongst the students. Some horrified, some refusing to believe that their own factions would do that, some that were asking for proof. Halvaren let them whisper and talk for a few minutes before he hit his cane to the stone, causing all talking to cease.

"The Black Wolf did not intervene immediately," Halvaren continued, voice steady, academic. "This era also marks the first *recorded emergence* of what scholars later classified as bloodlust within the Black Wolf lineage."

The word struck like a knuckle to bone. Inside me, something braced. Muscle memory took over. Jaw locked. Spine straightened. Fingers curled once against the desk, nails biting wood before I forced them flat again. Breathe in. Count. Anchor. The monster pressed forward anyway, teeth bared behind my eyes.

They speak of it like rot, it whispered. Like weakness. Halvaren's gaze swept the hall and paused on me. Expectant. I didn't rise to it. He can fuck right off if he thinks I'll turn this into a confession. "Can anyone tell me," Halvaren said, "what bloodlust is. And why it does *not* manifest in all werewolves?"

A hand shot up. Vampire. Smiling. Fangs just visible when he spoke.

"Isn't it just what happens when wolves can't control themselves?" he said lightly. "A defect. Cull the line and the problem solves itself."

The room laughed. Those that did not carry any wolf blood at least. I didn't. A sound tore out of my chest before I could stop it. Low. Vibrating. Not loud. Not wild. A warning.

The desks closest to me shuddered. Glass rattled. Several students flinched hard enough to scrape chairs. The vampire's smile died instantly, colour draining from his face as instinct screamed louder than pride.

The wolf surged, incandescent with rage. Say it again, it urged the male. See what happens. My hands tightened until the wood creaked. If it were possible, the vampire lost what little colour his recent feed had given him, the scent of fear saturating the room quickly not just from him from every natural in this room.

I didn't look for Caspian. If I had, I wasn't sure what I'd see on his face. Fear would have been easier than understanding or worse sympathy. I honestly have been doing well ignoring his existence I think, he should be looking to dissolve this bond in no time. My wolf's bloodlust amplified. Halvaren moved fast.

"Enough," he snapped, planting his cane sharply against the stone. "That will do." His eyes flicked to me. Not reprimand. Calculation. "Miss Black," he said evenly looking directly at me, his expression held an underlying fear that he would not be able to save the male from me, but duty compelled him to try, "you are heard."

I held his gaze for a long second, murder still coiled tight behind my ribs, before forcing it down. The growl faded, but the silence it left behind was heavier than sound. Halvaren turned back to the class, his shoulders visibly sagging with relief, and that gave my wolf just a slight soothing notion to her bloodlust vibrating through our body.

"No," he said coldly. "Bloodlust is not lack of control. And it is not a genetic defect to be culled by those who fear what they do not understand."

Another student spoke, quieter now.

"Isn't it when a wolf goes feral?"

"Partial," Halvaren replied.

Then a pure-blood gamma rose. Calm. Measured. Respectful.

"Bloodlust is both a disease *and* a consequence," she said. "It develops when a wolf is severed from pack regulation for extended periods."

The room stilled.

"Wolves aren't meant to carry sustained violence alone," she continued. "Pack hierarchies exist for a reason. Alphas to command. Betas to stabilise. Gammas to absorb overflow. Rituals. Touch. Shared grounding."

The monster listened.

The wolf approved.

"When those systems are removed," the gamma said, "instinct doesn't disappear. It sharpens. Power accumulates with nowhere to bleed."

Her eyes flicked briefly to me. Not judgment. Recognition.

"The disease forms when survival becomes constant," she added. "When violence is required without recovery. Once established, it alters a wolf's instinct permanently. That's why it *appears* hereditary, even though it isn't born that way."

Halvaren nodded once.

"Correct, Gamma Pinebane" he said. "Bloodlust is an acquired pathology. Born of isolation, imbalance, and prolonged survival stress, that can be passed down generationally."

He let the words settle. I look over to the Gamma female and I assess, *she is smarter than the rest,* my wolf tells me we should consider her. I scoff at my wolf, and what make friends, or are we picking up the argument from before we came here to the Academy about finding a pack. My wolf goes silent frustration clear in our mind, *you know we will eventually need one for the bloodlust,* and like I told you we will find another way first and let binding ourselves to a pack be a last resort. She retreats into the back of my mind, the monster inside satisfied with my self-preservation tactic in this argument. Trust gets you killed.

"And the Black Wolf lineage," he finished, "was designed to endure exactly those conditions."

His gaze returned to me. I met it without blinking letting the craving for violence to enter my eyes, daring him to continue on with talk about the bloodlust any further, his gaze swiftly leaves mine and he takes in a deep breath as if shaking off my violent intent.

The monster eased back, not gone, but satisfied. Good, it murmured. They remembered how dangerous we are. Another image. Fire again. But this time movement. Figures fleeing. Being carried. "He burned the land," Halvaren said. Continuing from the bloodlust and back into The Grove's history. "And smuggled survivors through Umbrakyn shadow paths into Druvenwald."

The wolf inside me exhaled slowly. *Saved,* she said. *Not destroyed.* "No one remembers that part," Halvaren added. "Because the survivors lived. Quietly. And the world prefers simple villains." I swallowed. Around me, students shifted. Reconsidered. *Good,* the wolf murmured. *Let them.*

Halvaren deactivated the projection. "The Academy records history as it was," he said. "Not as it flatters us." His gaze swept the room. "And if this unsettles you," he finished, "good. That means you're learning." The professor looked over everyone and hoit his cane to the stone a few times "that's all for today, get off to your next class" dismissing everyone. No one moved.

The wolf leaned close inside me, voice low and insistent now. You will remember, she said. When you are ready. I didn't answer. But for the first time in that room, I didn't want to leave. I needed to know more since I had to dig for information on Veyloris growing up, this was the most upfront and easiest information I had gathered especially on the black wolf.

Chapter Nine: The Interrogation & Intelligence

"There are some that only employ words for the purpose of disguising their thoughts."

— *Voltaire*

Allyssa POV

"Deep beneath the Verdfall Enclave Mother Nature's most magically fortified land where the ley-lines hum and the forest outside bends instinctively around the Academy's will." The interrogation and intelligence simulation room smelled like salt and steele, down here, in the lowest ring of the Academy, the level only hunters and professors saw. Walls lined in blackstone. Wards humming under the floor, pulsing faintly with the same tri-coloured glow that sometimes flickered in the sky over Veyloris when the ley lines shifted. My thoughts wander for a moment about how the Academy's halls *reek of power, but not half as much as the ones watching from above*, glass panes above where the fully pledged Hunters sat watching like gods peering down on mortals. They came from every corner of Veyloris; Druids of the Lyrravene Wilds, pale Tribunal elites imported from Calyxion, and stray pack-born wolves trained in the Frostpine Expanse. We were beneath them. Where truths bled. Every lesson here is a test. Every test a trap. And I refuse to be caught in anyone's snare but my own.

The faelight shard above us flickered with the soft teal native only to Aureslong; the Seelie capital whose mirrored lakes could hold magic like breath. Professor Vyn stood at the head of the platform, all in black, with a voice like surgical precision. "Control," she said, "is the art of giving your subject the illusion of choice; while removing every actual exit." She turned slowly, surveying the room. "Physical pain is a crutch. Crude. Predictable. You cut a man's finger, he tells you what he thinks you want to hear. But if you find what he *fears* losing?" She smiled. "Then he tells you what he never wanted anyone to know. Remember: the mind is a kingdom built on illusions. A kingdom you must rule with precision, not force. The difference between dominance and submission is always choice; or the illusion of it". The professors' eyes find mine as she recites that last one as if I needed to know this for another reason, then she looks over the rest of the students.

Half of them were scions of Iseryth and Umbrakyn, bearing faint faelight or onyx-ink sigils. A few wore the silver-threaded cuffs of Shadefen's Shadowkin accords. Others, like me, carried nothing visible at all. The most dangerous kind. One that has no kin, no place where I belong.

Students murmured behind their crystal screens. Most of them watching the other pairs. Only a few were watching me. Kael was one of them. "Today's simulation," Professor Vyn said, stepping aside, "is a live interrogation under limited arcane influence. No truth spells. No mindwalking. Just psychology, leverage, and instinct." She looked at me directly. "Hunter Allyssa. You're on." Time to play. People always told you who they were if you gave them enough rope.

Kael swaggered into the interrogation chair like it was a throne. He leaned back, legs spread, arms loose across the rests. Arrogant. Golden-haired. Confident in the kind of way males get when they've been told since birth the world was theirs for the taking. He'd been raised between Iseryth's Seelie courts and Academy drills, although he thought he was better than wolves he carried the same superiority seen in the Stromglen's warrior sons in the Frostpine packholds. Groomed to take command posts in Calyxion's patrols one day, if the Tribunal had its way.

Behind the glass, I heard a female whisper, "Gods, he's hot." Another scoffed. "Yeah, until he opens his mouth." Kael glanced toward them and winked. "Try not to fall in love, ladies. The collar's strictly decorative." Laughter ensues throughout the students.

INT. INTERROGATION ROOM

Wards hum low under the floor. Cold air tastes like salt and steel. A single table and two chairs sit at the center, lit by a shard of faelight overhead.

Professor Vyn (calm, deadly)

(voice echoing through the crystal)

"Begin."

Kael

(slides into the chair with a cocky smirk, legs spread, golden hair tousled like a war banner)

"Let's not pretend this is a fair fight, half-blood. You want the phrase? You're going to have to dig deeper than pretty words and sharper claws."

Allyssa

(*Inside: Gods, he's beautiful when he's this sure of himself. All that confidence... it's going to taste so much better when it shatters.*)

(slow smile, predator's amusement flickering in my eyes)

"Oh, I plan to. The thing is, Kael—"

(leans forward, palms flat on the table, voice velvet and lethal)

"—I'm not here to be fair. I'm here to see how much you'll give me before you break."

Kael

(grins, teeth bright, voice low and smooth)

"You think I'll fold for you? I've been trained for this, half-breed. I know how to hold my ground."

Allyssa

(*Inside: Oh, sweet boy, how I love a challenge. The harder you fight, the sweeter the surrender. Let him think he has a choice. Let him cling to it like a shield—until he realises I'm the only thing he'll kneel for*) (I chuckle softly, circling him, my boots silent on the blackstone)

"Oh, I know you do. The perfect Hunter. The academy's prize thoroughbred, never a hair out of place."

(I stops behind him, voice a whisper in his ear)

"But here's the truth, Kael, no one's ever really seen you. Not the male behind the discipline. The male who wonders if he's just another pawn in their games."

Kael

(his jaw tightens, a flicker of vulnerability quickly hidden,)

"I'm not your toy, Allyssa."

Allyssa

(*Inside: He wants me to believe that. Wants it so badly he's practically shaking with the effort. Gods, it's almost endearing.*)

(my smile grows wider, sharper)

"No. You're not. But you're about to be mine."

I move in front of him, sliding into his lap in one fluid motion. Gasps echo from the watchers behind the glass.

Kael

(breath hitches, hands clench on the chair arms)

"You think straddling me will break me?" he growls, but there's a tremor in his voice.

Allyssa

(*Inside: You're already breaking, Kael. You just don't know how to fall yet.*)

(tilting my head, gaze hungry and clinical)

"No, Kael. That's just the opening move."

(my claws trace a line from his jaw to his throat, just enough to make his breath hitch)

"You're here to hold onto your precious phrase. But you're already shaking. Do you know why?"

(I lean close, lips brushing his ear)

"Because I see the cracks in your perfect mask. The part of you that wants to be seen. That's what's going to break you, not my claws."

Kael

(teeth clench, breath ragged)

"You're... you're nothing but a tool," he spits, but his voice wavers.

Allyssa

(*Inside: He's trying so hard to hold on. Gods, I could almost admire it—if I wasn't about to ruin him anyway.*)

(smiling sweetly, voice dripping like honey laced with venom)

"And you're terrified you're nothing but a pretty blade the academy forged to die in someone else's war."

(I cup his face, forcing him to meet my eyes)

"Tell me the phrase, Kael," I whisper, "Tell me the truth you're not allowed to say out loud."

Kael

(shakes his head, voice raw)

"No. I won't."

Allyssa

(*Inside: Oh, I'm going to enjoy this. Gods, I'm going to enjoy every fucking second of this.*)

(leans back, my gaze calculating, almost gentle)

"You want me to take it from you?"

(I lets my alpha aura flicker—crackling electric in the air, making Kael's back arch with instinctive submission)

"Or do you want to give it to me willingly?"

Kael

(eyes wide, breathing hard)

"Why does it matter?" he chokes out.

Allyssa

(*Inside: Because this isn't just about the phrase. This is about making you want to break. Want to give in. Because that's what makes it so delicious.*)

(smirk, leans in close enough our noses almost touch)

"Because if you give it to me, Kael, you get to be more than the academy's perfect Hunter for once. You get to be seen. Understood."

(my voice softens, dangerously intimate)

"Don't you want that? Even if it's just once."

Kael

(a shudder runs through him, eyes closing briefly, His voice trembles; not with fear, but with relief. Like he's been waiting for someone to strip away the lie of control he's lived in all his life)

"I... I'm not... I'm not just a soldier," he whispers.

Allyssa

(*Inside: That's it, pretty boy. Show me the real you—let me see what you've been hiding.*)

(I hum approvingly, my lips brushing his skin like a promise)

"Then prove it."

(I kiss him—slow, deliberate, claiming, my claws pressing just enough to draw a bead of blood)

(*Inside: I didn't do it for the mission. I didn't do it for him. I did it because I wanted to. Because making him break like this... gods, it's everything.*)

"Tell me the phrase," I murmur into his mouth. "Say it." *(I feel it in his breath, in the way his shoulders sag. His body is telling me yes even before his mouth does. That's the sweetest part watching the mind try to hold out while the body confesses everything)*

Kael

(voice breaking, trembling against her)

"Mercy is... mercy is for the weak."

(his head drops forward, breath ragged, eyes squeezed shut in shame and relief)

Allyssa

(*Inside: There it is. His truth. His surrender. Mine.*)

(pulls back, satisfaction gleaming in my eyes)

"Good boy," I say softly. "That's all I needed to hear."

I stand, smooth and effortless, brushing off my clothes like he's nothing but dust on my skin. Kael slumps in the chair, dazed and humiliated, but there's something else in his eyes; freedom and ruin, tangled together.

Allyssa

(*Inside: Let him think I did this for the Academy. For the mission. Let them all think that. The truth? I did it because I love the way a male looks at me when he's finally broken. When he's finally mine.*)

[INT. INTERROGATION ROOM – DEBRIEFING

Professor Vyn stands at the head of the room, crystal eyes cutting through the silence. Her posture is calm, but the energy in the air crackles like a live wire. Kael keeps sneaking glances to me, but I don't give him any of my attention, I got what I wanted from him and I take a long swig of the redcap press to rid the taste of Kael and his arrogance from my mouth. The win was sweet, the Kael aftertaste not so much. The redcap berries are fermented to create a burn down my throat that I actually enjoy with a sweet aftertaste of the honey they pour through the drink. Soon the taste of Kael is gone, the bond surges behind my ribs demanding attention, I close it off firmer. Focusing back to Vyn.

Professor Vyn

(voice as cold and clear as ice)

"Impressive, Allyssa. You didn't just break him. You *convinced* him to shatter himself. The Academy doesn't just breed Hunters,

Allyssa. It breeds rulers. And you? You're learning to rule them in the only language they understand"

(a thin smile, like the ghost of a blade)

"You found his want. His need. You *weaponised* it."

Allyssa

(leans back against the cold stone wall, arms folded, face calm)

"Was that not the point of the exercise?"

(*Inside: I'm not apologising. Not for this. I didn't just follow the lesson—I made it mine, and what is this about making me a ruler, this stuff keeps coming up, I might need to chat with the director shortly about this weird shit*)

Professor Vyn

"True. But there's a difference between breaking someone... and making them *want* to be broken."

(she steps closer, her gaze sharp)

"You gave him the illusion of choice. You made him believe he was seen. That's a rare skill, Allyssa. One that can't be taught."

A beat. Her eyes flick over my face, searching.

Professor Vyn

(softer, almost amused)

"Tell me—did you enjoy it?"

(the question is almost rhetorical, but it lands heavy)

Allyssa

(tilts her head, a slow smile curving her lips)

"Why wouldn't I?"

(*Inside: I did it because I wanted to. Because watching him come apart under my hand... that's what I am. That's what I love.*)

Professor Vyn

(smile deepens, her tone approving)

"Good. You'll need that edge. But remember—this was just a simulation. In the real world? Sometimes the ones who break the easiest are the ones who'll make you bleed for it later."

(she inclines her head, a subtle sign of respect)

"Dismissed."

I step out of the room, shoulders squared, chin lifted. In my head, there's no guilt, only the taste of victory and the memory of Kael's breath hitching in the dark.

I didn't do it for him.

I did it because I *could*. The queen in me enjoyed the stillness.

As I exited the room, someone muttered, "Fucking half-breed psycho." I smiled. I feel another presence watching, something colder, older. The blue-haired man. His eyes don't see just me; a cold pulse that smelled faintly of Umbrakyn shadow, the kind found only in Dubhlinn's night palaces; I wonder where he has been, he no longer smells of Draethen, how does he change his scent like that. Part of me wants him to watch. To see me burn. Then I caught a pulse in the bond. A spark. A flare. Caspian. Watching from the shadows. Jealousy churned through the tether like acid. Not possessive. Protective. But wild. I didn't turn. Because if I did; I wouldn't walk out. I'd kiss *him* instead. And that? That wouldn't be a tactic. It would be a *surrender to a desire I am in no way in control of, which is unacceptable.*

Caspian's POV

The corridor is silent except for the low hum of wards and the thud of my heart in my chest. My knuckles are white where they grip the railing. I should let her pass. I should give her the space she's demanding. But I can't. I can't let her walk away without knowing I'm still here.

"Allyssa."

She stops. Turns with a slow grace that makes every muscle in my body tighten. Those turquoise eyes lock on me, cold and knowing, and I swear I feel them carve through every lie I've ever told myself.

“Pretty boy,” she says softly, her lips quirking in amusement. “Shouldn’t you be off somewhere polishing that white knight halo of yours? Or did you enjoy the show?”

My pulse stutters. I force myself to meet her gaze. “I’m not here for the show,” I say quietly, and even I can hear the ache in my voice. “I’m here for you.”

She arches a brow. “For me?” She steps closer, her body language all sinuous, controlled power. “And what is it you think you’re here for, Caspian? To rescue me? To fix me?”

My jaw tightens. “No,” I say, my voice low. “I don’t want to fix you. I don’t want to save you. I just... I want you to let me in.”

She circles me slowly, her presence like gravity. My breath hitches as her fingers brush my shoulder, trailing down my arm. It’s a caress and a warning.

“You think you’re ready for that?” she murmurs. “You think you’re ready to see all the ways I’ll break you if you let me?”

I swallow, my throat dry. “I’m not afraid of you,” I whisper.

She stops behind me, her breath warm against my neck. “Oh, Caspian,” she sighs, and the sound is almost tender. Almost. “You should be.”

I close my eyes, drawing in a shaky breath. “Maybe I am,” I admit. “But I’m more afraid of what happens if I let you keep pushing me away.”

A pause. Then she laughs softly, and the sound is both beautiful and cruel. She moves to stand in front of me again, and I feel her eyes on me, peeling back every layer I’ve tried to hide.

“You’re sweet,” she says, her voice a soft mockery. “Too sweet. And sweet things... they break so easily.”

“I won’t,” I say fiercely, stepping closer so there’s no space between us. My heart’s pounding, but I don’t back down. “I won’t break. Not for you. Not because of you.”

She searches my face, her expression unreadable. For a moment, I think she might say something—admit something—but then she just smiles. Slow. Dangerous.

"You're saying all the right things, pretty boy," she says, her voice like silk on steel. "But words are cheap. And next time I test you... it won't be like today."

I nod once, my jaw set. "Then test me," I say, my voice hoarse with everything I'm not saying. "Push me as hard as you need to. I'll still be here."

For a heartbeat, she just looks at me. And there's something in her eyes—a flicker of hunger, of something she doesn't want to name. Then it's gone, shuttered behind her mask of calm indifference.

"Careful what you ask for, Caspian," she murmurs, stepping even closer until I can feel her breath on my lips. "Because I don't play nice. And I don't play fair."

"Good," I say, and my voice shakes but I don't care. "Because neither do I."

She studies me, her head tilted slightly. And then she reaches out—fingertips brushing my jaw, her nails just scratching enough to make my pulse jump. Her touch is soft and hard all at once, and my breath stutters.

"You're so sure," she whispers, her lips curving in a small, cold smile. "But here's the thing, pretty boy... I don't want to be saved. I want to be worshipped. And I want you to know that when you kneel, it won't be because I asked."

My stomach flips. My wolf growls low inside me, but I keep my voice steady. "Then I'll kneel," I say, each word like a promise carved in bone. "If that's what it takes to prove I can stand with you."

She laughs again, quiet and knowing. "We'll see," she says, turning away. "We'll see how far you're willing to fall."

As she walks away, her scent lingers in the air— Crisp mountain air and Caramel and something that's already sunk its teeth into me. My wolf rumbles low in my chest, not in warning—but in want. Like he knows she's the only one he'll ever kneel to. And in that moment, I know:

She didn't say I failed. She didn't say I passed. She just told me the truth—she's not done with me yet. And when the time comes... I'll be there. *She's going to test me again. She's going to drag out every fear, every weakness, and see if I'll still stand. And I will. Even if it kills me. Because what she doesn't see yet—what she doesn't believe—is that I'd burn the world for her. And maybe... just maybe... she wants me to.) Beyond the stone, beyond the Academy's forested cradle, Veyloris stretched: Dravenwald's ancient canopy in the north, Shadefen's whispering warrens in the east, and the corrupt red ash plains of The Grove further south.*

Chapter Ten: Lessons in Loyalty

"The true test of loyalty is how it endures in the darkest times." — Unknown

Caspian POV

The arena sat on the southern rise of the Academy. From here, the world unfolded, the Sapphire Coast glittering to the west, the storm-scoured Draethen brooding to the south, and the pale ghost-line of Lyrravene's forest crowns stretching across the north.

Combat training was supposed to be routine.

Paired sparring, elemental resistance drills, pressure zone enchantments; the kind of things you survived through sheer muscle memory. Not today. Not when my entire body was still vibrating with the memory of Allyssa kissing Kael like she was dissecting him from the inside out.

Professor Drayk stood on the stone dais above the arena, voice sharp as steel and twice as cold. "Interrogation wins wars. Combat maintains peace. But loyalty? Loyalty prevents the worst of both." He turned, gesturing to the arena wards, glowing faintly under the sunlight filtered through the domed glass roof. "Today you will fight your bonded partners. Not to win. But to learn what triggers their collapse. Your bond is both shield and blade. Use it or be buried by it."

Whispers skittered across the arena.

"Bet Blackie kills him."

"No way. He looks like he'd cry if she growled."

"He's got that tragic golden retriever energy. Would absolutely die for her."

"Or get pegged by her."

"You mean again."

I ignored them. But I felt Allyssa flinch through the bond. Not physically. Soul-deep.

She stood across from me. Relaxed. Dangerous. Beautiful. Mine. The thought came unbidden. Not possessive. Not really. But when I caught a fae female from Water Division eyeing me from the stands, her giggle slipping past her fingers, I felt the bond spike.

She sauntered over during warm-up, twirling a water glyph on her fingertip like it was nothing. She had the accent of Aureslong's lake courts; soft, musical, shaped by floating sanctuaries and mirrored halls. "Caspian, right? I've seen you train. You're kind of impressive. For someone who's bonded to death incarnate." I smiled, trying to be polite. "Thanks, I guess?" "Maybe sometime you can show me how your magic works. Up close." I was about to respond with something appropriately awkward and sweet when a sound sliced through the air like a blade. A low, guttural growl.

Every student turned. Allyssa was still standing in the ring. But her head was tilted slightly, wolf eyes glowing, lips curled back just enough to show teeth. "Step. Back." Each word punctuated with bearly restrained malice. The female flinched. Magic rippled in the air between us. Not a spell. Just pure intent.

She scurried away.

I stared at Allyssa.

Gods, she was terrifying.

And something inside me loved it.

"No bond flares. No uncontrolled shifts. No excuses," Drayk barked. His gaze lingered on Allyssa, then flicked to me. He knew. They all knew. We were paired again. Of course. Not because it was strategic. Because it was entertainment. Drayk stepped back.

"Begin."

The fight started clean. Strike. Dodge. Pivot. Grapple. A rhythm. Sweat started beading down my back. But I was off. Distracted. She wasn't. She was fighting like she had something to prove. Like every student watching her was an enemy in disguise. Like she was holding back the wolf with nothing but sheer willpower and a pulse of loyalty she hated admitting existed. Adrenaline sang through her, I could feel it through the bond, sharp and bright. The world narrowed around her movements, every strike precise, every breath measured. There was a thrill there, undeniable. The monster stirred at the edge of her control, pleased by the damage she inflicted, I could tell by the dilated pupils and the way she inhaled just a little deeper when one of her blows caused some blood trickling from the split lip.

She kept it leashed. Barely.

I stumbled. The moment I did, it happened. A blast. Not from her. From the crowd. A student in black moved too fast — not clumsy aggression, but trained intent. He hurled a cursed blade toward me. The sigil on his wrist flared as he moved. A broken flame. I knew it. My father had once called them heretics. "They believe trials should never have been refused, that with them, the plague of the black wolf wouldn't have been lost them their loved ones was their rhetoric" he'd said. The Severed Flame. The blade wasn't practice steel. Real silver. Poisoned.

Allyssa moved before I could blink.

She caught the blade mid-air.

Her hand bled instantly. The poison flared.

She growled, eyes flashing black before returning to turquoise. Then she turned to the attacker.

He was already trying to disappear, a glamour cracking around him.

"Tribunal?," she snarled. One word. The student froze, caught in place by an ancient binding spell, the Professor taking charge of the situation and two pledged Hunters came up beside the attacker, and hauled him off. "Maybe not" I pondered to her "perhaps it's The Severed Flame" I told her and the look told me she knew who they were. Gasps echoed around the arena. Drayk moved instantly, dragging the attacker away with a warded chain. He didn't question her command. He didn't even look at her. That alone told me everything. Someone had sent him. And they hadn't expected her to save me.

I stepped toward her, heart hammering. "You okay?" She stared at her bleeding hand like it had betrayed her. "I almost didn't stop it," she said. "I almost let it hit you." "But you didn't." "Because you're mine," she hissed. "And no one takes what's mine." The words scorched through the bond like fire. I didn't answer. I couldn't. Because the way she said it made something primal rise in my chest. Not fear. Need yes. But I also wanted to push back. Test the chain. Rebel against the collar she didn't even realize she was tightening. And gods help me; I wanted her to tighten it. She pulled back before I could speak. Turned. Walked away. And everyone was still watching.

Later, I stood in the hallway outside the med wing, hands braced against the cool stone, trying to steady the echo of silver and poison still ringing through my pulse.

That's when Laya found me. Soft steps. Softer smile. Ginger curls braided back to look harmless. Her scent carried that faint metallic tang again — bloodroot and ritual smoke. I'd smelled it before in Dravenwald after Druidic rites that were never officially recorded. I felt myself relaxing in her familiar presence.

"That was insane," she said quietly. "You okay?"

"I'm fine."

She studied me like she didn't believe that. "You know she would kill for you, right?" she added gently. "Allyssa. She moved like instinct. Like her body decided before her mind did."

"She's like that."

"She is," Laya agreed.

She stepped closer. Not flirtatious. Measured. Like she knew exactly where my comfort ended and how far she could lean without crossing it. It has been tense between us since the bond.

"That kind of bond," she continued softly, "it burns hot. The legends always say that. Fire and prophecy and devotion."

Her fingers brushed the wall beside me, casual.

"But fire consumes," she said. "It doesn't ask what survives the ashes."

Something in her tone shifted. Not warning. Assessment. "You ever wonder," she asked, eyes steady on mine, "what's left of the gentler one... when the storm finally finishes reshaping him?"

There it was. Not about Allyssa. About me. About whether I would still be myself. About the future we talked about each of us wanting, and if it was still on the cards. I felt the bond hum faintly at the back of my ribs — Allyssa alive, volatile, unapologetic.

"I'm not kind because I'm fragile," I said quietly.

Laya smiled.

"No," she agreed. "You're kind because you choose to be."

A pause.

"And choice," she added lightly, "is the first thing prophecy eats."

The words settled wrong. Too clean. Too rehearsed. As if she'd practiced that sentence. I looked at her properly then. Not at the braid. Not at the soft smile. At the steadiness in her gaze. She wasn't just jealous. And six months ago that knowledge might have been the best news I had herd, perhaps give me enough confidence to finally ask her out. But now I just saw past that, She was measuring durability. And I suddenly had the uneasy sense that I was being evaluated. For something I hadn't agreed to.

She stepped back before I could answer. "Just don't lose yourself," she said. "Some fires don't mean to burn everything. They just... do." Then she walked away. And this time, the metallic tang in the air lingered longer than it should have.

I looked down to the orb pulsing in my pocket and pulled it out. My brother's name with a message shone on the surface of the orb. I pulled my thumb across it to read it, of course it was a voice message. "Heard about the bond. You alive? Call me. Dad's pretending not to worry. And Emily will not let up with making sure your safe." A small amount of guilt lodges in my chest, Asher is extremely patient and calm, he would have waited for me to talk to him. He is going to make an amazing Alpha for Frostpine.

I wondered if the pressure from our father and Emily have pushed him so much and then another wave of guilt hits me, Asher really has enough on his plate. Having me contribute to it, feels wrong. I make a mental note to call Asher later, he hates messaging, Ill explain everything to him, and it will be good to talk to someone about Allyssa. I think Asher will get what I am feeling. Even though he hasn't found his mate yet, I have always been able to go to my older brother with anything.

That evening, I stood outside Lakemond's office. My hands were fists at my sides, the ache in my chest more than just the sting of combat. It was the weight of everything I didn't know; about her, about us, about what we're meant to be. Naturals here gossip like my grandmother with her group of friends back at Frostpine, not that I can blame them, their communication orbs are set to only communicate with those inside the Academy. Privileges of being a son to the Frostpine Alpha family I guess.

Lakemond opened the door without a word. He was already waiting. "Come in," he said quietly. His office smelled like cedar smoke and old magic, the shelves heavy with tomes older than the Academy itself. In the flickering lamplight, he looked tired. But his eyes were sharp. "You're wondering why," he said. "Why the Academy keeps pushing you together. Why we watch. Why we don't intervene, even when you both seem ready to tear each other apart."

I swallowed hard. "I just... I need to know what she is. What I am." Lakemond nodded once. Reached into his desk and pulled out an ancient scroll, the wax seal bearing the Academy's crest. He unrolled it carefully, and the words carved there burned with old magic:

⟐ The Prophecy of the Triskelion

"When the blood of kings and the fury of the Black Wolf merge,
When the White Wolf's light steadies the storm's edge,
When the Warlock of Secrets binds them in shadow and truth,
The Triskelion shall awaken—three souls woven in one fate.
From the ruin of empires and the ashes of kings,
Their bond will forge a throne unclaimed by mortal hand.
Through them, the Hunt shall rise and the old orders shall tremble,
For the Black Wolf is not just fury, but the promise of reckoning.
The White Wolf is not just mercy, but the quiet strength of night.
The Warlock is not just cunning, but the keeper of all that was lost.
The Academy shall stand as silent witness, its halls bound by ancient pacts,
Vowed to nurture the Black Wolf's rise, yet shackled by duty to the shadows.
In secret they watch, their loyalty woven into the walls themselves,
Guardians of the prophecy's breath, awaiting the Queen's call.
Together they stand—wolf, fae, warlock,
Three threads of the world's last hope and final ruin.
In their union, the fractured realms shall find peace or perish.
And in the shadow of their love and rage, a crown will be claimed."

He paused. Met my eyes. And for the first time, I felt the edges of doubt—the whisper of a voice that sounded suspiciously like Laya's, asking if this bond could really last, if I really wanted to exchange the future I had dreamed of for this. If I was strong enough to carry my half of it. Lakemond's eyes narrowed, just briefly. "There are others who would prefer the prophecy die with you both. Quiet voices in high places. And quieter ones much closer than you think."

"You and Allyssa are two parts of that," he said. "The Black Wolf. The White Wolf. The Academy stands behind you. Not the Tribunal. Not the old ways. The Academy alone. Because this prophecy? It's older than any crown. And it's why we exist."

I stared at the scroll. The words were a promise, and a threat. Lakemond's voice softened, like he was telling me a secret only the stones themselves remembered. "This isn't just about love, Caspian. It's about balance. It's about our realm itself. And it's about the choice you both must make."

A choice. Not fate. I straightened my shoulders, feeling the bond between me and Allyssa pulsing like a live wire. "Then I choose her," I said hoarsely. "No matter what this prophecy says. I choose her." Lakemond's lips twitched, almost a smile. "Good," he said. "Because the realm isn't going to let you forget it." As I left his office, the final words of the prophecy echoed in my head:

"...In the shadow of their love and rage, a crown will be claimed."

And I knew: whatever it costs, whatever it takes; I'll stand beside her, even when the third piece of our bond returns from the shadows to claim his place. As I walked back to my room, I pulled out the communication orb and called my brother. If there ever was a time I needed someone that was way more experienced than me to talk to, it would be now. Ashers face shows up from the hologram a few minutes later and he smiles at me and just like that all my worries about the bond and the prophecy just go away knowing my brother will have my back.

Chapter Eleven: Proximity and Pressure

"The most courageous act is still to think for yourself. Aloud." — Coco Chanel

Caspian POV

A month later, we'd hit the final stretch of the winter cycle, the Midwinter Assessment block. Every cycle came with academic testing, a quiet reminder that the Academy didn't run on hope. It ran on standards. If you fell behind, you didn't get comfort. You got cut. For the career-track Hunters, that meant failure and dismissal. For the cross-blooded like me, it meant something simpler. We were in it all the way, or we didn't leave at all.

Room 7-B reeked of magic, testosterone, and bad decisions. The windows on the far wall faced the Verdfall Enclave's protective groves, the Lunar Grove among them, where Black Wolf rites used to echo under triple moons.

The moment I stepped inside, I knew it was a setup. Two beds. One shared bathroom. No personal quarters. A single desk wedged between us like a monument to conflict. Wards shimmered along the walls, tracking enchantments bright under the surface, privacy spells stripped down to bone. We weren't just housed. We were staged. And we were being watched.

Allyssa leaned against the wall like she owned it, arms crossed, hair wild, eyes sharp. Her aura coiled tight, the kind of controlled pressure that promised detonation if anyone misread the distance.

"Director's orders," she said flatly.

I dropped my bag by the door. "You're thrilled. I can tell."

"Only slightly less than I'd be for a root canal without sedation."

My bruised ego rose up before my better judgment could stop it. I lifted a brow, pure challenge. "Well. I snore."

She didn't hesitate. "I bite."

My thoughts dove straight into the gutter. What would it be like to wear her mark, teeth and claim and heat? I swallowed the reaction before it could touch my face, and we held the stare anyway, stubborn as wolves. The silence thickened, turning the air into something you could drown in.

I tried again. "We don't have to make this weird."

Her eyes glinted. "Too late. You exist."

So much for diplomacy.

I'd honestly thought things would feel easier after the call with my brother. I'd reassured him I was alive, that the Academy hadn't fed me to anything with fangs, and then I'd made the mistake of telling him about Allyssa. How we met. How she crashed into my life like a threat with a heartbeat. He growled through the ugly parts, then laughed when I got to her arrival, as if the sheer audacity of her had won him over on the spot.

I told him about the Snow Moon Rite, about the version of Allyssa I'd seen that night. Curious. Watchful. Asking questions about my family like she was cataloguing the shape of me. He listened, and that gleam came into his eye before he said, too pleased with himself, "She sounds sexy and dangerous. You're a lucky male, Caspian."

My wolf surged hot at the word sexy, sharp with possessiveness. Asher laughed it off immediately. "Relax," he said. "I said dangerous too. Keep talking. I want the whole story."

He gave me advice I already knew I wouldn't follow. "Use the sweet charm," he said. "Use the diplomacy. But don't crowd her. Stubborn females need space. Give it to her."

In my defense, I had. I'd kept my hands to myself. I'd kept my mouth careful. I'd kept my hope tucked behind my ribs like a shameful thing. But the absence of touch was turning brutal. The bond kept pulling, urging, insisting we finish what it started, and the worst part was how unbothered she looked. Like distance didn't scrape at her skin the way it scraped at mine.

Torture, I thought. And she was going to enjoy every second of it.

We barely spoke the first two nights. Except in training. There, it was war.

Every mission simulation, urban recon, magical restraint, threat neutralisation, turned into a lesson in pain and control. The bond didn't help. If anything, it sharpened everything. She flinched when I got too close. I burned when she pulled away. Even our dreams tangled: hers soaked in blood and broken teeth, mine haunted by her laughter and the phantom sensation of her breath against my throat.

But then came infiltration class.

Task: neutralise a simulated Fae trafficking ring in under twenty minutes.

The tunnels were modelled after routes running from Umbrakyn's lower citadels into Calyxion's black markets, corridors the Tribunal pretended didn't exist. A high balcony wrapped the chamber for oversight. Professor Vaughn stood above it all, dry and sardonic, watching like disappointment given a body.

"Black Wolf. White Wolf," he called, voice echoing through the glass theatre. "Let's see what bonded strategy looks like under pressure."

The moment the timer flared gold above the door, she dissolved into motion, pure instinct wrapped in lethal precision. She moved through the glamoured halls not just unseen, but unfelt. No sound. No displaced air. Shadows folded around her like they were glad to have her back. Her magic pulsed low beneath her skin, wildfire leashed by will alone. She is so fucking beautifully lethal.

The simulation mimicked an underground fae smuggling corridor, obsidian-carved tunnels layered with confusion wards, false rooms nested inside other false rooms. Illusions over reality. Traps inside traps. Every turn demanded intuition and calculation in equal measure.

Allyssa thrived in it.

One moment she was scaling a balcony with nothing but clawed fingertips; the next she slit the throat of a glamour-shielded decoy and stripped his keycard before his body hit the illusionary floor.

"Bet they didn't prep for sadistic fairy godmothers," she muttered.

A few warlocks in the gallery laughed.

And then I hesitated.

She moved too fast. I tracked her down a service hall, hit a mirror illusion at the wrong angle, and the world fractured for half a heartbeat. Enough. I triggered a dormant tripwire charm and the ceiling flared gold with simulated alert runes.

Up above, Vaughn tsked audibly. "White Wolf. Try not to die before you reach the objective."

Heat flushed through me.

Allyssa was suddenly there.

In my space. Too close. Her magic crackled against my skin like static. Her eyes; sharp turquoise and unreadable; locked on mine.

She didn't raise her voice. She didn't need to.

"Speed is the essence of war," she said quietly. "But without coordination, speed is suicide."

Vaughn had drilled it into us since first year. Hunters do not fight alone. Triads win wars. Breaker. Shield. Arcane. Frontline. Flank. Spell lattice. Two without the third is vulnerability. Three is survival.

Allyssa must have been studying what she missed before arriving. Or maybe she understood instinctively what some of us needed textbooks to explain.

Her fingers tapped once against my chest plate. Not unkind. Not gentle either. Deliberate.

"We win together," she said. "You cover my shadow. I break their lines. They're watching us. Not me. Us. Show them why we are who they want to bond with."

For half a second her mask cracked. Not doubt. Pressure. This mattered to her. Not just the mission. The architecture of what we were building.

She didn't know the full shape of the prophecy yet. Lakemond had told me he would inform her when the time was right. But she felt the gravity of it. I could see it in the way she squared her shoulders.

I swallowed my pride and reset.

This time I stayed tighter.

When she broke wards, I sealed the rear. When I drew hostile glyphfire, she slipped past unseen. When decoy slavers burst from opposing doors, she ducked between them, claws flashing; I shattered their sigil lattice mid-cast and drove one through a false wall with a kinetic strike that cracked stone.

We weren't chasing each other anymore.

We were moving.

She flashed a grin at me. "There you go, White Wolf."

Up above, Vaughn's voice crackled through the crystal relay. "Better. Let the observers pay attention. This is what partnership looks like when both sides earn it."

Observers.

The warlock gallery wasn't here to flirt. They were here to evaluate structural integrity. A Hunter triad is military architecture, not romance.

Three selection glyphs flared faintly along the upper ring. Intent. Calculation. Interest.

Allyssa glanced upward as we advanced toward the objective chamber. "Let them scramble," she murmured. "I'm only interested in the ones who see what we are. Not just what I am." That was new. Not dominance. Discernment. Maybe she did just need time. She didn't grow up here, perhaps she needed time to filter and come to terms with everything. Her arrival here was less than a normal arrival.

We breached the simulated holding cell — arcane locks folding under her control — when We breached the simulated holding cell when Vaughn's voice cut in again.

"Observers. Covenant Protocol is active. If you are considering bond candidacy, you may demonstrate strategic value. You are not auditioning for courtship. You are offering alliance."

The gallery shifted.

A tall warlock in violet stood. High cheekbones. Obsidian hair. Confidence sharpened into arrogance. He leaned over the railing, voice magically amplified. "Lady Allyssa," he drawled, "if you ever tire of playing predator, I'd be delighted to teach you the pleasures of restraint. We warlocks are exceptional with ropes." Silence fell. Not scandal. Assessment. He hadn't just insulted her. He'd revealed he misunderstood the structure.

Allyssa didn't pause. Then she tilted her head. "Oh, darling," she said softly, "if you're going to open your mouth, make sure it's to apologise. Or scream." A flick of hexlight. His robes ignited in controlled glamour-fire, heat without harm. His belt snapped free mid-laugh; trousers collapsing as every rune inked across his torso flared bright as a drunken constellation.

Gasps. Laughter. Rapid note-taking. "She didn't even gesture," someone whispered. Allyssa finally looked up. "You're disqualified." She turned to the rest of them. "No one chooses us. You're not picking a partner. You're being evaluated. Conduct matters. Intelligence matters. Respect matters."

Three who had been whispering stiffened. "You're out," she added calmly. Professor Vyn raised a hand. "Candidates removed under Conduct Clause Seven." No one argued.

I stood beside her, silent not because I was overshadowed, but because she was correct. She wasn't posturing. She was filtering. She didn't know the full weight of the Triskelion. But she was already eliminating instability. And in that moment, something in me shifted. She didn't feel like a storm I was trying to survive. She felt like a structure I wanted to help build. She was already building a court.

I looked at her again. Really looked. The way she stood at the centre of chaos without chasing attention. The way her shadow moved like it understood her before she understood it. There was something sovereign in it. I wanted to stand beside her. To fight with her. To hold the line when she burned too bright. And yes— There was something in me that wanted to kneel. Not in submission. In recognition.

The violet warlock thought he was clever. She dismantled him without blinking. Gods help the ones who think they can own her. She looked back at me as if nothing had happened. "You cover left," she said. "I'll breach." We moved. Behind us Vaughn chuckled darkly. "To lead, one must command not just fear, but precision. To command both is to reign. Well, played, Black Wolf." We finished the simulation with the syndicate leader bound at her feet.

Applause rippled through the chamber. As we exited, our fingers brushed. Accidental. Neither of us pulled away. Her pulse skipped. I felt it through the bond like lightning threading bone. For the first time since our bond sparked into existence, I didn't feel like I was chasing her. She wasn't outrunning me. She was circling back. Maybe Asher was right about the giving her space thing. I hate when he is right. And somewhere above us, unseen, a selection glyph burned steady. Not eager. Not amused. Patient.

The announcement hit the theatre like a thrown blade.

"Black and White Wolves now eligible for third-bond selection," Professor Vyn declared.

Chaos bloomed instantly.

Warlocks packed the velvet-stepped gallery like carrion drawn to fresh blood. Robes of every rank and colour swept the tiers in waves of arrogance and ambition. Draethen silks brushed against Sangreal crimson. Shadefen ghost-ink shimmered faintly. Professors lined the outer ring, quiet and tense, more than one tracing warding glyphs beneath their breath.

The last time this many warlocks gathered in one chamber, a southern district imploded.

The ceiling shimmered with containment wards.

Just in case.

I stood beside Allyssa at the centre of the floor, the bond pulsing like a second heartbeat beneath my ribs. She hadn't spoken yet. Warlocks heckled from the balcony rows, voices overlapping like blades on glass. "Why fight for scraps tied to a half-breed and a brooding golden retriever?" Laughter followed. Controlled. Tense. The kind of applause you give a predator in a cage because you hope the bars hold. Allyssa didn't look at the speaker. She looked through him. And the temperature of the entire theatre dropped.

My thoughts flickered back to the prophecy etched into memory like runes in stone.

When the blood of kings and the fury of the Black Wolf merge...

Three souls woven in one fate.

Did she feel it yet?

Because her gaze swept the gallery not with hesitation, but with calculation.

Not fear.

Hunger.

She stepped forward. And growled. It wasn't loud. It didn't need to be. The sound cracked through the hall like ancient thunder; echoing through marrow, vibrating through stone.

"You're not choosing us," Allyssa said, voice low and precise. "We choose you." Each word landed clean. A warlock in emerald robes leaned forward. "You talk like you're royalty." She smiled. "I am." Then she turned to Professor Vyn. "Remove him." Vyn didn't hesitate. Candidate dismissed under Conduct Clause Seven."

The emerald glyph on his chest flared once, then vanished. His future severed. "You can't just. She cut him off "I just did." Allyssa's voice dropped, colder than midwinter cycle steel. "Disrespect me, and you disqualify yourself, this isn't a popularity contest."

A voice from the back muttered, "That's not how power works."

I stepped forward. Calm. Cold. "Power is earned," I said. "You want in? Respect the bond. Respect her. Respect the structure. Or walk." Silence tightened. Someone whispered, "Soft." My smile was thin. "Try me."

I may be the sympathetic one in Allyssa presence but I am far from soft. Our bond may have thrown me this year but in that moment I remembered myself and where I came from. Laughter. A few claps. Several whispered "She'll break you" under their breath, but the mood was volatile.

Then came her again. Allyssa didn't bother with a speech. She nodded to professor Vyn and the warlock that muttered soft their evaluation glyph on his chest flared once; then vanished. Just like the last warlock that disrespected Allyssa. Exasperation filled Alyssa's expression and she shook her head not lowering herself to have to repeat her earlier warning. Her eyes swept the room; razor sharp, predator bright.

Then a female warlock in obsidian-threaded robes spoke, sharp-featured and venom-smiled.

"And what if we're not interested in being leashed to something so clearly... unhinged?"

The room froze. Allyssa tilted her head. "You haven't seen unhinged," she said softly. Ropes snapped into existence, gold-threaded and precise. They bound wrists, lifted arms, pulled posture into forced presentation. Not pain. Exposure. The warlock flushed crimson. "Disrespect," Allyssa said conversationally, "is submission in denial." The ropes vanished. "You're disqualified."

A voice from the balcony cut through the tension. "Now that," it purred, velvet-dark, "was impressive." All heads turned. Mazzer leaned against the carved railing in slate-grey silk, formal and unsettlingly restrained. No leather. No smirk. Just stillness. Those gold-ringed eyes never left Allyssa. Whispers rippled.

"Is that Mazzer?"

"The Warlock of Secrets?"

"He never attends selection."

He didn't move. He didn't need to.

Professor Vyn clapped once. The sound shattered the tension like lightning. "Enough," she said. "Three candidates will be chosen. One will accompany the hunters during a collaborative combat sim. One during a conflict mediation trial. One during an infiltration exercise. Your success will not be measured in magic or muscle, but in coordination, compatibility, and composure."

A warlock in silver sneered. "You're testing us more than them." Allyssa's head tilted. "You're not being tested." Her magic danced in her fingertips again, barely held at bay. "You're being exposed." Gasps. A few more muttered complaints. She turned to three whispering candidates. "You're out." "What?" one of them snapped. "That's not...." She'd already turned away. Didn't even offer them another breath. I stepped forward again, pulse steady.

"You want our bond?" he said. "Prove you can carry it without shattering."

Professor Vyn raised her hands. "Warlocks; interest glyphs active now. You get one submission." Maverick finally stood straighter above. His smile didn't falter. Didn't grow. But his fingers moved; a whisper of a flick, barely visible; and his glyph flared. He didn't say a word. Allyssa's hands didn't rise. Her smile did.

Maverick POV

There. The smallest recalibration. Her weight shifted before her magic did. The others flinched at rope-spells and spectacle. They saw dominance. I watched alignment. Her shoulders squared a fraction too early. Her spine adjusted as if anticipating impact that never came. Predatory readiness. Older than the wolf.

Her eyes didn't blacken fully this time, not like I had been watching in other moments. The change lived in the stillness between blinks. The moment when her gaze stopped seeing and started measuring. Distance. Risk. Outcome. It surfaced. Receded. Fascinating.

I felt it press against the edge of my awareness like a knuckle testing glass. And gods help me, my breath caught. Not with fear. With want. I wanted inside her mind. Not like a thief. Not like a conqueror. Like a cartographer staring at an unmapped continent and realising it might finally ruin him.

I imagined the structure of its instinctive corridors, sealed rooms, pressure points laid down by necessity rather than choice. I imagined the place where that thing lived. The sentry. The blade. The part of her that learned pain could be turned outward and sharpened into protection.

Beautiful. No. Dangerous. Better.

The surge passed. She reined it in with a breath, with a smirk that told the room she'd *meant* to look like that. Control snapped back into place with practiced ease, like a collar she wore because she chose to.

The room exhaled. I didn't. I leaned forward slightly, fingers curling against the stone, pulse loud in my ears. I knew this architecture. Not the specifics. Never this exact shape. But I had walked minds fractured by power and terror before. Survivors. Rulers. Wolves who learned early that softness was a liability and restraint was the real triumph.

This wasn't madness. This was a defensive sovereignty. A Crowned Fracture. The thought slid into place with a thrill sharp enough to border on reverence. And then, inconveniently, honestly, something else hit me. I was obsessed. The realisation didn't come with shame. It came with clarity.

I had memorised her routines. Cross-referenced her file against sealed histories. Followed the scars of her past through the minds of those that knew her, teachers, neighbours, teachers, neighbours, witnesses who saw my Queen suffer and did nothing. I told myself it was duty. Curiosity. Strategy. Lies.

This was fixation. The anger that rose at their indifference was proof enough. And standing there, watching the monster behind her eyes stretch and settle, I understood I had crossed a line long ago and never once tried to step back. Worse. I didn't want to.

The craving surprised me in its intensity. For not only her body, because well fuck it was perfection but also to her mind, to the *knowing*. To sit inside her thoughts. To trace the boundaries between Allyssa and the thing that kept her alive when she was too small to do it herself. To see where the monster ended. And whether it saw me yet.

My mouth curved into a slow, private smile. Not yet, I decided. I would not reach out. I would not name it. But I would watch. Because whatever lived behind her eyes was not a flaw to be cured or a beast to be slain. It was a guardian. And guardians, I knew from experience, always noticed when they were being studied.

Allyssa POV

The queen chose spectacle. The other part wanted blood. Something was wrong. Not loud. Not magical. Wrong in the way a room goes quiet before violence. I froze without deciding to. The Monster surged first. *Look away. Move. Exit.*

My pulse spiked, sharp and immediate. Not fear. Preparation. Someone was looking at me. No.

Watching was too passive. *Evaluating.*

The Monster dragged my awareness inward, rapid-fire inventory snapping into place the way it always had when I was small. Distance to exits. Lines of sight. Who could reach me first. Who was pretending not to notice.

There. Upper tier. Shadowed. Still. My eyes did not go to him. The Monster didn't need them to. The pressure of his attention pressed against my skull like a blade laid flat against skin. Not hostile. Not hungry. Interested. Focused. Appreciative. That was worse. My stomach twisted. The Monster bristled, claws scraping the inside of my ribs.

Too calm, it warned.

Too close without moving.

Danger.

I shifted my stance by instinct, weight rolling forward, ready to spring. I didn't remember deciding how to do that. I'd never had to. The Monster had taught me long before words mattered. When stillness was survival. When softness got you hurt.

The Wolf stirred then. Not alarmed. Curious. A low, ancient hum rolled through my chest, slow and unsettled. Recognition without context. Like a scar aching before a storm. The Wolf didn't understand what it felt. Only that it felt... old.

No, the Monster snapped, sharp and absolute. *Away from him.* My breath caught, not auditable. The disagreement inside me crackled, tension pulling tight between instinct and something deeper. The Wolf leaned toward the sensation, not trusting it but not rejecting it either.

He is not a threat, the Wolf murmured, uncertain.

Not like the others.

That's how they start, the Monster hissed.

Pretty. Patient. Watching.

Anger flared through me sudden, unbidden. At him. At myself. At the pull I didn't want and hadn't asked for. For half a second, my gaze lifted on its own. Met his. The look he gave me was wrong. Not dominance. Not challenge. Appreciation. Interest sharpened by restraint. Something warm and electric snapped through my chest and the Monster recoiled violently, slamming itself between that feeling and my heart like a shield raised too fast.

Do not let him closer, it snarled. *He will cost you control.*

The Wolf bristled in irritation at the fear, hackles raised not at him, but at the Monster's panic.

You feel him, the Wolf said quietly.

You're afraid because you do.

That landed like a blow. I tore my gaze away first, jaw tightening, forcing my posture loose. Bored. In command. Let the room see what it expected. Let the warlocks fear the Wolf and never see the fracture beneath her skin.

But the Monster stayed upright. Agitated. Pacing. Watching him watching me. Noting the way his attention never wavered. The way he didn't flinch when my power flared. The way he looked like someone who had waited a very long time to see something like me.

He will not chase, the Monster whispered, unsettled.

He will wait.

That scared it more than any blade. I swallowed hard, fingers curling into my palm until the tension bled off in manageable increments. The Wolf settled, uneasy but intrigued, sensing a thread it didn't yet have the language to name.

I told myself it was nothing. Just another warlock. Just another watcher. But the Monster did not let me cage it again. It stayed coiled. Which I am secretly glad for. Because something about him had reached too deep, too fast. And whatever bond the Wolf felt stirring; The Monster wanted it burned before it could grow teeth.

Laya POV

Below me lay Greenhollow; beyond it, the wounded red valley of The Grove, where it's believed the cult had carved its sanctuary into the Broken gathering hall in the mountains. Outside the warded window, I sat atop the east tower's balustrade, the cold night wind dragging red curls across my cheek like fingers of fate. From here, the entire warlock hall still glowed with residual magic; echoes of rope spells and power plays lingering like perfume in the dark. My legs dangled over the edge, boots tapping softly against the ancient stone. I didn't blink. Didn't breathe. I watched.

Allyssa stood at the centre of it all like a storm with a crown she hadn't earned. Cloaked in her arrogance. Drenched in her power. And still; Caspian looked at her like she hung the damn moon. My jaw clenched, lips bloodless. I'd watched it happen in real time. The way he stood beside Allyssa without hesitation. The way his voice steadied hers. The way his eyes softened; even now; as she walked away, victorious and violent and untouchable.

The Black Wolf. The same bloodline my elders swore had butchered my ancestors in another life. The same half-breed the cult had promised to erase if the prophecy ever stirred again. And yet here she stood. Beloved. Bonded. Untouchable.

Fate is such a stupid, breakable thing.

I closed my hand into a fist. Beneath my gloves, the branded glyph of the cult pulsed once warm against my palm. A secret concealed that I carried like a knife beneath a gown. "She won't win," I whispered, not caring if anyone heard me. "She won't keep him. Not when he learns what she truly is." I won't loose anyone else I care for. The cold didn't bother me. I liked it, actually. It reminded me of the winters after the slaughter, when grief tasted like iron and silence became holy.

Caspian had been kind to me, we became good friends. He was gentle. Too gentle. *That's the problem with men like him,* I thought bitterly. *They confuse empathy for love. Loyalty for destiny.* I saw the way he flinched when Allyssa lashed out. How he smiled anyway. How he thought *gods help him;* that he could save her.

But I knew better. You didn't save storms. You survived them. And eventually, Caspian would drown. I will be there to pull him free. I will be there when his loyalty broke under the weight of what Allyssa had done; when the old memories clawed their way up and bled through the bond. When the truths buried in that cursed female's soul came out screaming. Then, he would see. He would realise. That not all bonds were meant to become lovers. Some were meant to be... something else. *Something softer. Something safer.* I'll make sure of it. Even if I must poison the whole Academy to do it.

I leaned back against the spire, gazing up at the stars. One hand pressed lightly to my glyph. It pulsed again; once, then twice; as if answering my thoughts. Waiting. Planning. Ready. Soon.

Chapter Twelve: Shadowed by Flame

"What is to give light must endure burning." — Viktor Frankl

Caspian POV

Three warlocks. That was the limit. The number the Academy allowed before chaos became liability.

The storm we invited with open hands and sharpened smiles.

Day One

Day One began as the sun crawled over the eastern spires of the Academy, casting fire across the sky like a warning flare. To the north, I could picture the faint glow of the auroras over Frostpine shimmering, a reminder that the wolf packs still trained under skies that bent to magic. The air shimmered with tension. You could taste it in the wards. You could feel it in the silence. It was the kind of morning that promised either disaster... or revelation.

Allyssa stood beside me on the training quad like a blade already unsheathed; arms crossed, cloak snapping in the wind, magic tethered but restless.

She wasn't braced for impact.

She was the impact.

The first warlock approached with curated confidence. Ciaran. Sangreal accent polished smooth as glass. Bloodmoon crimson robes. The kind of arrogance born from a life that had never said no to him. Even though warlocks and witches call Draethen home, there are those that live all over veyloris taking work in the courts, with the Tribunal and the lord houses of the vampires. And taking jobs with the packs not unheard of but rare. None are allowed in druid territory. Training to take contracts with Hunters being most favourable to their schools.

"I appreciate the opportunity," he said with a bow that stopped just shy of mockery. "I'll be unobtrusive."

"If I can hear you breathe," Allyssa replied, "you're doing it wrong."

Ciaran grinned.

"Noted."

We began in Alchemy. Professor Bane didn't so much teach as set fires and see who lived.

Containment wards. glyph arrays. Fire channeling without collapse. It was brutal. Precise. Deadly. Allyssa was magnificent. Her glyphs carved through the air like scripture. Fast. Sharp. Ruthless. When Ciaran's array collapsed for the third time, she didn't gloat. She *smirked.*

By midday, Ciaran was soaked in sweat. "Do you always train like this?" he asked, panting. "Only when she's trying to kill someone," I said. Allyssa didn't correct me.

Combat simulation. That's when it turned bloody.

Fae-illusion combatants; taller, faster, wild with glamour-blades; filled the arena. Ciaran barely kept pace. I held the perimeter with shield charms. Allyssa tore through the enemy like a hurricane wrapped in silk. She vaulted over one illusion, claws dragging across its throat, and landed without a sound. The illusion flickered, shuddered, and collapsed into light. She licked a smear of blood from her wrist, eyes glowing that beautiful turquoise.

"You're enjoying this," I muttered.

She bared her teeth. "Of course I am." More energy to her steps.

Professor Vyn clapped once from the balcony.

"This," she said, "is what a bonded pair looks like."

Ciaran wheezed beside us. "You two are *terrifying.*"

Allyssa smiled. Not kindly. "You have no idea."

That evening, the final two arrived. Neris, elegant and silent. Silver rings forged in Calyxion's mirror-spires, gleaming like cut ice, pale hair, eyes like obsidian knives. Veylin, all rakish charm and danger in silk, with the soft dusk-lilt spoken in Dubhlinn,

Umbrakyn's shadow capital. The kind of predator who preferred parlour games to battlefields, typical cultural norm for the unseelie court even if you're not fae. "Quite the specimen," Veylin purred, eyes raking over Allyssa. "I could get used to following your orders."

She didn't flinch. Didn't blink. "Flirt with me again," she said, "and I'll show you how long it takes to peel a man's face from his skull while keeping him conscious." Neris snorted. "And yet you're still somehow more attractive." She turned away with a hum of disinterest. Veylin trailed behind her like a moth to a funeral pyre.

Later, in the library courtyard, Neris approached me.

"Caspian," he said smoothly. "You're the structural centre of this bond. She's fire. You're gravity."

He stepped closer. "What you need isn't dominance. It's equilibrium." His fingers brushed my shoulder. And then; She was *there*. Smoke and shadow and flame. Between us. "Touch him again," Allyssa said, voice low, edged in razors, "and I'll make you regret the day your mother didn't swallow."

Neris raised his hands. "I meant no...." She cut him off brutally, "No?" Her claws clicked free. Slow. Deliberate. "You meant to seduce *my* bonded. Without *my* permission?" She stalked closer. "Let me make this simple. You do not breathe near him without my say. You do not look. You do not speak. And if you *ever* touch him again....." She smiled, sweet and sharp. "I'll extract your spine through your throat and make your ribs into wind chimes."

Neris paled to the roots. I didn't say a word. I just reached for her hand; fingers tangling with hers. Her pulse flared like a star between us. She glanced down. Then at me her eyes becoming softer still possessive and a little crazed. "Still yours," I said softly. "You know that, right?" Her eyes lingered too long, searching for my lie. Then she looked away. "Don't forget it."

Later, walking side by side beneath the lantern-lit arches, she muttered, "I hate this." "The warlocks?" I ask. "The watching. The games. The idea that someone could get close to you without bleeding for it." I paused. "You want someone who doesn't flinch." She nodded but had a contemplative look on her face. "But you also need someone who *understands*. Who doesn't try to tame you. Who loves the violence as much as the grace." I say, trying to keep the conversation going. I can hardly believe she is freely discussing something with me, even more taking on my input. I get so excited I reach to entangle my hand in hers, she looked down at it curiously.

She tilted her head. "And you think that's you?" challenging me, testing me again. "No," I said, pulling in as much confidence as I can, straightening my spine, looking directly into those beautifully dangerous eyes that always keep me captured. "I *know* it's me."

She looks directly back into my eyes, searching again a flare sparks and she is silent for another minute She must have seen something in my eyes because she finally whispers, "You're too soft for this world." I heard her loud and clear; tension crackled between us like a spark waiting to turn into an inferno. I smiled. "I'm just soft for *you*." I see her full body cringe at my statement and the previous tension falls away. But she didn't argue, and she just squeezed my hand tighter, before walking away. I can feel my grin splitting my face as I watch her.

Above us, the Warlock of Secrets leaned against the highest railing, slate silk instead of leather, still as carved obsidian. He hadn't spoken. He hadn't needed to. His eyes tracked Allyssa with unnerving precision. Something about that patience unsettled me. Because it didn't feel like pursuit. It felt like inevitability.

Day Two

Day Two dawned beneath a ceiling of tarnished steel clouds. The air smelled like rain and restraint. Conflict Mediation. Not her strength. Here I can hold my own a little, the perks of being a son of the largest and most powerful Alpha and pack in Veyloris. Blades were easier than diplomacy.

I felt Allyssa's mood before I saw her; raw, coiled, predator-sharp. She waited outside the mediation chamber like a weapon left too long in the forge. "This is a bad idea," she muttered. "Most good ideas start that way," I replied. She didn't smile.

Inside, Professor Elion stood with all the grace of a blade in velvet. Her robes shimmered the colour of bruised plums, and in her arms rested a grimoire bound in bark, roots curled around its cover like it had grown from the ground itself.

"Today's trial is a simulation," she said. "But the tensions, the stakes, the histories; they are all real. Dryads and Shadowkin. Broken accords. Blood feuds old enough to turn stone into soil. Your task: de-escalate. Diplomacy under pressure. You'll be watched. Judged. Scored. Not by outcome; but by how you carry the fire." Allyssa didn't react right away. It wasn't avoidance. She'd heard it. I was sure of that. Her attention was just... elsewhere.

Her gaze drifted past the instructor, past the warded archways, skimming the upper balconies like she was mapping something that hadn't been mentioned aloud. Not anxious. Methodical.

I followed the line of her sight without meaning to. Stone. Runes. Sightlines. Nothing out of place. When she looked back, her expression was composed. Almost bored. But something didn't line up. Her breathing was slow. Too slow for someone who'd just been thrown into a political exercise designed to provoke mistakes. Her shoulders were relaxed, but her weight had shifted subtly onto the balls of her feet, stance adjusted for movement she hadn't been asked to make. Making herself ready for any threat just in case.

The instructor finished speaking. Still she didn't move. I leaned closer. "Allyssa?" Her eyes flicked to me then. Not startled. Not annoyed. Assessing. For half a second, I had the uncomfortable impression that she wasn't deciding *what to say*. She was deciding whether I mattered to the situation at all.

The thought landed hard enough to steal my breath. Then it withdrew, not vanished, withdrawn. She turned fully toward me, expression smoothing into something familiar. Dry. Sharp. Controlled. "Relax," she murmured. "I was listening." I nodded, though the words didn't settle right. Because she had been listening. Just not to the same thing the rest of us were.

Veylin, assigned to observe today, gave a long-suffering sigh. "Ah, politics. The art of lying prettily while everyone sharpens knives under the table." He muttered "Consider this your table," Allyssa growled. "And my knives visible."

The illusion shifted into the shape of Dravenwald, its moss cathedrals, its root bridges opposite the sharp, starlit geometry of Shadefen's shadow courts. The illusion shimmered, and the chamber became a forest-court hybrid. Twisted roots for chairs. A canopy of woven starleaf. Dryads to the left; antlered, ethereal, bitter. Shadowkin to the right veiled, venom-eyed, their glamour cloaking centuries of hostility. Tension crackled like kindling. I stepped forward first. "We recognise the pain on both sides," I said calmly, hands visible. "But pain doesn't have to end in more graves."

A Dryad elder hissed. "Words from a youngling who bleeds light and knows nothing of rot." Veylin leaned toward them with that lazy, amused drawl. "He bleeds more than light, I assure you." I didn't look at Allyssa, but I felt her fury rise like a tide through the bond. "Shut up," she said simply. Her voice could've shattered bone. Still, the factions escalated. Accusations flung. Territory lines drawn in illusionary blood. One of the Shadowkin slammed his blade into the bark-table, snarling about dishonoured vows.

Allyssa stood. I stiffened; expecting violence. But she didn't reach for a weapon. She spoke, her words clipped and annoyed. "You want blood?" Her voice was raw thunder. "Fine. Spill it. But understand; if you draw first, there won't be a second breath." The Dryads went still recognising the threat for what it was. Even the

Shadowkin faltered darkness recognising darkness. She paced now, slow and deliberate. "You think vengeance honours the dead? No. It dishonours them. It makes their sacrifice meaningless. We don't come here offering peace because we're weak; we offer it because we're dangerous. And if we choose war, it won't be by accident."

Elion watched silently, her quill marking something on the scroll. I stepped in beside Allyssa. Close enough to steady the air bringing my calming aura with me. "But we are offering peace. Not as a gift. As a choice. You want someone to blame? Blame the silence between you. The pride that let rot take root. Or; start something better. Right now."

There was a beat of silence. Then the Shadowkin prince spoke. Low. Measured. "What guarantees do we have?" I met his eyes. "You have our names. Allyssa and I don't make promises we won't burn to uphold. On top of that let us come to an agreement to the details needed, Hunters for reinforcement and protection where you feel its necessary to come to an accord." The prince turned to the Dryad matriarch. She inclined her head.

Professor Elion finally spoke. "Resolution achieved. Bonded synergy: intact. Score: exceeding expectations." Even Veylin remained silent for a full three breaths. Then he muttered, "Well. Fuck."

Outside, Allyssa collapsed onto the nearest bench, breathing hard. Not tired; just full of too much. "That was..." I began. "Awful," she groaned. "I'd rather eat nails." I sat beside her. "You were brilliant." She looked sideways at me and I think I can see a little sparkle of pride in her gaze before she says. "You didn't flinch. Not once." I shook my head in confirmation "Not from them," I said. "Never from you." Her fingers brushed my knee. "Don't get soft on me, White Wolf." I smiled. "Not soft. Sharp."

She leaned back, exhaling slowly. Veylin wandered past, all mockery and silk. "You two are insufferable." Allyssa flicked her eyes toward him her indifferent mask firmly back in place. "Insufferable, but effective." He paused give her one last longing look. "She's going to change everything, you know." I tensed. He looked at me, gold eyes flickering with intent. "The question is... will you survive the fire, or become part of it?" I didn't answer. Because the truth? I already knew. I was burning. But gods; so was she. And for once, we were burning together.

Maverick POV

The first time I saw her, truly saw her, she was covered in blood and didn't care who was watching. The second time, she smiled as a warlock screamed.

Now? Now she stood before a tribunal of ancient spirits, face tilted slightly toward the firelight, hands folded behind her back like a monarch inspecting her court. Calm. Still. Dangerous.

And gods, I was starving.

I leaned against the carved obsidian rail of the observation balcony, a deliberate picture of detachment. Slate-grey robes today—silk, not my usual infernal leather. Formal. Quiet. Unassuming, at least on the surface. But I knew every gaze in the room tracked me with the wariness of something sharp kept barely sheathed. Good. Let them watch me watching her.

Caspian stood beside her; shoulders squared, jaw clenched, golden and tragic as always. I could almost pity him. Almost. He thought this was about leadership. About loyalty. About keeping her grounded. It wasn't. Not really. This was about hunger. Raw, aching hunger. For freedom. For power. For surrender. She just hadn't figured out which kind she wanted yet. But I had.

I watched them like someone who'd witnessed five eras collapse Frostpine kings, Seelie sanctums, the burning of The Grove, and survived all of it. I have watched five before her walk this razor's edge. Five Black Wolves. Five storms wrapped in different names and different skins. Each chosen. Each falling to silence. Each leaving me with another mark beneath my ribs, like branded with another failure. The Academy thought it was tradition that I observed. That I advised. That I guided. They never asked what it did to me. They never asked what I gave. And now came Allyssa. Half-fae. Half-wolf. Half-mad, and all breathtaking. All mine. Eventually.

I studied the room below with half-lidded eyes as the second day of trials bled toward its end. The conflict mediation had been more revealing than I anticipated. Shadowkin threats, Dryad demands, centuries of blood and broken treaties hanging like fog between the factions. She had been brutal in her truth. Soft in ways that hurt. Precise in a way that only those born for pain understood. And Caspian? He hadn't folded. Hadn't begged for calm. He'd stood beside her like he belonged there. Interesting. There was steel under that golden male shine. Maybe not enough to survive her fire. But maybe enough to enjoy it.

Below, Veylin looked like he wanted to die for her. Neris looked like he wanted to own her. Fools, both of them. You don't own a storm. You kneel in its path and hope it spares you. That's the difference. I wouldn't fight her wildness. Wouldn't try to soften her teeth. I'd train her to use them. That's what the others never understood. Bonding with the Black Wolf was never about control. It was about offering yours, open-handed. Because she doesn't want a partner. Not really. She wants a witness. A shield. A toy. A blade.

And gods, I could be all of those things.

My eyes traced the elegant lines of her posture, the subtle twitch in her jaw as she processed yet another veiled insult from a warlock trying to appear unshaken. I could teach her. Not just combat. Not just strategy. But *discipline*. The art of surrender forged through domination. Most people feared power like hers. I wanted to taste it. Bare-chested. Bound. Begging.

Because in the end, she'll need someone who can take everything she gives and come back asking for more. Someone who doesn't flinch when the claws come out. Someone who offers their throat not to be spared; but to prove they're worthy of being marked. I smiled. Soft. Slow. Private. The kind of smile you wear when you know the game is already yours. She looked up just then. Glanced toward the balcony. Her eyes passed over the crowd, then landed on me.

I didn't wave. Didn't blink. Didn't breathe. And for half a second; just half; she held my gaze. Not recognition. Not interest. Curiosity. Like something inside her had already named me without knowing how. And damn did that look make my blood turn to lava and I even blush at how intense that gaze stilled me. Blush.... Me.... That's a new one.

Below, Vyn clapped and ended the trial. Caspian brushed her hand on the way out. She didn't pull away. But she looked back, just once. Not at him. At me, and my heart nearly seized in my chest with the knowledge she needed to look at me before leaving. I straightened slowly and turned into the shadows. Let her wonder. Let her burn. The Warlock of Secrets was patient. But gods help the world when I finally drop to my knees for her. Because when I do? She won't need to ask me to beg. I'll already be whispering her name.

Day Three

Day Three tasted like ozone and unfinished sentences. A storm rolled over the Academy overnight, and lightning stitched the sky behind heavy cloud.

Infiltration. The trial no one could fake. Professor Vaughn stood at the dais, a sheaf of illusion-paper floating beside him.

"The mission is simple," he said, dry as ash. "Infiltrate the Citadel vault under the guise of rogue operatives and extract the enchanted relic from the target room. Fail to remain unseen and

the simulation ends in exposure. This isn't a game of power. It's precision. Coordination." He turned his eyes on Neris. "And trust."
Neris offered a slim smile. "Trust is a rare commodity."

"So are second chances," Allyssa replied, already wrapping glamours around her skin like armour. I felt her pulse shift through the bond. Alert. Fluid. Dangerous. And then we moved. The Citadel simulation was layered in nested illusion—glamoured corridors, illusory guards with real teeth, motion-triggered alarms linked to hexfire cannons. We split into triangle formation: Allyssa on point, Neris rear, myself middle for arcane modulation and glyph weaving.

Allyssa didn't just lead. She vanished. She moved like shadow given purpose. Slipping through sensor fields, deconstructing wards mid-stride, slashing through magical tripwires like they were silk. She never hesitated. Never slowed. Her magic glimmered on her fingertips, alive but chained. Neris kept pace; barely. I caught him watching her, curious, calculating. Not lustful like Veylin. Not mocking like Ciaran. Just... studying her. As if he couldn't decide if she was the weapon or the prophecy itself.

We reached the central vault after ten minutes of silence. Too smooth. That's when the system triggered a failsafe; arcane heat flooded the floor, the illusionary ceiling began to collapse, and magical sentries blinked into view. No time to plan. Allyssa launched upward, claws out, catching the ledge above and vanishing into the shadows. I dove right, sending a burst of silence-field glyphs to confuse the sentries. Neris... hesitated. One moment of fear. One breath too long. He faltered beneath a collapsing hexbeam.

Allyssa dropped from above like a falling star, tackled him from the impact radius, and snarled through her teeth: "Move or die."
Neris coughed. "I was recalculating...."She stopped him with a look "You don't get to recalculate when someone else is dying for your

hesitation." But she didn't let go. She helped him up. Then flicked me a look. "Left corridor. There's a break in the wards. I'll breach." We moved like we were one thing. Not perfect but getting there.

When we reached the vault, the lock was already active; runes shifting in complex pattern loops keyed to the bond resonance of the intruders. It wasn't strength we needed. It was synchronicity. I looked at Allyssa. She looked back. And without speaking, we placed our palms to the glyph. Bond pulse. Unified. The lock melted open.

Professor Vaughn's voice crackled through the arcane relay. "Mission complete. Time: fourteen minutes. Observers' notes incoming. Warlock compatibility under stress: functional. Bond coherence: escalating."

I exhaled for the first time in what felt like an hour. Neris nodded, sweat at his brow. "That was... instructional." Allyssa cocked her head. "You mean humbling." He didn't argue. Wouldn't dare.

Back in the hallway, as we waited for Vaughn's final marks, Allyssa leaned beside me on the stone balustrade. "You did well," she said. Her voice was quiet. "You did better." I counter. She shrugged. "I was born for infiltration. I'm not used to waiting for others." "You didn't have to wait." I didn't want to be the one to slow her down, guilt and shame gnawed at my stomach. "I did anyway." She simply replied either unaware of my churning emotions or just not giving them voice.

I looked at her. "Do you think any of them are right for us?" She didn't answer for a long time. Then: "One, maybe." I blinked. "Neris?", gods I hope not, he was a complete waste of time. I didn't expect her actual answer though. She smirked. "No. I mean you." I swear I was near floored with

As we exited the chamber, I caught the warlock of secrets silhouette at the end of the hall. Still watching. Always watching.

He gave no sign of approval. No mockery either. Just a slow tilt of the head. Waiting. Choosing. Allyssa's spine straightened beside me. Her eyes narrowed. But she didn't look away. And neither did he.

Chapter Thirteen: The Director's Office

"The mind is its own place, and in itself can make a Heaven of Hell, a Hell of Heaven." — John Milton

Allyssa POV

A week after the warlock trials, the Academy stopped treating it like spectacle and started treating it like strategy. Rumours calcified into assessments. Wagers hardened into quiet alliances.

And one of the Hunters had decided to follow me around like a time bomb with a heartbeat, counting down to something no one had bothered to name.

He couldn't even tail someone to save his life. At least the others assigned to "make sure Allyssa doesn't murder everyone" duty had the decency to make it interesting.

I didn't knock. I never do. My wolf refusing. A instinct that has become even more pronounced since being here. The door swung open beneath my palm like it understood the hierarchy, and inside, Director Lance Lakemond looked up from glowing rune-scrolls as if he'd been expecting the storm.

He didn't flinch. He never does. That's what makes him dangerous.

Maps of Veyloris lined the walls; Frostpine's glacier coast, Lyrravene's bioluminescent forests, the drifting sanctums of Aureslong, Dubhlinn's shadow rivers, Bloodmoon's crimson citadel, Centenary's obsidian desert, and the scarred ash valley where the Severed Flame once ruled.

I scanned the room. Empty. But not unoccupied. My wolf lifted its head inside me. There. A scent. Familiar. Unplaced. The pull stirred again. I forced it down and turned back to Lakemond.

"Allyssa," he said, nodding once. "To what do I owe the pleasure of this silent rebellion?" I didn't answer. He gestured to the chair. I stayed standing. Distance is easier than vulnerability. "I take it you're still refusing to train with Caspian." "You already know the answer." "I do," he said mildly. "I'm wondering if you do." His tone was gentle. Which made me bristle.

His voice was maddeningly gentle. Like he was walking me toward something I already knew but refused to name. The silence that followed pressed like a blade to the throat. He rose, moved to a carved cabinet, and poured water into two stone glasses. No whisky. Not this time. He handed me one. I ignored it. He sipped his own without missing a beat.

"I saw what you did in the Warlock Hall," he said. "How you let them insult you, test you, provoke you; just to see which ones would flinch." "They all flinched," I muttered. "Not all," he said. "Two worshipped you. One tried to challenge you and now likely needs trauma counselling. But it wasn't the disqualifications that interested me. It was your reaction when they flirted with Caspian." I stiffened. He continued, "You didn't even *look* at him. You looked at them. Like they were already yours to bury."

"He's mine," I said before I could stop myself. "And yet you won't let him get close to you, to nurture your bond," Lakemond said. "Won't train with him. Won't let the bond breathe." "That's why," I snapped. "Because I *am* his. And I'm dangerous." There it was. He leaned back slowly, expression unreadable. "You think you're protecting him." "I know I am." I defend. "No," he said, voice like iron. "You're breaking him." It felt like a slap to the face, yes I'm aware of the emotional whip lash I am producing but fuck, logic and reason does nothing in the face of this bond apparently.

Lakemond didn't hesitate. "Caspian will remain assigned to you," he said. "His bond stabilises your output. That isn't negotiable." I didn't argue, just narrowed my eyes at him, my wolf feeling the challenge to her authority and not appreciating it one bit. That alone should have been warning enough.

A soft exhale behind Lakemond to his left. Almost a laugh. Glamour peeled from the far corner of the room like smoke withdrawing from glass. He stepped forward. Of course he had been here. "He's right," the warlock said lightly. "You're better with him close." The words landed like fingers at the base of my spine. Not rough. Not gentle. Certain.

The Monster snapped awake.

Too familiar.

Too confident.

He speaks as if you are already decided.

My jaw tightened. The warlock went on, unbothered by the sudden chill in the room. "It's not the magic," he added. "Anyone with eyes can see that. It's what happens when she doesn't have to guard every breath." There it was. The soft place. The Monster surged forward, furious. *He names the soft place, break him.*

My pulse spiked. Heat flared low and sharp in my gut, the kind that preceded violence or flight. My shoulders squared before I caught myself. Across the desk, Lakemond's gaze flicked sharply to the warlock. A warning look. He noticed. Of course he did. His mouth curved, just a fraction. Amused. Unapologetic.

Lakemond cut in, voice iron-flat if not a little exasperated but resigned to it. "Mazzer is an ally of the Academy." That is all he said, nothing more, no other explanation. No reassurance, *he is hiding something;* Both my wolf and the monster inside agreed. Well fuck that was a first. Looking between the two men I kept watching.

Mazzer inclined his head, the gesture smooth, practiced. Not submission. Acknowledgment. "As I said," he murmured. His eyes found mine then. Not lingering. Not invasive. Assessing.

The Monster bared its teeth inside me.

He is enjoying this.

The wolf stirred beneath the agitation, ancient and steady.

He is not enemy, it rumbled.

But he is not harmless.

My weight shifted subtly onto the balls of my feet. Ready for any attack that might come my way. Mazzer's gaze flicked downward. Clocked it. His pupils dilated, just a touch. Interest. Then he leaned back against the stone wall, attention withdrawing as if he'd already taken what he came for.

The pressure eased. The Monster stayed coiled, pacing like a caged blade. *He thinks he knows you now.* I exhaled slowly. Because the worst part wasn't that he'd tested me. It was that he'd done it smiling. As if I would fold, as if I would agree without further argument, I turned to Lakemond.

My fists clenched and continued my conversation as if the warlock wasn't there, ignoring him seemed to be best in this situation, make sure not to let him see he has a reaction within me. "He doesn't understand what I am. What I could become." Lakemond stepped around the desk, came to stand in front of me, arms crossed. "Do you think he hasn't *seen* what you are?" he asked. "Do you think he hasn't already chosen to stay?" "It's not about choice," I whispered. "It's about fate, even you have no idea of what I truly am."

Mazzer stood abruptly "well now, that is my queue, I will catch up with you again soon Lance". Lakemond inclined his head and the warlock left his strides sure and graceful and I utterly despised how hot it was to watch him walking out that office door. I snapped back out of it not wanting to give up this argument with the director.

His gaze sharpened. "Interesting. Because I was about to say the same thing." He moved back to the desk and pulled a black cloth from a scroll. Its seal shimmered with three interlocking spirals; the mark of the High Grove's deep prophecy archives. "The Triskelion prophecy had been preserved not just in Dravenwald's High Grove but whispered across all realms feared in Centenary, forbidden in Bloodmoon, studied in Aureslong.," he said, laying it flat. "Three souls. One fate. You've heard of it?" I didn't answer. "You and Caspian are two of them. And the third?" This war had started before I ever agreed to fight it, do I accept or let it all crumble, choices.. choices... choices.... Sun Tzu words a comfort on the situation I find myself in.

He didn't finish the thought. He didn't have to. "Maverick," I said, before I could stop myself. Lakemond froze. Slowly, he turned to face me, eyes narrowing with something that looked a lot like *shock*. "What did you just call him?" I blinked. "Mazzer," I repeated. "The Warlock of Secrets."

"No," he said carefully. "You didn't. You called him Maverick. That name hasn't been spoken in Centenary since the shard storms of the last century, nor in Dubhlinn since the shadow-plague. Only one place would remember it: the Academy." The name echoed through the room like a pulled thread unraveling something ancient. My stomach twisted. I hadn't even noticed. It had slipped out like a breath. Like instinct.

Lakemond approached me slowly. Not afraid. Just... studying me. "No one calls him that," he said. "That's not his name anymore. Not to anyone. It hasn't been for over a few hundred years." "I—" I hesitated. "I don't know why I said it. It just felt... right. Now we are both over dramatizing this, it's just a name." I huffed at the both of us.

He was already shaking his head "You've never met him outside this life," he said softly. "Never spoken to him before this bond formed. And yet... you know the name he hasn't heard aloud in a century."

A chill ran down my spine. "What does that mean?" I asked, voice hollow. "I don't know," he admitted. "But it means *something.*" He moved back to his chair, slow and deliberate. "You were never just chosen," he said. "You were *called.* The prophecy wasn't about power. It was about *return.* About bonds that echo across time." "And what?" I demanded. "You think Maverick's one of them?" He didn't answer directly. "I think he's been waiting for you," he said. "Maybe longer than you've been alive. Goddess knows he was here with instructions when I came into the Director chair, even I don't know much about him, only the rumours."

My pulse thundered in my ears. "He unnerves me," I confessed. "Not because I don't trust him. But because... something in me already *does.*" "That's your soul remembering something your mind hasn't caught up with yet," Lakemond said. "And it's why you need to stop running from the people fate is pushing toward you."

I shook my head, the bond pulsing in my chest like a wound. "I don't want to destroy Caspian." "Then *train with him.* Let him prove you won't." He is imploring me to see reason now. "He's soft," I said, but it came out strangled. "He's soft for *you,*" Lakemond corrected. "And you're not nearly as heartless as you pretend to be." I cringed again at the use of me and soft in the same sentence and turned away, breath shaking.

He added quietly, "Joint combat training starts tomorrow. No excuses. No substitutions. The Academy's watching. And so is he." "Maverick?" Lakemond didn't answer. He didn't need to. As I reached for the door, he spoke one last time. "He's not afraid of your darkness, Allyssa. He's afraid you'll never let him carry it with you." I paused. Fingers tightening on the handle. And for a moment; I wanted to. Gods help me, I *wanted to.* But want was weakness. And weakness broke things. Still, I didn't slam the door when I left, and didn't object anymore to his suggestions. That counted for something. Below the window, the Verdfall Enclave breathed, the last neutral land in a realm carved by wolves, fae, blood, shadow, and secrets.

The door to Lakemond's office closes behind me without a slam.

That alone feels like growth. Joint training with Caspian begins tomorrow. Non-negotiable. The Director didn't say it in anger. He didn't have to. The prophecy is no longer theoretical. The Hunters are reporting fractures across the realm. Missing shipments. Unmarked assassins. Severed Flame agitation. Im nothing if not observant, if he didn't want me to know then he wouldn't have left his notes and open reports both written and one open on a communication orb. Something is coming. And I am at the centre of it.

The bond pulses. Caspian's emotions brush against mine like open palms instead of blades. He does not barricade them. He was raised to tend bonds, not survive them. Pack. Bloodline. Ceangal doscartha ties. They are meant to be fed. Strengthened. Honoured. He reaches for me instinctively when I recoil. And gods help me, I don't recoil.

That's the problem. His touch doesn't ignite revulsion. It doesn't scrape against memory. It settles. Warm. Steady. Infuriatingly safe. My body responds before my mind can categorise it. That is unacceptable. Maverick, no Mazzer is worse. Because with him, it isn't safety. It's voltage. And I don't trust electricity in my hands.

I trust control. I trust dominance. I trust the clean silence that comes after pressure is applied with precision. Emotion is unpredictable. Power is not. The bond disagrees. It pushes. It presses. It insists I feel. So I do what I was built to do. I compartmentalise.

Maverick POV

I watched a couple on the main floor of the Hollow Vein getting ready for their performance. The velvet lounge in the back corner was my favourite, it had a clear view of the main stage for performances, but it was also a direct line of sight to the main door, while also being next to the entrance to the kitchens, escape routes, Cath would be proud. Speaking of my best friend, bodyguard, deadly assassin druid, former lover, former submissive, and current co-conspirator in what I've decided to call my *fuck it* era. He strides over to me all smirks, broad shoulders and a face that others would describe as rugged and takes a seat next to me. He doesn't say a word just keeps smirking, I know he is waiting for me to ask, but as with every time we play this game I have about 400 years on him and do not like losing.

After about ten minutes Cath huffs in annoyance and clears his throat. "You have a customer, the one you have been watching and pushing to come see you", I smirk before schooling my features into a fake offended expression and just to add to the drama I gasp at him. "I would never push someone to take or need my services, what kind of 800-year-old mind manipulation warlock do you take me for Cathbad" He just rolls his eyes at my antics "800 years old my ass" he quips and my lips lift into a genuine smile at my oldest friend. Very true, I am significantly older than 800 but that is the story I am sticking to this year.

Cath looks over to me "Why did you need this one so much?" the question was a fair one, I don't usually hunt for my clientele, and this one would have come to me eventually but it seems that my patience that I am known for means absolutely nothing when it comes to Allyssa. This client could have information I need to understand my gorgeous obsession and apparently that was enough to make me become an impatient warlock. I look at Cath and I tell him the truth, he has always been my confidant, and I have always been able to be truthful with him. "He retired from the Tribunal archives, was a background figure in the chambers and I need to know what they were up to twenty-two years ago, to gain a better understanding of someone" A note of longing in my voice.

As soon as I finished speaking Cath's whole body language shifted from attentive and intrigued to all tense lines, he stood without warning and I just cocked my eyebrow at the suddenness of it. The shift was fascinating to watch, but also, I'm not sure I understand the abhorrence coming from him.

He remained standing at my shoulder, arms crossed, posture loose in the way that meant anything but. His gaze stayed fixed on the Vein's main entrance, not the floor, not the stage. Watching. Assessing.

I followed the line of his attention and found nothing immediately threatening. No weapons. No raised wards. No blood-intter that didn't belong. Interesting.

"You're tense," I observed mildly.

"You're distracted," he returned without looking at me.

I smiled. Not because he was wrong, but because he was pretending this was about vigilance.

"Am I?"

Cath's jaw tightened. "You don't usually let clients circle this long."

"I let them ripen," I corrected.

"You let them bleed."

"Same thing."

That earned me a sharp glance. The kind meant to cut conversation short. Instead, it confirmed what I'd already suspected. Cath wasn't concerned about the Archivist. He was concerned about why *this* one mattered.

"You don't trust him," Cath said.

I lifted a brow. "I don't trust anyone."

He exhaled through his nose. "You don't care about most of them."

Ah. There it was. Cath had never begrudged my lovers. Not the fleeting ones. Not the dangerous ones. Not even the ones that stayed long enough to learn where I kept my knives. But this wasn't about a lover. This was about focus.

"You're reading too much into it," I said lightly.

He didn't respond. Didn't argue. Didn't retreat. Just shifted half a step closer to me. Protective. Instinctive. Old habit. The Vein pulsed around us, sensing the tension and mistaking it for anticipation. I let the moment pass. Some fractures didn't need to be named to be acknowledged.

"Bring him in," I said at last.

Cath hesitated. Just long enough for me to notice. Then he turned toward the entrance, shoulders squared, expression unreadable.

"If this goes sideways," he said quietly, "I end it."

I smiled again. This time, softer.

"You always do."

I watched and waited as Cath brought the archivist through a tall lean frame, still beautiful even knowing his age, straight blond hair that seems to have a shine to it still, eyes that shone with arrogance, ahhh there is the seelie in the male.

He waited longer than most. That alone told me how desperate he was. How easy it was to push him to move just a little faster in my direction. A well-placed rumour in his building, a success story at his barber.

The Hollow Vein breathed around us, low-lit and layered in velvet shadow. Contracts hummed softly beneath the floor, old magic woven so deeply into the structure that even silence felt observed. He stood about 30 meters away, spine straight, chin lifted, trying to look like a man who had come by choice.

They always tried that first.

"I was told," he said at last, voice low, careful, "that you deal in... restorations."

His accent marked him immediately. Lower Seelie Court. Not noble enough to command outcomes, not disposable enough to vanish quietly. The kind of man who survived by keeping his head down and his records immaculate until the world moved on without him.

"I deal in what survives," I replied mildly.

That earned me a flicker of irritation. Then fear. Good.

He smoothed his robes, fingers brushing the faint sigil stitched into the inner seam. Tribunal archival mark. Retired, officially. Forgotten, functionally.

"I require a service," he said. "A summoning."

Ah.

Not curiosity. Not ambition.

Grief.

"Be specific," I said.

He hesitated. Long enough that the Vein itself seemed to lean closer.

"My wife," he said finally. The word caught. "She died seventeen years ago. A border skirmish near the southern ley-rift. Official cause: collateral spell collapse."

Official causes are always tidy. Death never is.

"I want her returned," he continued, forcing the words through clenched restraint. "Not permanently. I understand the limits." A pause. "Twenty-four hours."

Cath stiffened behind him. I did not look away from the Archivist.

"Conjured," the man added quickly. "Anchored. Whole. As she was. I want to speak with her. To hear her voice. To know—" His breath hitched despite himself. "—to know if she hated me for surviving."

There it was.

Not memory.

Not power.

Absolution.

"That service is not cheap," I said.

"I know." His jaw set. "I was told payment could be... abstract."

I tilted my head. "You were told you could offer a secret."

Hope flickered. Foolish thing.

"One of my choosing," he said carefully.

I smiled.

"That," I said pleasantly, "is the lie clients tell themselves so they can sleep before coming here."

His pupils dilated.

"You don't choose what you give me," I continued. "You choose whether you proceed."

Silence pressed in. The Vein thrummed softly, waiting.

He swallowed. "And if I proceed?"

"Then you get your twenty-four hours," I said. "And I take what you owe."

A beat.

"You won't remember giving it," I added. "Or what it cost you to keep it."

His shoulders sagged. Just slightly. Relief and terror in equal measure.

"Will she know?" he asked quietly. "That she's—"

"No," I said. "She will be as she was. Unafraid. Unburdened."

That decided him.

He nodded once.

"I accept."

The Vein exhaled.

And somewhere deep inside his mind, a sealed room cracked open.

The contract snapped into place.

Not a signature. Not a sigil.

Intent.

The secret surfaced immediately.

The moment it broke free, I felt it.

Not shock.

Recognition.

My magic tightened, instinctively precise, as though it had been waiting for this particular shape of truth. The Vein dimmed around us, sound folding inward, the world narrowing to the slow, deliberate unfurling of something that had been circling me for weeks.

Twenty-two years.

The number rang through me like a struck bell. Too exact. Too deliberate.

Answers slid into place with unsettling ease, even as new questions bloomed behind them, sharper and more dangerous than the last.

I had lived long enough to know the difference between coincidence and design.

And I had spent far too long circling one woman whose presence felt... heavier than it should. As though the world leaned, just slightly, whenever she entered a room.

I kept my expression pleasant. Neutral. The archivist didn't need to see the moment curiosity tipped into something closer to hunger.

Gods help me, I thought distantly, I should not want this to be true.

The thought barely finished forming before I acknowledged the lie.

I wanted it desperately.

Somewhere behind me, I felt Cath's attention sharpen. Not fear. Not suspicion.

Possession.

I ignored it. Some truths required silence to mature.

I felt it unfold as I guided the magic toward a memory he didn't realise was dangerous to have. One that he wouldn't remember giving me.

A closed Tribunal session.

Observers cloaked.

Archivists rendered invisible to avoid contamination.

He had stood silent in the corner, unseen, unimportant.

Listening.

"...the Unseelie King will not yield without leverage," a voice had said.

"He requires an heir capable of shadow command, all his other heir's have either died trying to prove themselves or not been capable of shadow command to which they are automatically unable to be his successor."

"Then we create one," another replied.

The conversation flowed from one to the next plans coming together. The Severed Flame was named. Not as a battlefield. As a resource. They have a scientist among them, a goblin that is capable of this kind of genetics, he was apart of the seelie and unseelie war and helped create the hybrids.

A controlled experiment. One that would see their victory in this power struggle. Hidden. Placed beyond court influence. Raised in the mortal realm, we will use the shadowkin to move through the veil to put her and a trusted ally to watch over her, teach her about veyloris. When we are ready we recovered the child.

The Seelie Archivist's breath shuddered as the truth surfaced through him, eyes unfocused now.

"There was a warlock there," he whispered without meaning to. "Cloaked. Severed Flame insignia. He didn't speak. Just... watched."

I noted that carefully.

The magic continued its work.

"They never discussed the outcome," he went on, voice distant. "Only the intent. Only the hope. When the veil gates opened three years ago the child vanished unable to find the child after a year, the project was... archived."

Archived.

I almost laughed.

The secret folded inward, sealing itself into the lattice of contracts etched through my soul. Another truth preserved. Another thread aligned.

I withdrew the magic gently.

The man sagged slightly, confusion already blooming behind his eyes.

"You will forget what you offered," I said calmly. "You will remember receiving relief."

His gaze flickered. "And the service?"

"Rendered," I assured him.

I reached out, brushing two fingers lightly against his temple.

The memory blurred.

Not erased.

Recontextualised.

By the time he stepped back, the weight was gone. The fear softened into a vague sense of unease he could never quite explain.

He bowed, shallow but sincere.

"Thank you," he said.

I inclined my head in return.

The Vein breathed again as the echoes faded, velvet shadows reclaiming the space like nothing irreversible had occurred.

But something had shifted.

The secret settled into me with deceptive neatness, answering questions I had been circling for months while simultaneously tearing open others I hadn't known how to name.

Twenty-two years ago, the Tribunal had tried to manufacture leverage. Control. A solution dressed up as inevitability.

And somewhere along the way, that solution had grown willful.

The shadows did not obey her.

They lingered.

As if waiting to see which version of her would speak next.

I catalogued the anomaly and set it aside. There were too many variables. Too little data.

Conclusions made too early were a liability.

Still—

The fact remained.

She had been removed from the realm at a critical age. Raised beyond factional reach. Exposed to survival without structure.

And whatever that had made of her, it had not broken her.

I folded the truth carefully into the lattice of contracts etched through my soul. Not for use. Not leverage. Not yet.

Timing mattered.

Proximity mattered more.

Whatever Allyssa Black was becoming, it was not something that could be understood through a single secret or reduced to intent scribbled in a Tribunal archive.

The revelation should have satisfied me. Should have cauterised the curiosity.

Instead, it sharpened it.

I was no closer to understanding what she was. Only more certain that she was *more* than anyone intended.

I realised, distantly, that she was no longer just the next Black Wolf under my protection.

She was the axis everything else had begun to tilt toward.

The thought was... inconvenient.
And entirely irreversible.

Chapter Fourteen: The Tribunal and the Observer

"In a time of universal deceit, telling the truth is a revolutionary act."
— Orwell

Thaelan – High Advisor to the Seelie Court | Arcanum Tribunal Operative

Indigo – Subject Watcher #37 | Codename: The Observer

Section I: Thaelan – Hall of Echoes

The Black Wolf has returned.

Moonwine catches starlight as I turn the chalice between my fingers. Below us, the scrying basin ripples, its surface fractured with scenes from the Academy. There. Allyssa. Caspian at her side. The tether sealed. Black and White. What was engineered as balance has become... something else.

Lady Vaelith stands beside me, spine perfectly aligned, hands folded within her sleeves. "The bond is stabilising her," she says.

"Yes."

"And destabilising our projections."

I allow myself the smallest smile. We did not create her to be simple. The basin shifts. Allyssa mid-combat. Shadow lingers along her spine a fraction too long before settling back into place.

Vaelith's voice lowers. "She is not Shadowkin."

"No," I reply softly. "She is not."

Only the royal Unseelie line commands external shadow. And even then, rarely. The Hall of Echoes hums faintly beneath Aurelensong's foundations. This chamber remembers every decree we have ever signed into inevitability.

"The Shadowkin remain compliant?" Vaelith asks.

"They remain contracted."

When the veil gates closed and Veyloris sealed itself from divine scrutiny, travel became leverage. The Shadowkin, newly severed from the Unseelie Court, sought sovereignty.

They were tired of walking armies into war. We offered recognition. They offered infrastructure. A thousand-year term. All veil-walkers registered. All inter-realm passage sanctioned. No independent contracts. Observational intelligence upon request.

They believed it protection. Fifty years remain. "And the clause?" Vaelith asks. "If a new Unseelie heir manifests royal shadow command," I recite, "and reintegration is formally declared, the contract voids." They tried to end the contract early when the portal gates reopened. But they are still required for travel, the gates are guarded by Hunters and they unfortunately do not answer to us. But we at least had sanctioned signed by all factions after that first wave of mortals and creatures from other realms tried to invade. That cost us in other plans but none the less we still have control over who is to travel between the gates for now.

The Shadowkin were not foolish. Merely afraid. The basin shifts again. A memory fragment surfaces. A laboratory ward. Sterile light. A sealed vial marked with sigil-code. Vaelith's voice remains even.

"The extraction was clean."

"Yes."

"And the Greenhollow containment?"

"Efficient."

We all played our parts. If shadow manifested, we would shape a throne. If it did not, royal blood still negotiates. Obsidian glass sustains half the wards above land. Trade is stability. Stability is power. "She was not meant to become the Black Wolf," Vaelith says.

"No."

That was variance. Black Wolves are volatile. Historical data confirms that. Which is why we layered contingency. The basin shows Caspian reaching for her, magic threading between them in visible arcs.

"The White Wolf stabilisation model," Vaelith says carefully.

"Yes."

The male is bound by fate to be the only natural strong enough to take out the black wolf when instability has taken over. Empathic. Loyal. Predictable. If the Black Wolf destabilised beyond acceptable thresholds, the White Wolf could be positioned as counterweight.

Public sympathy.

Moral fracture.

Justified removal.

It was clean. Instead— They reinforce one another. Bond reciprocity exceeds initial modelling thresholds. The Council has noticed. "They are uncomfortable," Vaelith says.

"The Council is accustomed to chairs that assume permanence," I reply coolly.

The basin darkens. Another thread surfaces. The Severed Flame. Agitation rising. They seek recognition. Specifically, the high warlock. He wants a seat. Legitimacy.

"He believe eliminating her proves their utility," Vaelith says.

"Yes."

"And if they attempt it?"

I set the chalice aside.

"Then either the problem resolves itself, the high warlock has his followers believing the black wolf is the end of our realm."

"And if it does not?"

"Then she resolves them."

We remain uninvolved. The basin flickers once more. Allyssa stands alone on a rooftop, shadow pooling wrong at her heels. "She was contained in the mortal realm longer than projected, she was supposed to have the knowledge of the realm and at the age of maturity we would have moulded her into what we needed." Vaelith says.

"Her first Watcher failed."

"Yes."

Clause 9.3 was invoked. Replacement assigned.

"The new Watcher?" she asks.

"Efficient," I say.

For now. Fifty years remain on a contract the Shadowkin believed temporary. If she manifests fully before expiration— The corridors close. And the Tribunal must adapt. We always do.

Section II

Indigo – Watcher Log #37

Codename: The Observer

Target: Alpha-Black (667-ALY)

Observation Position: Verdant Athenaeum

Glamour Layers: Three

Detection Risk: Minimal

She pauses more frequently now.

External shadow adherence extends beyond natural drift by measurable margins.

Unconfirmed manifestation.

Monitoring.

Log Entry 1192

Age: 20

Status: Fully Activated

Ceangal doscartha: Confirmed

Projection Deviation: 17% and rising

Contract Expiration Window: 50 years

Predecessor terminated under Clause 9.3. Failure to maintain mortal containment. He believed the mortal realm safe. He underestimated absence of magic. Alpha-Black disappeared at sixteen.

I traced her through mortal power networks and mortal gang cells. She was searching. Not for magic. For origin. Then she crossed a gate in the chaos of a horde of demon from another realm and returned to Veyloris.

Report submitted. Reassignment ordered. I continued observation unofficially. The Shadowkin contract was not conquest. It was exhaustion. They left the Unseelie Crown because they were tired of being deployed as weapons. Now they escort Tribunal envoys into realms that never requested oversight.

They observe.

They report.

Their intelligence has cost cities.

Entire bloodlines erased in quiet adjustments.

They became what they fled.

The void clause remains intact. If an heir manifests royal shadow command and reintegration is declared— The contract dissolves. The Tribunal does not dissolve with it. Alpha-Black exhibits early-stage external shadow response. I have not reported this. If confirmed and submitted— Acceleration protocols trigger. Containment. Or elimination. The White Wolf contingency model was their failsafe.

Instead, the bond deepens. Severed Flame agitation rising. If they attempt removal— Public sympathy recalibrates. If she survives— Momentum shifts. No outcome is stable. She lifts her head again. Shadow tightens at her back. Listening. I close the log. And remain silent.

Personal Addendum [Encrypted: Watcher Clearance Only]

There is something in the way she restrains herself. The way she blinks back instinct instead of unleashing it. I see it in the tension between her fingers. In the slow exhale before she chooses words over violence. The Black Wolf was never born mad. They were driven there. By betrayal. By isolation. By being named "monster" before they learned their own name.

This one—Allyssa—still hesitates. Still chooses. Still pulls the blade back when she could let it fall. Maybe she will not fracture the way the others did. Maybe she will not become the weapon they expect. Maybe she will rewrite the ending. And if she does—

Then the Tribunal will not survive her mercy. Because if they give the order...

If they decide containment means execution—

I am no longer certain I will obey.

Maverick POV

The Hollow Vein was already awake when I returned.

Music bled low through the stone. Velvet shadows shifted across the main floor as contracts beneath the foundation hummed in quiet adjustment. The Vein has always preferred anticipation to chaos.

I paused just inside the threshold, letting the wards recognise me fully.

There is comfort in systems that obey.

Unlike Councils.

"Eastern rotation's dragging," I said as I crossed the floor. "Give them elegance before appetite."

A warlock inclined his head.

"Yes, Warlock."

"And tell the kitchens no stimulants tonight," I added. "I want desire, not frenzy."

That earned a flicker of surprise, quickly smoothed away. Orders were obeyed. Questions were not.

The Vein settled as I took my usual seat in the velvet lounge. Clear sightlines. Clean exits. Old habits built by centuries of not dying. Cath appeared briefly at my side, close enough to speak without being overheard.

"You're back early," he said.

"I wasn't needed longer," I replied, only acknowledging to myself that I stayed longer than I needed to just to watch her a little longer.

He studied me for half a breath longer than necessary, then nodded once. No commentary. No probing. Good. He'd learned when silence was the wiser play.

A figure approached from the bar — tall, ink-dark skin faintly luminous beneath the Vein's lighting. Shadowfin. Her name is Vireth. She moved with the careful control of someone who never entirely trusts the room to hold her shape. She set the drink before me without bowing.

"Warlock."

"Vireth," I acknowledged.

Her shadow pooled cleanly beneath her feet. Controlled. Self-contained. No external command. No royal bleed. "How are your elders?" I asked casually. Cath went still. Vireth's expression did not shift, but the shadow beneath her tightened a fraction.

"They endure," she said.

"Endurance is rarely satisfying."

Silence stretched.

"And the contract?" I continued lightly. "Any movement toward... interpretation?"

Vireth's gaze sharpened.

"No formal revisions," she replied. "The elders remain in consultation."

Consultation. Translation: disagreement.

"And my suggestions?" I asked.

Her pause was answer enough.

"Seers are not legislators," she said carefully.

"No," I agreed. "They are rarely listened to until hindsight requires them."

Vireth inclined her head slightly — not submission. Acknowledgment of shared memory. I dismissed her with a nod. When she moved away, Cath leaned back, arms folding. "You're still pushing them."

"They're still bound."

"They chose it."

"They chose fear."

Cath's jaw tightened.

"They were being used," he said.

"I know."

And that was the problem.

I remember the Hall of Ink. The original Shadowkin elder stood before me, his form flickering at the edges from strain. Even then, too many of his people were losing cohesion. Too many returning from Unseelie campaigns unable to maintain corporeal shape for more than a few hours at a time.

"We are tired of being corridors for slaughter," he had said. "And you think signing with the Tribunal changes that?" I asked.

"It gives us sovereignty."

"It gives them jurisdiction."

"They offer protection."

"From one crown," I replied. "In exchange for another."

He had held my gaze. "The Unseelie King commands shadow," he said. "He commands us."

"The Tribunal commands law," I countered. "Law endures longer."

Silence had stretched between us. "You rely too heavily on prophecy," he said at last. "I rely on pattern," I answered. I had brought the Seer to them. She saw threads. Not certainty. Possibility. A royal shadow line re-emerging. A convergence of blood.

A contract void clause triggered by heir manifestation. The elders had listened. Then they had looked at their children. At the Shadowkin who could not hold form for more than minutes after returning from Unseelie wars. "At least with the Tribunal," the elder had said, "our very being will not be commanded. We will be used under law."

Law. They thought that would make it cleaner. I told them then: "You are trading one misguided king for a council that will call exploitation governance." They signed anyway. Fear shortens patience.

Back in the Vein, I lift the glass and watch the liquid catch the low light. Fifty years remain on that contract. Fifty years until expiration. Or earlier, if the void clause triggers. "She's manifesting," Cath says quietly. "Early stages," I reply, at least I believe she is.

"And if she completes?"

"The corridors close."

"And the Tribunal?"

"Will adapt."

Cath's gaze sharpens.

"And you?"

I consider that. I once argued against the contract. The Seer may have been wrong. Or she may have been early. Vireth moves across the floor again, serving patrons, her shadow perfectly obedient to her form. I watch it. And I wonder how many of her people remember the day they believed they were choosing freedom.

"Client waiting," Cath added distracting me from my thoughts. "Walk-in."

I hummed. "Species?"

"Satyr."

That narrowed my attention a fraction. Not suspicion. Assessment. Interesting. "Send him in when he's done pretending, he doesn't need this," I said.

Cath snorted quietly and disappeared again. I leaned back and let the Vein breathe around me. Walk-ins came for all sorts of reasons. Grief. Obsession. Fear dressed up as curiosity. Most of them thought they were unique. Most of them were wrong. Still, I listened. Because sometimes, buried beneath the ordinary desperation, was a question worth answering. And sometimes, even when I wasn't looking for anything at all, something unexpected surfaced anyway.

He smelled of iron and moss when he entered the Vein. Not the clean green of untouched forest. Not the bright snap of cultivated ley-fields. This was earth pushed too hard. Overworked. Compelled. Satyr. His hooves were polished, silver-capped, etched with stabilisation runes meant to dull instinctual surges. His horns had been trimmed short, the tips bound in ornamental filigree that screamed wealth.

Cath noticed it too. His posture shifted half a degree. Defensive. Ready. I raised a finger. Stay. The satyr stopped just inside the contract ring, spine straight, chin lifted. He bowed shallowly. The bow of someone who had not knelt in a very long time.

"Warlock," he said. Educated accent. Careful diction. Fraying control. "I was told you offer... corrective services."

"I offer resolution," I replied. "The distinction matters."

His jaw flexed. Already annoyed. Already afraid. Petty satisfaction coils in my chest making me smirk without remorse.

"I need something removed," he said. "Before it becomes... irreversible."

I tilted my head. "People usually say that *after* the damage is done." A flicker of something dark crossed his eyes. Not guilt. Anticipation.

"She is a nymph," he said quickly, as if speed might soften the truth. "River-born. Employed in bio-reactive stabilisation. Exceptionally intelligent. Painfully uninterested."

Cath shifted behind him. Disgust, sharp and immediate.

"You've been pursuing her," I said.

"I've been restrained," the satyr snapped — then visibly reeled himself back in. "I mean... I have tried to be."

Tried.

"She doesn't run," he continued, voice tightening. "She doesn't provoke. She simply exists. That should not be enough to—" His breath hitched. "—to unmake my focus."

The Vein hummed, displeased.

"I know what my kind becomes when desire curdles," he said, quieter now. "I will not be that creature."

I studied him properly then. This was not a monster seeking absolution after indulgence. This was a man standing at the edge of a cliff, staring down, and realising how much he wanted to jump. "What happens if you don't intervene?" I asked, curious to see if that gives him pause, testing his commitment to resist instinct. Cath calls it playing with my food. I call it understanding thresholds.

His lips parted. Closed again. "She would not survive the attention," he admitted finally. "Not intact." Honesty. At last. "I want it gone," he said hoarsely. "The fixation. The hunger. Strip it out. I don't care how." That surprised him, when it left his mouth.

Cath's fingers twitched once.

"I don't erase instinct," I said calmly. "I redirect it. Recontextualise it."

"I don't care," the satyr said. "Do it."

Desperation always made people reckless.

"Payment will be required," I said.

He nodded instantly. Too fast. "A secret."

"Yes."

"One of my choosing?" he asked, hope flaring despite himself.

I smiled.

"That," I said pleasantly, "is the lie clients cling to so they can walk in here."

His pupils dilated. His hooves scraped stone.

"You don't choose what you give me," I continued. "You choose whether you proceed."

Silence pressed down. For a moment — just a moment — I thought he might retreat. Cath did too. I felt his readiness spike. The calculation flicker behind his eyes. If the satyr turned now, Cath would retrieve him before he reached the door. Not violently. Efficiently. The obsession would be stripped anyway. Quietly. Permanently. Some lines could not be left uncrossed once approached.

The satyr swallowed.

"And if I refuse?" he asked.

"Then you leave," I said. "And someone innocent pays the cost of your restraint failing."

That decided him.

He bowed his head. Lower this time. Truer.

"I accept."

The Vein exhaled. The contract formed. I slid into his mind and opened a secret at random; I held no interest in his science experiments and the dealings of a no-name innovation company. The secret surfaced softly, almost apologetically. And I nearly missed it.

Schematics. Procurement chains. Design constraints that made no sense until they did. Magic calibrated downward. Stabilised.

Blunted. Built for hands without resonance. For nervous systems that could not channel. Human-compatible.

I stilled. Not shock. Curiosity. I had lived long enough to know better than to underestimate anyone. And still, I had.

Who, I wondered distantly, had been speaking to mortals long enough to know their tolerances? Who was preparing to arm them? The questions burned to be answered. The satyr didn't know. He thought it an annoyance. A limitation imposed by unseen investors. He had cursed the inefficiency more than once.

I folded the knowledge away carefully. Not leverage. Not yet.

The obsession burned out next, clean and precise. Desire untethered from fixation. Memory rewoven until hunger lost its teeth. When the satyr sagged, it was relief that broke him, not loss. "It's done?" he asked quietly.

"Yes."

He bowed properly this time. "Thank you," he said. "For stopping me."

I inclined my head. Cath waited until the satyr was gone, the Vein settling back into velvet hush.

"That one," he said carefully, "wasn't worth much."

I smiled faintly.

"No," I agreed. "He wasn't."

I touched the sealed knowledge again. Human hands. Mortal limits. Someone, somewhere, planning very carefully. "But the questions he carried are."

Somewhere beyond the Vein, someone was teaching humans how to hold magic without understanding the cost. And I had just learned enough to know where to listen next.

Chapter Fifteen: The Warlock Who Saw Too Much

"One is not born, but rather becomes." — Simone de Beauvoir

Allyssa POV

Three days after Lakemond's ultimatum, the bruises from joint training had already begun to fade. The bond had not. Caspian trains like he was raised to tend something fragile. Even when we spar, even when I drive him into the sand hard enough to crack bone, there's restraint in him. Not weakness. Intention.

He touches my wrist to correct form. My shoulder to steady balance. My waist to pivot through a throw. Learning to fight in a pair is harder than I expected. I was built to fight alone. He never lingers. He doesn't have to. The bond does. It stretches between us during drills, threads tightening every time skin meets skin. Not hunger. Not exactly. Something quieter. Persistent. He doesn't flinch from it. Doesn't try to cage it. He was raised to nurture bonds. Pack. Blood. Ceangal doscartha =ties. They are meant to be fed. Honoured.

I was raised to survive them. Three days. Three days of training beside him. Three nights of sealing the bond and feeling it bleed through anyway. I haven't let him touch me outside what the drills require. I haven't let myself. And that restraint is starting to fracture.

The bond hums. The ley-lines around the Verdant Athenaeum shift with it, as if the whole Enclave reacts to my instability. Caspian's pain lingers like a phantom hand around my throat. I feel the guilt. The regret. The yearning. So much emotion, hasn't he ever heard of compartmentalisation before fucking hell. So, I do what I do best and I run. Because I don't do feelings and Caspian's are unfiltered and raw, but what I do is dominance. I do survival.

Those are necessary all the other emotions that try to surface are put into their boxes and analysed at a later date if at all.

The bond is fighting me every step of the way, every time I try to protect him it fills me with a pain that travels all through my body trying to force me to concede. I know what pain is and my threshold is high, but my mind feels like I'm unravelling, thread by thread.

Caspian's emotions aren't guarded. They never are. They crest through the tether like waves against glass. Concern. Patience. Hope. Hope is the worst of it. I shove it down. Seal harder. Layer shields until my skull feels packed with iron.

It doesn't work. Need presses through. Not his. Mine. The realisation tips something inside me sideways.

"Allyssa."

Pinebane's voice is low, steady. She's watching from the edge of the courtyard, arms folded. Shatter Bay scent — salt, cedar, storm-wet fur. Gamma calm. My thoughts come in one-word punches. I can't hold anything longer than sensation.

"You're shaking."

"I'm not."

"You are."

I can feel it now. Micro-tremors under skin. Pulse too fast. Vision narrowing.

"Ground," she says gently. "Five breaths. Name what you feel."

I don't feel. I catalogue. That's different. Her gaze softens. That's when the monster moves. Softness is exposure. Exposure is weakness.

"Don't," I snap.

"I'm not your enemy," she says.

I step forward. She steps back. Not out of fear. Out of understanding. That infuriates me more.

"Back off," I growl, voice low enough to vibrate.

She holds my gaze one heartbeat too long. Then she lets me go. The mask slides back into place like a blade into its sheath. Controlled. Contained. Almost.

That's when I smell him. Spiced citrus. Old parchment. The smell of rain and lightning scorching earth. I have never known anyone with such a complex scent. I drink it in; I can't seem to stop myself in my state. Precise. Controlled. Warlock. Him. The scent cuts through emotional noise like a knife through silk. My pulse shifts. Not chaotic. Focused. Danger is easier to manage than feeling.

He moves through the lower corridor toward Lakemond's wing. Alone. Or pretending to be. Suspicion sharpens everything inside me. He tested me in that office. He watched. He knew.

What does he want? Information? Leverage? Me dead? The bond recoils at that thought. I don't give it time to argue. I slip into shadow. Magic folds around me like muscle memory.

Predator mode is quieter than panic. Easier than hope. And if Maverick thinks he can read me—

He's about to learn I read back.

He enters Lakemond's office without knocking. I reach for the fae magic inside me and set a single intention. *Cloak.* Most fae have to gesture. Direct their element. Fire, wind, water, earth. Their magic answers to what they are born to. Mine never has. I've never manifested an element. No flame. No tide. No storm.

But I don't need to. Darkness has always listened. I fold into it easily, the way other fae summon sparks or frost. No words. No sigils. Just will. Warlocks and witches cast through language. Precise spells. Structured power. Werewolves carry magic in blood and bone, transformation and strength woven into muscle. Druids and dryads carve runes and sigils into weapons and structures to fight their battles. Hunters are different. We're built for war. Which is why we're paired in triads. Hunter. Hunter. Warlock.

I become the shadow at Lakemond's wall.

Lakemond pours two glasses of whiskey, the tension in his shoulders coiled and brittle.

Mazzer. Not Maverick. Get it together.

He drops into the chair like it belongs to him. Like every room does. "She's not like the others," he says, voice smooth as glass.

Lakemond sighs. "No. She's not." "She's the kind of fire that burns the hands that try to hold it."

"Then don't try to hold it," he replies easily. "Kneel. With respect."

"And fear," Lakemond mutters, like the word costs him. Mazzer smiles, tilting his head. "Good," Mazzer says. "The world should."

My gut coils. That shouldn't land.

But it does That I'd rather be feared than adored.

That dangerous feels safer than beautiful.

That weapon is easier than woman.

"She needs help," Lakemond mutters. "Control. Restraint, maybe even a fucking therapist if I could ever get her to see one." Mazzer doesn't blink. He leans back slowly, spine folding into the chair like a man settling into a throne built from the bones of his past. One ankle crosses over his knee, casual and blasphemous in its ease.

"Let her descend," he says, almost reverent. "Power doesn't always bloom in light."

His voice carries storm-forge cadence. Centenary steel.

"Sometimes it grows teeth in the dark."

Lakemond's frown deepens. "She needs balance." That makes Mazzer pause. Just briefly. His grin twitches, falters for a breath. Then he recovers, golden eyes glinting like firelight catching the edge of something sharp. "No," he says, softer now. "She needs someone who won't flinch when she bares her teeth. Someone who doesn't mistake her survival for sin.

"Caspian will be her balance. You know that. But the prophecy was never about balance alone."

His gaze sharpens.

"Mother Nature didn't write it. The Fates did."

My breath stutters. Not enough to be obvious, but enough that I feel it; like a missed step on a familiar path. A tiny betrayal. I shouldn't care what he says. I don't care. But apparently I do. It's like he reached inside and touched something I didn't give him permission to see. I shouldn't want that. Shouldn't need it. But maybe I do. Because what does it say about me that being called dangerous feels like the closest thing to intimacy I can stand? That maybe I'd rather be a monster people admire than a female they pity?

His head turns.

Directly toward me.

"I know you're there, darling."

Lakemond blinks in confusion, looking around. "What?"

"Didn't expect the Black Wolf to play spy," Mazzer drawls. "Thought you preferred the direct approach."

I drop the hold on my magic. The air shivers with silver light as magic lifts from my skin like fog. "Cute trick," I say coolly. "Didn't know your ego had sonar."

Mazzer's lips curl. "Not ego, love. Experience. I knew your scent the moment you stepped into the arena."

I narrow my eyes, voice like a blade testing bone. "You were watching me?" I knew that he was, and he knew it too, it was like a game between us in front of the Director. Mazzer's lips twitch; not in embarrassment, but something far more dangerous. "Oh, obsessively." He rises with the slow grace of someone who knows how to weaponize stillness. His posture is fluid, languid even; unthreatening to anyone who doesn't know how to read predators. But I see it.

The way his shoulder blades tighten beneath his robes. The subtle shift in weight over his heels. The stillness isn't relaxation. It's restraint. Like a spring waiting for permission to snap.

"I watched your blade drills," he says, voice dipping into something silkier. "Your interrogations. The way you moved when you didn't think anyone was watching. Focused. Precise. Ruthless." He steps forward, not touching, but close enough that I feel the heat radiating off his skin. "And the moment you licked blood from your claws mid-battle," he breathes, "I knew..." He pauses. His eyes lock on mine; no glimmer, no smirk now. Just intensity. Heavy as prophecy.

"You're exquisite," he says quietly.

"Terrifying."

"Chaos disciplined into steel."

My body reacts before my mind can stop it. A flicker in my chest. A pulse in my throat. A tightening that has nothing to do with fear.

I scoff, sharp and defensive. "Creep."

"Admirer," he corrects, and steps closer. Not enough to threaten. Just enough to test me. Like he's daring me to push him away. Or pull him in. His gaze dances across me. Not lustful. Not exactly. It's... reverent. Analytical. Worship twisted into curiosity.

"You came all this way for fashion advice and unsolicited dick-stares?" Lakemond groans into his drink. Mazzer grins. "You're vicious. No wonder I can't get you out of my mind."

I tense. A beat. My spine locks, every muscle coiled so tightly it hurts. That single sentence—so simple, so confident; slides under my skin like heat through frost. "Excuse me?" I say with one eyebrow raised. Mazzer doesn't flinch. His voice drops, not for drama, but intimacy. "You're not like the others," he says, slow and deliberate.

"The last Black Wolves were powerful. Tragic. Symbols carved by fate." He leans in, just slightly. No smirk now. Just reverence and danger braided in his tone. "But you," he murmurs, "you were born sovereign." My heart skips. No; it *stumbles.* Like it wasn't ready for that word. That weight. Sovereign.

The word settles heavy in my ribs.

I roll my shoulders, force my voice into ice. "Keep talking, warlock, and I'll crown you with your own spine." He exhales; soft, almost amused. But there's no mocking in it. "Say that like it's a threat." I narrow my eyes at him "It is." And then he meets my gaze. Not like a man ready to challenge me; but like one *willing to kneel.* "I'd still kneel." He purrs. My mouth opens. Closes.

A second passes.

Then another. The silence between us is no longer empty. It *aches*; thick with something unspoken and ancient. Like a wire pulled too tight between predator and offering. And gods help me... Part of me wants to pull.

"Are you flirting with me," I growl, "or offering yourself as a chew toy?" Mazzer's smile curves like it was sculpted for sin. "Why not both?" Heat crawls up the back of my neck like a brand. My pulse spikes, traitorous and loud. I don't move. I don't breathe. I *won't* let him see that. So I force my expression into blankness; stone cold and sharp-edged. My jaw clenches. My eyes narrow just enough to signal warning. *He's not allowed to reach me. No one is. Not there.*

"I don't want loyalty," I say. "I want control."

The words taste like truth.

The words hang in the air. Raw. Real. More honest than anything I've said in weeks. His response is wordless; yet deafening.

He bows.

Not theatrically.

Not as submission.

As invitation.

"Then command me," he says softly, like a secret passed between teeth and soul. And somehow, it doesn't feel like surrender. It feels like power being placed gently into my hands.

Lakemond rubs his eyes like he's already regretting asking. "Enough. Mazzer. You had a proposal." Mazzer's grin fades. His expression rearranges itself into something polished and clinical, the kind of mask you wear to speak in rooms full of judges and executioners. "I want to take her to my club." Lakemond blinks, then narrows his eyes. "The Hollow Vein? Beneath Draethen's Portal Gate?"

"The underground one." Realisation dawns like a sunrise no one wanted. Lakemond goes still, the color draining from his face. "*That* club?" Mazzer lifts his glass in salute, the ice clinking like a dare. "The very one." "You want to throw her into a sex dungeon?!" Mazzer shrugs, nonchalant. "I prefer to call it a sanctuary of consensual dominance and therapeutic power exchange but yes. That's the idea."

Lakemond chokes on his drink. "You think *that* will help her?" Mazzer sets his glass down gently, then clasps his hands together like he's presenting a theory to a tribunal. "Yes. Because it's not about sex. It's about *control*. Structure. Ritual. Boundaries. It's the one place where instinct isn't punished; it's negotiated. Where power is *asked for*, not taken." He turns to me, and something in his posture changes. The edge dulls. His eyes meet mine, and for the first time tonight, they don't burn; they *glow*. "It's about reclaiming power. On your terms. For once."

The word *sex* hangs in the air like smoke. And I inhale it by accident. Too fast. Too deep.

My chest tightens. My lungs constrict. A memory surfaces; not full, not clear. Just *sensory*. A voice that wasn't mine. Fingers that left bruises. A locked door. A silence I was forced to swallow. *Flash*.

Hands. Shame. No voice. No exit. I flinch. It's small. Instantaneous. The kind of involuntary reaction you train out of yourself over time. But this one escapes. And he sees it. Of course he does. His gaze flickers; not with pity, but something deeper. Recognition. A knowing so sharp it might cut if I let it linger.

So I do what I do best. I strike. ""Did your last Black Wolf love you," I ask softly, "or did they just use you like a leash?". The words echo. The silence that follows is colder than any blade. But he doesn't flinch. He doesn't scowl. Or sneer. Or retaliate. He just looks at me. Like he *knows*. Like maybe... he understands. And then, softly.... "That," he murmurs, "was ruthless." And somehow, it feels like a compliment. And godsdamn me... I like the way he says it.

Like it's not an insult. Like it's a rite of passage. Like it's a name I've earned and he's the first to say it without fear. My heartbeat stutters. I swallow it whole.

Mazzer tilts his head, then exhales softly; as though filing the moment away. He shifts his stance slightly, shoulders squaring, tone pivoting to strategy. "None of the other warlocks will work," he says. "They're afraid of her. Or they want to own her. Neither will survive her."

I think of Caspian. Of the quiet conversations in the dark. Of him watching me, not with awe or fear; but respect. I remember what I told him. "You need someone who doesn't leash it. Who enjoys it."

Mazzer steps closer, his voice dipping like a secret just for me. "Let them try. Let them fail. I'll still be here." His breath ghosts across my cheek; warm, deliberate, intimate in its restraint. Not close enough to touch. But close enough to *promise*. He looks at me like I'm gravity, and he's already decided to fall. "Let them fumble for your leash," he murmurs near my ear.

"I never needed one."

Maverick POV

She storms from the room like a blade pulled too fast from its sheath. I don't follow. I watch. The door rattles in her wake. I slip back inside and take a seat in one of the armchairs, staring at our latest game of fates table putting my hand to it and pushing my intent making the next move and sitting back. Lakemond exhales like he's aged a decade. I remain seated, hands folded loosely in my lap, pulse steady despite the storm she leaves behind.

Recognition hums through me. Lust. Infatuation. Need. Curiosity. She is not ready. Not yet. There is still too much resistance in her. Too much shame welded to strength. But she's closer than she realises. She thinks control means containment. She thinks dominance means suppression. She has not yet learned the difference between rule and restraint.

But the fractures are there. Hairline cracks in the armour she forged from trauma and sharpened into a crown she refuses to wear. She felt it when I knelt. That tremor was not fear. It was recognition.

Lakemond watches me carefully. "You're playing a dangerous game."

"I don't play games," I reply lightly. "I dismantle them."

And she is the most intricate one I have ever seen. I lean back, gaze drifting toward the shadow she vacated. The Black Wolf.

The missing archive.

The anomaly no one will name.

She carries Unseelie blood.

Royal, I suspect.

Proven? No.

The trail fractures in the archives. Redactions where records should breathe.

The Tribunal has hidden something. Possibly several somethings. And for all my reputation as the Warlock of Secrets, even I cannot pull answers from parchment that no longer exists. It irritates me. I dislike incomplete patterns.

But this I do know: They expected a hybrid weapon.

A controllable variable.

They did not expect sovereignty.

They expected volatility. They did not expect restraint. The White Wolf was meant to be the blade if she fractured.

Instead, he bonded.

That miscalculation unsettles them. I can feel it in the political tremors. The Severed Flame tests the perimeter.

Assassins disguised as students.

Opportunists wearing ideology. If they remove her, the Tribunal's hands remain clean. If she removes the cult, the Tribunal consolidates power. Either way, they believe they win. They are comfortable in their chairs. Comfort breeds blindness. I do love a game of fates table.

Lakemond wants the prophecy to unfold. The Tribunal wants control. I want truth. And perhaps... something more dangerous. I rise slowly.

"She will come," I tell Lakemond.

He studies me. "You're certain?"

"She doesn't tolerate unanswered questions."

And I have made myself one.

When she stood before me tonight, fire coiled behind her eyes and fury masking fracture, I saw it clearly. She does not crave submission. She craves safe control. There is a difference. She needs ritual. Structure. Containment chosen, not forced. She needs somewhere her instincts are not labelled monstrous. The Hollow Vein is not a vice. It is architecture. And if I am correct, she will step into it like she was always meant to rule it.

I pause at the threshold of Lakemond's office. Not to admire her rage. To calculate. If she manifests shadow fully, the contract shifts. Fifty years remain. Fifty years until renegotiation. Unless a legitimate heir emerges. Unless the clause triggers. Unless the realm changes faster than the Tribunal expects.

The seers once warned the Shadowkin elders of this path. I warned them too. They chose survival over patience. Perhaps they were right. Perhaps I was. Choice is a dangerous variable in prophecy.

She is not ready. But she is close. And when the crown stops feeling like a threat and starts feeling like inevitability—

I will not stand before her. I will stand at her side. Not as master. Not as leash. As weapon. And if she commands it—

As devotion. The Spring Cycle approaches. The Academy shifts beneath it. So does she.

Chapter Sixteen: Verdant Bloom

"A seed grows with no sound, but a tree falls with huge noise."

— Confucius

Caspian POV

The Academy courtyard had transformed overnight.

Ivy swallowed stone. Saplings spiralled around the dais under druidic hands. Petals drifted in deliberate arcs, wind-charms holding them aloft like suspended breath.

At the centre stood the Bloom Pyre. The central dais where Director Lakemond addressed students was encircled by young saplings coaxed into spiral growth by druidic hands.

Not fire. Living wood.

Branches gathered from every territory in Veyloris, braided and seeded with dormant buds waiting for the Rite's crescendo.

This was not sacrifice. It was tending.

Renewal instead of conquest.

Every faction would prove today whether they understood the difference.

I stood with Frostpine's delegation, formal but unarmoured. White tunic. Crest at my shoulder. My wolf restless beneath my skin. Because she was here. Allyssa stood across the courtyard, half-shadowed by a flowering trellis. She did not soften for the ritual. She never did. But something about the living canopy above her made the air around her feel... steadier. Not tamed. Rooted. She was dangerously gorgeous.

Students parted around her without realizing they were doing it. She did not seek space.

Space yielded. And then—

Him.

Mazzer leaned casually against one of the ivy-wrapped pillars near the Vein delegation. Deep green suit. Gold ivy threaded along the lapel. Shirt half-buttoned. Too much chest for a ritual. I roll my eyes, warlocks never arrive quietly. No insignia. His gaze was not on the ritual. It was on her. Irritation slid down my spine. I didn't like how easily he looked at her. As if he'd already calculated something I hadn't.

I looked back to Allyssa beneath the canopy. She wasn't watching the ritual. She was watching everyone else. As if a threat might come from any direction. I wanted to go to her, my wolf urging me to do just that. I didn't. I stood with Frostpine's delegation. I was here as a representative.

I once imagined a future beneath trees like these.

A pack-bonded mate. Strength. Protection. Pups tumbling through frost-kissed forests.

Emily used to tease me about it.

Asher said I should focus on being strong enough to face the Black Wolf first.

I wondered what Emily would think of Allyssa.

Asher already knew. He'd been blunt about it, as always.

But Emily...

I've read her messages. Every one of them.

I just haven't answered.

She keeps calling on the orb. Asking questions I don't know how to explain.

Not about the bond. Not really.

About her.

I don't know how to put Allyssa into words that won't make my sister worry.

Or worse—judge, more than she already has, if her messages are anything to go by.

Guilt sits heavier than armour some nights.

I had not imagined prophecy. I had not imagined her. And yet now, watching her, I understood something I hated admitting: The future I once wanted felt small. I wanted to be more than just the White Wolf. More than the half-breed son of Frostpine's Alpha.

Laya stepped beside me. She had chosen green tonight. A deliberate shade. Frostpine-adjacent without being so. Her smile was warm. Familiar. Careful. "You're quiet," she said lightly. "I'm thinking." I reply. "That's dangerous." She quips. A joke. Old rhythm. Once, it would have been easy to lean into that comfort. Before the bond. "You've barely spoken to me since Winter," Laya continued, softer now. "Did bonding really change you that much?"

It had. But not in the way she meant. "I didn't expect to be part of a prophecy," I said honestly. "I expected to become strong. Defend the realm. Find a mate. Build something simple." Her gaze sharpened. "And now?" Now I stood here watching a woman who terrified half the Academy and fascinated the other half. "Now I don't think simple was ever an option."

Laya's jaw tightened just slightly.

"She's already pulling you into storms," Laya murmured. "Now she's collecting warlocks too?" I stiffened. "That's not how this works." "Isn't it?" she asked softly. Across the courtyard, Allyssa's head turned slightly. She looked between Laya and me.

Then her gaze swept down my body, searching for injury.

Heat followed wherever her attention lingered. Possessive. Claiming.

The bond brushed mine—probing. Concern. Sharp and unfamiliar from her. She looks me in the eye once more and then turns her attention away.

I wanted her to cross the courtyard. To stand beside me. To make it unmistakable. The thought was possessive. Primitive. My wolf approved of it far more than I did. I forced the impulse down and fixed my gaze on the ritual instead. Allyssa stepped closer to the ritual circle, instinctively—not seeking attention, not claiming space. Just moving where she felt pulled.

Some noticed. Some didn't. Pinebane did. Gamma Pinebane of Shutter Bay had been watching since the courtyard filled. She moved like she always did—quiet, deliberate, never wasted motion. Broad-shouldered, steady, eyes sharp as cut bark. She did not approach Allyssa directly. Brave. She positioned herself. Between. Not blocking Laya. Not confronting her. Just standing in a line that said: Enough. Laya noticed. So did I. My eyebrows rose in response.

Pinebane didn't look at Allyssa when she spoke. But her voice carried low and certain. "Growth protects its own." It wasn't directed at anyone. But it landed. Laya's smile thinned. "Is that a warning?" Pinebane finally turned her head. Not hostile. Not aggressive. Just... assessing. "I recognize pack structure when I see it." Silence fell between them. The ritual circle pulsed brighter.

Allyssa glanced over her shoulder then—just briefly—taking in the dynamic without reacting. She didn't ask for help. Didn't acknowledge it. But she didn't reject it either. And that was new.

Laya shifted tactics. "Caspian," she said smoothly, stepping closer to me, "you don't have to carry something just because it chose you." There it was. The gentle invitation back. Back to safety. Back to the version of me that existed before all this. I almost wanted it. I sliver of being caught with Laya imbedded in, like I did something wrong before I let it go.

Then the Blooming reached its peak. The living throne split open—and from its centre rose a single sapling of silver-veined bark, its leaves shimmering like tempered glass. The crowd inhaled as one. Renewal. Not destruction. Not chaos. Reclaiming. The roots shifted again.

Not toward the druids. Not toward the Shutter Bay delegation. Toward Allyssa. Just a subtle lean. A bow so faint most wouldn't see it. Pinebane did. Her posture changed. It wasn't dramatic. It wasn't kneeling. But it was recognition. A Gamma's instinct aligning before her mind consciously allowed it. Not submission. Acknowledgment. I felt it through the bond before Allyssa did. She stiffened slightly. Not at the movement. At the weight.

Laya saw the root's direction too. Her breath caught. Mazzer saw it. His posture shifted slightly. Interest sharpened. And for the first time that evening, something like real fear flickered across Laya's face. Not jealousy. Not rivalry. Loss. Because this was no longer about affection.

The courtyard erupted into celebration—wine passed, music rising, laughter spilling into the night. But beneath it all, something had shifted. Not loudly. Not violently. Just enough. Pinebane stepped closer to Allyssa at last, voice low. "Some trees grow alone," she said quietly. "Others gather forest around them." Allyssa's mouth curved faintly. "I don't gather."

"No," Pinebane agreed. "You don't." A pause. "But forest gathers anyway."

And that— That was the moment I understood something I had been resisting since Winter.

I had not been chosen to protect her. I had been chosen to stand beside something that would reshape the ground itself. And Pinebane had just seen it too. I glanced toward Mazzer.

He looked as though he wanted to cross the courtyard as badly as I did.

A druid at his side placed a hand on his shoulder and murmured something low.

Mazzer's expression shifted—calculation replacing impulse.

His gaze moved to me. Then to Laya. Then back to Allyssa.

The magic in the air illuminating her skin and making her hair look as soft as silk.

I felt the brush of magic before I saw it. Not aggressive. Not sharp. Warm. Alive. A thin current of green-gold slipped through the air like sunlight threading leaves. It coiled once above Allyssa's head before blooming into form. Deep violet tulips unfurled slowly, petal by petal, forming a crown that did not sit on her hair so much as grow from it. She stiffened instantly.

Her hand rose toward her temple. And then— The magic shifted. Softened. A whisper of power traced along her cheekbone. Light. Almost reverent. A caress disguised as ritual residue.

My wolf bristled. I did not need to look to know who had done it. Mazzer. He stood across the courtyard, one hand still half-raised, expression composed but eyes dark with something far less composed. He was not smirking. He was watching her. Living for her reaction. Allyssa's jaw tightened. Her gaze cut across the courtyard, hunting the source. When her eyes found him, something flickered across her face. Not anger. Not embarrassment. Something sharper.

Awareness. The magic lingered for half a breath longer against her skin before dissipating like breath in spring air. A kiss he knew he wasn't allowed to give. And from the way his chest lifted when she found him— He would do it again.

I took a step toward Allyssa, ready to demand an explanation.

Someone stepped into my path.

"A moment, if you have it."

Of course she chose tonight.

I forced myself to turn back to Frostpine's delegation. I was an Alpha's son before I was prophecy-bound. Discipline did not vanish because desire grew complicated.

The future I once imagined had not been destroyed. It had evolved. And if I was to stand beside her— truly beside her— I would need to grow with it.

I recognised her then. Trinity.

My sister's mate.

"Since when are you formal with me?" I asked lightly.

"Since you stopped answering Emily," she replied just as lightly.

I sighed and gestured toward the dorm wing. Better private. Better contained.

We walked in silence until the music dulled behind stone walls.

Trinity didn't look at me right away. She leaned against the corridor arch, arms folded, posture relaxed but assessing. She always did that. Made it feel like you weren't being evaluated while she evaluated you anyway.

"You've changed," she said calmly.

"Bonding does that."

"Bonding reveals," she corrected.

I exhaled slowly. "Emily sent you."

"Emily worries," Trinity said. "I am an alleviator of worries."

I huff a laugh at that description of my sister in-law.

"What kind of Natural she is," Trinity said. "Not what she can do. What she is."

I held her gaze.

"My bond," I answered first.

My wolf stirred at that. Approval. Possessive and absolute.

Trinity's brow lifted slightly. "That's not what I asked."

I knew.

"She's not unstable," I said carefully. "She's disciplined. More than most."

She bleeds control, my wolf murmured inside me. *Even when she wants to tear.*

I didn't disagree.

"Does she know where she comes from?" Trinity asked. "Fully?"

The question tightened something in my chest.

"She knows enough," I said.

Not everything.

Not who her parents are. Not whether they ever searched for her.

But enough, for now.

"Origin shapes allegiance," Trinity said quietly.

"My allegiance shapes hers," I replied before I could stop myself.

That surprised both of us.

My wolf approved again.

Pack before politics.

Trinity studied me.

"And if her origin contradicts Frostpine?"

There it was. The real question.

Pack versus prophecy.

Blood versus bond.

I didn't answer immediately.

Because the truth was complicated.

If Allyssa stood against Frostpine for power? I would fight her.

If Frostpine stood against her because they feared her?

My wolf bared its teeth.

We do not abandon our bond.

I exhaled slowly.

"She's not collecting power," I said. "She's trying to survive it."

Trinity didn't interrupt.

"She doesn't crave a throne," I continued. "She resents being pulled toward one."

That was the part most people missed.

Trinity's tone softened.

"Is she safe?"

Not for the realm.

For you.

I understood that.

I looked back toward the courtyard. Toward where she stood under bloom and magic and scrutiny.

"She's dangerous," I said plainly.

Trinity's shoulders tensed.

"But she chooses restraint."

That mattered more than anything.

My wolf leaned forward in my chest.

She chooses us.

And that was the truth I hadn't fully admitted aloud until now. Because as much as there is a push and pull, she hasn't rejected our bond either.

Trinity watched my expression shift.

"She frightens you," she observed.

"Yes," I said.

Silence.

"And?"

"And I would still stand beside her."

Not because of prophecy.

Not because of obligation.

Because I wanted to.

That was the part that changed everything.

Trinity exhaled through her nose.

"Emily needs to hear that from you."

Guilt pricked sharper than any blade.

"I know."

"You don't have to protect her from the truth," Trinity added gently.

My wolf rumbled at that.

We protect both.

"I'm not protecting Emily," I said quietly. "I'm protecting Allyssa."

That was the real fracture.

Trinity saw it.

She tilted her head.

"Then tell me this," she said. "If the Tribunal turns on her... where do you stand?"

That question settled heavy.

Not hypothetical.

Not political.

I didn't hesitate this time.

"With her."

My wolf surged in approval.

No doubt.

No fracture.

Trinity watched me for a long moment.

Then she nodded once.

Not agreement.

Assessment complete.

Chapter Seventeen: Through the Cracks

"The wound is the place where the light enters you." — Rumi

Caspian POV

The bond is supposed to be quiet.

That's what I tell myself when I feel her at the edge of my mind—lightning on a distant horizon. Charged. Beautiful.

But tonight she bleeds through.

She thinks she's shielding me. That the iron walls she's built are enough.

They're not.

Rage crackles sharp and volatile. Shame follows, metallic and bitter.

And beneath it—fear.

Not of me.

Not even of the lies spread from the severed flame about the black wolf.

Of herself.

A scent. Citrus and smoke. Heat. Silk against skin.

And her.

Her walls shaking—not from battle. From restraint.

Someone's pushing her. I jolt awake. My chest heaves like I've surfaced from drowning. The sheets are tangled around my legs, soaked with sweat. My hand grips the side of the bedframe so hard it creaks beneath my fingers.

It's not the first time. I've felt pieces before. Shards of her mind pressing against mine like broken glass under silk. She thinks she's keeping me out. But the bond doesn't care about permission. Not when one of us is fraying. I sit up, dragging a hand through my hair, damp at the roots. My skin buzzes. My pulse won't settle. My heart is trying to tell me something my mind doesn't want to hear. I know that scent. That heat. That *presence* in her thoughts. Mazzer.

My jaw tightens until it aches. She's been different since the selection. Sharper. Quieter. Guarded in a way that feels deliberate. Like she's hiding a blade behind her silence. And I thought....I *hoped*......that maybe we were getting somewhere. That maybe I mattered. But now I get it. She's scared. Not of *him*. Of what he *sees*. Of what she might become; with someone who doesn't flinch when she bares her teeth. And that terrifies me more than anything. Because for all my strength, my loyalty, my light; I don't know if I'm enough. Maybe this was always the design.

Not one tether.

Two.

She needs both of us. The rage and the reason. The war and the peace. The hands that hold, and the hands that strike.

The bond flares again, even the wards along the Verdfall treeline thrum in response, the Greenhollow wind carrying the sharp taste of unsettled magic. Not words. Not images. Just a *pulse*. Like her heart is screaming without sound. Like she's clawing at the inside of her own mind. And this time, it's worse. Because I feel what she felt in the Director's office. That moment where everything inside her buckled under the weight of restraint. how right it felt to take control in a place built for dominance.

She recoiled from that truth. And now she's trying to bury it. Mother Natures celebration last night must have been a convenient distraction for her to bury the emotions.

I double over, hand reaching for my shoulder blade, where our bond mark curls like ink made of starlight. It burns. Then it *freezes*. A wall slams down. Not gently. Not gradually. It drops like a guillotine between us. And her warmth is gone. What's left behind isn't rage or grief. It's nothing. A cold void. Ice that burns more than fire ever could. I gasp, falling to my knees. Clutching the mark.

Shaking. She's trying to kill it. The part of her that can still feel. I whisper: "You don't have to protect me from you."

Because I already chose this. Chose *her*. Even if it breaks me. Even if one day I have to stand against her. I will still love her. Through the fire. Through the madness. Through the cracks. But gods help me; I need to find her before she seals them shut forever.

I'd stopped when I heard her voice because I thought she was speaking to someone else.

"I know," Allyssa said quietly. Not sharp. Not commanding. Soft in a way I'd never heard from her before. "I know you want that. But not yet."

I stayed where I was, half-shadowed by the archway. The corridor was empty. No one stood with her.

She exhaled slowly, fingers curling against the stone railing. "No," she murmured. "I didn't forget. I'm just not ready to let you have it."

A pause. Long enough that my skin prickled.

"I *will*," she added, firmer now. "I promise. Just... not like that."

Silence answered her.

She straightened after a moment, shoulders settling, spine aligning like armour sliding back into place. When she turned, she saw me instantly. Too instantly.

"How long have you been standing there?" she asked.

"Not long," I said. It was true. It still felt like a lie.

She searched my face, something wary flickering behind her eyes, then nodded once. "Good."

I wanted to ask. Gods, I wanted to ask so badly my chest ached with it.

But the bond hummed. Not warning. Not denial. Something else.

Don't.

Not fear. Not secrecy. A boundary.

So I swallowed the question and said nothing.

She passed me, close enough that our shoulders brushed, and for just a second I felt it.

Not power.

Not the wolf.

Something smaller. Quieter.

And deeply, terrifyingly alone.

Then she was gone.

I told myself the worst had passed.

It hadn't.

The surge hit again—raw, unfiltered. She tried to slam the ward down over our bond. It cracked under the pressure.

The backlash was fucking agony.

The halls are silent this late; cold stone corridors echoing only the sounds of my footsteps and my heart, still racing. I didn't know where I was going until I see him. Mazzer. Leaning casually against the frame of a side archway near the training courts, as if he'd known I would come. His arms are crossed, the slate-grey sleeves of his warlock robes hanging loose, hands tucked beneath them, the faint southern dust of the Draethen still clinging to his boots. His expression is unreadable; but his golden eyes gleam, reflecting the faint blue witchlight lining the hall.

I stop. My hands curl into fists before I even speak. "You did something to her." His head tilts. Not guilty. Not smug. Just watching. "No," he says, voice quiet. "*She* did something to herself." I take a step forward, fury tightening my throat. "She's cutting herself off so deeply I can barely feel her. You were in her head. You *did* something."

"I offered her a mirror," Mazzer replies, voice too calm. "She looked into it. That's all." "Bullshit." I move closer, chest tight. "She was opening up. She trusted me. She started letting me in; until *you*. Now she's trying to erase the part of her that can even *feel*."

Mazzer's jaw tightens. Just barely but he couldn't hide the worry in his eyes. "And what would you have had me do, Caspian? Coddle her? Pretend she's not drowning beneath her own fear of who she is?"

"She's not drowning. She's *choosing* to sink because you showed her the undertow!" His gaze sharpens. "I didn't create her darkness. I just didn't look away from it." We stand there; two stormfronts colliding in silence. "She was never going to make it to the end on her own," he says finally. "And neither were you."

I flinch. Because I *know*. "You think you're part of this prophecy?" I ask, low. "You think you belong with us?" He steps forward. "I *know* I do." I scoff. It sounds weaker than I intend.

"You're not part of this bond." A lie, I know the prophecy talks about him being part of it, but I am angry at his arrogant ass and the peace I was working up to, vanished when I felt her emotions. Mazzer smiles, but there's no humour in it, just clear and full confidence. "Not yet." And I frown at him not because I don't believe him but because I kind of do believe him. His next words drop like stone in water: "The Triskillian bond was never meant for two." My mark pulses. Fucking asshole warlock. I don't say a word though.

"You are her anchor. I am the part that teaches her how to survive herself".

I look away. My hands shake. "I don't want to take her from you," he says, gentler now. "I want to stand with you. Because she won't survive if we don't and neither will the world." A long silence stretches between us. I hate him for being right, and mature and a million other reasons as well. The bond flares again cold this time. Sharp as frost. I gasp, one hand clutched over my shoulder. "She's slipping."

Mazzer's expression hardens clear determination and devotion lines his annoyingly handsome face. "Then let's go. Before she disappears." I hesitate. He steps beside me. "I don't need your permission, Caspian. Only your help." We move together. Cutting across the training fields that overlook Verdant Lake, past the overgrown amphitheatre carved during the founding of the Athenaeum. Not as rivals. Not as opposites. But as the only two beings in the realm who refuse to let her vanish. Just two tether points trying to reach the one who's slipping into shadow.

We find her in the ruins behind the Academy grounds. A collapsed ceremonial space from the first age of Mother Nature's disciples one of the last surviving structures from before Greenhollow existed. The old first-age amphitheatre ruins; half-crushed by time, tangled in ivy, moonlight slicing through the cracked stone like judgment. It's quiet here. Too quiet.

She's not training. Not pacing. She's sitting on the edge of the broken dais, back straight, hands resting on her knees like she's preparing for war. Her eyes shift—black, turquoise, steel, dull blue—cycling through something unstable and uncontained. Her magic coils around her like a storm locked behind glass. Still. But seething.

"Allyssa," I call softly. She doesn't turn. Mazzer takes a step forward. Then another. But when I reach for her through the bond, I feel it again; *ice*. Sharp. Impenetrable. Her emotions locked so tightly it feels like standing outside a sealed tomb. So Mazzer does the unexpected. He kneels.

No words. No theatrics. Just silence and presence. Her gaze shifts. Barely. She sees him.

She sees *me*. But she doesn't move. "Why are you here?" Her voice is raw and flat. A whisper dragged over coals. "To find you," I say. "You already did," she murmurs. "You should've left me there." "Why?" I ask, stepping closer. "So you could bury the last part of yourself that still feels?"

"I'm not burying anything." Her voice sharpens. "I'm surviving." "No," I say. "You're numbing. You're turning your heart into a weapon because it's the only part of you you've never been taught how to use." She stands slowly, and gods, the way her eyes meet mine, they're not fire now. They're frost the colours of her eyes still shifting from one to the next. "I don't want to feel," she says. "Not if it means wanting. Needing. Hurting." Mazzer stands beside me, eyes on her, calm but unyielding. "That's not peace," he says gently. "That's self-destruction in a prettier cage." She glares at him. "And what would you know about it?" He doesn't look away. "Because I've worn it too." I step closer.

My hands ache to reach for her, but I don't. "You don't have to do this alone," I say. "You never did." Her lip trembles; barely her eyes stay in that dull blue colour stating at me. She blinks it away. "You don't understand," she whispers. "If I let myself want this... if I let myself *need* either of you..." Her breath hitches. "The world won't survive it and I will have become the very thing everyone says I am, I will become exactly what they fear".

"You will," I say. "Because we're not asking for all of you. Just the part you won't kill." The bond trembles. I feel it shift. Fracture. Then surge. A flare of wild magic bursts around her almost like shadows springing forth; dark and violent. And just as quickly, it folds back in, like she's terrified of what it could do. She stumbles. I catch her elbow. Mazzer steadies her back. We don't speak. We just hold her. Not her power. Not her fire. *Her.* Her breathing slows. Her shoulders drop. Her head bows between us. "I don't know how to survive without killing the part of me that wants this," she whispers. My hand finds her cheek. Mazzer's finds her other cheek.

"You don't have to," I say. "We'll teach you how." Her breath catches. But the moment breaks, eyes pure black look back at us. Her magic lashes out without warning; raw, reflexive, explosive. A sharp crack in the air, and the energy surges like a whip of force through the space between us. I brace, shielding with instinct. Mazzer doesn't move. He takes it. The blow hits him square in the chest. He grunts, staggering back several feet as the force lifts him off his feet and slams him into the fractured stone wall. Dust explodes. Debris rains down.

"NO!" Allyssa gasps, horrified. Her hands tremble, magic still dancing along her skin like lightning within shadow being held at bay.. Her eyes go wide, then flood with horror. "I didn't....I didn't mean...." Mazzer groans. He rises slowly, wincing, his robes scorched and his ribs likely fractured, but his eyes are steady. Focused. And then; He drops to his knees before her. Not in surrender. Not in weakness. In *offering*. His head bows. His arms rise, palms up, hands outstretched above his head. Devotion made visible. Allyssa shakes, chest heaving. "You... you're insane," she breathes. He smiles despite the blood on his lip which Allyssa can't look away from. "Probably." He replies lightly.

I kneel beside him—not because I agree with him, but because I refuse to leave her standing alone in her own fear. "Not because we're weak," I say. "But because we believe in your strength; even when you don't." "You don't have to do this alone," Mazzer echoes. "You don't have to destroy the part of you that craves us. That makes you more than a weapon." "The part that turns you from monster," I whisper, "The part that makes you more than what they call you.".

Her hands cover her mouth. Her knees buckle. She falls to her knees too. Between us. Silent. Shaking, a vulnerability she will allow no one else to see. But finally, finally; *feeling*.

Chapter Eighteen: Mr. Lakemond & The Tribunal

"No man chooses evil because it is evil; he only mistakes it for happiness." — Mary Wollstonecraft

Lance Lakemond POV

The wards were humming again.

Verdfall Enclave breathed with it, the forests around Greenhollow rustling in unnatural synchronicity. Not the quiet ambient pulse Lakemond had lived with for three decades. This was tension. A string drawn too tight.

He stood in the centre of his warded study, back to the hearth, stormleaf whisky untouched in his hand. He hadn't poured a glass in weeks. Not since the Tribunal auditors.

Tonight, restraint felt foolish.

The air itself felt heavier. Dense. Charged. Allyssa's magic had flared like a solar wound, then collapsed inward. The ley lines shuddered hard enough to knock a book from his shelf.

Then silence.

He didn't need a scrying mirror to guess what had happened. She had reached a threshold. Someone had steadied her.

And Mazzer had been near.

I exhaled slowly through my nose, tipping the glass back and letting the bitter fire of the stormleaf scorch a trail down my throat. So the Triskillian bond had begun to stir. I activated the rune-carved desk. Blue glyphwork unfolded into the air.

Watcher nodes flickered across the projection—Verdfall perimeter, Seelie border near Aurelensong, Starweave Crossing toward Calyxion.

Two shockwaves registered within the hour.

One hers.

One the bond.

Resistance.

Then surrender.

I could still see her. The way she had looked that first night, soaked in blood not her own, eyes like an eclipse. Beautiful. Terrifying. And fragile. Fragile not in strength, but in belief. In the notion that she was anything more than what the world had made her. I reached out, brushing my fingertips through the projection, scanning for magical interference. None. Not yet. But I knew it was coming. I turned from the light and stared out the tall arched window that framed the eastern wing of the Academy. The moon hung low, blood-orange and heavy over the ruins behind the field. I could almost see her there; kneeling among the broken stone, both males flanking her like twin blades.

This was not how the prophecy was supposed to unfold. They weren't ready. Caspian was supposed to *lead* her. Stabilize her. Anchor her light to the realm. But she had anchored him just as much. The prophecy was not dying.

It was accelerating.

I activated the binding rune on the wall behind my desk. The room shimmered in response, sealing to full privacy. No echoes. No stray listening spells. No judgment. And then, quietly: "She's not falling," I said aloud. "She's choosing." The Tribunal never accounted for agency.

Or love.

I did not sit. Instead, he reached for the communication orb Frostpine's science company had given me, Stealth orb, I chuckle at my own joke, glad no one was here. The orb had been created to have secured connections with others of the same model . Ice-veined quartz, threaded with Alpha sigils. I pressed my palm against it.

The surface frost-glowed. A moment later, the projection sharpened into the broad-shouldered figure of Frostpine's Alpha.

"Director," the Alpha said, voice low and steady as winter ground. "I felt it."

Lakemond inclined his head. "Of course you did." The Alpha's eyes narrowed slightly. Not alarmed. Assessing. "Is my son alive?"

"Yes."

A beat.

"Is he well?" He asked emphasis on the last word. Asking in no subtle terms if he is psychologically and emotionally well.

"Yes."

Another pause.

"And the female?"

I considered the question carefully. "She nearly chose erasure," I replied. "And then chose not to."

That earned the faintest shift in the Alpha's posture. Interest.

"Good," Frostpine's Alpha said.

I watched him carefully. "You approve?"

The Alpha's mouth curved slightly. Not soft. Not warm.

"Your Black Wolf arrived at an interrogation lesson with Draethen healing elixir already concealed on her person," he said evenly. "Before the instructor clarified the parameters."

Lakemond allowed himself a small nod.

"She anticipated the curriculum," the Alpha continued. "Understood that 'information through any means necessary' was not theoretical."

A pause.

"She opened the Seelie candidate without hesitation. Controlled depth. Controlled bleed. No arterial severance."

"She then tipped Draethen witch's elixir over the exposed organ," he added. "Watched the flesh knit while the female screamed. Only after she had the information."

My jaw flexed faintly.

She did not raise her voice," the Alpha continued. "She did not tremble. She did not rush."

Another beat.

"She did not kill when she easily could have."

I finally spoke.

"She never lost control."

The Alpha's gaze sharpened.

"No," he agreed. "She did not."

I folded his arms.

"That is not savagery. That is preparation."

Silence hung heavy between them.

"She embarrassed Ciaran because she had already decided what the outcome would be," the Alpha added. "No improvisation. No ego. She entered that hall knowing exactly how far she would go."

I studied him.

"And your conclusion?"

The Alpha did not hesitate.

"She is not ruled by her violence. As much as the others in power in our realm seem to think she is."

A faint smile edged his mouth.

"She uses it."

I nodded once. Agreement.

"And her retorts," the Alpha added dryly. "Delicious."

My brow lifted.

"She does not cower before authority," Frostpine's Alpha said. "Good. My son requires a bonded who will not."

There it was. Not political approval. Personal.

"Then Frostpine stands?" I asked.

The Alpha did not hesitate.

"Frostpine stands."

A beat passed.

"But," he added, voice cooling, "if the Tribunal moves prematurely, we move first."

My gaze sharpened.

"That is already accounted for," I said quietly.

The Alpha studied me for a long moment.

"You've been preparing."

"For three years," I replied.

The Frostpine Alpha nodded once.

"Then keep my son alive."

"And the Wolf?" I asked.

A flicker of something fierce crossed the Alpha's face.

"If she falls," he said evenly, "it will not be because we failed her."

The crystal dimmed. The connection severed.

I stood alone once more. Negotiations with Frostpine had not begun tonight. They had been unfolding for months—quietly, deliberately. The cult had hunted Caspian for years. Not to kill him. To claim him. To forge him into a blade against the Black Wolf. Frostpine had bled for that.

And now the Academy stood openly aligned with her. I had not been certain, until tonight, whether Frostpine's loyalty leaned toward protection... or preemption. Whether fear might eventually align them with the Tribunal—or worse, with the cult's logic.

But the Alpha's approval had not been reluctant. It had been deliberate. As if he had been waiting for my invitation.

My gaze drifted to the Fates Table set across the corner of my desk—Mazzer's last move still bleeding faintly in silver light. I pricked his finger with a claw-tip and pressed a drop of blood to the board. The pieces shifted. Tonight's ripple wasn't just power. It was grief. Forgiveness. Surrender. Which meant... She was still capable of choosing the light. But for how long? The click of the outer door broke my thoughts. I walked over to the warding rune behind my desk and Margaret stepped in. "Let me guess," she said, not looking up from her clipboard. "You need me to talk the Black Wolf out of another terrifying decision." I offered a dry smile. "She's already made it."

Margaret's head jerked up. "She agreed to *Mazzer's* proposal?"

"She did." I slowly nodded.

Margaret set the clipboard down slowly, as if afraid it might explode. "And you signed off on this madness?"

"I did." She let out a long, theatrical sigh. "Goddess help us." I poured a second glass and pushed it toward her across the desk. "Relay the standard schedule changes. Add Mazzer to her advisory file. Inform no one else of her whereabouts. And if someone asks, I need to know about it immediately.

Margaret didn't argue. She just nodded, took the glass, and exited with the air of someone preparing for a siege. I returned to the hearth. The warmth didn't reach me. Not this time. Because just as the door clicked shut behind her, the wards pulsed again. A new kind of cold swept through the room; sharp, silent, absolute. I didn't flinch as the shadows in the far corner of the study thickened and moved, shadowkin opening a portal. A figure emerged. His robes bore the angular sigils of Calyxion's Crystal Spire—cold geometry marking Tribunal authority. Robes black as pitch, stitched in obsidian thread. A mask shaped like the skull of a beast long extinct. No eyes. Just presence. Just weight.

"You should have told us sooner," the emissary said. His voice was velvet wrapped around a blade. I didn't turn. "About the bond?"

"No. About the fracturing." So. The Tribunal had been watching. "I assumed you'd notice," I replied evenly, keeping up with appearances.

"It was never my intention to hide her from you. Only to give her room to choose."

"Choice," the emissary hissed, "makes prophecy unpredictable." "Good." There was a pause. Tension shimmered between them like frost on a wire.

"You have one season," the emissary said. "At the first breach, we intervene."

My fingers brushed over the rune-lined desk edge, activating a quiet current of protective warding.

"And if she doesn't fall?" I asked with more than a little knowledge on their real motives. The investigation has brought many things to light.

"Then the wolf has outrun the trap." With that, the emissary vanished. No sound. No flash. Just absence. I stood alone once more. But not at peace. I knew without a doubt that the tribunal will never just leave it at that. And with that; war, I have been preparing for three years since I took over.

Inner sanctum of the Tribunal in Calyxion

At the apex of Calyxion's Crystal Spire, where geometry replaced wilderness and crystal eclipsed root, the Inner Sanctum glowed with measured restraint.

Calyxion did not grow.

It was engineered.

Below, the city shimmered in precise lines of conduit and steel, ley power channelled through regulation instead of instinct. Order perfected.

Within the Sanctum, seven figures hovered above a sigil-locked dais. Suspended. Contained. Identical in silhouette, differentiated only by the sigils stitched into obsidian thread.

The Tribunal convened.

A projection burned between them—fracture signatures radiating from Verdfall.

"She crossed threshold," said the figure marked with a crescent sigil.

"And stabilized," replied another.

The projection shifted. Three pulses intertwined: Black. Silver. Gold.

"She binds to both."

"Earlier than forecast."

Silence.

"The Frostpine Alpha has aligned," one observed coolly.

"Strategic alignment," corrected another. "Not devotion."

"She almost severed herself," the crescent figure said. "And did not."

"That is the concern."

A pause.

"She is integrating power instead of fracturing under it."

The air thinned.

"She must be tested under sustained pressure."

A new projection surfaced—cult sigils flickering along border territories. Shadowed enclaves. Dormant cells.

"They have been requesting latitude," one of the robed figures said.

"Denied," another replied.

"For now," said the lowest voice.

Silence stretched.

"If we intervene directly, Frostpine unites with Verdfall."

"And the Academy solidifies around her."

The gold-threaded figure inclined its head slightly.

"Then we do not intervene."

The projection sharpened.

"We grant the cult operational tolerance."

No flourish. No ritual.

Just policy.

"Unrestricted?"

"Escalated."

"Documented?"

"Internally."

"Externally?"

"Non-attributable."

A beat.

"They believe they hunt the Black Wolf."

The lowest voice answered:

"They may test her instead."

"And the white wolf?"

"Collateral strain."

"And the third?"

"If he fractures, he was never viable."

The sigils beneath them pulsed once in agreement.

No spells were cast.

No portals torn open.

Just permissions adjusted.

Far from Calyxion, dormant cult lines brightened like veins under thin skin.

The Tribunal did not unleash chaos.

They authorised it.

And their hands remained clean.

Chapter Nineteen: The Reassignment and the Hollow Vein

"Between the idea and the reality... falls the shadow." — T.S. Eliot

Allyssa POV

The message arrived at dawn.

A velvet pouch. Deep violet. Delivered by a third-year whose hands trembled so violently the drawstring slipped twice before he placed it on my desk. He didn't meet my eyes. I smirked.

The bond pulsed once. Warning. Anticipation. I opened it anyway. Inside lay a communication orb—but not the standard Academy issue. Ice crystal threaded through the core. Frostpine design. Gold braiding fused into the casing, shaped to stretch and contract like living metal. Caspian's influence.

I turned it over in my hand. A rune glowed faintly along the back—new. Unfamiliar. I pressed it. The orb activated instantly, sealing against my thigh with a soft magnetic suction. Clever. No bounce. No loose weight when I ran. No distraction in combat. Lakemond thought of everything. The cloudy surface shimmered. Joint combat training. Effective immediately. No substitutions.

It didn't make me laugh this time. Because everything had changed. Because I had changed. I wasn't just attending the joint training because I was told to. I was doing it because I needed to.

Since the ruins. Since the old boundary stones between the Academy and the Lyrravene Wilds, where I nearly erased myself. Since magic tore from me sharp enough to kill. Since Maverick took the strike without flinching—and knelt in the dust with arms open. Since Caspian dropped beside him. Not in fear. In faith. Something inside me had cracked. Not broken. Opened.

I hadn't spoken much since. There are no words for being seen at your most monstrous—and still chosen. They chose me anyway.

Maverick, with all his knowing. Caspian, with all his quiet loyalty. They hadn't just accepted my darkness. They'd embraced it. Held it. Anchored it. So, I didn't laugh. I just stared at the communication orb letting me know my session for joint combat was in fifteen minutes, let the magic hum through my fingertips, and tried to remember how it felt; to be held without breaking.

The bond no longer burned like wildfire. It pulsed. Steady. Intentional. Present. A second heartbeat threaded through mine. Not weakness. Not dependency. Connection. And I hated how much I didn't want it severed.

Margaret delivered the follow-up herself. "Report to Sector Seven," she recited, scroll clutched tightly. "Combat pairing revision. Allyssa. Caspian. Permanently reassigned." Her eyes lifted once to meet mine—then dropped. Respect. And fear. I could smell it. Sharp. Metallic. Interesting. "What if I decline?" I asked evenly. Colour drained from her face. She swallowed.

"Then Director Lakemond instructed me to remind you," she said carefully, "that your extracurricular placement has also been finalized. Effective tonight." Extracurricular. My jaw tightened. I hadn't agreed to anything beyond joint combat. "What placement?" I asked softly. She hesitated. "He said," Margaret added quickly, "that you would understand."

I didn't speak. I didn't threaten. I didn't even snarl. Because I did understand. The lightbulb moment had already happened before she spoke again Maverick. Of course. Because Lakemond was many things; but subtle wasn't one of them. And now that the bond was stabilizing, now that I hadn't shattered the world in a flare of grief and magic, he would test the new edges of my control. My balance. My hunger. But this time, I wouldn't go alone. This time, I went not as a weapon or a wound; but as something forged from both.

That night, as the moon bled over the eastern spires and the wind whispered the names I hadn't earned yet, Black Wolf, Commander, Your Highness; I followed the call in my blood. And I went to find the only warlock who had already offered me something no one else ever had: The tools to master myself.

The Wisteria trees were in bloom again. One of the sacred groves planted by the first black wolf after the founding of Verdfall Enclave. Not the delicate kind that grew near the herbalist greenhouses; but the old grove, tucked behind the wards, where petals hung thick as smoke and the air shimmered with forgotten magic. This place remembered things. Wars. Lovers. Oaths. Blood. Perhaps that's why Maverick waited here. I found him in the heart of it, standing barefoot in the soft moss beneath the lowest branches, head tilted back as if listening to something only he could hear.

"You came," he said without turning. "I said I would," I replied. "Didn't think you'd come quiet." He muses. "I'm not quiet. I'm considering." Because I just couldn't help myself feeling affronted even if he was right. "Dangerous habit." He smirks. "Necessary one." I counter defensively. "Did you enjoy the show earlier?" I asked changing the subject to get rid of the unwelcomed feelings of nervousness. Maverick smirked. "Which one? The new assignments or Margaret nearly pissing herself? He continued "Both. Though I give your dramatic pause a solid 6.5. You could've gone full brooding." I chucked a little easing some of that tightening in my chest.

He turned then. No smirk this time. Just that maddening calm. That warlock serenity that always felt like it was one breath away from becoming a storm. "I thought we'd start here," he said. "Not at the club?" I lifted an eyebrow in question. "The Hollow Vein isn't a destination," he replied. "It's a mirror. It shows you what you carry. If you're not ready, it will break you with your own reflection."

I crossed my arms. "And you think I'm ready?" "I think you've already survived the worst mirror of all; yourself." We stood there a long moment, the breeze stirring the branches between us. "I don't want to lose myself in this," I said.

Maverick's eyes darkened; not with doubt, but with something deeper. Affection sharpened by reverence. The look made me internally shiver. "Then don't. That's not what this is. This isn't about becoming something new. It's about peeling back the layers they buried you under. The 'monster,' the 'commander,' the 'threat.' Let them go. What's left is you." My throat tightened. I hated how easily his words could reach me now. "And if what's left is just fire and teeth?" I ask genuinely curious to his thoughts. "Then we teach you to forge it into something sacred." He stepped forward, slow enough that I didn't flinch. "I won't tame you," he said quietly. "I will stand where the heat doesn't scare me."

A silence fell between us. Not awkward. Holy. And then he offered his hand, not in submission, not in command. In ritual. "Come with me." He said simply. "I'm not into handholding, warlock." because he looked so serous in that moment and I had to cut the tension in my body somehow, comedy sarcasm seemed to be my go-to. He smirked. "Pity. I was going to offer a piggyback." He playfully supplies. Loving the easy banter I responded, "I'd rather ride a hydra." He didn't miss a beat and said "Noted. Next time, I'll conjure one."

I didn't ask where we were going. I didn't need to. Because I'd already decided. I reached out, and for the first time in my life, I wasn't afraid to take. The portal opened like the unfurling of some ancient eye; silent, slow, and watching. One moment, the grove behind the Academy shimmered with soft moonlight and blooming wisteria. The next, a door to another world breathed open before us. Maverick didn't say anything. He didn't need to. The magic between us had already shifted; no longer coaxing, no longer testing. Tonight, it waited. So did I. I stepped through. And the air shifted from the gentle pulse of the Enclave's ley-lines to the harsher, fractured magic of Draethen.

The Hollow Vein was not a club. It was a creature. Just beyond Draethen city centre, beneath the portal gate, where magic flowed like a river and my senses kicked into overdrive. I knew I had arrived. This wasn't chaos. It was a map. And maps could be learned. I reach for my book in my cloak pocket and sigh in relief at its familiar feel in my hand as I walk with Maverick.

The first thing that struck me wasn't the scent or the heat; it was the pressure. The way the air thickened, pressing against my skin like a lover's breath and a blade's edge all at once. Every step forward felt like trespassing into a cathedral where reverence was measured not in prayer, but in the willingness to be seen; utterly, fully, without armour.

The corridor was long and bone-curved, ribbed in glossy obsidian that arched overhead like the fossilized remains of a forgotten beast. Veins of red rune-light pulsed within the stone, shifting rhythmically, like a second heartbeat syncing with my own. The floor beneath my boots shimmered. Not with glamour, but memory. Each step awakened glyphs embedded deep into the rock; each one whispering fragments of moments past: cries of pleasure, gasps of surrender, the echo of magic cast not in war, but in longing.

"This place is alive," I murmured. Maverick's voice was a velvet hush beside me. "It is. It remembers everything. Especially you." I looked at him "How does it remember me, I haven't been here before?". He gives me an appraising look before he answers "It remembers your soul, the spirit the Black wolf is tied to of course". Said as if it is something that is obvious and I can't help rolling my eyes at his behaviour. He went on. "I watched your classes. Your combat trials. Your interrogations. You don't just fight to win. You fight to study. You catalogue." He tells me with absolute certainty.

"That's creepy, even for you." I quip. "Don't pretend you don't like it." And I shrug non-committal and didn't answer. Because he was right. "This is not about control over others. It's about control over yourself. You will not kneel. You will command. But first, you must know what it feels like to decide who you are." He states.

We passed beneath an arch of silverleaf ivy that writhed as we crossed beneath it; sensing, testing. The moment I passed, the tendrils stilled. The doorway *opened.* Then came the main chamber; and I stopped breathing. It was not a room. It was a world.

The Hollow Vein unfurled into a vast, multi-tiered sanctum carved into the very roots of the mountain. Balconies spiralled upward like gilded ribs, each one lined with loungers, silks, and masked figures drinking from chalices that shimmered like molten dusk. The central floor dipped into a shallow amphitheatre of runes, where bodies moved in magic-drenched rituals; some dancing, others fighting, a few simply standing still, and somehow commanding more attention than any spell could. I didn't look at them as people. I never had. My mind sorted them the way it always did when we walked into concentrated power.

Warlocks first. Easy. Magic clung to them like residue, bleeding from skin and breath, eyes too sharp, bodies searching. Every one of them carried contracts behind their ribs, bargains etched so deeply they no longer bothered hiding them. Dangerous in the way men are dangerous when they believe themselves clever.

Druids stood apart, even here. Grounded. Rooted. Their magic moved slowly, like growth you didn't notice until it split stone. Bark-slow patience. Ancient memory. They watched me with the calm of creatures who understood endurance better than dominance, two of them even inclined their head to me. Not sure what to make of it I kept cataloguing.

Vampires lingered in shadowed alcoves, breath unnecessary, hunger leashed by discipline rather than denial. Their attention tracked pulse, heat, weakness. Predators who had learned the value of waiting.

Shadowkin were harder.

Corners bent wrong where they stood. Space folded around them like a held breath. Some weren't fully visible, only impressions where light refused to settle. Watching from places that shouldn't exist, as if the room itself had learned to keep secrets.

Then something else caught me, a scent. Salt. My steps slowed before I meant them to.

Sirens. They stood near the Vein's inner edge, skin faintly iridescent, colours shifting like light through deep water. Their presence wasn't aggressive or invasive. It was... poised. Controlled. Voices low and unraised, carrying the soft pressure of tides rather than the pull of song.

Beautiful. Our curiosity flared sharp and immediate.

I had dealt with merrows before, once or twice, on the black markets of Shatterbay. Traders. Runners. Smugglers with webbed fingers and sharp smiles. Useful, dangerous, and never inclined to linger.

But sirens were different.

Older. Political. Deliberate.

The Sea does not bargain with the land.

History surfaced unbidden. The sea dominions ruled themselves. Unified. Patient. Watching the surface fracture itself over and over again while refusing to step in. They had said they would come to the table only when the land learned restraint.

And yet here they were. My gaze lingered. Not for danger. For information. What changed? I couldn't help but wonder. Or who? The Monster didn't snarl. It only watched. The wolf stirred, unsettled but curious. Old water remembers old blood. My eyes followed that of the siren and found Maverick. Of course, he nods in her direction and then continues to walk.

If sirens walked the Hollow Vein, then someone had once convinced the sea to bend. Not through force. Not through conquest, I instinctively know that wouldn't work. Through desperation perhaps... or trust maybe.

And if that agreement was old enough, if it had been struck before the surface splintered the way it had now, then it meant Maverick had been there. Watching. Surviving. Making himself necessary long before she had ever drawn breath.

A new thread of fascination sparked in my chest.

I wanted to know what kind of man left footprints deep enough to reach the sea and last centuries. I dragged my attention back to the room. None of them felt harmless. Good. Neither was I.

Above it all, the ceiling stretched into a dome of mirrored crystal, capturing light and heat and throwing it back in kaleidoscopic fragments. Mazzer saw my eyes taking it in and whispered "Rumoured to be crafted from a shard of the Mirrorbridge in Calyxion; stolen a few hundred years ago before the Tribunal started monitoring the portals to the city" He winked. I said nothing too in awe of my surroundings. Spells curled through the air like smoke. Glamours flickered like phantom fingers brushing over bare skin.

To my left, a series of alcoves housed more private performances; suspended nymphs tangled in shimmering rope that changed colour with every moan. A vampire knelt at the feet of a veiled fae, collar aglow with glyphs pulsing in time with his heartbeat. Another booth held only silence; a Seer with golden eyes, watching me. Everyone was masked. But not hidden. Here, masks were permission. Not a lie. A promise. My skin hummed with every breath. Maverick's voice found me again, low and steady. "This isn't about sex. It's about *power.* The raw kind. Intention made visible. Desire without shame. Control without cruelty."

"And pain?" I asked. He tilted his head. "Is sometimes a door. Sometimes a language. But never the point."

A figure detached from the upper balcony before we reached the stairs. Tall. Lean. Brown toned skin like that of a tree marked with old warding ink along his throat. Eyes too sharp to belong to someone relaxed. I had seen him with Maverick before at the spring celebration.

He did not look at me first. He looked at Maverick. "You brought her," the druid male said flatly. Maverick didn't break stride. "I did. Allyssa this is Cathbad, my best friend and head of security." I nodded. Cath's gaze slid to me then. Measuring. Not impressed. "You're the Wolf."

"I am," I replied evenly. He stepped closer than courtesy allowed. Too close. "What are your intentions with him?" Cath asked. Not playful. Not polite. Protective. Possessive. Ah. Maverick opened his mouth to answer. I didn't let him.

"My intentions?" I tilted my head. "With your warlock?" Cath's jaw tightened. "You misunderstand," I continued calmly. "If I wanted him broken, he would already be." The air between us shifted. Cath moved closer again. Testing. His hand brushed my shoulder as if to move me aside.

Mistake.

The dagger found its way into my palm without ceremony. Cold steel pressed gently against the front of his pelvis and I held my ground. He didn't react at first. He smirked instead. "Bold," he said softly. "You think—"

I added pressure. Just enough. His breath hitched. Subtle. Almost invisible. My smile widened. "You guard him," I said quietly. "Good. Continue." Another fraction of pressure. "Next time you invade my space, you'll limp for a week." Now he looked down. Realization flickered. The smirk died. Maverick laughed. Fully. Unbothered.

"Cath," he drawled, "go sulk somewhere useful." Cath stepped back slowly, eyes still locked on mine. He did not like losing, I could read it all over his body. He respected it, however. He left without another word. I sheathed the dagger. "You didn't need to do that," Maverick said mildly. "Yes, I did." He studied me. Satisfied.

He guided me up a staircase of black glass, the banister etched with shifting glyphs that warmed beneath my palm. At the top, the hallway narrowed, lit only by torch-crystals sunk into the floor. The room he led me to was warded; a circle of runes carved into the stone like old magic had bled into the architecture. The door itself was made of living wood, deep brown with black veins that pulsed like breath.

"This is where we begin," he said. "What is this room for?" I asked really curious now. Maverick smiled, but it wasn't mocking. It was reverent. "Presence. This room teaches you how to take it; and how to own it. There are no ropes. No chains. Just you. And the weight of your *will.*" He stepped aside. Let me enter alone. The door sealed with a hush. I stood in the centre of the circle. The walls mirrored my reflection a thousand times. Not perfectly; distorted slightly. Just enough to make you question what was real. Each version of me stood tall, straight-backed, impassive. But inside? I was spinning. Then the runes lit. And the air changed.

The room reacted not to movement, but to *intent.* When I squared my shoulders, the glyphs brightened. When my breath stilled, the mirrors rippled. Every hesitation dimmed the light. Every decision sharpened it. Maverick entered quietly. "Control isn't about suppressing who you are," he said, voice low. "It's about choosing which part of you steps forward. In this room; you decide." I met his eyes. And for the first time in my life, I stepped forward as Allyssa; Not the Black Wolf. Not the bondmate for the triskelion. Not the broken little female with teeth in her grief. Just a female who finally understood: Power wasn't the absence of fear. It was the ability to *stand anyway.* Maverick inhaled sharply. Just once. But it said everything. The training began.

Maverick turned to me, rolling up his sleeves like a surgeon preparing for alchemy. "This room is not about pain," he said. "It's about awareness. Command. Consent." He continued "Consent is the first rule. And the last. You don't earn control until you can wield it without needing to prove it." I mulled it over and what was meant to be an internal comment came out of my mouth for all to hear "Huh. Sounds like therapy, but with leather."

"Exactly," he said, annoyingly pleased.

He walked over to the centre of the rune-ringed floor. "There are five basic hand signals used here. Every submissive is trained in them. Every dominant is required to memorize them." He demonstrated: one fist closed = *stop.* Palm out = *slow.* Two fingers pointed downward = *ground.* Palm flat against chest = *overwhelmed.* Hand slicing through the air = *scene end.* I mimicked them, my movements stiff at first. Then again. Smoother. Sharper. "You learn these," Maverick said, "and you ensure the person under you never has to find the words to beg." I curled my lip in indignation "I don't make people beg." He doesn't even bat an eye and responds with. "You will, But not for pain. For release. From control. From fear. From the past. You'll offer them safety in surrender. That's power, Allyssa. Not just fear."

"Eye contact next," he said, his voice low, like velvet-wrapped steel. "You enter a room, and you see everything. But you offer nothing. You don't chase attention. You *command* it. Presence isn't loud, Allyssa. It's deliberate. It's how silence becomes a blade." I arched a brow, but he didn't flinch. Just gestured. So I walked. Turned. Walked again. Each step sharpened with intention; not practiced, not performative. Owned. I didn't just move across the room. I claimed it. Shoulders relaxed, chin lifted, gaze flat and assessing like a predator not yet hungry, but aware of its power. He made me enter, exit, turn again. Each time, I imagined a dozen eyes tracking my every breath. I gave them nothing. No tell. No invitation. Just stillness wrapped around steel.

"Posture," he said next. "You don't need to tower to dominate. You need to hold space like it owes you rent." Voice. Tone. Volume. How to speak in a register that made people lean closer without realizing why. How to pause just long enough that silence became weighty, suffocating. He showed me how to end a sentence with a whisper that carried more threat than any roar. "Never rush your words. Never fill the quiet. Let it ache. Let it *pull.*"

He taught me how to offer a hand without promise, how to hold eye contact without dominance, how to own the silence without letting it consume me. "Touch is a language," he said, close behind me now, but not touching. "You don't touch to control. You touch to communicate. Even air has texture when you mean it." I moved my fingers through the air slowly. Like I was tracing the line of a spine. A shiver went through me. Maverick nodded. "Good. Now again. With intent." I raised my hand. Closed my eyes. And this time, I felt it; not the air. *The choice.*

His voice had dropped to a rasp. He moved behind me; not close enough to touch, but enough that I *felt* him. Like gravity. Like a threat that didn't need to strike to be real. "My wolf wants out," I muttered, not voicing that the monster also wants control when the scent of fear hit my nose, the air thrumming around my fingertips my skin starting to inch with the need to shift. "I know," he said softly. "Let her listen. But not lead. Let her see, smell, taste the fear in the room; but let *you* decide what to do with it." His words landed in me like stones into still water. Slow ripples. Deep. That was the difference. Between survival and control. Between the monster they feared and the queen I could become.

He moved toward a padded bench against the wall and pulled out a rolled scroll. Inside: sketches of poses. "Submissive postures," he said, gesturing. "They aren't about weakness. They're about transparency. This one?": he pointed to a kneeling figure, head down, palms up: "complete surrender. This?": a standing pose, spine straight, hands behind back: "readiness. And this...." He showed a position that was somehow reverent and defiant at once. "That one's my favourite," I muttered. He grinned. "Naturally." And it *was*. Something about that pose..... sitting on a red velvet wingback chair or throne knees spread apart, ancles crossed arms relaxed and looking downcast as if everyone that dare speak to me should be in my line of sight at my feet. It didn't feel vulnerable. It felt regal. Intentional. For the first time in a space built on sex, I didn't feel hunted. I felt sovereign.

Maverick watched my expression change. "That one's called 'Throne and it is the only position not for a sub but of a domme, I put in to test you and see if it stood out for you.' It fit, although I didn't appreciate being tested like that. We moved through the poses, but I kept coming back to that one. It grounded me. In presence.

By the time the session was over three hours had passed by, my skin felt electric. Not from magic, but from clarity. I hadn't fought myself once. I hadn't run. I had led. Maverick stepped in front of me. His eyes glowed You command without flinching," he said quietly. "I would rather kneel for that than serve a coward." Waiting for the punchline. The smirk. The strings attached. But he just stood there. Steady. unmoving. Like he meant it. I undid the collar and held it out. "Then follow well." He took it with a smile that was entirely too reverent. "You will change everything, Allyssa. The Hollow Vein already whispers your name."

For the first time in years, I smiled without threat. Because in this place, I wasn't just the Black Wolf. I was something more.

And later, as we walked back through the glowing halls, Maverick added: "You don't want someone who flinches." I nodded, recognizing my own words. "But you also need someone who doesn't fear you," I added. "Who enjoys it. Understands it. Doesn't try to leash it." Maverick smiled. "None of the warlocks in the selection understand that. They want your power, not your purpose. When you and Caspian realize that, I'll be waiting."

"You think that's not manipulative?" I quip "I think it's honest. Rare currency in this place." He replies. "And why did the others fall?" I question. "Because they believed the world wanted to save them. You don't. And that's your strength." He answers. "What if I want to?" I challenge. "Then that's your war." He started into my eyes intently. Something inside me twisted. I shoved it down. Laughed. Fully comprehending my experience, because tonight, I had found something I thought I'd lost forever: Control. And gods help the world if I ever decided to keep it.

Maverick stayed behind to debrief with the Vein's inner circle. Some sort of ritual re-cleansing, he said. For the room. Not for me. I didn't need cleansing. I needed silence. So, I took it. The hallways whispered as I passed, old wards pressing against my skin like hands checking for fever. Old Marches wards acknowledging a sovereign magic they had not felt since the last true warlock-queen. I walked alone, boots tapping out a rhythm steadier than my breath.

For once, the bond didn't roar. It hummed. Caspian, his name brought a small tug of a smile to my lips. I felt him stir, felt his awareness bloom like light cracking beneath a locked door. He didn't push. He didn't invade. He just *was* a question unasked. And I didn't shut him out. I didn't answer either. But maybe that was its own reply.

I passed a polished obsidian column, and for a moment; just a flicker; I caught my reflection. My pale moon kissed skin was bright and illuminating, my black hair shimmered around my face that had a slight flush from Maverick and our lesson. I saw not a monster. Not a child clawing for control. A queen. A wolf with teeth bared not in fear, but in *rule.*

"If they insist on calling me monster," I murmured, "then they will learn what kind." I thought that would appease us all, my monster had other ideas on the matter. I stopped to talk with the protector inside; I needed to stay in the drivers seat this time.

Maverick POV

I stopped because I thought she was arguing.

Not loudly. Not violently. Just enough steel in her voice to cut through the corridor as I rounded the stone bend overlooking the lower practice ring.

The Vein was quieter at this hour. Magic hung low. Sweat and secrets clung to the air like incense that refused to burn out.

"I said no."

Short. Controlled. Final. I slowed. There was no one with her. Allyssa stood half-lit beneath guttering witchlight, arms crossed tight against her ribs. Her shadows were not drifting tonight. They were drawn inward—coiled. Muscled. Waiting. She wasn't posturing. She was negotiating.

"You don't get to decide that," she said quietly. "Not this time." A pause. Her jaw tightened. Her left hand curled, then deliberately relaxed. The magic that had been edging toward the surface retreated, replaced by something colder. Calmer. Sharper. A swap. I felt it in my chest like a pulled thread. Gods. She exhaled slowly through her nose. "I know what you want," she murmured. "And I understand why."

That was when it struck me. Not metaphor. Not memory. She wasn't speaking about something. She was speaking to it. Her jaw tightened. Her left hand curled, then forced itself open. Magic edged forward—then withdrew. Deliberate. Controlled. She wasn't suppressing the Monster. She was bargaining with it.

My pulse thudded loud in my ears. I stayed perfectly still, pressed back into the stone, every instinct screaming at me not to interrupt whatever fragile equilibrium I was witnessing. Her gaze dropped to the floor, unfocused; inward. "No," she said again, more firmly now. "I'm not weak for wanting this. And I'm not putting him at risk just because you think pain is safer."

"You don't get to take over just because you're scared." The air shifted. Not explosively. Not dramatically. But the shadows flexed—then stilled. Blade sheathed. Authority reasserted. Gods. I'd walked fractured minds before—tyrants, survivors, prophets who mistook trauma for divinity. Most breaks were chaos. This wasn't. This was governance. A Monster, yes; but not a rabid one. A sentry. A blade that only slept when commanded.

And Allyssa didn't suppress it. She reasoned with it. Gods help me, I wanted inside her mind. Not to break it. Not to heal it. To map it. To trace the seams. To understand who held the knives, who held the crown, who stood watch when she slept.

Her head snapped up. Not startled. Not panicked. Alert. Her eyes found me instantly, shadows flaring a hair's breadth before settling. The Monster surged; not outward, but *toward* me. Fight or flight. Measure and mark. I inclined my head slightly. No challenge. No submission. Acknowledgment.

For a heartbeat, I thought she might bare her teeth. Then she inhaled, slow and deliberate, and the tension eased. The shadows withdrew. The blade went quiet. She hadn't meant for me to see that. I straightened, stepping fully into view. "Maverick" she said like she was about to scald me. I was floored she just called me Maverick. I never told her that was my name. I was in so much awe of my name on her lips I was quick to explain myself. "I didn't mean to eavesdrop," I said lightly. "Your walls could use work."

A lie. A courtesy. A gift. Her eyes narrowed, but there was no denial. No embarrassment. Just calculation. "Did you hear anything you shouldn't have?" she asked. I smiled; slow, private, reverent. "Only enough to know I was right to be patient." Her gaze sharpened. Dangerous. Intrigued. Good. Very, very good. Because whatever lived behind her eyes wasn't a flaw to be cured or a beast to be slain. It was a guardian. And guardians always noticed when someone was learning their patrol routes.

She stepped through the portal I opened back to the Academy. I held it open a fraction longer than necessary. Long enough to consider breaking every rule I had just taught her. Long enough to imagine pulling her back into the dark and asking her to stay. I didn't. Patience has always been my greatest weapon.

Allyssa POV

I was halfway between the Wisteria grove and the upper barracks when the air cracked sideways. One second, I was alone beneath the stars, boots crunching softly over moss and fallen petals. The next; a ripple tore through the veil in front of me. A portal bloomed without warning, slicing into my path like a summoned storm. The shimmering edge tinted with the red hue of the Tempest Barrens, where Maverick's magic draws its heat. Instinct didn't wait for reason. My fist connected with the intruder's face before the magic had even fully closed. A sharp grunt. The satisfying thud of knuckles against bone.

"Ah," he breathed, one hand lifting in surrender while the other cupped his face. "Yes. That was earned." I flexed my fingers, assessing the sting in my knuckles. "By the moon, you reckless fool," I snapped. "You do not portal into a trained predator's line of sight." He winced. "I believed you'd recognize my signature." "I did," I said flatly. "A fraction too late." He eyed me like he didn't believe me. To be fair I could probably have put more effort into stopping. "Technically, I did knock first." I arched a brow. "With what? A flare and a death wish?"

"Consider it a... dramatic reentry," he muttered, then added with a wince, "and possibly a mild concussion." I sighed, crouched beside him, and shoved his hand away from his face. "Let me see." He looked up. Eyes gleaming, nose slightly crooked. And still, still, he smirked. "I've seen prettier," I muttered, fingers grazing his cheekbone as I tilted his face toward the moonlight. "But only just." "Are you flirting with me while inspecting your own assault damage?" he asked. "Depends. Are you going to bleed on me again?" His smile grew. "Not unless you ask nicely." I snorted and stood, offering my hand. "Come on, warlock. Up. Before I decide to finish the job."

He took it; of course he did but didn't stand right away. Just stayed kneeling, one hand still in mine, looking up at me like I was the moon and the blade that cut it in half. I need to do something before you leave tonight please come back with me to Hollow Vein I just need another Fifteen minutes," he said quietly. "Mo dhorchadas.". The Irish rolled from his tongue like a vow. My darkness. The endearment has me pausing and despite myself I nod and follow Maverick back to Hollow Vein.

Chapter Twenty: The Fifth Oath

"What we achieve inwardly will change outer reality." — Plutarch

Maverick POV

The forest was too quiet. Wisteria sagged beneath its own bloom, violet heavy in the Lunar Grove of Verdfall, where Mother Nature's wards breathe like sleeping beasts and druid-forged ley lines hum beneath the soil. Moonlight fell in blade-thin shards through the canopy. I stood barefoot in moss, letting the cold earth anchor me. The petals whispered. She would come.

She always came. Even when she hated herself for it. Especially then.

My hand flexed at my side. Not because the oath was done. Because I had already chosen it.

The ritual had not been performed. Not formally. But the decision had hollowed something inside me. The Triskelion bond could wait. She was only twenty. Caspian needed time to grow into what he would become only being a year older than Allyssa. She needed time to rule herself without a crown pressing against her skull.

But I—

I needed to bind something real. A blood oath. By choice. No prophecy. No Tribunal. No fate. Just me. And her

I had paced the Hollow Vein for hours before coming to collect her for her training session tonight. Obsidian corridors carved by the first warlock cabals of Draethen. Storm memory etched into every surface. Too soon. She is not ready. You will frighten her. You will bind her before she chooses. Five oaths. Five lifetimes. And this—this last one—

Belonged to her. Not for duty. Not for prophecy. Because I could not stop dreaming of her restraint. Because she knelt in her own ruin and did not shatter. Because she governs the monster instead of feeding it. Allyssa is not fire. She is the fucking forge. And I am done pretending I have not already stepped inside it. Tonight proved just how much.

The portal tore open before I could reconsider. I emerged five paces ahead of her. A mistake.

Her fist connected with my jaw before the rift sealed. Impact. Stars. Blood. For a heartbeat, I saw her fully. Not just a female. Not commander. Tempest. "Ah," I breathed, lifting my hands. "Yes. Earned." She flexed her fingers. "You do not portal into a predator's line of sight."

"I believed you would sense me sooner." I complained a little. "I did," she said. "A fraction too late.". I eyed her full suspicion in my gaze, pink flooded her cheeks, did she just blush. Little liar. I said nothing, however. She crouched beside me. Eyes assessing damage with clinical detachment. "Let me see." I tilted my face into her hands. The moon caught in her hair. Her thumb brushed blood from my lip. Something in me tightened. Not pain. Want. "I've seen worse," she murmured. "Flirting while evaluating structural damage?" I asked.

Her gaze darkened. "Depends," she said quietly. "Will you bleed again?" Gods. I would. Without hesitation. "Only if asked properly," I replied. She stood. "Up," she said. "Before I reconsider." I took her hand. And stayed where I was. Kneeling. Not submission. Not theatrics.

Choice.

I looked up at her. Not as a warlock. Not as a strategist. As a male who had just decided to alter the architecture of his own soul. "I need fifteen minutes," I said quietly. Her gaze sharpened.

"Why?"

"Because tonight," I answered, "I begin something that cannot be undone." "Fifteen minutes," I said softly. "Mo dhorchadas." Her breath caught. Just barely. The words are not just possession. They are recognition. She is darkness. And I choose it. She hesitated. Measured. Decided. One nod. That was all. The portal opened again. This time, she stepped through first.

I followed. And the grove exhaled behind us.

The club breathed as we entered. Not like lungs. Like a beast. The arches shuddered. The glyphs flared. The floor beneath us sighed with recognition. Allyssa didn't ask where we were going. She didn't need to. The Vein welcomed her like it had been waiting. We moved quickly through the lower halls, past the echoing domes and watching masks, up a flight of midnight stone steps that glowed where her feet touched. I could feel the room I'd prepared resonating ahead.

The room beyond was nothing like before. No mirrors. No glyphs. No props. Just a dais of black glass. And three altars. One with a bowl of my blood. One with a collar; white leather, gleaming like bone. And the last with a blade. Allyssa stopped in the threshold. Her eyes moved across the space; first to the bowl, then the collar, then the blade. She didn't breathe. Didn't blink. "I've seen this before," she said quietly. "In the dreamscape... or maybe a memory. Things have been coming to me when I close my eyes, memories that aren't my own, this is similar to one of them." Her voice sharpened as realization struck. "The fifth oath."

I nodded a sense of pride in her for that brain of hers seeking information, analysing it and coming to the correct conclusion, fucking beautiful. My knees found the floor. My hands lowered to the first altar.

The bowl. Not just any blood. My own. Poured under moonrise, ritually offered, not spilled. The essence of past oaths. Four names burned into my chest and my memory, each one a soul I had knelt for. Protected. Loved. Lost. Each carved during a different era of Veyloris—Aurelensong, Dubhlinn, Bloodmoon, and the Heartwood Age This would be the last. Not because I am weary. Because I have chosen where I will end. “This oath binds my life to yours,” I said quietly. “If you fall, I follow.” “If I fall, you remain.” Her gaze sharpened. Sacrifice understood.

“I’m not offering this because you need it,” I continued. “I’m doing this because *I* do. Because the oath doesn’t bind me to you; it *frees* me. From the past. From the silence. From pretending I haven’t already chosen you in every way that matters.” She said nothing. But the Vein pulsed once, like a heartbeat. I reached for the blade. Silver and obsidian, etched with oath-runes that shimmered against the skin. I held it up; palms open, blade resting across them.

Allyssa’s fingers lifted before she realised she was moving. They traced the faint lattice of scars already carved into my skin. Old oaths. Older promises. Marks laid down long before her, layered one atop another like history written directly into flesh. Curiosity burned first. Sharp and immediate. Then came something colder. Not jealousy. Not anger at me.

"Allyssa," I said, voice steady, ancient magic thick in the air between us. "I swear loyalty unto you. I vow to stand beside you against all threats, to raise my hand in your defence and my blade at your command. My faith is yours. My soul is bound to your purpose. As I have done for every Black Wolf before you, I now do for you." I drew the ceremonial blade from the third dias, its blood red edge humming with arcane heat.

Without hesitation, I asked for her finger, resolute in my decision now. She started at me for a good thirty seconds and I thought fuck she is going to run but to my utmost delight and shock she held up her palm to me, maybe she saw the desperation in my eyes, maybe she has chosen me too.... No can’t think of that right now. I sliced her index finger and pulled her finger above the bowl of my blood were three drops went into and mixed with my blood, I stirred our blood together and used my index finger to draw a perfect "A" across the centre of my chest. The other four scars flared faintly as I worked; old, jagged, and still burning under the surface. The Vein *shuddered.* "By fire and will," I whispered.

A surge of warlock magic ignited from my palm, searing the letter into my skin with threads of eternal flame. It glowed for a moment, radiant and painful. Then it settled, becoming the fifth.

Allyssa stood silent, her eyes unreadable. But I saw the slight shudder in her frame, like her soul recognized something her mind hadn't caught up with. I felt the bond tug, just for a breath. Then it vanished. She brushed it off.

The collar lifted into the air, glowing with light, runes spiralling along the edges. Allyssa stepped forward, I thought she was going to grab the collar, I closed my eyes in anticipation.

The mark burned. Not pain exactly. Pressure. Recognition. The kind that didn't ask permission and didn't care whether you were ready. I welcomed it. The Fifth Oath flared across my chest, light sinking into flesh, sealing itself among scars that had never truly faded. I didn't move. Didn't breathe. I knew better than to interrupt a moment that was deciding how much of me would survive it. Then I felt her. Allyssa's hand lifted, slow, uncertain, as if she hadn't yet decided whether she was allowed to want this. My eyes opened and I looked at her. Her fingers hovered for half a second before making contact, tracing the ridged lattice of old marks already carved into my skin.

Not gentle. Careful. She followed the lines the way a reader follows marginalia, recognising that what lay beneath the surface mattered more than what was new. Each scar was an oath given to a Black Wolf who was not her. Each one a life I had knelt for. Bled for. Remembered.

I felt the shift in her before she spoke. Curiosity first. Bright and sharp. Then something tighter. Colder. Fear. Not of me. Of permanence.

Her touch lingered, then stilled, fingers pressing flat against my chest like she was grounding herself against something unseen. I knew that feeling intimately. The moment where want and retreat collide, and only one is allowed to win. "How many?" she asked quietly. Not accusation. Assessment. I didn't soften the answer. She deserved better than comfort. "Enough to understand what it costs," I said. "And enough to know that choosing you doesn't erase them."

Her breath hitched. Just slightly. A fracture she didn't know I was watching for. I held her gaze, unblinking. "It means I choose knowing the cost." The silence that followed was not empty. It was heavy. Watchful. Like time itself had leaned closer to see what she would do next.

She withdrew her hand. Not rejection. Protection. I didn't reach for her. Didn't try to reclaim the contact even though I was burning to feel her skin on mine again, the loss of it was like dragging the oxygen from my lungs. This was not the moment for reassurance or persuasion however and I clamped down on the storm forming within me. This was the moment where she learned something about herself. About how deeply she wanted, and how afraid she was of what wanting implied.

I felt the weight of it settle. Not just on me. On us. This would be remembered. Not by witnesses. Not by record. By something older than either of us. And gods help me, even knowing that, even feeling the seal tightening around my soul, I would do it again. Every lifetime. Every cost. For her. She didn't speak. She didn't stop me. She *watched.* And in that moment, I felt something ancient shift. The kind of silence that comes before thunder.

"I am yours," I said, voice hoarse now. "Not as a servant. Not as a shadow. As a shield. As a storm. As a man who chooses the fire, and the woman who walks through it." The collar hovered between us. Waiting. And the bond between us pulsed; not as tether. But as *invitation*. Allyssa's expression didn't flicker. Not in fear. Not in doubt. If anything, it deepened; into something unreadable. Something ancient. Her gaze dragged back to mine. "You don't know what you're asking of me," she said, voice low, sharp. I just smiled.

The collar hovered between us still, now spinning slowly, slow enough for the weight of the moment to hang in the air like ash before a storm. Her fingers closed around it. She didn't tremble. "Once I do this," she said, softer now, "there's no taking it back." "Good," I replied. "Because I've never wanted anything I couldn't bleed for." A long pause. Then she moved. No flourish. No drama. Just intent, as sharp as a blade and as quiet as a burial. She raised the collar; bone-white, rune-bound; and set it around my throat. It snapped shut with a sound like thunder inside my chest.

The room erupted. Light arced from the runes. The altar shattered. The magic surged up my spine and down into the ground, anchoring something that had never been spoken aloud. *This one is mine*. My head dropped forward, breath hitching as the magic claimed every scar, every shadow, every secret I'd ever held; and turned them into *vow*. Her hand touched the collar once; just once; and I swear the Vein itself went still. Then her voice, like silk over steel: "Kneel if you must. But never forget; I didn't ask. You *offered*." I laughed, ragged. Holy. "Gods, I love you." It escaped before I could stop it. She blinked. Once. Twice. Then....."Yeah," she muttered. "You're definitely concussed." But she didn't pull away. Not immediately. And that pause? That breath? It was everything. Because for once, she didn't run. And neither did I.

When we reached the long corridor just past the training arena back at the Academy, she stopped. I nearly walked into her. Her voice, when it came, was quieter than I'd expected. "You really meant it." I blinked, startled. "You thought I wouldn't?" "No," she said. "I thought you'd hesitate." She turned to me then, that same guarded brilliance in her eyes. It wasn't mistrust. Not anymore. It was memory. "I've had people give me promises before," she continued. "Swear to protect me. Stay. Help. None of them burned themselves alive to prove it."

I shrugged. "Guess I'm not most people."

"Guess not." Her mouth twitched. "Idiot."

"Sadist," I shot back.

"You like it." She accused, but I was too giddy and replied honestly. "Terrifyingly true."

We stood like that for a beat; quiet, scorched, slightly drunk on the new bond. Then she looked down at the collar again. "You didn't flinch," she said. "Not once." "I'd flinch for a thousand things," I said. "But not for you." That landed harder than I meant it to. Her gaze snapped up, searching. Testing. Then accepting. "I don't know what to do with that," she murmured. "With someone who sees the worst of me and doesn't run."

"Don't do anything," I said. "Just let it exist." She looked like she might argue. Instead, she reached out; and with the softest touch, brushed the collar again. Her eyes flashed different shades and in quick succession. And for the first time, *it looked like she didn't fight it.*

Hours later, I stand alone in my private chamber beneath the Hollow Vein. The stone here predates the Realm's borders. Cut from dark rock that remembers vows older than kingdoms.

My fingers trace the fresh scar across my chest. The fifth. Each mark is different. Each given to a Black Wolf who needed something no one else could offer. Guidance. Restraint. Power. Sanctuary. None of them survived themselves. But Allyssa—

Allyssa is not like the others. She carries more than rage. She carries memory. Legacy. Reclamation. And power—raw and untethered—that calls to everything sacred and dangerous within me. She should not exist. Not with the man who broke her still walking this world. Not with the Tribunal watching. And yet she does. Defiant. Radiant. Unapologetically dangerous.

When she walked through the Vein, the shadows shifted.

Not in submission.

In awareness.

The walls warmed.

The magic aligned.

She does not know it yet, but this Realm already weighs her name in its silence.

During our session, I watched her the way a scholar studies a spell forming for the first time.

She catalogued everything. Tone. Breath. Posture. Silence. Controlled. Measured. And yet—

There were moments. When her laughter slipped free before she could cage it. When her eyes sparked with unguarded amusement. When I said, "This place feeds on hesitation," and she replied, "Good. I do not."

Underneath the barbs and sarcasm, I read the truth in her posture. The tension when I stepped too close. The way her fingers curled when I spoke of control, not chains. She hides her scars in sharp words and sharper wit. But I've seen enough broken empires to recognize someone who built a throne from the rubble. I was once a guardian of her line. Now, I find myself something more. Fascinated. Drawn. Bound. Not just by oath. But by desire. She thinks I want to serve her. She has no idea how much I ache to worship her. If I must stand beside her as storm and shadow so she never becomes the monster they expect—

So be it.

Let the world test her.

I will remain.

Outside, the Draethen storms rolled low across the Tempest Barrens. Old warlocks say the sky answers when an oath is accepted. Tonight, it did. Cath joined me without sound. He stood at my shoulder, gaze fixed on the horizon rather than on me.

"You sealed it," he said.

Not a question.

"Yes."

A long pause.

"With her."

"Yes." As if there had ever been another choice. His jaw tightened slightly. Barely noticeable. Most would have missed it.

"You trust her," he said at last.

That was the question beneath all others.

"I do." I made sure my conviction bled into my response.

Another silence. He did not argue. He did not question prophecy. He did not question her right to rule. Cath believes in destiny. He believes in strength. He believes in fate. What he does not believe in—

Are unstable hearts. "She burns hot," he said finally. "Hot things consume what stands too close." I almost smiled. "She governs the fire," I replied. "You saw it."

"I saw control," he said evenly. "Tonight."

A beat.

"I worry about tomorrow."

There it is. Not rebellion. Fear. For me. "For once," I said quietly, "let me choose the risk." His eyes flicked to the scar at my chest. Then to the collar. He had asked for me for a collar once. A long time ago. Before we became what we are now. When he once knelt before me, waiting our scene to begin.

"I always let you choose," he said. He stepped back toward the Vein. But before disappearing inside, he added: "Just make sure she chooses you too." Then he was gone.

Allyssa's POV

The air still smelled like smoke and devotion. Even after I left the Hollow Vein, it clung to me; richer than incense, heavier than sweat. Iron. Heat. And under that his scent spiced citrus. Old parchment. The smell of rain and lightning scorching earth. Still so complex. It settled beneath the skin. Into the bone. Maverick's words echoed louder the farther I got from him. *"I swear loyalty unto you... My faith is yours... My soul is bound to your purpose..."* Not just vows. Not theatre. Not some elaborate display to impress me. No. This had weight. Ritual. History. *Blood.* And gods help me, it *meant* something.

When he pressed that blade to my skin and used our combined blood to carve the fifth *A*, when he burned for me; because of me; I felt the pulse of something older than either of us stir. Not love. Not even lust. Something... more feral. More sacred. *Recognition.* Like a door opening inside me I didn't know existed. One I'd padlocked shut with years of rage and shame and hunger, only for his magic to slide through like it had always known the way. It terrified me. Because I didn't stop him, because I *let* him kneel. Because I *liked* it. And because deep in my marrow, I knew it wasn't about ownership or submission. It was about devotion.

I sat on the edge of my bed at the Academy that night, not really seeing the stained-glass moonlight scattered across my arms. My hands had stopped shaking, but my mind hadn't. He knew when to advance. When to kneel. When to strike. When to wait. That wasn't impulse. That was strategy.

Everyone seemed to be asleep. Peaceful. As if the world outside hadn't just changed shape. I pressed my palm to my chest, to the hollow place just above my heart. The bond was quiet. For once. No fire. No screaming. Just a low hum Not Caspian's. Maverick's. A new thread. Not a chain.

No one pledges themselves to me without wanting something. That's the rule. The first rule. I've buried people who broke it. The memory hit like a blade to the ribs. Years ago; or was it another life? It's getting harder to tell with the awaking memories in my dreams. A druid young male with forest-fire eyes had knelt in front of me with a vine-woven token and a promise of loyalty. I was younger then. Hopeful. Desperate to believe someone could see me and not just the darkness that trailed in my wake. He'd pledged his soul in ritual tongue. Said I was worthy. Said I was *safe*. Three nights later, he sold my location to the highest bidder; an Unseelie warlord who wanted to dissect the Black Wolf and make a blade of her bones. I slit the druid's throat with the same ceremonial dagger he'd offered me. Buried him under roots that wouldn't take. Cried only after the blood dried under my fingernails. *Never again*, I'd sworn.

So why did I let Maverick do it? Why did I *want* him to? Maverick doesn't look at me like I'm broken or dangerous or in need of saving. He looks at me like I'm something divine. Something *honoured*. Worshipped. Not for being pure; but for being powerful. Even Caspian—gods, Caspian—loves me like I'm something he's trying to protect from myself. He loves me in a way that makes me feel like a storm he's trying to hold at bay. But Maverick? He wants to drown in it. When he branded himself, it wasn't submission. It was reverence. It felt like prophecy bending toward me. And something inside me; some long-dead part that once believed I could be more than a weapon, *ached* to rise to meet it. I don't know what that makes me. A goddess? A tyrant? Something in between?

But I do know this: My wolf didn't growl when he pledged himself. She *purred*. And maybe, just maybe... she's not the monster they warned me about. Maybe she's the *judge*. And maybe she's been waiting for someone who didn't try to leash her. Someone who offered *power* instead of permission. Maverick said the Hollow Vein whispered my name. And I think... part of me whispered back. Because tonight, I didn't just survive. I didn't just reign. I *was chosen*. And this time... I might choose myself back.

Caspian POV

She returned changed. Not in some obvious, theatrical way; no new scars, no bloody confrontation, no declarations of destiny. No, it was subtler than that. Quieter. She moved differently. Like the air parted to let her pass. Like she'd stopped begging the world to let her exist in it and simply *took her place*. Even her silence felt stronger. Not hollow. Not distant. Contained. Like she found release and control all at once. And the moment I felt it; the moment her feet touched Academy stone and the bond between us lit like kindling; I knew. Something had happened in the Hollow Vein. Something that wasn't mine. Something sacred.

I sat alone in the shadowed colonnade beside the East Wing, where ivy clung to the stone like memory. Moonlight pooled between the columns, casting fractured silver across the marble floor. My hand drifted over my shoulder, fingertips brushing the place where her mark lived; inked into me like a sacred burn, just beneath the fabric of my tunic. It pulsed faintly beneath my skin. Still hers. But no longer frayed at the edges from strain or silence. Now, it beat with rhythm. With weight. With something *new*.

With *others*. Mine, the wolf growled.

Ours, I corrected.

I didn't shatter. But something inside me cracked. A quiet grief, sharp in its honesty. Some selfish shard of me still hoped I could be enough. That I could hold her with both hands and not watch her slip through my fingers like smoke.

She didn't need correction that night in the amphitheatre. She needed someone who wouldn't flinch. And when he knelt first, and I followed, that was not surrender. That was choice. That was the first thread of the Triskillian bond weaving itself into place.

She didn't need just me.

She never did.

And that truth still cut.

Allyssa was not made for one pair of hands. She was built for balance. For power shared without being diminished. She was born to command armies. Hearts, blades, magic all bent to her will not through cruelty, but truth. She sees all of us

The bond between us is not a circle. It's a triangle. The strongest shape in the world. The prophecy knew exactly what it was doing. Mazzer is not an intruder. He is a point of stability. A third axis.

And if loving her means standing beside another man while she rises into what she was born to be, then I will stand.

I don't need to be the only one she leans on.

I only need to be someone she chooses.

Every time.

If she is the storm, I will not try to cage it. I will build with it.

Chapter Twenty-One: Teeth and Temptation

"The most important kind of freedom is to be what you really are." — Jim Morrison

Allyssa POV

The courtyard training ring had never felt smaller, set atop the ancient amphitheatre stones of The Academy, the heart of Verdfall's magical convergence. I could feel the magic thrum like beating of tribal drums building up a rhythm of anticipation for the crowd. Rings of students circled the perimeter, whispers thick as smoke. Caspian stood across from me, already in stance, shoulders loose, gaze steady, jaw tight. Too tight. He was holding something back. Interesting.

He usually lets his emotions spill through the bond. Today, he's locked them down.

Intriguing .They'd all shown up for the spectacle. Word had spread fast. Black and White in the ring, the anticipation of the crowd forming was stifling. Bound. Fractured. Burning. The words slithered through the crowd and fed my wolf's possessiveness. I flexed my fingers, bones cracking. Let them talk. Let them stare. Their fear was a currency I'd long since learned to spend.

The order had been simple: demonstrate bond synchronization in a live-combat session. Observe and report. Of course, the Tribunal's emissary was watching from the bleachers, an emissary from Calyxion, the Tribunal's glass citadel, where every breath is measured and every gesture recorded; hidden behind glamour, but I could still smell him. Like sulphur and sanctimony. And of course, Maverick was there too. A thrill ran through me as I felt Maverick's bond pulse. The memory of him kneeling in front of me flits across my mind and an unwelcomed feeling of need rose up before I shoved it down. Fucking not the time or place Allyssa, stupid fucking sexy warlock.

He was of course lounging like a smug bastard in the crowd, boots up, smile sharp. Watching me. Ass. I looked back at Caspian, and he was staring daggers at Maverick and then lightbulb moment happened, I never actually talked to him about what had happened with Maverick in my training or the blood bond that we performed. Fuck sakes, I don't know how to do this — the part where other people's feelings matter. Now I understand why Caspian looks like he wants to simultaneously punch something and throw up. Fuck me, I'm going to have to sort that out after this, have a chat with him so he is brought up to speed. I should probably feel guilty or remorseful however those are feelings I have always struggled with to either comprehend or allow myself due to them causing hesitation. That meant weakness and that was something I couldn't afford to be.... Weak....

Professor Vyn droned on about tactical trust and infinite variation. I'd memorised the passages years ago. Caspian probably still was. I snicker to myself and Caspians gaze collides with mine a question unanswered in his gaze. I shook my head but apparently that was the wrong thing to do since his expression hardened and he sneered. Is it wrong that pissed off Caspian is fucking hot cause that is exactly where my mind is going.

"Begin," Director Lakemond called. Caspian moved first, not just fast *lethal.* His steps were fluid, but sharp with intent, like every motion was pulled from a blade he hadn't yet unsheathed. I barely had time to shift my stance before he was on me. I kept blocking each strike and jumping and dodging each sweep and roundhouse to the point where I was actually working up a sweat before I decided enough was enough.

If we don't prove we are synchronized, the Tribunal will fracture us themselves. So I studied his moves as I defended the commander inside pushed forward noting, every movement of his feet positions to his left swing going a little too wide and his shoulder dropping from exhaustion typical right handed dominant that left is always a little weaker. *Left side weak. He's tiring. Strike now,* my wolf purred agreeing with the commander. *Remind him who leads this dance.*

He was pushing harder than necessary. Testing me. Or himself. Then he left his left side exposed again and fuck it if I wasn't going to use the opening. I answered swiftly snarling at him in clear disapproval, I caught his strike on my forearm and let it slide past me. One step inward. One breath. My elbow drove into his ribs before he could pivot. Our clash was precise, brutal, beautiful.

Apparently that only fuelled his determination to win this little match between us. The arena floor hums beneath my boots. Stone etched with ward-lines. Containment lattice. He is drawing on his well, the area responded, safety precautions and all. Observation runes burning faint silver overhead. The Academy pretending this is instruction and not measurement.

Caspian stands opposite me, shoulders squared. Calm. Too calm. His magic doesn't lash outward. It settles into him. Reinforces bone. Strengthens muscle. Sharpens reaction time. A quiet amplification. He moves first again. A shard of broken stone rips from the arena floor and launches toward me. Not elegant. Efficient. I pivot. It whistles past my cheek and shatters against the barrier. I smile a feral smile. Another follows. Then a third. He's controlling the debris field. Herding me like an animal.

I bare my teeth. I dip into my well and let raw force answer him. A pulse through my palm. The next stone detonates mid-air, fragments scattering like hail. The impact reverberates up my arm, delicious and sharp. He's closer now. He throws up a shield — not visible, not dramatic — but I feel the resistance when I strike.

My fist meets something that isn't air. The contact jars through my knuckles.

He's reinforcing the space around him. Not projecting. Condensing. Smart. I circle. He advances. We trade momentum. Magic for leverage. Stone for bone. I slam a fractured column toward him; he absorbs the impact with that steady, infuriating well of his. It isn't brute strength. It's endurance. He's gaining ground. Having the experience and already having manifested his affinity.

My boots slide half an inch across dust and grit. He's anchored himself — pouring magic into balance, into stance. Every time I push, he holds. The bond flickers. Not bright. Just... present.

He shifts his weight to step into me — to close distance, to take control of the centre. And something in me refuses. Not fear. Refusal.

My wolf snarls beneath my ribs. *We do not back down she growls in my head.* He presses harder. Anchored. Stable. Unmoving. I reach — not for power — just for ground. For something solid. For resistance. The arena light flickers. Barely. His heel lifts — and sticks. Dust shifts strangely at his feet, like the stone held him a fraction too long. His balance falters. Confusion flashes across his face. The commander in me takes the driver seat and we are moving before I can think.

Pivot. Hook my arm under his and twist with the opening he shouldn't have given me. He hits the stone hard. Air leaves his lungs in a sharp rush. I'm on him before the echo fades, knee braced at his chest, forearm at his throat. The wards flare briefly at the impact. One female near the front practically swooned, hand clutched to her chest like this was some kind of royal mating ceremony. Another druid whispered, "I thought she'd tear his throat out." Another muttered something obscene about watching Caspian dodge like a fae prince. I caught it and before I could stop myself,

I growled possessively; *mine,* my wolf whispered, claws itching beneath my skin. *Not for their eyes. Not for their fantasies.*

Caspian blushed furiously and that made him falter. I used that to slam him into the arena floor harder, claw at his throat, his hand was already pressed to my chest. "You going to kill me?" he asked, grinning like he didn't care. "Thinking about it," I growled, has he lost his mind, my wolf was in no state for his death wish. "Good. Means you're still here and want me." he confesses. We froze like that, breathing each other in, our bond glowing so violently it hurt. My wolf surged forward trying to take control and claim him and I pushed her back with a growl only now realising how far she had brought me to his lips, mine grazing over them before I pulled away.

Silence floods the arena. His gaze locks on mine. Not angry. Need, then it cleared. It turned perplexed. I frown faintly. "You hesitated." I accused. "I didn't." he responded indignation coating his words. The bond hums, unsettled. For a moment, I almost believe him. Because I felt it too. That half-beat. That drag. But it wasn't me. Was it? I withdraw, rising fluidly. Offer him a hand. He takes it after a beat.

Afterward, while the students were dismissed, Lakemond ordered us to remain. Maverick joined us all confidence and a knowing smirk. Caspian stiffened next to me, yep, I definitely needed to talk to him about Maverick. I smirked at Maverick. "Here to critique our footwork, Warlock?" "Only the part where you almost gutted your bonded," he said his accent slipping into the old Draethen cadence warlocks only use in ritual or danger. "Very romantic."

Caspian rolled his eyes. "You watching all our training now?" Maverick grinned even more, fuck he is going to say something with an inuendo, I braced myself for it. "Only the sweaty ones." And he winks, fucking winks at Caspian. There it is.

Caspian growled and stepped forward. I caught the back of his neck and held him in place without looking away from Maverick. His smirk lingered a heartbeat too long. Then his chin dipped. Subtle. Deliberate. No one else would have noticed. I did. Something in me settled.

Lakemond cleared his throat. "Enough. I saw connection. The Tribunal saw fracture. That opening display resembled disunity."

Caspian stepped forward. "We're not a threat to each other." "No," Maverick said, voice suddenly sober. "But you are a threat to what the Tribunal wants you to be." I crossed my arms. "Good." I look over to Lakemond. And what is your position with the Tribunal, its not like you have clued us in, just letting them spy on us. Why, cause I am the black wolf, or something more? His gaze flicks to Maverick. I look back to Maverick but his gaze is studying my body language, my controlled breath, the twitch in my claws I hadn't managed to suppress. "You restrained yourself," he said quietly. And is that disapproval in his tone.

"Observation training," I replied a bit more bite than before. "I didn't want to break the arena. Or him." Caspian arched a brow. "Comforting." Maverick chuckled, but there was heat in his gaze; not just lust. Reverence. I didn't look at him. "You were about to answer my question."

Silence. When he still didn't speak, a low warning growl slipped free. "I do not enjoy being kept in the dark, Director."

Maverick shifted at the edge of my vision. I ignored him. Lakemond exhaled slowly. "I was not keeping you in the dark, Allyssa. You've been adjusting. Training. I wanted to give you as much time as possible before... complicating things."

"Complicating how?"

His jaw tightened. "The Tribunal has shown particular interest in you. More than procedural curiosity. I don't know if that means they possess information about your origins... or if they were involved in them." A chill threaded through my spine. "I've requested birth records. Contacted the packs. Sent inquiries to the Unseelie Court."

I cut him off. "Why the Unseelie Court?" He looked between Caspian and me. Something like realization dawned. "Allyssa," he said carefully, "have you not examined your bond mark?" Humour ghosted through his tone. We bristled as one. "Do I look like I asked for another question?" I snapped. "Answer mine." I had seen the mark. The first night. Then I had chosen not to look again. Pretended it wasn't burned into my skin. Pretended I wasn't permanently tied to someone else.

Lakemond straightened under my challenge. "My apologies. I meant no disrespect." He drew a measured breath. "The broken crown within your mark is the crest of the Unseelie Court. That symbol does not appear by accident. It suggests your bloodline originates there." For a fraction of a second, my mask slipped. A lead. Gods. I hadn't had a lead in years. "What else?" I demanded.

"You're an Alpha wolf," he continued evenly. "We've been tracing Alpha bloodlines across the known packs. So far, no claims. No acknowledgments. No matches. But we are still looking."

Silence settled heavy between us. Unseelie. Alpha. Hidden. And suddenly the dark didn't feel accidental. I held Lakemond's gaze. There was something I hadn't told him. Something I had ripped from a man who deserved far worse than I gave him. My mother was a werewolf.

Ray had sworn it between screams. The faint echo of them now, brings me a sick sense of peace that I have owned for some time now. If Lakemond suspected Unseelie blood, then that left only one direction for the rest of it. But saying that aloud meant explaining how I knew. It meant admitting I hadn't discovered it through archives or court whispers. It meant admitting I'd carved the truth out of a monster with my own hands. The hunters who pulled me off him had written their reports. Lakemond had read them.

But reading something and hearing it from my mouth were different things. I couldn't guarantee the monster wouldn't slip free and reveal just how much we enjoy the memories of not just Ray but others. If I gave him that truth, he would ask questions. And questions meant I would have to say I couldn't find the rest alone. I hated that more than I hated the silence. I had carved my own scars rather than let them fade. I could endure silence a little longer. So I would not give Lakemond that leverage. Not yet.

Indigo POV

I was not assigned to this arena. Officially. My reassignment placed me back in the mortal realm. Blending. Observing softer variables. Humans are easier. They scream louder when things break. Yet here I am.

The new emissary, on the other hand, is very much assigned. He sits three rows down, posture rigid, blade visible, like a child showing off a stolen trophy. I follow the line of his hand to the hilt. Grove wood. Not just Grove wood. Charred. Polished. Preserved. A souvenir carved from the remains of the dryads who burned in the Great Grove fire. Not only illegal. Repulsive.

Using the dead as ornamentation. Very "villain monologue in the third act." I half expect him to pet it while explaining his master plan. Subtlety is not his strength. I adjust my stance and let the bleachers swallow me again. Below, Lakemond gathers the Wolf, the Healer, and the Warlock. I lean into my hearing. And hear nothing. Interesting.

A shimmer folds around them — thin, precise, elegant. Warlock work. Of course it is. Maverick doesn't waste power. If he is muting sound, then whatever is being said matters. The emissary leans forward, irritated. Good. Serves him right for being a terrible version of Jason Bourne.

He does not know I am here. He also does not know I am not required to be. Technically, I should leave. Technically, I should report only from my assigned post. Technically, this is not my concern.

Pros of reporting:

– Compliance with Tribunal directive.

– Preservation of position.

– Avoid suspicion.

Cons:

– Strengthening the Tribunal's case.

– Accelerating interference.

– Possibly handing the Wolf to people who carve dryads into weapons.

-Loss of entertainment

I tilt my head. The Wolf's posture has changed. She isn't defensive. She's calculating. The Wolf stands cantered. The Healer leans toward her without realizing it. The Warlock watches both of them as though gravity has finally chosen a direction. Three. Not accidental. I was present when the first murmurs of that alignment crossed Tribunal archives. I know what the pattern looks like. This is it. I exhale slowly. If this were a mortal film, ominous music would swell right about now and someone would whisper something dramatic about destiny.

I fold my arms. Am I supposed to observe? No. Am I bound by contract? Yes. Not the Tribunal's contract. The older one. The one written before Veilwalkers pretended neutrality was virtue. She is a convergence point. And convergence points are never boring. Entertainment is not a valid reason to violate reassignment. But, maybe it is as well.

I glare at the emissary anyway. Some of us still prefer precision to intimidation theatrics. Not all Shadowkin require spectacle to feel important. He shifts slightly under my stare. Good. He can't see me. But he feels it. Below, the silence bubble holds. Whatever is being said is not for Tribunal ears. I consider filing a partial report. Selective phrasing. Omission without falsification. An art form.

The Wolf glances upward. Not at the emissary. Higher. For a moment, I have the uncomfortable impression she is looking at me. For a fraction of a second, her eyes lock on mine. And she smiles. Small. Knowing. Then she turns away, the Healer and Warlock falling into step beside her as if it had already been decided. I resist the urge to step back.

"Excellent," I murmur under my breath. "This is exactly how all catastrophic power convergences begin." I was waiting for someone to whisper do you want to play in a haunting mortal child voice.

Instead, the arena remains quiet. Which is worse. Maybe. I remain. I do not report. Not yet.

Chapter Twenty-Two: Quiet Burn

"Nothing can dim the light which shines from within." — Maya Angelou

Allyssa POV

The dormitory halls were empty. For once. No whispers. No stares. No warlocks lurking in shadows or professors with too-sharp eyes. Just the rain cascading outside, I took a deep breath and the smell soothed my soul. Then the scent doubled and Carmel was added, Caspian He leaned against the balcony rail at the far end of the East Wing, overlooking Greenhollow and the distant glow of Calyxion's glass spires on the horizon. Shirt rumpled, hair damp from the training ring, his bondmark glowing faintly on his shoulder blade, the glow penetrating his thin white tunic; two interlocking circles etched in soft white light, my initials curled into the smallest orbit Not my initials. A.M. Not A.B. Another clue I had ignored out of sheer stubbornness. I would examine that later. He didn't turn when I approached. Didn't need to.

"You always stomp like a wolf trying to scare prey?" He asked, I smirked. "You always wait up for nightmares?" His smile tilted, tired and gentle. "Only the ones I want to understand." I stepped beside him, shoulders almost brushing. Almost. The air pulsed. The bond hummed. Too close. Not close enough. My wolf urging me to claim what is ours and almost pushes through "*He is ours. Weakness is death. Take him*".

"You were incredible today," he said. "And terrifying." He rubbed the back of his neck, embarrassed. I studied him instead — the way his pulse moved beneath his skin, the shift in his breathing. Reading him without crossing the bond. Gods, emotions are going to be the death of me. "You say that like it's a compliment." I said. He immediately responded nodding his head clear awe in his eyes. "It is." I didn't answer. Just stared at the stars above the courtyard, the Veyloris's sky shifting between constellations tied to pack lore in Frostpine and old prophecy in Druvenwald, too bright for a sky this dark. Too quiet for a world preparing to kill us. The god trials that were mentioned in history paying on my mind.

He looked at me then. Really looked. Like I was something fragile, turning my stomach into a tsunami of nausea at the idea of being pitied. Then his expression changed he looked at me like I was dangerous. I was pretty unstable when they both came to find me, perhaps he just felt responsible to do the right thing since we are bonded. Not all bonded Hunters were lovers. I'd asked. Most were comrades. Siblings in arms. Best friends at best.

Caspian and I had never felt like that. From the first moment his scent hit me, it had been something else. Even our bond mark is different from the others. Though I suspected that was due to the prophecy.

My wolf growled again this time more insistent *we will claim what is ours even if I have to break through to do it for you Allyssa.* I was so distracted I almost didn't hear his comment.

"Mazzer said you smile like a predator." He spoke. I huffed. "That's rich, coming from a male who owns a dungeon." The words slipped out before I could stop them. He Chuckled. "Wait when did you talk to Maverick? I mean Mazzer." Red stains his cheeks as he admits "We may have ran into each other as you went back to your room for a shower." He didn't elaborate more. Then he sobered. "What if I said I wanted to understand your darkness?"

I turned. Slowly. Met his eyes. "I'd say you don't know what you're asking." "Maybe not," he said. "But I'd still ask. Because you protect me. Even when you think I don't notice. Even when you think it's better to push me away." His voice lowered. "But I see you, Allyssa. The real you. Not just the bond. Not just the beast. And I'm not scared.

The word see twisted something inside me.

He didn't see me in the warehouse.

Blood up to my elbows.

Bodies buried for less.

Part of me wanted him to.

Part of me wanted to be more than prophecy and claws.

I looked away, not wanting him to see how conflicted I was, didn't want to ruin him no matter what Lakemond said if he falls for me I will ruin him. So I thought I would be as honest as I could in this moment. "You'll die if you love me." He touched my hand. Just once. Fingers barely brushing. "Maybe," he said. "But I'll live more honestly than anyone else in this realm." Silence. Then I did something reckless.

I leaned in. Pressed my forehead to his, don't do this. He's too bright. And I am everything that eats light. "You're mine," I whispered. Not soft. Not gentle. Feral, tinged with the voice of my wolf, so there would be no mistaking that we both wanted him, to claim him. "I know," he replied. And I felt him smile. It didn't fix anything. But it made the world quieter. And for a moment, we just breathed. Together.

And then I kissed him, slow and unhurried, He answered immediately, hands settling at my hips. Mine slid up to his jaw, angling him deeper. The world narrowed to heat and breath and the taste of him. His fingers flexed on my hips pulling our bodies flush and then he moaned into my mouth, fucking moaned the sound went straight to my throbbing clit. The bond opened. Need. Longing. Heat. White-gold light tangled with something darker beneath my skin — not a brand. A promise. For a moment, it felt like balance. I pulled back first, resting my head against his. In Veyloris, every bonded pair knew one truth: Touch anchors the soul. And I had been denying the both of us.

“I need to tell you something.” He stiffened slightly. I explained. Maverick's blood bond. What it meant. His intention to stand as our third. The Triskelion. Caspian tried to interrupt. I pressed a finger gently to his lips. “Let me finish.” I told him about Hollow Vein. About control. About needing discipline before I lose it again. About how sometimes even his presence isn’t enough to anchor me.

Sadness flickered across his face. Understanding followed. Resignation. I stepped back. Distance. Necessary. “I can’t claim you,” I said quietly. “Not yet.” Everything in me screamed to take. My wolf slammed against the barrier in my mind. Sweat beaded at my temple. My nails cut crescents into my palm. Still she pushed. Caspian stepped toward me, ready to argue.

I lifted my hand. Stop. He froze. “I can’t give you softness,” I continued. “I don’t know how to be that yet. I’m not sweet. I’m not gentle. I don’t know how to love without teeth.”

His eyes filled — not weakness. Grief. I felt it through the bond and almost broke. One day.

I would give him what he deserved. Just not tonight. Before my wolf tore through restraint entirely, I turned and walked back to my room.

Maverick’s POV

They don’t know I’m watching.

Not in the crude sense. Though the kiss was fire, and in that moment it almost felt voyeuristic if the inconvenient state of my body is anything to go by. Though part of me is cataloguing the angles of her mouth, the way she tilts her head, calculating how to earn a kiss like that. Focus. I watch as something older than strategy. As someone who remembers what it means to want. They stand on the balcony, two silhouettes cut from the same storm; Caspian, radiant and raw form emotion; Allyssa, spine straight, expression unreadable. And yet the air between them thrums like magic laced with gunpowder. I can feel it from here. Even the Vein responds; my private scrying portal flickering with their shared pulse.

She pressed her forehead to his. Claimed his lips. He accepted, gods but then she pulled away and denied herself, I sigh knowing what we need to do in our next training session. Because when a Black Wolf loves, she does not soften. She annihilates anything that threatens it. Even herself. Caspian is her light, her anchor. And I intend to make sure she does not lose him.

And me? I thought I was only loyal. Only devoted. But I was wrong. I fell in love with her. Not because she is beautiful; though she is. Not because she is powerful; though she terrifies the realms. But because she *chooses* restraint. Because she *knows* she could destroy and still reaches for restraint. And because, gods help me, when she looked at me in the Hollow Vein, like she saw something in me worth trusting, it nearly broke me. And Caspian? He's no longer just her light. He's mine too. Whether I like it or not.

I didn't mark her. Nor did I ask her to mark me. Not yet. I activated the bond on *my* side only; my initials burned beneath her mark, waiting, dormant, unclaimed. It was too soon. She wasn't ready. I wouldn't force her to carry me; not while she still carries so much else. But I needed to feel her. To know she was safe. Because she and Caspian? They're the future. They were my future. And I'm meant to protect it. To protect them. I've served four Black Wolves. None like her. None who made me believe there could be another way. That a Black Wolf could *survive* without being tamed, or slaughtered. This bond we share; me, Allyssa, Caspian, it's incomplete now. But I can feel its edges forming, tightening like the promise of thunder.

She will choose. When she is ready. And when she does, it will not merely be sacred. It will be unstoppable. Caspian is her light. I am her shadow. Together, we will be her edge. But first, the world will try to tear her apart. The Tribunal watches. The Huntstone is waking. Veyloris will stand trial again. They will come for her. Good. Let them. We will stand as champions for this realm — not because we were appointed, but because we are necessary.

There is no version of the future where she falls. I did not swear loyalty lightly. I swore it knowing the cost. And if the realms demand fire to protect her, then I will oblige. The old magic stirs beneath Hollow Vein. Not everything whispers her name in reverence. Some whisper it like a warning. Some like a death sentence. They may not be wrong.

I get myself back to the Vein to get some work done and hopefully avoid Cath's ever present jealousy, and disapproval. I took my usual seat and just took a breath, ready to get the rest of my night done so I can go to bed. The press of metal on my straining cock reminding me that discipline is rarely comfortable — though the discomfort is its own indulgence.

The Hollow Vein dimmed without being asked. Not the usual prelude to indulgence or spectacle. This was a different hush. A lowering of sound, a drawing-in of velvet and shadow as something old crossed the threshold. I felt her before I saw her. Grief has a particular gravity. It bends magic. It warps rooms. My need and arousal evaporated in an instant.

She did not wait to be announced. The Unseelie noblewoman stepped into the lounge with the quiet certainty of someone who had once commanded entire corridors with a glance and no longer had the strength to try. Her glamour was still intact, but muted, like a crown left too long in ash. Silver-black hair braided low. "Maverick," she said.

No title. No pretense.I rose. "Lady Rhiannon," I replied, inclining my head. "It has been... a long time." Her mouth curved, faint and humourless. "Longer for me." She looked past me, taking in the Vein with eyes that had once been sharp enough to read betrayal in a breath. Now they were tired. Not dull. Worn. Cath had already withdrawn. This was not his place.

"You still sit where you can see every exit," she observed.

"And you still count the ones no one else notices," I said gently. That earned me the smallest exhale of a laugh. It died quickly. She moved closer, stopping just short of the contract ring. Hands folded neatly. Spine straight. Pride clinging to posture long after hope had abandoned it.

"I am here for a final petition," she said. I studied her. Really studied her. The King's first concubine. The first to bear him a son. The one history had reduced to a footnote after grief made her inconvenient. "You know the cost," I said. "I do." Her voice did not waver. "I also know you will not refuse me." That was not arrogance. It was certainty born of knowing exactly how little one has left to lose.

"What service do you seek?" I asked. Her fingers tightened once. Just once. "My son," she said. "Conjured. Anchored. As he was. Twenty-four hours." The Vein stilled completely. I did not interrupt her. "I do not wish to be absolved," she continued. "I do not wish to forget. I wish to see him laugh again. To hear his voice without it echoing through a battlefield." Her eyes lifted to mine. Raw. Unflinching. "And when the sun rises the next day," she added softly, "I will be finished." There it was. Not despair. Resolution. Relief even.

I let the silence hold us. Let the magic measure intent. "You understand," I said, carefully, "that I do not prevent death." "I am not asking you to," Rhiannon replied. "I am asking you to make it... bearable." For the first time in centuries, I felt something dangerously close to anger at the world itself. "Payment," I said at last. Her lips curved. Sad. Knowing. "A secret," she said. "One I have carried long enough for it to rot, one I am sure you will find is worth your time."

She stepped forward. The contract accepted her without hesitation. I entered her mind gently. This was not a theft. It was an offering long overdue. The secret unfolded slowly. Deliberately.

A court heavy with silence. Servants bribed. Enchanted linens. A careful, methodical betrayal carried out not for ambition, but revenge sharpened by grief. I saw the moment she had decided that if the King would move on, if he would build a future that did not include the child they lost, then she would ensure that loss meant something. That it left a scar.

Tribunal intermediaries. Quiet exchanges. Promises made without understanding the scale of what they were being handed. And underneath it all, the truth she could no longer outrun: She had helped set something into motion that would outlive her. The secret sealed itself into my lattice with a weight I had not expected. Rhiannon sagged slightly as it left her. Relief and horror braided together.

"You will forget this exchange," I said quietly. "But not the grief."

"I don't want to forget him," she said.

"You won't."

That mattered.

I moved to the cabinet behind me, withdrawing a vial no larger than my thumb. Clear. Unassuming. "Peace," I said, setting it between us. "Not pain." She nodded, fingers closing around it without hesitation. "Thank you," she said. Not for the poison. For the child. For being seen. The conjuring would take place at dawn. She would leave this world the following night.

I watched her go, shadows parting for her like mourners. Only when she was gone did I allow myself to breathe.

The secret settled heavily. Not as leverage. As context. Twenty-two years ago, a woman had acted out of grief and vengeance and set a future into motion she never lived to see. And somewhere in the world now, the consequence of that choice was learning how to survive.

I closed my eyes briefly. Some secrets do not ask to be used. They wait to be understood.

And this one had just finished breaking my heart.

Laya's POV

They think I'm just watching. They're not wrong. But watching is how you learn where to cut. Allyssa and Caspian stand too close to the edge of something dangerous. I can feel it thickening around them. The air warps when they share a glance. The bond between them isn't fragile anymore. It's rooting. That should frighten me. It does.

The Black Wolf always finds an anchor. That is how the cycle survives. Katarina had one too. And when she died, she burned half The Grove in her name. My parents burned with it. That is what the elders told me. The Academy tells a different tale, doesn't even mention the loss of the Black Wolf's bonded. That justice demanded sacrifice. That the Wolf devours what it claims to protect. That Veyloris forgets its dead too easily.

They fed me truth in fragments. Just enough. Just enough to keep the fire alive. I should hate Allyssa. Instead, I study her. She is not reckless like Katarina was. She is colder. More controlled. When she fights, the room bends. When she commands, people listen. And Caspian steadies her. That is the threat. A Wolf alone can be hunted. A Wolf with a pack becomes inevitable.

The elders warned me this would happen. They said prophecy would try to right itself. They said I was placed here for a reason. My communication orb warms in my palm before I even reach my quarters. Encrypted. Sealed with the Severed Flame's sigil.

I lock the door and mumble the sound shield activation spell before answering. The orb blooms with muted crimson light. His silhouette forms within it — tall, robed, voice disguised but unmistakable.

"Report."

No greeting. No affection. Just expectation. "The assassins breached the southern perimeter," I say evenly. "They reached the lower ward before being intercepted."

"Intercepted by whom?"

"The warlock."

Silence stretches. Disappointment hums through the orb like static. I thought the warlock was occupied with Caspian and Allyssa was alone in her room. "You assured me the Academy's outer lattice had weakened."

"It had," I snap before I can stop myself. I swallow the edge from my voice. "It was calculated."

"And yet," he replies softly, "the Black Wolf still breathes."

The words strike harder than accusation. Failure. I was entrusted with recruitment. Placement. Access. I hired them. I guided them. I secured their entry. And they failed. "You were chosen because you understand loss," he continues. "Because you know what the Wolf cycle costs."

I do. I see my parents every time Allyssa smiles. "Do not confuse proximity with influence, Laya," he says. "You are not there to admire her." The reprimand lands where it hurts. "I do not admire her," I lie. "Good," he says. "Because if she bonds fully, if the triad stabilises, the Huntstone will not judge her alone. It will empower her."

His voice lowers. "And then the realm will burn again." The orb dims slightly. "You will not fail me twice." There it is. Not anger. Expectation. The kind that feels like approval withheld. "Yes," I whisper "I will find the right angle". The connection severs. The room feels colder without him. I sit for a long moment, staring at my reflection in the darkened glass. I wanted someone to blame when my parents died.

The elders gave me a name. The Severed Flame gave me purpose. And he gave me direction. Watching Caspian laugh at something Allyssa said on the balcony earlier, It twists something sharp beneath my ribs. Not just jealousy. Something worse. What if the elders were wrong? What if this Wolf is different? No. I can't afford that doubt. Three points to a bond.

One always fractures. If I cannot break the Wolf... I will break the anchor. And when he looks for comfort—

I will be there.

Chapter Twenty-Three: The Trial of Silence and Command

"What is food to one is bitter poison to another." — Lucretius

Allyssa POV

Hollow Vein Training Session Two

The Red Room was sweltering heat designed to strip you raw, the chamber set deep below Draethen, closer to the volcanic roots that surfaced in Sangreal, closer than any student was meant to go. There were no distractions here. No furniture. No symbols. Only scent: old leather, citrus oil, sweat, and iron. The walls pulsed faintly with breath-like pressure, as if the Vein itself was watching. Testing. Maverick stood barefoot at the far end, dressed in slate-grey silk. His arms were behind his back, chin lifted, collar at his throat softly glowing with our bond. The moment I stepped inside, the air shifted. Dense. Expectant.

"Today is non-verbal," he said. "Hand signals only. One gesture per command. No voice. No magic. If you default, we start again." I nodded once. He handed me a small card, an illustrated guide. Fourteen hand signals for the compliant male. Codified. Clear. Each one designed for instant obedience if projected correctly. A twitch of a finger could kneel a man. A raised hand could still his tongue. He knelt before me, eyes down. "Begin."

I raised my hand; index finger up.

Listen. Don't speak.

He froze, perfectly still. Breath shallow. Watching. Waiting.

I let the silence linger. Drew my shoulders back. Then shifted my hand; two fingers down, pointing.

Come immediately. Stand at the point.

He rose without a word and moved to the centre of the circle etched in glowing runes.

Next, I extended my hand, palm out, then tilted it downward; the kneel order.

Kneel at the point, eyes down.

He dropped smoothly. The movement was graceful. Controlled. But I wanted more.

I stepped closer, let the heat between us build. Then I added the locked-hands kneel; index and middle fingers together, curled downward.

Kneel, legs spread. Arms locked behind back.

His shift was slower this time. Shoulders tensing as he found the new posture. I circled him like a hawk over prey.

Palm flat, fingers closed. Hands and knees at the point.

He dropped again, posture perfect.

Each new gesture layered command atop command. Sweat prickled at my brow, not from the heat, but the precision this required. One mistake, one flick of the wrist too weak or uncertain, and he wouldn't move. Maverick obeyed *power*, not mimicry.

I moved on.

Fingers angled down. Knees bent.

Elbows lowered. Chest to the floor.

Hips lifted in submission.

He shifted again, the movement more reluctant, like the pose cost him something. I felt it, the flicker of resistance, just a heartbeat of hesitation. It excited me. And it angered me. Control requires surrender — and surrender must be chosen. The runes beneath him glowed faintly brighter. Or perhaps that was my imagination.

I walked around him slowly. Let my foot slide along the back of his calf. Then, without speaking, I made the "Go now!" symbol.

Fist out, thumb extended backward.

His task was known. He performed it. Flawlessly.

And I was *drained*. Not because of him. But because the effort to control—not just him, but myself—required more strength than any battlefield ever had. The coil of my power was moving beneath my skin. The air thickens with it.

By the time I gave the final signal; one finger pointed to the floor: Sit at the point. I could barely lift my hand. But he obeyed. Of course he did.

I walked to him. Raised a hand.

Index and middle finger held up; Silent. Remain silent until otherwise instructed.

He held.

Then I spoke the only words I'd allowed myself the entire session.

"You serve well."

He looked up; eyes glassy, lips parted in breathless reverence and whispered:

"You lead better."

The Hollow Vein was colder tonight. Not in temperature. The arcane fire still pulsed through the obsidian veins of the walls, steady and alive. But the silence had changed. Anticipation hung in it. A breath not yet taken. The kind of quiet before judgment. Maverick waited in the Reflection Hall, barefoot upon the bloodglass circle etched in primal glyphs. No mirrors tonight. No distortion. Only clarity. Only tension wound tight between us.

"Strip to your base layer," he said without turning. I obeyed. The command slid under my skin like frost. Tonight was not seduction. Not ritual. Control. Precision. The difference between dominance that inspires fear...

...and dominance that commands it. "You did well last time," he said as I stepped onto the circle. "But you relied on instinct. On heat." He turned then, eyes dark and bright all at once. "Tonight, you learn frost."

Two fingers lifted. Come. Stand at the point. I crossed the circle and stopped exactly where he indicated. "You will obey only through sign," he continued. "No voice. No language. No magic." A flick of his wrist. Kneel. I dropped instantly, my wolf bristling but not fighting. This was not surrender. This was study. I had to keep reminding us.

The stone bit into my knees. Another signal. Hands behind back. Legs apart. I shifted. "You hesitated." My stomach tightened. "You interpreted," he corrected, circling slowly. "You anticipated. Dominance is clarity so absolute the body moves before the mind argues." Again. He signaled. I responded. Signal. Position. Correction. Again. Again. The drill became rhythm. My muscles burned not from motion but from restraint. From stillness held too long. Sweat slicked my spine. My thighs trembled as I forced them steady.

This was harder than commanding him. Harder than battle. Because I was not ruling chaos. I was mastering it. My wolf paced beneath my ribs, furious. Hungry for escalation. For impact. For a fight. Maverick did not strike. He watched. And when I moved too quickly — when the heat flared through me — he stopped me with a single raised finger. Listen.

No correction. Just stillness. Time distorted. The Vein hummed faintly, reacting to the pressure building beneath my skin. Not magic unleashed. Magic contained. Something darker coiled, testing the edges of discipline. I held. That was the test. He approached without sound. His fingers brushed my jaw, barely there, lifting my chin.

"You are not the female who must demand fear," he said softly. "You are the one it answers to." The words struck deeper than any blow. He stepped back. One final signal. Sit. Remain. Silent. I lowered myself, breath measured, pulse steady only by force of will.

He circled once more before stopping. "You've crossed the second threshold," he said. "Now comes subtlety."

He tossed something at my feet. Parchment. "Homework." I arched a brow. "I'm serious." He said. I unfolded it. Five signals. Nonverbal. Controlled. Public. "Practice them in the open," he said. "Students. Professors. Anyone. No power flares. No voice. Just presence. You will know you are succeeding when they respond before you finish raising your hand."

Subtle power. Invisible command. Queen work. I looked up. "You have potential, Black Wolf," he said. "But you are still learning the difference between a Queen... and a Tyrant." I did not speak. But I rose differently than I had knelt. And for the first time, his smile held no edge. No seduction. Only pride. That felt more dangerous than any blade.

The East training quadrangle pulsed with motion.

Students sparred in tight formations. Professors barked corrections. Elemental magic arced between bodies like disciplined lightning. The last warmth of Spring thinned toward Autumn; the breeze carried the dry promise of change.

I stood at the edge of the sandstone circle. Still. Spine straight. Shoulders relaxed but squared. Chin lifted. Not arrogance. Claim. Maverick's voice echoed in memory. *Control begins before a word is spoken. Presence first. Command second.*

My wolf stirred beneath my skin. Not hungry for blood for once. Evaluating. A small cluster of third-years drilled at centre — two druids, a storm witch, and the twins from infiltration module.

Rhian and Rhordyn. Sharp. Clever. Disrespectful. Perfect. I stepped into the circle slowly. This time, I didn't just rely on posture. I let it breathe. Not force. Not the crushing weight I had once slammed across the arena floor. Something subtler. I drew a breath and let my alpha aura expand — controlled, intentional.

A steady pressure that speaks of rank and bloodline and pack instinct. Then, beneath it, something colder. Older. I feel regal. Not glamour. Presence. It slid outward like frost beneath a door. The courtyard didn't freeze. It quieted. Spellwork faltered mid-incantation. Laughter thinned. The air grew attentive. Rhian stilled first. His shoulders lowered by degrees he did not choose. His gaze dipped without instruction.

Rhordyn sneered. "You here to spar," he called, "or just pose, Black Wolf?" Mockery. But his pulse quickened. I could see it at his throat. I let my aura sharpen — not louder. Clearer. I lifted three fingers. Stand still. Prepare. Rhian obeyed instantly. Rhordyn hesitated. I stepped closer. Boot against stone. Measured. Two fingers. Eyes on me. Do not move.

He tried to resist. And then he felt it. Not fear. Recognition. Hierarchy settling like gravity. I felt a pull from within me, growing stronger, but before I could grab a hold of it, it slipped through my fingers. Professor Elion noticed something too it seemed. Her breath caught on the terrace above. I held Rhordyn's gaze. Did not blink. Did not smile.

The Unseelie thread in my aura cooled further, threading through the Alpha weight like dark silk beneath steel. The colder thread in my aura deepened, weaving through the wolf-blood in my veins. Since learning my heritage, I could almost name it — that quiet, sovereign edge. Not domination.

Order.

Rhian dropped to one knee. Rhordyn followed a heartbeat later. The courtyard exhaled as one. Something clattered to the floor. Someone swore under their breath. I let the aura recede — not vanish, just fold back into place. Control. I lowered my hand. Said nothing. Then turned and walked away. Behind me, the kneeling remained. And for the first time, I understood the difference between being feared...

...and being obeyed.

Three days after the quadrangle, I was still thinking about bloodlines. Not dominance. Not obedience. Blood.

The Academy archives had become my refuge between training sessions. Stone corridors. Dust-heavy air. Stacks of vellum that smelled older than most of the realms' alliances. I started with the Unseelie Court — not the ruling family. Not yet. The land first. The structures. The lesser houses. The natural factions that pledged beneath their banner. Perhaps I belonged to one of the less noble houses. Perhaps I belonged to one of them. Surely, if I were the daughter of a prominent house, there would be a record.

There was not.

The illustrations shifted as I turned the page, and I could not look away.

At first glance, it resembled any deep forest region on the Academy maps — same painterly wash of light, same silver-thread rivers cutting through terrain, same muted horizon glow to orient the eye. But the canopy was wrong. Not sickly. Not corrupted. Deeper.

Emerald-black layered over muted violet undertones, as though twilight had been absorbed into leaf and bark. The light filtering through it wasn't golden — it was diffused, softened into a living dusk that never quite surrendered to night.

The trees rose ancient and slightly exaggerated, trunks twisting with deliberate elegance rather than decay. Their silhouettes leaned inward, almost conspiratorial, as if they shared secrets across centuries. Bark spiralled in subtle helixes. Roots surfaced and braided above the soil before diving back into earth like deliberate script.

Creeping vines threaded between branches in arching sweeps, not strangling but claiming — wrapping trunks in slow, intimate spirals. They didn't choke the trees. They adorned them. A pale green-grey mist clung low to the forest floor, drifting just above moss and loam. It did not obscure the ground so much as soften it. Nothing in that forest was fully revealed at first glance.

That felt intentional. The flora hinted at something watchful. Thorned undergrowth curved inward rather than outward, protective instead of defensive. Tendrils coiled in patient arcs, not snapping but waiting. Some ancient tree hollows curved in shapes that, from the right angle, resembled partially opened maws — not grotesque, not monstrous — just... aware.

Alive in a way other forests were not. The margins described it clinically. "Unseelie woodland biomes exhibit heightened sentience in root networks and predatory botanical species. Territory defense mechanisms are adaptive and layered." Defense mechanisms. I traced the image with my finger. It didn't look hostile. Structured. Intentional. Cold without cruelty. And beneath my skin, that same colder current stirred — not in hunger.

Recognition. I exhaled slowly. For the first time since learning what I might be, the word *Unseelie* did not feel like accusation. It felt like geography. Like inheritance. Like standing at the edge of a forest you have never seen before and knowing exactly which path would open for you. Home.

The Observation Chamber was designed to contain volatility. Arched with spell-reinforced glass. Wards braided into the stone. The air shimmered faintly as I stepped inside, magic already bracing for disruption. Word had spread. The Black Wolf would attempt psychic dominance outside of combat. Let them whisper. Maverick's instruction had been simple.

Break their will without touching them. No physical pain. No blood. Only control. He called it mind-play. I called it proof. Professor Elion stood above on the upper tier, arms folded, expression unreadable. Students lined the chamber walls — Druids braided in living vines, Seelie twins with mirrored poise, a witch humming faint curiosity.

Across from me stood Arlen. Seelie. Illusion-craft specialist. Confident. He smirked. "This a new performance piece, Wolf?" I didn't answer. First lesson: stillness unsettles faster than threat. Elion's voice carried. "Begin." I did not raise my hand. I did not speak. I simply looked at him. And let the silence stretch. Not emptiness. Pressure. I allowed my aura to expand again — not violently, not crushing. Measured.

Arlen did not kneel. Not fully. He lowered one knee — then straightened again, chin lifting as if something inside him refused to bend. His glamour flickered gold at the edges. I felt it then. Why he resisted better than the others. Seelie blood. Old blood. Royal adjacency. His aura tried to push back with dominance. He smiled slowly. "I am third cousin to the Seelie Crown." he said, voice strained but steady.

A ripple moved through the chamber. "My line bows to no one, royalty itself" he continued, breath tightening as my pressure increased, "certainly not to a half-breed psycho that lived among weak mortals."

The word hit. Half-breed. My aura sharpened. "Even your own parents didn't want you," he sneered, teeth flashing. "Abandoned you to dirt and rot in the mortal realm."

Something inside me split. The alpha pressure surged. Not louder. Heavier. The air thickened. Arlen's spine jerked upright as if invisible hands seized him from within. His breath hitched. "You—" he started. Then he choked. My aura wasn't just pressing now. It was forcing. A physical gravity crushing inward. His hands clawed at his own ribs. His back arched. A strangled cry tore from his throat.

The chamber wards flickered. A thin line of red slipped from his nostril. Then another. Blood spilled over his lip. Gasps broke around the circle. I did not move. A burst of power had the dirt swirling around us, blocking everyone's view. Then something behind me did. The shadows at my feet stretched. Not outward. Toward him. They coiled around his ankles. Up his calves. Not binding. Holding.

He trembled, suspended upright even as his knees failed. That wasn't instinct. That was me. I felt it. The thread I had brushed before. The colder current. It surged up my spine like liquid night. My vision darkened at the edges. Arlen screamed. The sound was wet now. Blood dripped to the obsidian floor. And the monster inside me purred. My wolf surged forward at the scent.

Teeth. Hunger. Satisfaction. The pressure increased without my permission. No. That wasn't true. It increased because I let it. I was moving the shadow. I didn't know how. But I was. The monster inside me uncoiled fully. Not snarling. Smiling. Arlen's body convulsed. His eyes rolled white. The wards shattered in spiderweb fractures along the glass.

"Black Wolf!" Elion's voice cracked like a whip. I barely heard her. My eyes burned. Heat flooded my skull. Then—

Everything went black. Not unconscious. Absorbed. My vision bled into ink. The room dulled. Sound thinned. The only thing sharp was the blood on the air. Peace. For the first time in my life, it felt simple. If I let go...

There would be no more push and pull. No more fracture between wolf and monster and girl. Just power. Just inevitability. Just me. Arlen sagged against the shadow that held him upright. A puppet on invisible strings. The thought of finishing it slid through me like silk. One more push. One more tightening. He would submit completely. Or break. And I would never feel small again. I almost chose it. I almost let the darkness consume the rest of me. Then—

Caspian. Not physically. A memory. The way he looks at me like I am something worth protecting. Maverick's collar glowing at his throat. The future they both see when they look at me. Not weapon. Not monster. A Queen. If I let go now—

There would be no balcony nights. No quiet touches. No chance to feel something other than rage. Only fear. They would kneel. Not out of love. The monster pressed harder. The bloodlust roared. But my wolf did something unexpected. She did not surge forward to consume. She turned. And shoved. Not at Arlen. At the monster. At the darkness caressing my skin. At the part of me reaching too far. We will not destroy what is ours.

The thought wasn't gentle. It was feral. Claim. Future. Pack. Family. I inhaled. Dragged the shadow back. It resisted, still responding to my emotional state. For one terrifying second, I felt how easily I could choose not to. Then I chose. The pressure snapped inward. The shadows recoiled. Obeying me.

Arlen collapsed fully to the floor. Alive. Breathing, sort of. Unconscious. Blood pooled beneath his cheek. The chamber silence crashed down like stone. My eyes burned. I blinked. The black receded. The monster not satified with the outcome. Glass wards still hummed, fractured but intact. Elion stood rigid, hand raised mid-spell. She hadn't been able to reach me. No one had.

I looked at Arlen. At the blood. At what I had almost done. The monster whispered. Next time. I swallowed it whole. Without a word, I turned and walked out of the Observation Chamber. No apology. No explanation. Just control reclaimed. Barely.

The forest did not recoil when I entered it. I walked until the Academy's stone dissolved behind bark and root. Until the wards and watchful towers were nothing but memory. Until the air felt wild enough to swallow sound. I did not stop when the trembling began. I did not stop when the sun shifted west.

By the time I dropped to my knees in a clearing ringed with low pines, the light had thinned to amber. Three hours. Maybe more. The monster no longer roared. It watched. Patient. Never apologetic for protecting me — even from myself. I pressed my palms into damp earth and forced my breathing steady. The forest smelled of sap and iron-rich soil. My pulse still echoed too loud in my ears. Control.

I reached for the silver blade at my thigh. Habit. Not thought. I lifted the edge of my combat vest and found the familiar patch of skin between leather and waistband. Old scars mapped there — pale lines layered over older ones. Proof of past attempts to quiet storms. My thumb traced one. I had learned young that pain sharpens focus. That it narrows chaos into a single point.

The blade hovered. I've needed it less over the years. Especially after Sionnach Rua. After Brian. The work I did there gave me the release I thought I'd been searching for — discipline carved into muscle, violence given direction. It taught me control in a different language.

For a moment, I almost pressed it down. Almost. The memory of the first time I used it like this flickered — desperation, not strength. Survival, not mastery. My jaw tightened. Is this still who I am? The monster did not need the blade. It wanted blood from elsewhere. My hand trembled.

I let the blade kiss the surface just enough to sting — not deep, not carving — just enough to feel the cold bite of silver against skin. My breath hitched. The sensation grounded me. Not release. It doesn't do that for me anymore. Not peace. Just interruption to the chaos in my mind and focus. I lowered the blade. Watched a thin line of red bead along the old scar.

It didn't fix anything. It didn't calm the shadow. It didn't erase what I almost became in that chamber. But it reminded me of one thing. I am choosing. Even this. My breathing evened slowly. The tremor in my hands faded. The forest remained steady around me. The monster watched. And for once —

So did I.

The dust cloud had been instinctive. My power had flared outward, creating a veil thick enough that no one saw what I did. They only heard Arlen's cries. Only smelled his blood. I had wanted isolation. And my magic gave it to me. That should concern me more than it does.

I closed my eyes. Reached inward. Past the wolf. Past the alpha heat. Down into the colder current. Shadow and something reverent. It didn't feel elemental. It didn't move like fire or wind or stone. It coiled. Listened. Waited.

When I brushed it with thought and asked for it to brush me back, it respond. Then it was gone, like I wasn't ready yet. In the chamber, I hadn't meant to command it. But I had thought it. Keep him down. Hold him. Don't let him rise. And that cold tendril had expanded, unfurled, flowed outward and done exactly that. Not violently. Precisely. The memory sent a shiver through me.

Shadowkin. The archives had mentioned them — Unseelie. Rare. Not rulers. Not noble. Not elemental. They do not control shadow. They are shadow. They give themselves form. They can shape their own darkness — not someone else's. But I had moved Arlen's. Not intentionally. But undeniably.

Maybe I am just powerful. Maybe I am just unstable. Maybe I am something the texts never anticipated. The thought pressed in. Freak. Perhaps I skip the royal's and find out more about the shadowkin. They are the closest I know of that would know about shadow magic.

I sighed out loud, It had been easier when I was just a half-breed. Now I am something no one has a name for. The wolf stirred. Not defensive. Considering. We chose. Yes. That was the part that mattered. I had chosen to stop.

The sound of careful steps through brush reached me long before scent. Caspian. He did not rush. Did not call my name. He stopped several paces behind me. "I counted three hours," he said quietly. I did not open my eyes.

"Go back."

"No. Please don't ask that of me."

Silence stretched. He didn't try to push through the bond. I had sealed it tight. All he could feel was static. "What happened in there..." he began, then stopped. He took a discreet sniff of the air; it was obvious to me though. Adjusted. "Do you want to talk about it?"

Not what was that power. Not what did you do. He only knew what the others saw. Pressure. Blood. Aura. Nothing more. "No," I said. He accepted that. After a moment, he moved closer but still did not touch me.

"Arlen's alive," he said. I nodded, not really caring. I cared more that I had lost control temporarily. "They're saying it was controlled. That you stopped before it crossed into lethal." I let out a slow breath. Chuckled a little. I almost didn't.

"I'm not proud of it," I said.

"You don't look proud."

That pulled my eyes open. He wasn't judging. He wasn't afraid. He looked... steady. "You blocked me," he said gently. Trying to conceal his hurt. A little accusation thrown in there for good measure. Mostly observation though. With a silent question at the end. "I needed quiet." I didn't elaborate, or acknowledge his quick glances at the skin showing between my waistband and combat vest. He nodded once. "Okay." The sun slid lower, light threading copper through the trees. "I don't know what I am yet," I said finally.

Not about shadow. Not about Shadowkin. Just the truth that fits. He crouched a few feet away. "You don't have to know tonight."

That simple. That infuriating. The wolf shifted, less restless now. "You stopped," he continued. "That's the only part that matters." I studied him. He truly believed that. He wasn't asking about the darkness. He wasn't demanding access. He was waiting. I did not tell him about the tendril. About the way the shadow responded to command. About how natural it felt. That part is mine. For now.

He stood and held out his hand. Not to anchor me. Not to restrain. Just to walk back together. I stared at it. Then I stood on my own. His face fell a little but then smirked and filled in step next to me. I leaned into him. He practically beamed and I shook my head trying to hide my smile. The forest did not close behind us. It watched.

Chapter Twenty-Four: The Silence He Earned

"The quieter you become, the more you are able to hear." — Rumi

Allyssa POV

Two weeks after the Observation Chamber, Maverick did not smile when he stepped through the wisteria trees. That alone told me this was not training. No flirtation. No testing banter.

No smirk to disguise what waited beneath. Just silence. And a portal. I followed.

The chamber beyond lay deeper than the Vein's usual halls. No velvet. No carved stone.

No ritual softness. Volcanic glass. I gave a low whistle before I could stop myself. Expensive.

Not Sangreal volcanic glass but Umbrakyn glass— born from the only magical volcano in Veyloris, deep beneath Unseelie Court territory where fire sprites rise screaming from the magma. That glass breathes magic. A material that swallows magic instead of shaping it. Wards layered into its veins made it nearly impenetrable. You could blast power against these walls all night and they would not crack.

Naturals fight wars over slabs of it. Set it into jewelry to blunt lesser spells. Line foundations with it to keep rivals from veiling through. I ran a finger lightly across the surface as we passed. Absorptive. Silent. Protective. It must have taken weeks to craft. Maverick does not build rooms like this for theatrics. He builds them for containment. My pulse shifted. This was not training.

Walls that swallowed light. In the centre — a chair. Strapped to it — A man. Human. For a moment, I did not recognise him. Stitches webbed across his face in jagged seams. Purpled flesh pulled tight over poorly mended bone. One cheek sagged slightly where muscle had once been flayed back. I stepped closer. And the world tilted.

Ray. Confusion hit first. How is he alive? The last time I saw him, he had been unconscious in a pool of his own blood. His face peeled back beneath my claws while I searched for something monstrous beneath the skin. I remember the bone. I remember the teeth. I remember thinking maybe if I cut deep enough I would find the demon that made him what he was.

He had been barely breathing. He should have died. It's why I didn't really fight the Hunters that came to collect me. My gaze tracked the seams again. The healing was wrong. Too clean in some places. Too smooth. Scarring that had sealed faster than mortal medicine allows. Magic. I turned slowly toward Maverick. Two questions burned hotter than rage. "How is the asshole still alive?"

Maverick did not flinch at my tone. He did smirk, but his eyes were blazing with wrath. "Healing potions," he said evenly. "Administered before mortal surgeons took over. They sealed smaller wounds and stabilized the lethal ones long enough for doctors to do their work." I stared at Ray. So someone had intervened. Saved him. Preserved him. For this? My jaw tightened. "And how," I asked quietly, "did you get him into Veyloris?"

Maverick's eyes darkened faintly. "The Hunters who retrieved you were permitted to use a gate," he continued. "They were held responsible for any... destruction you might cause." Destruction. The word almost made me laugh. "And you?" I asked. His mouth curved faintly.

"I am very old," he said. "And I am called the Warlock of Secrets for a reason. Currency in Veyloris is rarely coin." He did not elaborate. He did not need to.

Ray whimpered. The sound dragged me back into the room. "Allyssa..." he rasped. "Please..." His voice was weaker than I remembered. Good. I stepped closer. And this time I let myself look properly. He was smaller. Not physically. Spiritually. The stitches could not hide the fear. The wolf stirred first. Not hunger. Recognition. Prey.

The little girl stirred next.

The cold floor.

The weight.

The breath in her ear.

The words.

You made me want you. Noone will believe you. My hands began to shake. The monster watched. The commander assessed. The queen stood tall. Five selves. One body. Ray sobbed harder when I drew one dagger. The look in my eye must have been particularly terrifying, I know my eyes have bled into ink now. Or perhaps it was the memory of what I did to him the last time we were alone.

"I didn't mean it," he said. The little girl wanted to scream. The monster wanted to peel. The wolf wanted to tear. The commander wanted order. The queen wanted finality. "I begged you once," I said quietly my voice coming through layered. He flinched. "I begged when I caught you with her." His breath hitched. "I begged when I was small enough to believe you might stop." I crouched.

Met his eyes. There was no rage in me. Just something colder. "You meant every touch." His head shook frantically. "No—" I ignored him. "You meant every whisper." I tilted my head slightly. "And you thought I would grow up too broken to remember or to fractured to get revenge." He began to cry in earnest. The sound did not move me. What moved me was the memory of my foster sister's laugh.

Bright.

Unaffected.

Still whole.

That was what he tried to steal. That was what he never understood. I rose slowly. This would not be frenzy. This would not be loss of control. This would be authored. I began with his hands. Because those were the first instruments of harm. I did not rip. I peeled. Blade sliding beneath skin at the third knuckle, separating flesh with careful pressure. He screamed. The monster leaned forward, fascinated.

The wolf watched his pulse. The commander kept my breathing steady. The little girl did not look away. One finger. Then another. Each dislocation clean. Each pop deliberate. "Did it hurt little Allyssa?" I asked softly. He choked. I moved to his knees. "You can take a little more darling" Crushed them slowly beneath my boot until the bone gave way. The sound was ugly. The satisfaction was not joy. It was balance. He sobbed, drooling. "Too loud," I murmured. "No need to cry darling, you know that doesn't make it stop." When I carved the runes into his chest, I did not choose chaos. I chose judgment.

Ancient Frostpine markings, that Caspian has been teaching me, to get me up to speed in everything that is Veyloris. Shadefen condemnations, that I learnt in conversations over the three years in Veyloris. Symbols of exile beyond redemption. Blood filled the grooves. He thrashed uselessly. I took his tongue before his throat. Not in rage. In statement. "No more lies," I said. The monster purred approval. The wolf stood tall. The little girl felt something unravel inside her. Not pain. Release. When I slit his throat, it was not dramatic. It was precise. Clean. Final.

He sagged. Blood spread. Silence followed. I stood over him and waited.

Waited for rage.

For trembling.

For collapse.

None came. Instead— Stillness. Deep. Settled. Peace. And as we watched the light drain from his eyes. The little girl did not cry. The wolf did not howl. The monster did not demand more. The queen stood. Something tugged in my chest. Maverick. His tether flared. He gasped in the shadows. He felt it. Felt the alignment. I had not accepted him. But in that moment of blood and reclamation, something in me brushed his thread.

Not surrender. Recognition. I sealed it immediately. My power snapped back into place. Maverick stepped forward slowly. Reverent. "You did not lose yourself," he said quietly. I looked down at the corpse. "I was never given peace," I said. "So I made it." He inclined his head. "The Vein stands with you." I did not respond. As I turned to leave, I glanced once more at Ray's face.

The stitches. The seams. The magic that had kept him breathing long enough to answer for what he'd done. For a brief, strange moment, I wondered who had decided he deserved preservation. Then I realised— Perhaps it had always been me.

Session five: The Lesson of Pain

It has been a week since I stood over Ray's body and felt something in me finally settle. A week of lighter mornings. A week of night terrors. They came back the first night. Not louder. Not worse. Just... there. Waiting. As if killing him had not erased the past, only silenced one voice in it.

When I wake from them, I train. Hard. Until my muscles burn and my lungs sting and the adrenaline bleeds out through sweat instead of memory.

What I don't understand is why this fucking terror remains. It is so frustrating.

I felt something leave me when I slit his throat. I felt capable. Unburdened. For one reckless moment, I thought maybe I could finally take Caspian and Maverick to bed without flinching from my own skin.

Instead, I showered. Lay down. Slept. And the nightmare found me anyway. I am not afraid of them. I am afraid of losing control and traumatising all three of us. If I am going to let anyone touch me — truly touch me — then I need to understand power inside the bedroom the same way I understand it in battle.

Controlled.

Chosen.

Measured.

So I return to the Vein. The Vein greets me like something awake. The doorway hums, magic pulled taut beneath its surface. Expectant. My boots strike obsidian as the portal seals behind me. No velvet. No low laughter. No sin-draped silhouettes. This is not indulgence. This is instruction. I need this. If I am going to step into intimacy with them — with both of them — I need to know where my edges are. I need to know that pain does not own me. That I own it.

The walls had been charmed to resemble polished onyx, and hanging along them were tools, rows of paddles, floggers, switches, and canes, each one warded in glyphs of safety and intent. Runes carved into the stone throbbed with magic, the ones for pain glowing a deep, wine-dark red. The ones for healing shimmered blue-white like lightning caught in glass. Maverick was waiting. Already inside. Cloaked in slate-grey silk that framed his bare chest like it belonged to a weapon. His arms were folded, his expression unreadable, but the glint in his eyes told me everything.

We were past the point of comfort. Tonight was about power. And the truth beneath pain. "Welcome back, Alpha," he said, and the word rolled like smoke. "Tonight, you learn how to break skin without breaking soul." He stepped aside, and there, kneeling in the centre of the room, bathed in blue light, was a male. Late twenties maybe. Bronze-skinned with the tell-tale patterns around his face of a succubi, lean muscle, head bowed, posture perfect. Naked but for a crimson wrap around his waist, modest yet deliberate.

His back already bore faint scars that shimmered like old starlight, testaments, not wounds. His tail flicking in anticipation that he can't control. He was calm. Unafraid. "He's a professional submissive. Trained and trusted by the Vein," Maverick explained. "He knows tonight is about your learning. He has agreed to offer himself to that purpose." The male lifted his head and met my gaze. No fear. No arrogance. Just certainty. "My safe word is 'midnight.' I will speak it if I must," he said clearly, respectfully. "Otherwise, I am yours to command, Dominant." And he resumed bowing his head, cutting eye contact out of respect.

My throat was dry and my hands twitched as if preparing to strike already, it felt like a rush of need, not sexual, but domination swept through me. Consent. Structure. Choice. Maverick steps behind me. "Pain given with purpose is a gift," he says. "You my fierce alpha must learn to give it without rage."

He gestured to the wall of instruments. "Choose." I walked forward. One step. Two. The weight of the Vein pressing into my spine. My wolf stirred, curious, hungry. She didn't growl this time. She watched.

I ran fingers along braided leather and cold chain. Some tools called to me like memory. Others repelled. Finally, I found it, a cat-o-nine-tails made of soft-treated suede. Weighted, balanced, designed to deliver sensation without tearing flesh. A beginner's weapon with master's potential. I turned and looked at Maverick. Maverick nodded once, pleased. "Begin the warm-up," he instructed.

The male; my submissive for the night; rose to stand, back exposed his tail becoming a little more frantic as the anticipation rises, his posture neutral despite his tail giving away his need beneath the practiced submission. I circled him once, letting the weight of the whip settle in my hand. Then, I struck. Lightly testing, just enough to make him inhale. "Too light," Maverick said from behind me. "You're hesitating. He volunteered, Allyssa. He chose this. Trust him to take what you give."

My second strike was firmer. Not cruel. But real. The suede kissed his skin with a sound like falling rain. His muscles flinched, then settled. "Better," Maverick said. "Now focus. Pain, to be pleasure, must be a rhythm. A conversation. Not a scream." With that Maverick put music on in the background, find the rhythm in the music and strike in time with it. I fell into it. A dance. A ritual. The flogger arced, landed, circled again. His breath kept time with mine. The bond between us; not magic, but trust, formed its own heartbeat.

He moaned once, a sound of surrender. His skin bore deep red impact markings a few had breached the skin and trickle of blood had started to peek through one. I stood there transfixed on the trickle. I was already turned on, but I could feel my wetness drenching me now. The monster within, came rushing to the surface *More* it demanded. I didn't allow the slip into the bloodlust craving I held my shit together.

There was a release deep within me in the males' moans and gasps that I thought I could only get from giving into the bloodlust completely. Maverick stepped closer, voice low at my ear. "See the way he breathes into the pain? That's submission. Not fear. Not trauma. Willingly given. Your power, received. Now test. Switch to sting."

I dropped the suede for a crop. The strike was sharper. A hiss escaped the males lips, but his hands didn't twitch. No flinch. No fear. Just offering. His tail curling around his upper right thigh, rippling with restrained pleasure, as if he was making sure it didn't reach for me. The feeling of release breathed out of me as I delivered five more, each precisely placed. Shoulders. Ribs. Left thigh. I painted with his breath and inked his skin in obedience. They created welts on all the areas I chose to mark but my eyes again drifted to where I had breached his skin.

I stepped forward without really knowing what I was going to do. A sense of possessiveness rushed over me. The need to claim and make sure he knew who he belonged to in this moment was overwhelming. "You take what I give," I murmur. He nods. Not trembling. Not broken. Present. And something shifts in me. I let my aura slip a little. The male quickly responded "Yes, Mistress." The queen inside purred her satisfaction.

I bent forward and licked my marks, making the male hiss and then moan in pure bliss. As I licked all my marks, the bloodlust that had been roaring in my ears comes to a stop and a deep sense of gratification curls its way through my body. While this revelation was coursing through me the male was panting and the smell of his arousal was so sharp that a predatory feeling was taking over.

Maverick moaned deep and guttural that it had a new rush spreading low coating my panties even more. He cleared his throat, readjusting himself and said. "You're ready," he added softer now, restrained to the point of pain. "Now finish the scene. Then offer care." I paused. I lowered to the male and placed a hand on his back. Warm. Reassuring. "You did beautifully," I said quietly. "You may rest." I walked over to the cabinet and grabbed a cooling lotion for my marks.

He exhaled, lowering into child's pose on the mat. I kneeled beside him to rub the lotion over his back, shoulders, and thigh but he asked if I could leave it this time, that my saliva is doing the work the lotion would have. I allowed the request and I covered him with a silken wrap and whispered, "Midnight." He smiled. I lay the crimson wrap. I didn't need to destroy the storm. I just needed to stand in its centre.

Maverick took the crop from my hand. "You controlled yourself," he said. "You learned. And more importantly, you listened." I didn't feel like a monster. I felt... powerful. Precise. And somehow, more whole.

The Hollow Vein's lounge was drenched in low amber light, casting flickering shadows against the velvet walls and marble hearth. It was quiet, dangerously so, like the aftermath of a storm waiting to be acknowledged. Only the occasional crackle from the fireplace disturbed the stillness. I sank onto one of the dark green couches, my muscles screaming from the precision strikes, my wrists still buzzing from the grip I'd held, the restraint I'd commanded.

My fingers trembled, not from fear. From everything else. The adrenaline had faded, but the high clung to my skin like sweat. Maverick entered soundlessly, like a ghost of the session just passed. His robes were gone, replaced by a loose black shirt rolled at the forearms, collar open. His hair was damp from the rinse room. He didn't sit right away. He looked over my shoulder and I followed his gaze. Cath, Maverick shakes his head and Cath just glares at me before leaving us. Maverick brought his eyes straight back to me, watching me with eyes that saw too much. "You didn't flinch," he said eventually, voice low, unreadable. "No," I whispered, then licked my lips. "But I didn't feel nothing, either."

A pause. Then he sank into the chair across from me but didn't lean back, elbows on his knees, hands clasped. His gaze held mine like a tether. "You were present. That's what matters," he said. "You didn't dissociate. You made decisions. You adjusted when your partner needed more or less. You delivered pain and monitored pleasure. That's not control, it's mastery in the making." I exhaled shakily. My hands curled into fists in my lap.

My throat tightened. "He trusted me. He moaned for me. And for a moment, I wanted to take everything. Push further. Just to see if I could." He nodded. "You didn't. That's what makes you different from the monsters who hurt you." The room pulsed with the weight of those words. My eyes burned. "I'm scared," I admitted. "Not of hurting them. Of how much I like it when they want me to." Maverick leaned forward. "You like being needed. Desired. Worshipped. That doesn't make you cruel. That makes you someone who craves control because yours was taken." I met his gaze again, but this time, I didn't look away.

"You felt me," I said quietly. "During Ray's reckoning. Through the bond." His jaw twitched. "I did." I swallowed. "What did it feel like?" He leaned back slowly. "Like standing at the edge of something divine. Terrible. Righteous. It hurt. But it was beautiful." We sat there, in that thick silence, for several long moments. "Does it scare you?" I asked. "No," he said without hesitation. "But it will terrify them. And that's why I stay." I looked at him then, really looked. Saw the man who'd waited lifetimes. Who had knelt without asking for anything in return. Who burned quietly, patiently, for me. "You were hard watching me," I said. Not a question. "Not just aroused."

"No," he said again. "I was proud. And... aching." He moved to sit beside me, not touching, just close enough to feel. "I wanted to hold you after," he whispered. "But you needed to hold yourself first." I bit down on a sob. Swallowed it. "I don't know how to let go yet."

"I'm not asking you to," he said. "But when you're ready; when you want to fall; I'll be the floor." Something broke in me then. Not shattered. Just... loosened. I turned, pressing my face into his shoulder. His arms encircled me, steady and warm. No demand. No dominance. Just presence. And for the first time, I let myself be held.

Chapter Twenty-Five: Shadows Between Us

"To be yourself in a world that is constantly trying to make you something else is the greatest accomplishment." — Ralph Waldo Emerson

Caspian POV

I was in the arena when it happened. Sparring drills, with some of the second year Hunter. I wanted to get the extra practice in, I wanted to be able to keep up with Allyssa. She picks up everything so fast. Five Hunters rotating in formation. And then—

The bond detonated. Not pain. Alignment. It slammed through my ribs and down my spine like a blade finding its sheath. I dropped to one knee mid-step. The others thought I'd taken a blow. I hadn't. I felt blood. Not physically. Emotionally. Satisfaction. Cold. Settled. Final. Allyssa. Something in her had... closed. And for one staggering heartbeat, she opened.

Not her mind. Her want. It hit me like a shout. Raw. Unfiltered. Him. Mazzer. Me. Her bed, in some very vivid details. Her hands travelling all over my body, wondering what I would taste like. Heat flooded my face so fast I nearly choked.

One of the female Hunters called my name. I didn't really hear her. Couldn't respond. All I heard was the echo of Allyssa's body saying *yes*. Not to him. Not to Mazzer. To both of us. And then—

It vanished. Sealed. Locked. She realised her block slipped. I stood there shaking while the others stared. They thought I'd lost my footing. They didn't know I had just felt the woman I love choose pleasure—

And then locked it back down.

I woke with her scream in my skull. Not sound. Emotion. The nightmare again, the one time she can't keep me blocked. She has it almost every night. Its always the same nightmare, I only catch glimpses, a large hand on her body, pain, shame, a mattress, a bed, a couch, a basement floor. She dropped into the nightmare so violently the bond caught the edge of it.

Dark floor.

Ray's breath at her ear.

His weight.

I tried to reach her. *Allyssa.* Nothing. I pushed harder against the bond. *Wake up.*

For a second she surfaced—

Rage. Not at the memory. At herself. Frustration burned hotter than fear. She had wanted us. She had almost allowed it. And now she hated herself for hesitating. Then she felt me. And snapped. The rejection wasn't cruel. It was panicked. *Don't.*

Not angry. Terrified of being seen unravelling. I was already moving down the corridor before I realised it. Her door. My fist raised. I hesitated. Too late. The door opened. She was composed. Too composed.

"Go back to bed, Caspian."

"You were screaming."

"I'm fine."

"You're not. Noone would be fine after enduring that night after night."

Her jaw tightened. "I can handle it."

"I can help, don't shut me out again. Ill just stay up with you, or do some reading with you. I have noticed you have been doing extra reading on the unseelie court, maybe I could tell you what I know about them. I could tell you about the different leadership of all the factions. You know I had to learn and meet a lot of them with Frostpine and my dad." I was absolutely sounding desperate. But she was not okay, and she needs someone to lean on. I want to be that for her. I want to know her better.

"No," she said sharply. "You can't help me Caspian, I know your heart is in the right place. I feel what you want. I have been trying, I just need more time."

Time.

Always time.

The door closed.

Not slammed.

Just... closed. I went back to my room, more deflated and not sure how to get her to let me in. How can I love someone so much, that I barely know. I think it's time for me to do a little homework of my own. Nothing to invasive, I have already been reading about where she grew up. Maybe there is more though. I could ask Asher to find some information. He is good at that stuff. I continue contemplating this as I fall asleep.

For the next two days I waited. Wanting her to let me in. Wanting her to lean. She didn't. Deep down I knew she wouldn't. She trained. She read. She ran herself into exhaustion. I think she does it on purpose to try and sleep without dreaming. She stubborned her way through it like survival was a solo sport.

She would not let me hold her. Would not tell me what Ray did. Although I am starting to get the picture from the little pieces that come through each night. Honestly with what I have been able to understand so far, I have been debating whether she was right. If it really is what I am suspecting. I have no idea how to help her.

Over the last few days, I have been researching the dreamscape and how the bond works. I finally had the great idea of trying to push a dream through our bond that makes her not have her nightmare, I am still struggling a little with it but I think I almost have enough of an understanding to try it tonight. She is back at Mazzer's for training tomorrow.

My communication orb came to life on my desk, when I saw Emily's name glow through I almost ignored it.

She's been relentless since speaking with Trinity — convinced I should reject the bond before it's cemented by mating. How she knows we haven't mated is beyond me.

I pressed my thumb to her name.

Her voice filled the room.

"Cas, I know we're not seeing eye to eye about the Black Wolf. But there's something you need to know. I just found out she was part of a group called Sionnach Rua. They eliminate anyone who interferes with their operations. Please. I'm your sister. Trust me."

I translated automatically. The Red Fox. That didn't sound chaotic. How does Emily even know this? She doesn't have mortal contacts like that. I let the message fade. Allyssa will tell me when she's ready. I just have to be ready too.

Until then I will keep going to her room when I feel her have a nightmare and use proximity and scent to help calm her as much as she will allow.

The bond shifted again days later. Not violence. Heat. Control. Rhythm. I was in the Athenaeum when it reached me. Measured breathing. Impact. Pause. Impact. Her. Focused. Present. And beneath that—

Pleasure. Not from blood. From restraint. It hit me low and sharp. She was learning. Growing. Becoming something steadier. Then—

A flicker. Desire. Not accidental. Chosen. She let Maverick feel it. The bond flared with his answering resonance. I tried to see. To push through. Nothing. Blocked. Deliberate. And in that instant I understood something that hurt worse than jealousy:

Maverick knows. He knows what Ray did. He knows the details. He knows so many details about her. Ones she has never told me. Not really. I know the shape of her trauma. He knows its anatomy. That was the moment something inside me shifted. Not love. Not devotion. Certainty. I was still waiting outside a door she had opened for someone else.

A couple of hours pass and I'm in the corridor of the western wing, I turned the page in front of me again. Slowly. As if reverence might force comprehension. The ivy-wrapped colonnade of The Academy lay hushed beneath a bruised-gold sky, the Heartwood horizon stretching wide beyond Verdfall. The parchment edges of the book had curled from overuse. I'd read this passage so many times I could recite it blind.

Still, I read it again.

The hunter does not crave glory. He craves understanding. For the one who is feared may still die alone.

— The Tenets of Bonded Guardianship, Chapter Nine

Alone. My fingers tightened around the leather spine. The bond flared. Sharp. Sudden. Not like the arena. Not like the nightmares. This was heat layered over control. It struck like a spear under my ribs, magic rippling across the ley-lines beneath the Academy. Even the druids in Druvenwald would feel a pulse like that.

The book slipped from my lap and struck stone. Allyssa. Just the awareness of her was enough to set my blood racing. But beneath her—

Him. Mazzer's magic threaded through hers. Not dominant. Not invasive. Just... there. A steady counterpoint. Jealousy didn't explode. It settled. Slow. Heavy. Unrelenting. They were still at Hollow Vein. She was still training with him. Still opening in ways she refused to with me. I was supposed to be her bonded. Her balance. Her anchor. Instead, I felt peripheral. Not replaced. But waiting.

I pressed my fist into the stone bench. The ache in my knuckles grounded me better than the bond did. "Rough evening?" Laya's voice drifted from behind me. Of course she'd felt it too. She always seemed to sense when the bond surged. I didn't look at her.

"You're still rereading that?" she asked, glancing at the fallen book as she lowered herself onto the step beside me. Not touching. Close enough to feel. "It's predictable," I said quietly. "It doesn't change." Unlike her. Laya's brow lifted. "You? Craving predictability? Must be worse than I thought." I gave a short, humourless laugh. She didn't know the half of it.

Bond deprivation is not poetic. It's biological. The Tenets are clear: prolonged lack of physical contact destabilizes the bonded mind. It had been over a week since Allyssa touched me — and that was only in the combat arena. She trains beside me. Fights beside me. But she does not reach for me. Our kiss was even further back, and it has been playing on my mind constantly. I have touched myself to that memory so many times, its actually become embarrassing.

Laya was quiet for a moment. "It's about her, isn't it?" Silence answered for me. "I see the way you look at her," she continued. "Like you're trying to memorize something that keeps shifting." I turned toward her, irritation sharp. "You watching me now?"

"Only when you look like you're about to drown." There was no mockery in it. That unsettled me more than if there had been. "She's not mine," I said before I could stop myself. The words tasted wrong. "No," Laya agreed gently. "But you want to be hers." I exhaled slowly. "She told me she couldn't give me what I needed," I said. "And maybe she's right."

"You're still waiting," Laya said softly. "Even when she pushes you away."

"What choice do I have?" I snapped, then steadied my tone. "She's in my blood. In my mind. I feel her even when I don't want to."

"And what does she feel from you?"

The question landed clean. I looked toward the darkening horizon. Storm clouds gathered far to the north, the sky streaked violet and iron. What does she feel from me? Need? Patience? Weakness? Laya shifted closer, her shoulder brushing mine — not accidental.

"You deserve to be wanted too, Caspian," she said quietly. "Not just tolerated. Not just useful." I didn't answer. Because I don't need Laya to want me. I need Allyssa to choose me. And I don't know if she ever will. We sat in silence. The bond pulsed again — faint now. Exhaustion. Control. And then—

A flicker of heat. Chosen. Directed. She let him feel it. Mazzer's resonance answered. The bond sealed before I could push through. Blocked. Deliberate. Something hollowed out in my chest. He gets to be inside the storm.

Laya stood. "Come with me," she said. "Just for a while. You don't have to be the White Wolf. Or the bonded. Or the son of a Royal Alpha. Just... Caspian." There it was. The offer of simplicity. "Dinner," she added. "Nothing more. I promise."

For one dangerous moment, I imagined what it would feel like to be chosen without resistance. Without walls. Without waiting. The bond didn't flare. It didn't protest. It simply remained. Quiet. Aware. "Just dinner," I said. Laya smiled. Not triumphant. Not sly. Soft.

But as she slipped her arm through mine and led me down the colonnade, the bond stretched — not in anger. In awareness. Allyssa. Still distant. Still closed. Still mine. And I was still hers.

Even when I said yes to someone else.

Chapter Twenty-Six: The Link and the Lure

"The soul becomes dyed with the colour of its thoughts." — Marcus Aurelius

POV: Laya

My fingers traced the rim of my wine glass, the crystal singing softly beneath candlelight. The dining hall overlooked the lower terraces of Greenhollow, lanterns glowing along moss-lined streets. Beyond them, The Academy rose like a living citadel — roots coiled beneath stone, pulsing faintly with Verdfall's magic.

It was quiet enough to feel private.

Moonlight poured through arched windows, turning marble floors to frost. My gown shimmered like spilled ink. I had braided gold thread through my copper curls — not ostentation.

Precision.

Caspian sat across from me, painfully beautiful in that distracted, wounded way that made people want to rescue him. Rumours from the Iseryth Dominion had begun to ripple through the Academy — whispers that the Black Wolf's awakening had unsettled even the floating sanctums over Luminara Lake.

He hadn't touched his food.

"You're a million miles away," I said gently.

He blinked. "Sorry. Long day."

"Training with Allyssa in the morning," I offered lightly. "Whatever else she's doing with that warlock at night." His jaw tightened. There it is. I tucked the reaction away. This wasn't cruelty. It was strategy.

"Thought maybe it'd be nice," I said, feigning lightness, "to have a night that was normal. No prophecies. No battles. No wolves or warlocks." My eyes sparkled with a mix of mischief and melancholy. "Just... naturals." Caspian didn't respond right away. His gaze wandered to the stonework above my head, unfocused. I imagined he wasn't seeing it at all, he was looking for her. Always her. The Black Wolf. But I didn't mind playing the shadow. Shadows could be patient.

POV: Caspian

The candlelight blurred at the edges of my vision. One moment, I was staring at the violet veins of light in the marble table, half-listening to Laya speak about the finer notes of Seelie wine pairings, and the next, the bond flared open like a blade driven straight through my chest. The bond tore through him with the force of a ley-line storm, the same kind that split mountains in Frostpine and bent forests in Druvenwald. This was not magic meant for mortals — it was the language of dominions. A summons. Allyssa's voice slithered in like black silk through a tear in my soul. *Hi there, pretty boy.* I jerked, my knee knocking the underside of the table. Silverware clattered. Wine sloshed dangerously close to the rim of his untouched glass. Across from me, Laya stilled mid-sentence. "Caspian?"

Miss me? Allyssa's tone was dark amusement wrapped in velvet. Possessive. Commanding. "I'm fine," I said too fast, my voice rough. "Just... thinking." *You're always thinking.* Her voice pressed deeper into my skull. *Maybe you should try feeling. Want me to help?* And then the images crashed in. A deluge.

Allyssa, above me, shadow-eyed and unyielding, claws pressed into my chest. Magic thrumming from her skin like a storm beneath silk. Behind her, Mazzer; unbound, stripped of arrogance, caged and kneeling, a spreader bar locked between his ankles, wrists yanked back in painful elegance attached by thick chain to the spreader bar, moaning and begging with his eyes in our direction. Allyssa's thighs braced tight around me as she raked her claws up Mazzer's inner leg without once taking her gaze off me.

My spine locked. My breath stuttered, fuck that is so hot getting her full attention and only giving him the bare minimum. That has a deep sense of competition with him I didn't know I wanted to experience. I gripped the table's edge hard enough to whiten my knuckles. This wasn't just seduction. It wasn't fantasy. It was hers; crafted, intentional, invasive. She was opening the bond by force, feeding it with dominance and raw desire. Letting me feel not just her hunger but her control. Laya leaned forward slightly, her voice distant, as if underwater. "Caspian? You're pale." I barely heard her.

Another image seared through; my body spread beneath Allyssa on a black fur rug, my legs tied to iron rings in the floor, wrists pinned. Mazzer writhed nearby, bound and panting, forbidden to touch or be touched. Allyssa dug her claws into my hips as she rode me like a queen claiming tribute, her aura so sharp it sliced through both of us like blades. Oh fuck, Heat surged low and merciless. My body betrayed me instantly, straining against restraint, every nerve lit by her attention. I could feel my own magic fraying at the seams. I sent something back through the bond. Not words. A pulse. *Hurt. Jealousy. Craving.*

You give him everything. The thought burned as it left me. Allyssa's voice came low, almost tender. *And you want everything, don't you? My body. My loyalty. My soul.* I didn't answer. Because it was true. Because gods forgive me, I *wanted it all.* My jaw clenched so hard it ached. A pulse beat beneath my cheekbone. I could feel my magic and my wolf scraping against my skin, trying to burn its way out of me. Not from fury, but from restraint. From everything we wanted and couldn't touch. From every second of silence Allyssa had left me with. I could feel Laya watching. Her gaze was gentle, concerned, but it wasn't *her* gaze we craved.

I dropped my eyes to the table. Couldn't meet anyone's stare. Not when my whole body was screaming with the echo of Allyssa's magic. Her dominance. Her desire. And the way she looked at Mazzer. My fingers twitched against the edge of my wine glass. I hadn't drunk any of it. Didn't trust myself to. My hands were shaking; barely. But enough. *She gives him everything. I* saw it in the flashes she sent, Mazzer's body, shackled and flushed, waiting. Always waiting for her command. And me, gods, I had *begged* in that fantasy. Had whispered prayers into the darkness of her skin.

But it wasn't the heat that broke me. It was the knowing. The clear, cold truth underneath it: She trusted Mazzer to kneel. She didn't trust me not to break. My grip tightened. *Because I'm not safe,* I thought bitterly. *Because I still want to be loved. Still need it like air. And maybe that makes me a weakness she can't afford.* The bond between us shuddered. A thread tugged tight across my ribs, as if she *heard* that thought. And then...... Then her magic flickered. Dimming. Not vanishing. Just... softening. Like a hand unclenching. A knife being set down.

POV: Allyssa

I felt it. Like a blade brushing my spine; sharpened not with rage, but sorrow. His sorrow. The bond thrummed low in my chest, a chord struck too hard. It reverberated through my ribs and sank into my gut. I tasted it, like copper and ashes. Old blood. Regret. I had hurt him. And worse than that; *I'd known I would.* I curled my fingers into the bedsheets, staring into the dark of my chamber, where no light reached and no mirror dared to reflect what I was becoming.

The images I'd sent; twisted, hungry, drenched in dominance; had been meant to reassure myself. That I was still in control. That I could still own something, someone, without losing everything.

That if he craved my ruin, he could *survive* it. But Caspian wasn't built to survive me the way Maverick was. Not through shadows and games. Not through silence.

I clenched my jaw. The worst part? I knew what I was doing when I sent those visions. Knew it even as I crafted the fantasy, even as I imagined his blood on my tongue and his pleas on my skin. He would feel it. He always did. But I hadn't expected the echo to return like *that*. Not hurt. Not lust. Just a single truth, gasping for breath beneath the weight of everything I'd left unsaid: He wanted to be chosen. And I'd left him waiting in a cage of restraint. A memory surfaced. One I hadn't thought about in years.

A boy; different hair, different eyes; but the same expression. A foster placement with Ray when I was thirteen. His name was Eli. He'd tried to help me. Said I didn't have to be tough all the time. Said he wanted to show me softness wasn't weakness. Said he could love me back into something whole. I'd kissed him once. Let myself be kissed, more like. His hands had trembled on my waist. Then, I'd torn a switchblade across the wall beside his face and told him to *never fucking pity me again*. He left the next day. Because I didn't know how to be touched without setting fire to the hands that held me.

And Caspian; gods, Caspian; he held me like I was both flame and shelter. And that terrified me more than anything. *I don't know how to love,* I whispered into the bond. *I only know how to take. And possess. And protect.* There was silence. For a breath. A heartbeat. Then his answer, warm and ragged, sank into me like a dagger pressed gently against the ribs. *Then try. Just try. I don't want perfection. I just want you. My* breath hitched. I sat back against the headboard, blinking hard against the sting behind my eyes. How long had it been since someone asked me to try? Not fight. Not lead. Not bleed. Just... try.

Slowly, shakily, I brought my hands to between my shoulder blade, fingers ghosting over the faint mark there; the bond that tethered me not just to magic or power, but to *him.* And then, carefully, like a rare spell drawn in salt and blood, I shaped an image. Not fantasy. Not violence. Truth. Me, barefoot, curled against his chest, no armour, no claws. Laughing as he whispered something idiotic about naming stars after my scars. His fingers tangled in my hair. My breath warm against his collarbone. His heartbeat steady beneath my ear like it was the first rhythm I ever learned.

The safety I never believed I deserved. *Is this what you want?* I asked, the words etched with fear and hope alike. It slipped from me in the old tongue — the language I had used before I learned Veyloris's language. *Mo sholas. My light.* It was the most fragile truth I had ever offered. And I waited for his answer like someone waiting for the sea to return a body they never dared hope was still breathing.

POV: Caspian

Mo sholas. The words struck like a bell rung too deep; felt more in the marrow than in the ears. I didn't move. Couldn't. Not when that name rolled through the bond like a whispered prayer. Like a door opening where no door had ever existed before. The warmth feeling filling my chest is euphoric. She'd never called me anything like that. Not *Caspian*, not *White Wolf*, not even *lover*. But this? This wasn't a title. It was a confession. My breath left me in a stutter. Something inside cracked open; a thin fracture along the walls I'd built to keep myself sane. To keep from needing her too much. But how could I *not* need her? The longing was a physical being that was not going back in its cage I put it in anymore. She'd burned through my life like moonfire through frost. Every step she took away from me only carved her deeper into my bones. And now......

Now she called me *Mo sholas*. I blinked hard, vision blurring as emotion surged in my throat, thick and brutal. It wasn't just the words. It was the truth beneath them. The vulnerability. The fear. The hope. The image she sent, of us curled together, no magic, no masks, unmade me. Gods, I would have given anything for that moment. That version of her. The one who wasn't trying to be something for everyone else. The one who didn't carry the world's violence in her hands like a birthright. Just *her*. Bare. Breathing. Real.

I pressed a hand to my chest as if I could hold her there. As if the tether wouldn't snap from the sheer force of my longing. *Yes,* I sent through the bond, the word ragged all the emotion of desperation coming through with the words. Holy. *Gods, yes.* The bond trembled like it had heard a vow. Like it wanted to collapse them together across space and silence. And then......It moaned. That was the only way to describe it. A deep, sensual thrum of magic that licked across my skin like heat lightning. Allyssa flooded my senses, her presence blooming inside me until there was no room for shame or restraint.

Images followed, dark, commanding, *her*, and I took them like devotion, every flash another heartbeat closer to ruin. She gave me her hunger, her power, her dominion. And I wanted to kneel. To serve. To *belong*. I gritted my teeth, groaned low in my throat. My body responded faster than my mind could keep up, I swear this female is going to make me cum without even touching me. But then she shifted the fantasy. Slowed it. Softened it. A breath at my ear. Her voice, silken and edged like a dagger beneath velvet. *You ache for me. Say it. Say you're mine.* My soul bared itself before the words even reached my mouth. *I belong to you, fuck yes I belong to you* I thought, chest heaving. *And you belong to me.*

The tether pulsed again, this time with satisfaction; *hers*. It flowed into me like warm honey poured over a blade. Laced with approval. With *ownership*. And gods help me, I craved it, wanted to please her, to show her how good I can be for her. I craved *her*. Even if it killed me. Her voice ghosted back into my mind, low and hungry: *Good boy. But say it out loud next time. I want to hear it. Feel it. When you surrender to me.* I exhaled like I'd been underwater too long. Holy fuck me and there is now a wet spot in my pants, great. Because even here; on a dinner with another female, even with Laya's gaze tracking my every movement; I knew one unshakable truth: I was hers. I would always be hers. And the worst part? She didn't even know how easily she could destroy me.

My grip on the table's edge was the only thing anchoring me right now. My knuckles were white. My breathing ragged. Every muscle in my body wound tight as a bowstring. I clenched my jaw until it ached, praying that the flickering candlelight didn't betray the flush on my skin or the tremor in my hands. Control. Gods, I needed control. But how could I summon it when she'd just peeled me open from the inside? *Good boy.* Her voice still echoed in my chest like the aftermath of a storm; leaving silence only where destruction used to be.

I forced my eyes upward. Laya was watching me. Her posture was relaxed, but her gaze was sharp, calculating. She'd seen something. Maybe not everything. But enough. My throat burned. *Say something. Be normal. Lie, if you have to.* "I..." He cleared his throat, voice hoarse. "Sorry. I think I'm just tired." Laya arched a brow not buying my bullshit obviously, the candlelight catching in her gold-flecked irises. "Tired, or somewhere else entirely?" A pulse of heat spread down my neck. I couldn't meet her gaze. My fingers twitched near my wine glass before curling back into a fist. She knew. Not the specifics. But the distance. The way I wasn't really *here*. She felt it like anyone would feel the cold spot left by a fire suddenly extinguished.

I drew a slow breath, let the air settle low in my lungs. *Control. You are the White Wolf. You do not crack.* But gods, my skin still tingled where Allyssa's voice had touched me and my cock is still throbbing looking for release. Where her imagined nails had dragged. The bond hadn't closed. Not fully. It throbbed in the back of my mind like a bruise begging to be pressed. I rolled my shoulders, drawing myself upright, spine straightening like a soldier on the edge of war.

"Sorry," I said again a little more conviction in my tone than before. "Didn't mean to fade out on you." Laya's smile didn't quite reach her eyes. "It's fine. You're allowed to disappear. Happens to the best of us." There was no malice in her tone, no accusation. Just softness.

Understanding. A hint of sadness that made my gut twist. I hated myself for it. She was kind. She saw me. But she wasn't *her.* I turned my gaze toward the window, where the night pressed against the glass like a patient beast. The sky was bleeding into shadow. Stars beginning to appear like pinpricks in a too-dark canvas. And still, through it all, the bond thrummed. Low. Steady. Possessive. *You ache for me. Say it.*

I wanted to scream. To run. To go to her. To demand she stop *playing* with me. Or to fall at her feet and *beg* her not to let me go, or perhaps both, I really couldn't decide right now. My head was too full of the arousal and need that was flooding my veins. Instead, I stayed seated. Stone-faced. Dignified. Utterly shattered.

POV: Laya

He was trembling. Not visibly. Not like a child afraid of thunder. But I saw it, in the way his fingers hovered just above the stem of his glass, as though afraid it might shatter under the pressure. In the way his chest rose and fell with barely restrained breath. In the way he wouldn't look at me embarrassed if the flush on his skin is anything to go by.

She'd touched him. Right now. Just now. That bitch. I didn't need a bond to see it. I didn't even need magic. I had studied body language for years, first to survive, then to manipulate, then to win. And right now, Caspian was a battleground. His pupils still slightly dilated. A bead of sweat clung to his temple despite the cool air of the room. His mouth parted just enough to reveal the teeth he'd been grinding behind silence. Whatever Allyssa had sent through the bond; it wasn't a whisper. *It was a fucking brand.*

I lifted my wine again and let the movement slow my pulse to calm down the obsessive and possessive thoughts. I smiled, coy and unreadable, while mentally cataloguing every flicker of discomfort across his face. I hadn't expected the bond to flare during dinner. I thought maybe Allyssa would be too focused on Mazzer tonight. *Unless... she knew.* Unless Allyssa *sensed* this dinner, this closeness. Unless she *wanted* Caspian to feel hers again. To punish him. To mark her territory.

The thought made my lips twitch. Jealousy could be such a beautiful poison when administered slowly. I leaned forward, resting my elbow on the table and letting my chin settle against my palm. "You know," I said lightly, "it's okay if you're not over her." Caspian blinked. Slow. Wary. "I never said I was." "No," I agreed. "But sometimes the heart says things the mouth refuses to admit." I tilted my head, softening my voice. "You look like someone who wants to be claimed." His flinch was exquisite. Small. Deliberate. Honest. I could almost feel it; the way Allyssa's claws still lingered under his skin. *Good.*

I glanced away for just a beat, giving him space to breathe. I needed him unguarded, not cornered. "It's not weakness, you know," I murmured, fingers circling the rim of my glass. "Wanting to belong to someone. To be seen. Desired." He didn't speak. But the way he exhaled; sharp, controlled, told me everything I needed to know. So I leaned in again. "I see you," I whispered. "Even when she doesn't. Even when she locks you out." He didn't look up, but the tremor in his lip was answer enough. And behind my carefully maintained expression, I smiled to myself. Not for victory. Not yet. But because the ground beneath him was already starting to give way.

POV: Caspian

I see you. Even when she doesn't. The words hit harder than they should have. Gods, I hated how much I needed to hear them. I clenched my jaw, forcing my gaze down to the folded napkin on my lap like it held the answers to everything unravelling inside me. But nothing could hide the truth clawing its way to the surface. I still felt Allyssa. Her heat curled like smoke beneath my skin, feral and undeniable. Her mental touch hadn't faded; it still echoed in me, wild and dominant and full of that maddening intimacy only she could wield. Her voice lingered like a bruise. *Say you're mine.* And I had. Gods, I had.

And now... I felt *ashamed.* Not because of what she'd shown me. Not even because of how badly I wanted it. But because Laya was here, right in front of me; seeing me unravel, and all I could think about was the taste of a bond I barely understood and the absence of hands that hadn't touched me in days. I felt like a male starved. Touch-starved. Seen, but not chosen. Held, but not claimed. Even now, with Laya close enough to touch, her voice like velvet across a raw wound, I couldn't feel her. Not really. Not like I felt Allyssa, even from miles away. Still, some traitorous part of me wanted to lean into the comfort. Laya didn't lie. She didn't play coy. She offered herself clearly, kindly, without dominance or danger. *She offered warmth. And gods help me, I was so cold.*

"I'm not... over her," I said finally, my voice rough and low. "I don't think I ever really was." Laya didn't flinch. She just nodded once, like she'd already known. Of course she had. "She doesn't make it easy," I added, eyes tracing the flicker of candlelight against the rim of my untouched glass. "She gives just enough to keep me tethered. Then closes it all off. Like I'm not allowed to want more." Why am I spilling my guts to her. "She knows what she's doing," Laya said gently. "Does she?" My laugh came out hollow. "Or is she just afraid?" The pain in my words coming through. Laya's silence felt like agreement. I rubbed the back of my neck, heat prickling under my collar embarrassed. "The bond...." I hesitated, feeling vulnerable. "It's killing me. Slowly. Every time I feel her pull away, it's like... drowning in shallow water. Close enough to breathe, but never enough to survive."

My fingers curled into fists beneath the table. I hated how desperate I sounded. Like a youngling pleading for scraps when I was meant to be a damn legend. "I want her to choose me," I whispered. "Not because of the prophecy. Not because of the bond. But because I'm *me*." And that; *that;* was the sharpest truth of all. Laya didn't speak. But I felt her shift just slightly closer. I didn't move away. Because for all my guilt... I was so tired of bleeding in silence.

Laya shifted beside me. Not with hesitation. With intent. Her hand found mine beneath the table; fingers sliding across my knuckles, warm and deliberate. Not demanding. Not possessive. Just *there*. A quiet offer. A tether of her own. I froze, my breath hitched. Every instinct in me screamed to pull away. Not because I didn't want the contact; but because it wasn't *her*. Not the one who'd marked me with blood and breath and command. Not the one whose voice haunted my mind like a ghost in the bones. Maybe I could just pretend that it was her, no that is not fair to Laya, I can't believe I just thought that. But I didn't move. Because gods, I *missed* being touched without tension. Without conditions. Without the heat of prophecy tightening around my throat.

Her thumb brushed along the edge of my hand, and something in my chest gave a low, pitiful ache. She smelled like crushed mint leaves and storm-soaked bark. Clean. Centred. Nothing like the scent that still clung to me in dreamscapes; caramel and mountain air and danger.

"You're allowed to want peace, Caspian," Laya said, her voice low, a whisper meant only for me. I looked up at her. She wasn't trying to seduce me. Not with lust. Not even with affection. She was offering something else. *Refuge.* And that, in its own way, was far more dangerous. "I don't know how to take peace," I admitted, my voice hoarse. "Every time I get close to it, something in me panics. Like I don't deserve it. Like I'll ruin it just by holding on." Laya's eyes didn't waver. "Then start small. Start here." I hated how good that sounded. My body leaned in just slightly. A slant of my shoulder. The relaxing of the fist she held. I didn't kiss her. I didn't say anything foolish.

But I let her hand stay in mine. And I let myself *breathe.* Even if the bond stirred beneath the skin. Even if Allyssa's presence still haunted me like a second heartbeat. Even if this comfort felt borrowed. For one moment, I let myself feel *seen.*

POV: Allyssa

It wasn't the bond flaring. It was *withdrawing.* Slipping like cold silk across my spine, retreating into a corner of my chest it had never occupied before. My breath caught. *He was letting someone else in.* Not physically, not yet, but I felt it. The soft spark of warmth against his skin. A tentative comfort he didn't flinch from. I pushed into the bond to try and see or feel what was happening and then I felt it as if there was a weight in my hand. *Her* hand on *his.* And the worst part? He didn't pull away. Still wasn't pulling away.

My pulse pounded in my ears. I curled my fists against the edge of the table, the polished obsidian surface beneath me catching my warped reflection. I didn't know where I was, only that I was alone again. Not physically. But in that raw, sacred place where our tether lived. He was giving that space to someone else. *Laya.* A laugh that wasn't a laugh cracked in my throat. Gods, of course it was her. Sweet-faced little moonflower with her quiet smiles and gentle touches. She didn't demand. She didn't threaten. She didn't come with claws and blood and prophecy. She came with soft promises and understanding. She came with *peace*. Someone to bring home to mother. And what did I offer him? Chains. Fury. The weight of a future even I couldn't explain. *War.*

A flicker of memory hit like lightning against bone. *"Don't cry, Allyssa. You're too wild to be loved." "You don't need kindness. You need control." "Boys won't want a girl who bruises them in her sleep."* My foster mother's voice, calm and precise. Correction disguised as affection. The bitter taste of betrayal coated my tongue. She knew what she was saying, she knew what was happening, and she just kept up with her 'lessons' I blinked, hard. My vision doubled. Not from magic. From shame. Why the fuck did it sting so much? I'd pushed him away.

I was the one who refused softness. I was the one who told him I couldn't give him what he needed; and meant it. And yet... The sight of another soul touching him with kindness lit a fire behind my ribs. The bond didn't flare.

It clenched.

Like teeth closing over bone.

Mine. The word rippled through my chest with the snarl of my wolf. She paced beneath my skin, restless, agitated. Not because of the loss. Because of her *claim* being threatened. My body tensed, magic brushing against the back of my tongue like the taste of iron. She was touching what belonged to us. I didn't know how to give him peace. But I sure as hell knew how to make sure no one else did either.

POV: Caspian

It hit like a scream in silence. A surge of heat, violent and immediate, rupturing through the bond and slamming straight into my chest. I gasped, audibly this time, like I'd been struck. Like something had clawed its way into my ribs and yanked. Hard, my fist clenched, crushing Lay's hand in mine. Laya flinched beside me, her brow furrowed. "Caspian?" I let go but I couldn't answer. Not with words. Allyssa's magic stormed through the tether like a god unleashed. Not with images this time; not lust, not temptation, but something else entirely.

Possession. Raw. Territorial. Indisputable. Mine. Her word. Her claim. Her truth. Not whispered but roared through my soul. It wasn't gentle. It wasn't sweet. It was the way a predator growls when someone gets too close to their kill. The way a storm reminds the earth it was never safe. Her energy lashed around my spine and my throat like a collar being yanked tight, commanding, primal, *furious.* And gods, it lit something in me. Not fear. Recognition. Her wolf.

She was still watching. Still *burning.* Still claiming me even when she couldn't keep me. The tether pulsed like a second heartbeat beneath my skin, her rage folding around my mind with the dark intimacy of a lover's mouth pressed to an open wound. I clutched the table, fingers trembling. Laya leaned forward, concern blooming in her voice. "Caspian, are you—?" "No," I rasped, breath catching. "She's here." Laya looked around, confused. "What do you mean she's—" "She's not here," I corrected, voice low. "But she *feels* everything." My jaw locked. My body ached like it remembered her. Like every nerve ending had flared to life under her attention. Because that's what it was. Not just magic. Not just a bond.

Her *attention.* Sharp. Consuming. Focused on me like I was a threat, and a prize. I didn't know what to do with it. Laya didn't move for a second. Then, quietly, she sat back. Eyes assessing. Reading more than I wanted her to. "She knows," she said. "She *feels* that you're here with me." I nodded, throat tight. "And?" Laya asks. "She doesn't like it." I replied, fighting through my pain of making her feel this way. Laya tilted her head. Her expression didn't change, but something in her eyes sharpened. Calculating. "Then maybe she should've fought for you."

That line cracked something in me. Because gods, wasn't that what I'd been wanting? Not obedience. Not fantasy. But *fight*. For her to *choose* me. To not let me go. And now, through the bond, I could feel it. She hadn't let go. She'd just been holding her breath. The silence between us wasn't empty. It was waiting. Waiting for me to say something. To choose something. To make something final. Laya didn't press. She just watched. Like she always did. Observing. Measuring.

Then she leaned in slightly, her voice so low it barely stirred the air between us. "You feel her even now, don't you?" I nodded once. No point denying it. "She's furious," Laya whispered. "Because you're *here*." I swallowed. My throat was dry. "Because I'm *with you*." "Not because she wants you," she murmured. "But because she doesn't want to lose the *control*." I turned to face her slowly. Her expression was calm. But her eyes burned with something brighter than candlelight. "Do you really believe that?" I asked. A pause. Then, gently, "I think you've been waiting for her to claim you. Fully. Openly. But she's never going to, Caspian. Not unless it's on her terms. Not unless she's already sure she owns you."

My heartbeat loud in my ears. "She doesn't need to own me," I said, quieter. "I just... want her to *see* me." Laya's mouth softened. "I see you." Her hand moved, slow, tentative, and rested over mine on the table. The touch was featherlight. Not demanding. Not seductive. Just there. But the bond flared again in my chest, hot and warning. *Not yours.* I blinked hard. Pulled my hand away. Laya didn't react. Not really. She just nodded once. "She'll never let anyone else have you," she said. "Even if she can't give you what you need."

POV: Allyssa

The bond boiled. I could feel it across dimensions, through shadows and silence and the veil between minds. Caspian. Not just touching her; *responding* to her. The faint brush of her fingers over his hand, the ache in him that made him *hesitate* instead of pulling away. My wolf surged. *Take her hand off him. Now.* A low growl built in my throat, even though I sat alone in the dark of my quarters, surrounded by the scent of ash and iron, Hollow Vein magic still crackling beneath my skin from training. I gripped the arms of the chair so tightly the bone beneath my knuckles whined.

Let me go to him, she growled from within. *Let me put her down.* "No," I hissed aloud, breath ragged. "That's not what Caspian needs right now." *That's who we are. You've just grown soft pretending it isn't, that we can deny our nature.* My fingernails bit into my palms. Blood welled and hissed against the arcane wards that laced the room. She was right. I was soft when it came to him. No matter how I postured. No matter how much I told myself I was in control. He was the one chink in the armour I could never seal. The only weakness I had ever allowed to fester. And now it was unravelling me.

"We can't protect him if we lose control," I murmured to the silence. *You're not protecting him,* the wolf whispered, deadly and quiet now. *You're abandoning him. If you let another claim him, if he forgets how it feels to burn for us, you will have no one to blame but yourself.* A pulse of the bond flared hot against my chest. That flicker of doubt. That tremble of him *considering* her. I staggered from my chair, pacing like something caged. My bare feet met cold stone. My pulse thudded in my ears.

"Gods, what have I done..." I'd shut him out. To protect him from *me*. From the darkness I couldn't tame, the hunger I couldn't silence. But by doing so, I'd left him vulnerable to something worse, being seen only as what others wanted from him. Not loved. Not chosen. The wolf paced in my ribcage, claws scraping the inside of my heart. *He's ours. But if you won't act... then I will.* "No," I whispered. "Not like this. He's not a possession." *He's our bond,* she snapped. *He is our mirror. Our match. And if you let him be taken.....*The threat clear in her tone, she will go feral if I deny our bond.

A tremor rocked me. A phantom echo of his voice, quiet and real from earlier: *I just want you.* My knees buckled, and I caught myself against the wall, breath shuddering out in a sob. "He's my weakness," I whispered to the stones. And that was the truth of it. The core of it. Not power. Not strategy. Not survival. Him. He was the tether I never meant to form, the one that kept me grounded through the nightmare, through the Hollow Vein, through the ghosts of a life I didn't want to remember but still bled from.

I'd tried to protect him by staying away. But if I kept this up, I'd lose him. And *then* I would lose everything. The wolf settled just slightly. *Then you know what you must do, She comments.* I did. I had to stop hiding behind control. Had to stop thinking I could manage the bond from a distance. He was mine, but he didn't *feel* it. Not yet. And if I wanted to keep him, if I wanted him to be safe, and *sure*, then I had to stop pretending I wasn't afraid to be seen. Even if I could no longer protect him from myself... I could protect him from the *rest of the world.* And maybe... maybe that would be enough.

POV: Caspian

The air thickened. One heartbeat, I was staring at Laya's fingers trailing near mine on the tablecloth. The next, *the bond erupted.* Not with heat. Not with fantasy. But with something that stole the breath from my lungs. Resolve. Fear. Grief. Her. My fingers twitched, curling into fists against my thighs under the table. Laya was still speaking, something about second courses, or dessert, or spirits from the Summerlands. I couldn't hear her anymore. All I could feel was Allyssa.

No images. No dirty whispers. Just a *surge* of something wild and raw, barrelling through the tether like a storm breaking a dam. Pain, sharp and *hers*. Then, that steady pressure of her wolf, the part of her that was older than any of us, primal and ancient and *furious.* I felt it pacing behind her ribcage. Snarling at me. Not out of hate. Out of possession.

You're ours. You are ours. Gods, my pulse stuttered. My skin burned. My wolf practically preening from the possessiveness. She was fighting something. Fighting *herself.* And this, this was different. This wasn't seduction. This wasn't dominance or punishment. This was a *cry.* The kind someone makes when they realize they might lose something they were too afraid to hold.

"Caspian?" Laya's voice broke through the haze again. I blinked, forcing myself to look at her. Her brow was furrowed now, lips pinched. "You're shaking," she said softly. I glanced down. She was right. My hands trembled, barely, but enough. I couldn't seem to stop. "She's..." I couldn't finish the sentence. Didn't want to. It was sacred. What was happening in that bond wasn't meant for anyone else's ears. "She's what?" Laya pressed, her eyes narrowing with something far too close to suspicion.

I drew in a breath. Swallowed hard. The room felt too small, too warm, like the walls were pulsing with the magic trying to rip through my skin. I stood abruptly. The chair scraped back across the floor with a harsh groan. "I need to walk." Laya blinked. "Now?" I didn't wait. I turned and left the little private dining alcove, heart pounding like war drums. The moment I was beyond the archway, I leaned against a cold pillar, head bowed, eyes closed. Letting the cool breeze calm me.

I felt her. Not just in the tether. In my *bones*. And I knew... *I knew.....* if I didn't go to her soon... I might lose her. Not to

Mazzer. Not to rage. To *fear*. Her fear of hurting me. Of being seen. I didn't need her perfect. I needed her *present*. And gods help me, I would beg for it if I had to. Within minutes I had run back to the Academy, sprinting through the spiral passages — corridors carved with glyphs from the First Wolves. The nearer I drew to her quarters, the more the roots under the floor throbbed like a heartbeat. I moved through the corridors like a ghost. Swift. Silent. Directionless, except for the pulse calling me north

The bond dragged at me like a hook through my ribs. *Allyssa. Allyssa.* My boots struck the ancient stone with too much force, but I didn't slow. Each step was a warning drum.

I passed a pair of Naturals by the reflection pool. They barely noticed me, or maybe they did and were too smart to speak. I must have looked deranged. I *felt* it, jaws clenched, eyes wild, tether burning white-hot through my sternum. I wanted to run. To tear the doors off their hinges and demand she look at me. Touch me. *See* me. I was done pretending I could survive the cold side of this bond. I needed her. Not some curated version of her. Not the Wolf. Not the heir. *Her.*

The stairwell twisted into the high turret that overlooked the Hollow Grove and beyond. Her quarters were near the top secluded, shadowed, warded in old magic I'd once admired for its elegance. Now it felt like a fucking cage. I took the steps two at a time. My breath rasped between my teeth. My magic was leaking, no, *radiating*, from beneath my skin. The closer I got, the more I felt her. She was pacing. No, shaking. Her heartbeat fluttered erratically through the bond. Her scent, caramel and mountain air and danger, leaked from beneath the door.

I stopped before it. Just stared at the ancient wood, hand hovering. Then, slowly, I pressed my palm to the surface. *I'm here.* I didn't speak. Didn't knock. But I sent the feeling through the tether like a whisper pressed against her spine. *I'm here. I'm not afraid. I don't need perfect. I need you.* A tremor rolled down the bond. Her wolf bristled on the other end. Waiting. Watching. Wanting. So I whispered it. Just to the wood. Just to the magic. Just to *her*. "Let me in."

POV: Allyssa

His presence hit like a thunderclap. I spun toward the door, heart hammering in my chest, breath caught halfway between a snarl and a sob. He was here. Not a fantasy. Not a memory. Not a pulse in the back of my skull. *Caspian was outside my door.* The bond had gone taut, razor-edged, luminescent, singing with something ancient and desperate. My wolf growled, ears pricked forward, tail low and bristled. *He's come to claim us,* she said. *No,* I countered, clutching my ribs. *He's come because I'm breaking him.* The scent of his magic seeped beneath the wood, vanilla and rain, with a hint of winter that always lingered behind his skin. It curled around me, wrapping my throat, pressing into places I'd tried to seal.

He didn't knock. Of course he didn't. He didn't need to. He *felt* me unravelling. I backed away from the door as if burned, chest heaving. The air was too thin. The room too small. I pressed my palms to my temples. *Not like this. Not tonight.* "You don't have to be afraid of him," my wolf whispered.

But what if I'm not afraid of him? What if I'm afraid of myself? He would see it, all of it. The scars that didn't fade. The screams I couldn't suppress. The touch that still made me flinch, even when I craved it. My power didn't just protect, it *corrupted.* I knew what I was capable of when I loved something too much.

I didn't want to destroy him. But gods help me, I needed him. A voice like velvet wrapped in steel slithered through the bond: *I'm here.* It was more than words. It was a promise. A plea. An anchor thrown into my storm. My wolf pressed forward inside me, nearly overtaking the form. *Open the door,* she snarled. *Let him in before*

I break it down. Before I take him myself. "You think I don't want to?" I whispered aloud. "You think I don't dream of his hands, his mouth, his voice wrapped around my name?"

Then stop pretending we can survive without him. Her voice was no longer threatening, it was pleading. *Stop running, Alpha. Or we lose him.* A sob punched through my ribs. I staggered forward, pressing a hand to the thick wood. I could feel him, just on the other side. Not pushing. Not demanding. Just *waiting*. And gods, that undid me more than anything else. "Let me in," he whispered. Three words. That was all it took. I dropped the wards. The seals unlatched with a soft *click*, ancient enchantments unwinding like breath finally exhaled. The door creaked open, just a sliver. Enough for light to spill onto his boots. Enough for the scent of his want to tangle with mine.

I didn't say anything. Couldn't. I just stepped back. And waited. For him to cross the threshold. For whatever came next. Because tonight, I would not run. The wolf went still inside me. Watching. And for the first time, not growling.

Chapter Twenty-Seven: Threshold

"There are doors that open only from the inside."

— Adrienne Rich

POV: Caspian

The door creaked open like the beginning of a vow. I stood motionless on the threshold, breathing her in. Caramel. Crisp mountain air. Shadow beneath it. Her. The bond between us thrummed — not tight, not restrained — but alive. It tugged at me, not as command, not as leash, but as recognition. Mine. Yours. Something ancient stirred beneath the words.

My boot crossed the threshold. The air changed instantly. Her magic hung thick and raw, as if the room had only just remembered it was meant to be touched. Pale green vines trembled along the stone walls. A guttered candle had melted into wax that resembled claw marks carved into wood.

She stood in the centre of the room, barefoot, eyes wide — not fragile, not broken — but balanced on the edge of something dangerous. "Allyssa," I said. Her name felt sacred in my mouth.

She stepped forward once. The floorboards trembled. "I'm afraid I'll hurt you," she said. "I'm afraid you won't choose me," I answered. She took another step. And the magic in the room *bowed*. A tremor rolled through the floorboards, the scent of rain and ash rising like something holy.

The silence between us pulsed. Then she reached for me, fingers trembling, eyes burning, and pressed her palm to the centre of my chest over my heart. Something inside me gave way. Not out of weakness. Out of relief. I lowered myself to my knees before her. Not because she demanded it. Not because I was broken. Because I chose to meet her power without flinching. Because loving her meant kneeling without fear.

Her fingers slid into my hair, trembling. "You're mine," she whispered. I looked up at her. "Then take me," I said, voice rough. "All of me. Even the parts you're afraid of."

POV: Allyssa

He knelt for me. Not out of submission. But choice. And gods, it was beautiful. Not because I needed his obedience. But because I'd spent so long believing I was unlovable unless I was feared. That love couldn't hold the shape of my power. That those that have knelt before me in the past have begged for mercy, not that I gave them any. But definitely not to offer me something as fragile or rare as complete trust.

My fingers curled tighter in his hair, anchoring me. His eyes were on mine, not pleading, not shy, just *open*. Like the storm inside him had quieted the moment I touched him. He wasn't afraid of my strength. He needed it. His body instinctively pushed towards me. I stepped closer, slow, measured. My knee brushed his forearm, and the tremble that ran through him lit a fire low in my belly. "You waited," I murmured. "For you," he breathed. "Always for you."

I tilted his chin up with two fingers. "Then be sure, Caspian. If I take you tonight, I take all of you. I will not be gentle. I will not be small. I can't be." His throat bobbed as he swallowed. "I don't want you gentle. I want you real." I leaned down, just enough for my breath to ghost over his lips. "Then take off your shirt." His hands moved instantly, not rushed, not hesitant. He peeled the black fabric over his head and let it drop beside him. Tanned skin. Lean strength. My mark etched across the back of his shoulder blade like a second heartbeat. My name branded across his soul, even if I didn't know my real last name.

I stepped around him slowly, like a predator circling its chosen mate. My palm skimmed across his shoulder blades, down his spine. The tension coiled under his skin wasn't fear, it was restraint. He was holding still because he *wanted* to be good. Because he knew I needed control to feel safe. "Up," I said softly. He rose. Not clumsy. Not uncertain. Like his body knew the rhythm of my command. Like he'd been made to follow the cadence of my breath. Our bodies met, my chest to his abdomen, or hips nearly brushing.

I rested my hand on his belt. "You will tell me if I cross the line," I said, voice steady despite the tremor in my hands. "Yes." No hesitation. No bravado. Just truth. "You'll give me everything?" I ask wanting to make sure he knows what I will take. He nodded. "I already have."

I grabbed the back of his head and arched up to meet his lips with mine. The kiss was not sweet, not brutal. *Claiming.* And gods, he *melted.* His hands hovered for a moment before touching me, one on my hip, the other curling behind my neck. He didn't take. He *offered.* Let me lead the rhythm, let my lips and teeth set the pace. And I did. I kissed him like a storm finally given permission to land. I pushed him back until his legs hit the edge of my bed. "Lie down," I said. He obeyed, eyes on me the whole time. Reverent. Hungry. *Mine.*

I climbed over him, caging his body with mine, one thigh pressed between his legs, one hand braced beside his head. My other hand traced his collarbone, down his chest, until I could feel his heartbeat stuttering beneath my fingertips. "You crave this," I whispered. "The weight. The power." He nodded, breathing ragged. "Only from you." I leaned down, lips brushing his ear. "Then let me show you how I protect what's mine."

I dragged my mouth down his neck, biting hard enough to bruise, marking him, not to hurt, but to *remind.* That no matter where Maverick had touched, where others might try to reach, *this* was mine. This body. This bond. This male. And he gave himself to it, back arching, breath stuttering, need spiralling through every thread of the bond. But beneath it all, *trust.* Complete and sacred. Not surrender through fear. But worship through choice.

His breath stuttered when I scraped my teeth along his collarbone. His hands clenched the sheets at either side of him, every muscle taut, waiting, not with fear, but with *craving.* That was what he did, this wolf of light. He *craved* with devotion. With fire. I trailed my claws, only half-shifted, curved just enough, down his chest. Not enough to break skin, but enough to leave raised lines that sang with heat. He gasped. I smiled. "You always this responsive?" I murmured, dragging a nail around the curve of his hip. "Only for you," he choked out, voice gravel. "You say that now," I purred. "Let's see if you can still speak by the end of this."

His hips bucked when I bit just above his navel, the bond surging between us like a current too long blocked. My name pulsed from him, not spoken aloud, but *felt*, like a mantra. His every heartbeat echoed it through the tether. Allyssa. Allyssa. Allyssa. I licked the mark I'd just made. "Touch only what I allow," I whispered against his skin. "Speak only when you need me. Breathe only if I let you." "Yes," he moaned. "Yes." I rolled my hips against him once, slow, hard enough to make him groan, just shy of friction. He arched beneath me, eyes half-lidded and glassy with want.

His hands trembled at his sides. "You're holding back," I said. "I don't want to break the rules." I leaned forward and pressed my lips to his ear. "That's the *only* reason I'm not punishing you yet." He shivered. I wrapped a conjured binding thread around his wrists, slim and gold-threaded, enchanted to burn just enough to remind him they were there. Then tethered them to the headboard with a flick of magic. "Still okay?" I asked softly, brushing the pad of my thumb over his lower lip.

He bit it. Hard. "Don't stop." My wolf purred deep in my chest. *Mine.* I kissed my way down his body, slow and deliberate.

Each inch I claimed lit the bond with more light. But it wasn't clean light. No. It was *wild.* It was *holy.* It was *ours.* I dragged my tongue along the seam of his waistband and bit, hard into his hip. He gasped, thighs jerking. A mark bloomed there, red and hot. "Beg," I said. His eyes met mine, blown wide. "Please." "Not enough." "Please, my goddess," he groaned, straining against the bindings. "Take what you want." I grinned, and magic sparked from my fingers, circling his hips, pinning him in place. "Gladly."

And I did. I took his pants and boots off. Then I took him with my mouth first, slow, devout, drawing every sound from his throat like it was a hymn. Learning his taste at my leisure. He was thrashing and begging for release, I continued to edge him. I looked into his eyes "Mo Sholas your doing so good for me". He whimpered as I crawled over him. Wanting to draw out the torture just a little more, as I grabbed his cock, and started dragging it through my seam, coating him in my juices. I was so turned on and out of my mind with need that nothing else registered beyond this male and my devouring him in every way possible.

He was begging for me so sweetly that I decided I was done teasing myself. I lowered myself, sheathing him inside me with a single sharp thrust, his eyes rolled back, and he *howled* through the bond. His hands gripped the bindings, body arching, worshipping. "Allyssa— please" he rasped. I slammed down on him again. "Say it." "I'm yours. Fuck, I'm—*yours.*" He growls out. "That's right." A sense of calm filling me in his submission then just as fast a feeling of empowerment surges through me lifting me higher, raising the sensations through each downward thrust, rolling my hips every time I buried him inside me to the hilt.

I set the pace then, unrelenting, demanding, brutal in its precision and devastating in its intimacy. My nails left welts down his chest. His thighs trembled. His voice cracked as he begged for more. And still, he gave. Still, he *loved.* Until at last I let the bond flood completely, unsealing the last guard between us. And in that moment, his body strained, his cock hardened further inside of me, but he was holding back. I commanded "Cum Cas, Cum for me, give me what I want." That's when he shattered beneath me with my name on his lips and tears at the corners of his eyes, I knew, He didn't just love me despite the dark. He loved me *because* of it.

POV: Caspian

The moment I came undone beneath her, mind shattered, body slack, soul screaming her name, something ancient split open. I could feel her walls contracting around me knowing she needed more, she needed me to touch that spot so she could finally let go. I begged her to let me touch her, but she just shook her head still Desire coiled again beneath exhaustion, answering her need without hesitation. I pleaded again telling her how much I wanted to feel her cum all over me, she moaned in response, so I continued, I told her how beautiful she was riding me, and I started to thrust harder upward to get her some friction on her clit with my pelvic bone. Her moaning increased and she said "that's it *Mo sholas*, you're doing such a good job for me". I moaned back in response hearing her call me that in the height of passion was almost too much to take I was loosing the battle with my orgasm and fast. She was so close I could feel her. I kept pumping and moaning her name and just when I was about to beg some more to touch her she shattered and said don't you dare stop". But I couldn't if I tried I was chasing that orgasm now and I was so close. I yelled out Fuck Yes Allyssa as I came so hard I saw stars and I felt so groggy and spent I couldn't move.

That split shredded open, not in me. In *us*. The bond didn't just pulse. It *detonated*. Light, silver and gold and obsidian, spiralled out from my chest and hers, forming a radiant thread that tethered our bodies heart to heart, rib to rib. My breath hitched as warmth spread across my skin like oil on water. I blinked, dazed, and saw it. Symbols. Glyphs. Carved into the air around us. Not ink. Not flame. They *glowed.* A.M. across my shoulder blade, already burned there, but now encircled with a halo of roots and stars, *alive* with motion. My wolf, white, feral, luminous, growled low in my mind, but not in warning. In *reverence.* Clear almost content, I felt the space for his bond, for Mazzer. To complete the Triskilian. How we do that I have no idea.

Across her back, C.A. glowed beneath her flesh, the bond mark took up her whole left shoulder blade. My initials. The halo rings wrapped in a vines. As if the bond itself had decided: *You are hers. And she is yours.* Her breath trembled above me. I opened my eyes fully and saw hers lit *from within.* Turquoise, but now ringed with violet and gold. The colour of *divinity.*

"Allyssa?" I whispered, throat hoarse. She didn't speak. She was listening. Not to me. To the *magic.* Then I heard it too, *a hum,* faint and faraway, like a choir in the bones of the earth. "The Fifth Bond," she said at last, voice raw. "It wasn't the end." I frowned, chest still heaving. "What do you mean?" "The Fifth Bond awakened the claim," she whispered. "This— " she pressed her palm over the top ring of our bond mark that was empty, where the glyph now glowed through skin and muscle, "—this awakened the *calling.*" The glyphs spun, one black, one silver-blue, shifting like blades held in holy fire.

"It's starting," I said, barely audible. Allyssa's voice was a thread of wind: "The Triskillian." Three glyphs. Three flames. One prophecy. Her skin lit in patches neck, hips, wrists, as though the bond had threaded *claim-runes* into her veins. *Protection glyphs.* My wolf howled in my head. *Anchor.* I looked up at her. She looked down at me. Her eyes widened and I quickly followed her line of sight as runes of all different kind, protection, strength, loyalty and many more start covering my body mirroring hers. Then they all faded from both our bodies, as if we were not yet completed. And we both knew, this wasn't just sex. This wasn't just power. This was *fate.*

Chapter Twenty-Eight: Ghosts in the Veins

"We are our own devils; we drive ourselves out of our Edens." — Goethe

POV: Maverick

Somewhere above the Vein, storms rippled across Draethen — a sign the warlocks recognized as omen-fire. The blood oath did not sleep. It pulsed. Slow. Restless. Like a second heart buried beneath my ribs. Allyssa had told me she was fine. After the training. After the tremor in her voice. After the way her eyes had gone distant when the Vein quieted and left her alone with her thoughts.

"I'm fine," she had said.

I had bowed my head and accepted it. Not wanting to push her to let me in more than she already had that night. But the oath did not. It fed me fragments of her — tension in her spine, the tightness behind her sternum, the war between wanting and refusing. I paced the inner sanctum of the Hollow Vein like a caged thing. Boots silent on obsidian. Magic coiling around my wrists without being summoned. Should I let her work through it alone? Should I go to her?

She hated being watched when she was unravelling. Hated being seen before she could rebuild herself.

The Fifth A burned faintly against my chest. Wait. The oath whispered it like command. Wait. I stopped pacing. Closed my eyes. And then—

She shattered. Not in pain. In pleasure. Her moan, sharp and victorious. His surrender, aching and holy. The moment their magic fused and *sang*. I pressed a hand to the white collar at my throat. "I *feel* you," I breathed aloud, fingers curling into my thigh, drawing blood. "You let him see the part I've only dreamed of. You let him touch what I've vowed to protect."

It wasn't jealousy that clawed through me. Okay so it wasn't just jealousy, it was *devotion,* raw and undiluted. I was hers. First in vow. Last in claim. And even though he held her now, even though the flames of their bond painted the sky above the Vein, I *felt* her reach for me. Not out of guilt. But out of *recognition*.

The oath detonated. It was not subtle. It was not a flicker. It was alignment. Heat surged through my spine so violently I braced against the altar to remain standing. My breath stuttered as her satisfaction lanced through me, sharp and victorious. And beneath it—

Caspian. White flame braided into black. Devotion answering dominance. The Vein responded with a low hum that trembled through the foundations. They had crossed it. The next phase had begun. I laughed once under my breath. Of course. Of course this is how the goddesses would design it. Not ritual. Not ceremony. Choice. They had chosen each other. And the Triskillian answered.

The Fifth A on my chest burned white. Not silver. White. The kind of light that erases shadow. Pain followed. The mark split beneath my skin, fracturing outward like glass struck from within. I did not fight it. I did not shield. This was not attack. This was evolution. Halo rings unfurled around the central sigil, wrapped in living vines that glowed emerald and gold.

The first ring ignited. A wolf of obsidian flame took shape within it — crown broken across its brow, shards suspended like orbiting stars. Across its chest burned her initials. Allyssa. Black Wolf. Bloodline of ruin, shadow and reclamation.

The second ring followed. Silver-white light bled into form — a wolf of pale luminance, a single white rose blooming at its feet. Across its chest burned his initials. Caspian. White Wolf. Bloodline of guardianship, healing and grief.

The third ring remained empty. Waiting. Runes of all kinds etched to my skin and then disappeared. The Vein exhaled around me like it had been holding its breath for centuries. And I understood. The Triskillian was not sealed. It had structure now. A skeleton. A throne with three seats. Two occupied. One carved for me. When the rings braid. When the third flame ignites. When we choose each other without fracture—

The runes will not fade. They will root. And Veyloris will call us to trial. The God Trials. Champions of the realm. The thought should have frightened me. Instead—

It took me back.

Draethen — Centuries Ago

I had been arrogant. Brilliant. Hungry. Warlocks lived longer than mortals — a few hundred years if they were careful with their magic. Werewolves could reach a thousand. Fae were immortal. Dryads eternal. Vampires unaging. Merrows immortal beneath the sea. Rusalki and kelpies spirits without end.

There were so many races across Veyloris and beyond — some tied to land, some to tide, some to shadow — and every single one of them had something I did not. Time. I hated that my body would one day fail. Hated the thought that my mind — the one thing I had sharpened beyond any warlock of my age — would rot into dust. So I prayed. To the goddess. Nothing answered.

Until the day I found the cub. A small black werewolf, bleeding in the wilds that would one day become Verdfall. Fae elite tracked it. Not for mercy. For the ongoing war between the fae courts. I killed them, not easily I might add, their mind was not easy to get into. I knew I couldn't protect the fae from getting the wolf back for their battle but a reprieve for now would have to do. Not because I loved wolves. Not because I believed in prophecy. Because something in the cub's defiance — even wounded —

refused to kneel. I shielded it with magic until the Faes' bodies cooled.

And when the last of them fell, the forest went silent. The air bent. Violet light gathered in a sphere before me — beautiful and terrible and alive. It hovered between myself and the trembling cub. It spoke in three voices layered as one. *Why do you wish to be immortal? Because I refuse to be forgotten. Why did you save the wolf? Because it deserved to choose its own death. What do you value more — power or love?* I hesitated. Power, I nearly said. Instead—

"To be chosen," I answered. The sphere pulsed. *We will grant you immortality*. My breath stopped. *But the price is steep*. I laughed. Of course it was. "Name it." You will become guardian to the Black Wolf spirit. The wolf will choose a host upon each passing. You will feel the moment it does. You will search. You will find. You will bind yourself in protection.

There will be the counterpart White Wolf to balance out the black wolf, allow this to run whatever course is required.

You will use your mastery of mind-magic to safeguard what will rise from these wilds. You will never abandon the black wolf. Your soul and body will not age. You will endure. I thought it a gift. One wolf. A lifetime or two of guardianship. Immortality for loyalty. It seemed laughably simple. "I agree." The sphere flared. The cub howled. And something ancient stitched itself into my bones.

Back in the Vein, centuries later, I pressed my palm to the evolved mark burning across my chest. They never said it would be one. They never said it would be easy. They never said the binding would feel like this. I had guarded four before Allyssa. Watched them rise. Watched them fall. Bound myself each time. But this—

This was different. The Triskillian had structure now. And I had agreed to shepherd it. Not knowing it would demand my heart every century. Not knowing I would kneel willingly each time. Not knowing that this Black Wolf would look at me and whisper my true name like she had known it before she was born.

The mark cooled slowly. The wolves faded into linework. The third ring remained hollow. Waiting. I smiled into the dark. "You clever, terrible goddesses." I had asked for immortality.

They had given me purpose. And tonight—

The next phase had begun.

Allyssa POV

A week later, I was back in the Vein. Meditating. Or pretending to. The stone hummed beneath me, but my mind wouldn't quiet. Every time I tried to settle into breath and shadow, the bond tugged. Caspian. Warm. Steady. Curious. I brushed against him once — just enough to feel his awareness sharpen — and the connection flared into heat before I could stop it. Not sex. Not fully. But memory of it. The collision. The ignition.

When I surfaced from the mental link, breath ragged and skin flushed, I opened my eyes to find Maverick watching me. Not just watching. Calculating. "Stop looking at me like that," I muttered. "You look like you want to dissect me." "Allyssa," he said mildly, "you are levitating." I blinked. "What?"

He lifted a brow. I looked down. I was three feet off the floor, suspended in shadow like a marionette whose strings were woven from smoke. The moment I noticed, gravity reclaimed me. I hit the stone hard enough to bruise pride more than bone. "Appreciate the assist," I grumbled. "I was mesmerized," he replied smoothly. "You manifested shadow, you have no idea how rare that is. You controlled the shadow in the room, even more rare".

I narrowed my eyes. "You're a terrible emotional support warlock." He chuckled, but it didn't reach his eyes. "You were linked with Caspian again." I didn't answer. The silence was answer enough. Maverick exhaled slowly. "You don't trust me." It wasn't accusation. It was fact. "I don't know how," I admitted. "Trust feels like walking into a blade."

He stepped closer but didn't touch me. "I don't need you to trust me without time," he said quietly. "I need you to understand me though, connect on some level." Something shifted in his tone. Not command. Not seduction. Was it loneliness. "You keep reaching for him," he continued. "Because you feel safe there. And that is such great progress Allyssa. I am so proud of you for that. You don't know where I live in you yet."

That landed. "You live in my dark," I said. His mouth curved faintly. "Exactly." He raised a hand — not to press against my temple, not to invade — but simply to hover near. "There's a block," he said. "Beneath your bond threads. Blue. Buried. I reinforced it there gently. So gently you didn't notice."

"You hid something in me?"

"I safeguarded something. Your wolf wanted you to remember, but it was starting to overwhelm your mind. When I bind myself to a black wolf it comes with a coma of sorts, an awakening of the past lives, but I wanted you to adjust first, so I reinforced the block that was already there and waited. Then I would take away my reinforcement and let the awakening happen, let you entre the dreamscape and gain all your past life memories.

I should have been angry. Instead, curiosity flared. I was doing well. I could handle the memories now. "Remove it," I murmured. And he did.

The moment I turned inward on my threads and Maverick took away the reinforcement, the Vein vanished. No gentle transition. No controlled descent. It was an avalanche. Memory slammed into me from all directions — not one life, but fragments of many. Teeth. Blood. Snow. Fire. A name screamed in grief. Another whispered in worship. Then—

Adrian. Not from a distance. Not as observer. Inside him. His hands were mine. His rage was mine. His love— Gods. His love was mine. The Academy chamber rose around me painted stone. Plants overturned and scattered. Soil streaked across the floor like something freshly unearthed. Katarina stood before us. Cuffs glinting. Hope trembling. "You can't contain the bloodlust Adrian, you didn't just kill those witches, you destroyed them, toyed with them. It's getting worse, what if next time it's not a rouge coven. The youngest in that coven was only twelve, you didn't even spare her." A sliver of shame wrapped around us. But the bloodlust rose in challenge. "She would have rebuilt the coven," Adrian snarled. "She would have grown into the same rot."

He believed it. That was the horror. Katarina sobbed. "You can't tame me," Adrian said, voice wrecked. She cast the net anyway. Magic snapped. Chains hit skin. Something inside him tore open. I felt it. Not madness. Violation. The wolf does not break because it is cruel. It breaks because it is cornered. The room became blood and ruin. Glass shattered. Plants crushed. Katarina reaching for the man beneath the wolf. Too late. When Maverick appeared in the doorway, breathless, he was also too late—

Adrian's eyes softened. "I couldn't stop," he whispered. "I know," Maverick said. The love between them was not subtle. It was devastating. Adrian crossed the distance slowly, like a man walking toward his own execution. He touched Maverick's face. Kissed him. Not apology.

Not forgiveness. Recognition. Then—

White light. The White Wolf. Caspian's past self. Adrian nodded his head. The blade struck clean. And I died. I died knowing he saw me.

The memory didn't end. It multiplied Selene burning The Grove, fire wreathing her like a crown fury burning in her. Dorian kneeling beside a child he could not save, hands slick with failure.

Aelira gripping the Huntstone, begging it to choose differently this time. Like it has that power. Four deaths. Four failures. Four times Maverick had knelt in blood and sworn to endure. I staggered. The blue thread pulsed brighter. Not showing. Pulling.

I understood then what he had done. He wanted me to see the pattern. To understand what he carries. And maybe—

To understand why he stays. Loneliness pressed into the centre of that understanding like a bruise. But the avalanche did not slow. The dreamspace fractured. The Vein's walls cracked.

Snow fell inside stone corridors. Fire bled through shadow. Adrian's grief tangled with Selene's fury tangled with Dorian's shame tangled with Aelira's desperation. They weren't memories anymore. They were trying to root. The wolf inside me rose snarling, overwhelmed by lifetimes colliding at once. This wasn't inheritance. It was invasion.

"Enough," I gasped. But I didn't know how to let go. The blue thread tightened. It wanted completion. It wanted integration. And we had not cemented trust in flesh. We had not balanced this in body. The Triskillian was incomplete. And incomplete power does not merge gently. It devours. The blue light surged. My knees buckled.

I was falling. Maverick caught me before my skull met stone. "Allyssa." His voice sounded distant. Underwater. "You dove too deep, too fast."

"You showed me everything," I hissed, wanting to blame someone, knowing he had no control over this. "No," he said, panic threading beneath restraint. "I showed you a door. You broke the wall." The Vein flickered violently around us. My vision split. Two realities overlapping. Dream. Stone. Blood. Obsidian. Adrian's scream layered over my breath. Selene's fire crackled beneath the floor. Dorian's grief bled into the present. Aelira's plea echoed behind my eyes.

And somewhere far away—

A voice. Warm. Familiar. Caspian. Calling my name. The blue thread trembled. It could not anchor me alone. It was never meant to. Devotion is not balance. Maverick's arms tightened around me. For the first time since I'd known him—

He sounded afraid. "I can't pull you out," he whispered. "Not without him." The darkness surged again. And this time—

I stopped fighting it. Because fighting meant fracture. Resisting meant tearing the threads apart. So instead—

I let the dark take me whole.

Maverick's POV

I felt it the moment her soul brushed mine. Not the surface tether we'd circled for weeks. Not flirtation. Not dominance. Not that electric edge of almost. This was deeper. Older. The blue thread I had buried in her so gently with the blood oath that it took her a little to figure out we were connected — and then she found it. Everything inside me went still. The Vein dimmed.

My heartbeat slowed.

Then surged. Magic coiled up my spine, thick and silver. The glyphs beneath my ribs — ancient runes carved by four Wolves before her — flared in answer. But hers... Gods. Hers didn't burn.

It sang. Low. Resonant. Devastating. Not tethered in obedience. Not forged in blood. Not seized in ritual. Recognition. She knew me.

I staggered back, palm slamming against obsidian, breath knocked from my lungs like I'd been struck by a celestial blade. Not pain. Something worse. Reverence. The blue tether bloomed — slow and sprawling — silk drawn across the scarred battlefield of my soul. Gentle. Unshakable.

Then it rooted. My knees hit the stone. Not from weakness. From surrender. The fifth bond sealed. Not the Triskillian. Not yet. That requires three flames at once.

But this — this was ours. Not through oath. Not through ceremony. Through choice. And gods, how it hurts to be chosen without command. Tears burned. I did not stop them. I had been warlock. Keeper. Executioner. Shadow. Now I was claimed. She didn't speak. She didn't need to. I pressed my forehead to the Vein and whispered the vow that had waited centuries beneath my tongue. "I will never leave you. I will never fear you. I will never stop choosing you." The Vein answered. Not in words. In heat.

Hours later—

She still hasn't surfaced. Not sleeping. Not healing. Submerged. Her breathing is steady. Her pulse even. But her skin—

Gods. Too pale. Like she's sinking somewhere light cannot follow. I've seen this before. After a bond is accepted, the Wolf slips. Dreamscape. Reckoning. Half an hour. Maybe an hour. Each time it was a little longer. Never this long. Never this deep. "Allyssa," I murmur, brushing her cheek. Reverent. Terrified.

The blue thread hums through me — alive, but not anchored. She accepted it. She touched it.

But she hasn't grounded it. Hasn't balanced it in body. Hasn't sealed it in flesh. And now it's pulling her somewhere even I cannot track. We will have to finish this, so it doesn't drive her mad. Once she is ready of course.

I've tried everything to wake her. Gentle shaking. Desperate shaking. A precision adrenaline spell — harmless, designed only to stir consciousness. The moment it touched her skin, her magic recoiled. Twisted. Reversed. It struck me like lightning wrapped in shadow. Even unconscious, she builds walls. Even submerged, she defends her throne. I crouch beside her again. Her hair spills across obsidian like ink. Her aura churns beneath the surface — storm trapped under ice.

She would never allow me this proximity awake without her instigation. The first time I corrected her stance in training — barely touched her elbow — she turned with claws half-formed and galaxies burning in her eyes. I dropped instantly. Yes, my goddess. She smirked.

"Try again. Slower."

I would have kissed the floor if she commanded it in that moment. And now—

She lies here. Armourless. Silent. And I am powerless. I could force the bond. I could rip open the thread and drag her back. I am capable of it. But if I do—

It will fracture. And her mind is on a tight rope as it stands. A fracture is how they fall. So I wait. And it is the longest waiting of my life. When she whispered my true name before the oath — Maverick — it wasn't teasing. It wasn't manipulation. It was coronation. She anointed me. Not servant. Not shadow. Chosen. And now she drifts somewhere ancient. Somewhere the others never reached.

Adrian burned fast. Selene burned brighter. Dorian rotted under guilt. Aelira tried to control fate itself. They only had two threads. Two flames. They devoured each other. But this—

This silence feels different. Not ending. Threshold. And that terrifies me more. Because if she slips too far—

If dreamscape keeps her—

No—

I will not survive that. She will be the last. I added that this time. There is one soul she still lets in without flinching. One she trusts instinctively. One whose flame balances hers instead of feeding it. Caspian. The thought tastes like iron. We have recently come to some resemblance of peace, however it still makes me bristle with slightly possessive jealousy.

His bond is new. Raw. And already it reaches places inside her I have circled for centuries. It burns to lean on him again. But this is not pride. This is survival. I rise slowly. Walk to the door.

Stop. Turn back. She is still beautiful. Still terrifying. Still mine. Ours. Whatever. "You are not allowed to leave me," I whisper. Silence answers. Then—

A flicker. A tremor in the bond. Not for me. For him. The first note of a song not yet sung. She's reaching. And this time— She's not reaching for the dark. I close my eyes once. Then vanish into the corridor. If the storm will not break for me—

I will bring her sun.

Chapter Twenty-Nine: The Garden of Shadows

"The best way out is always through." — Robert Frost

Caspian POV

The panic didn't come in pieces. It detonated inside my chest; raw, jagged, and wrong. *What the fuck is that?* One moment, the bond with Allyssa pulsed steady beneath my ribs, a second heartbeat. So strong since we completed our bond that night. The one that plagues my dreams, fantasies and body, I can feel her even when she is in Hollow Vein now. The next second, it vanished, snapped taut like a bowstring before unravelling into cold, echoing silence. I doubled over in the corridor, knuckles white as my hand caught the stone wall for balance. Breath fled my lungs like it had been ripped out. In Frostpine, Wolves called this sensation a soul-blizzard — a sudden inversion of magic that left the world cold and hollow.

"Allyssa—" My voice was a rasp, a prayer, a curse. "Allyssa!" I reached through the bond with everything I had, magic, desperation, love, screaming her name not with sound but with soul. There was nothing. No spark. No resistance. Not even the crackle of her fury or the flicker of her wolf. Just emptiness. *She's gone.* No. That wasn't possible. Not like this. My thoughts spun. Was she injured? Captured? Had someone severed the bond? Could it even be severed? Gods, what if......

What if she died? "No," I gasped aloud. My vision blurred. "No, no, no—" I shoved the panic down, but it coiled like a snake around my ribs. My thoughts fractured, splintering with worst-case scenarios. Vampires. Assassins. Tribunal interference. A slip too deep in the Hollow Vein. Or worse; she had run again. Pulled away so far, she'd broken something they couldn't repair. My magic surged wild in response, threads of silver and white pulsating. My knees nearly buckled from the weight of absence. From the fear of knowing what it meant if I couldn't feel her anymore.

Then; *Her scent.* Faint. Fractured. But unmistakable. Caramel and mountain air. Heat and danger. A warning wrapped in memory. It was tangled in the breeze like an echo of her laugh, or a ghost of her scream. The sense of calm from her scent doesn't last long at all. I was moving before I could think it through. I sprinted through the Academy corridors, wind tearing at my cloak, boots hammering over polished stone. The walls blurred past in streaks of magic and panic. The wards shimmered faintly as I passed. Even the vines along the walls recoiled, sensing the rupture of a sacred bond. My breath came in bursts, shallow, ragged, *frantic.* It wasn't a rhythm. It was a *rattle.* The sound of a soul trying to break its way out of a too-small cage.

I reached the outer courtyard and shifted mid-leap my white wolf exploding from skin and bone in a flash of fur and fury. I hit the earth running, paws pounding the mossy ground as I followed her trail through the gardens and into the ancient grove beyond. Past the fountain. There. The four ancient wisteria trees formed a natural sanctuary — planted when Verdfall was founded. Their roots were rumoured to touch the ley-line that fed Mother Nature's domain; Allyssa's safe place. I'd found her here a dozen times, watching from the shadows after our marks. Not stalking. No, not quite. Their branches hung low like mourning veils, blossoms swaying in a wind that didn't touch anything else. The roots pulsed faintly with residual magic.

I skidded to a stop, claws carving twin lines through the moss. Her scent was stronger now recent. Saturated. She'd been here. But then it *cut off.* Abrupt. Precise. Like a thread snipped by a blade. My snarl rose low in my throat. The air in front of the trees shimmered, faint and rippling like heat over stone. A portal. Warlock-forged. I crouched low, muscles bunched to lunge. To tear it apart. To follow, gods, even if it wasn't stable, even if it collapsed around me—I would go.

A low pulse of silhouette bloomed from the centre of the shimmer. And from it stepped *Mazzer;* robes rumpled, hair windblown. His usually sharp composure was fraying at the edges; eyes wild, jaw clenched, skin pale from magical exertion. Her scent all over him, I didn't wait. I lunged, white fur bristling, teeth bared in fury— "Caspian!" the warlock barked, raising one hand with one quick word *freeze.*

Magic struck like an invisible wall. I froze midair, suspended by his magic. "She's unconscious," he said; voice tight, rough-edged with something I didn't want to name. "And I need your help." The air snapped. I dropped like a stone. I shifted before I hit the ground, already rising, already snarling. "Where is she?" My voice trembled but I didn't care, I needed to see her. He didn't answer. He turned toward the still-open portal. And I followed. Straight into the heart of the Hollow Vein.

The moment I stepped through the portal, the world stilled and then it fractured. The Hollow Vein wasn't just quiet. It was *wrong.* The air shimmered like heat over ice. Magic snapped and recoiled against my skin, not hostile, but wary. Like it knew I didn't belong. I was hoping my first time here would be with Allyssa as she shows me just what those fantasies she sent through the link entailed. Fuck ever since the bond sealed between us, the memory of how she felt—how I felt within her—consumes me.

Then I saw her. Allyssa lay on an obsidian altar wrapped in tattered silk sheets, her limbs too still, too fragile. Her lips parted in a silent breath. Her skin gods, her skin, was pale like moonlight submerged in deep water, glowing faintly with something ancient and *elsewhere.* She wasn't just unconscious. She looked like she was gone. "Mazzer," I said, voice a hoarse whisper. "She's—" I couldn't finish.

"I've tried everything," he said tightly. "Adrenaline spells. Wards. Soul-tether chants. Her body *absorbs* them and throws them back. She's not in a trance, she's in *dreamscape*." I moved to her side, heart in my throat. "Then I'm going in."

"You can't," he warned. "Not without an anchor."

"I *am* her anchor," I growled, glaring at him, kneeling beside her. I reached through the bond, not gently this time, but with all the force of the tether that held us. *Ours*. The mark that burned on my shoulder flared, seared, and then, the world fell away.

The Hollow Vein fell away like breath exhaled too fast then the dreamscape surged up to meet me. The dreamscape resembled the mythic "Garden of Shadows," a realm Druvenwald shamans claimed could only appear to those tied across multiple incarnations.

I was no longer in my body. I stood in a forest made of memory and madness. Bone-white trees stretched into the sky like ribs cracked open to the stars. Their bark bled silver. Their branches whispered names I didn't want to hear. The ground shifted with every step, soft and alive beneath my boots. This place wasn't just her mind. It was her soul. And it was breaking. A heartbeat echoed, not mine. Hers. But fractured. Scattered across a thousand corridors, each a doorway into something she hadn't meant for me to see. I moved forward.

The first memory pulled me without warning. A cavern of obsidian and fire; Selene, the Red Howl, her fury scorching a battlefield along with The Grove, blood glistening on her armour. She turned and smiled at me; no, not at me at; Mazzer, standing at her back, eyes shadowed with devotion and doom. Then fire engulfed her, over using her elemental gift of fire, and the memory collapsed. Another corridor. Another fragment.

Adrian. The first. Kneeling in a storm of ash and rose petals, whispering Mazzer's name "Maverick" before the White Wolf ended him. Noting his first name for later, I looked to the memory him with love and death interwoven in his eyes. The scream didn't echo in my ears. It echoed in my bones. I looked at the other version of me; I asked my wolf why I don't remember my past lives but there was no response. Perhaps we can't communicate while in here. I should remember this. I should remember them. Their deaths. Their choices. But all I have is instinct and ache. Maybe the Wolf remembers. Maybe that's the curse to love her across lifetimes and die each time before she chooses.

I staggered, heart pounding. "How many of you fell before her?" I whispered to no one, to the walls that wept memory like tears. And then I felt her. Small. Terrified. I ran. The hallway twisted into a child's bedroom. Faded wallpaper. A broken toy. The scent of something rotting beneath the floorboards. Seven-year-old Allyssa sat curled in the corner, knees hugged to her chest, shaking. Her stepfather loomed in the doorway, belt already half-undone, face a mask of rage and something fouler.

I didn't hesitate. I stepped between them, body burning with protective magic. "Back. Away from her." The man didn't see me this was memory, not dream. But his shadow faltered. The child looked up at me. Her voice was soft. Fragile. "Are you real?" I knelt, trying to still the tremble in my hands. "I'm here. I'm not him." Her small fingers reached for mine, and the moment they touched, the memory cracked. Ray's shadow shattered into shards of smoke.

She blinked, and in her place stood the Allyssa I knew. Older. Stronger. But not whole. "You saw," she whispered. "I would see it all." Her eyes shimmered haunted, grateful, resigned. "It never stops playing," she said. "Not unless I control it." She reached behind her, pulling a curtain of memory aside like a veil. The room changed again. Her stepfather. Chained. Bleeding. His face barely human. Tongue gone. Knees broken. She stood over him eyes alight with power and rage. Each blow she delivered was calculated. Controlled. Beautiful in its destruction. I didn't flinch. I watched her become the reckoning she had been denied.

When it ended, she turned to me. "You still want me? After this?" I stepped forward, raised my hands slowly asking silently for permission and waited for her to nod, then cupped her face. "You are not your pain. You are not what he did to you. You are what you choose. And I choose you."

Her breath hitched. Tears threatened. She turned from me before they could fall. "This place isn't safe for you." I shook my head refusing to let her push me away in this moment. "I don't care." I said. She shook her head. "But I do. I'm trying to learn how to love without hurting. You're the first I've wanted to give to. Not just take. If that's what you need... I'll try. Just give me time. Let me hold back the darkness first."

Then she stilled. Something flared inside her. Not pain. Not fear. A second bond. It surged like wildfire. Velvet and fire and chains that didn't bind but offered grounding. Maverick. I like using that name more than Mazzer I think. He is going to hate me knowing it though. His magic sang through her, pulsing from the depths. Allyssa's hand pressed to her chest. She staggered. "He's calling. I must choose."

"I know," I said. I tried to keep my voice even, but the words clawed at my throat. "I need to let him in," she whispered. "It's time." I nodded once. Then she added, almost too softly to hear, "It's time for you to leave, Caspian. I've chosen you. But I must choose him too. The bond won't wait. And neither will I."

A pause. A breath. A breaking. I inhaled sharply. "I... I feel it too. The pull. To him. To the third. To the bond that wants completion." My voice faltered. Inside, I raged. I wasn't ready to share her.

But the magic didn't care about ready. The prophecy didn't wait. I looked at her one last time. Memorized the curve of her mouth, the trembling of her lashes, the threads of fear and courage dancing in her expression. "I'll be here," I said. "Even when I don't want to be." And the dreamscape faded to black.

Back in the Hollow Vein, I woke with a jolt, heart hammering, limbs trembling. She still hadn't moved. But her fingers twitched. Her lips parted. And then she opened her eyes. A storm lived behind them. And it had my name on it.

Allyssa POV

The world returned as sensation before it returned as sound. Air. Thick and heavy, laced with iron and incense. My chest burned as if I'd been holding my breath for centuries, not hours. The altar beneath me felt too cold, too solid stone forged from something older than stone, humming beneath my spine with residual magic. Of course, I'd wake up half-naked and magic-drunk on a warlock's favourite piece of furniture. Can't even pass out in peace around here.

I tried to move. Pain wasn't the first thing I felt. It was *absence.* A silence where Caspian had been. Where his heartbeat used to echo against mine. The link was still there.....distant now, pulled thin like light refracted through fog, but he was gone. No, *not gone.* Just... waiting. The part of him that had held me steady through the nightmare was retreating, respectfully. So I could face the other one. My eyes fluttered open. The ceiling was black marble veined with silver, and above me, a figure leaned forward—no, not a figure. *Him.* Slate-grey robes. Pale gold eyes. Shadows gathered around his shoulders like willing disciples. He looked like a villain halfway through seducing the heroine—and it was working; damn him I always did love the villains. Maverick.

"You came," I whispered, unsure whether it was memory, dream, or truth. His breath hitched. "I never left." Something in my chest twisted, then released. I sat up slowly, my limbs trembling with the weight of too many selves. Past lives clung to me like smoke. Selene's rage. Adrian's devotion. That girl in the corner with blood in her mouth and fear in her bones. "You saw me," I said quietly. "I *see* you," he corrected, reaching for my face with hands that shook just slightly. "Every piece. Every shadow. Every flame."

I didn't flinch. Not this time. My fingers found the mark on my shoulder blade, Caspian's. Still glowing faintly, still *mine*. I felt around and there was a pulse waiting for another sigil, his sigil. I felt it waiting. Like an invoice from the universe I hadn't agreed to, 'Congratulations! You've unlocked Bond #2: May contain obsessive magic and kneeling warlocks.' Maverick inhaled sharply, then laughed. He felt it too. The bond. "kneeling warlocks' huh" he said. I gasped. "Did you just read my mind".

I rose to my feet, every muscle aching, but it didn't matter. "No gorgeous, you said it out loud" I turned to him, to the warlock who had waited lifetimes, not because he was owed, but because he *chose* to. Over and over.

I closed the distance between us until our breath mingled. Until my lips were close enough to feel the tremble in his. "I remember you," I said softly. "All of you. And still, I choose you." Maverick's hands twitched at his sides. "Say it again." "I *choose* you." I pushed his shirt open and found the mark of the triskillian waiting for activation. He hadn't shown it to me yet, but now that I remember him, all his tells and insecurities. The mark was beautiful. It was dulled and my brows furrowed. "I'm confused, isn't that how you did all your other oaths?" Your mark should be active now, I accepted it and choose you in the dreamscape like the others did."

He smiled up at me. "Yes that is how my oaths normally work with the black wolves. As you can see the mark is clearly not the same as the others, because with you it is the triskilian. The bond will not activate until we are all choosing each other together."

I blinked "So you and Caspian have to fuck as well?" Caspian starts coughing in the corner, I look over to him and he is so red in the face that he looks like he is about to pass out. Maverick laughs big "No, although with your dialated pupils you are more than interested in the idea, we just have to choose to share you." Caspian quietly sniffs the air and he must recognise the arousal in my scent, cause his answers just as fiercely.

Maverick plops himself down in front of me, eyes dazed with wonder. "How does it feel?" I asked. "Like I've finally come home," he said. Then, softer—"You let me in." Of course," I said, grinning. "You do have an excellent track record with doors. Especially ones marked 'do not enter' I murmured, tracing the line of his cheekbone. "But make no mistake, Warlock. The only one who owns me, is me."

His grin curved slow and dangerous. "I wouldn't dare dream otherwise." I turned, the weight of both bond's curling inside me like twin blades. Caspian's restraint. Maverick's surrender. Two halves of a whole. And somewhere beyond this moment, I could feel the prophecy stirring again. I twisted my hands into his hair and pulled him to me, kissing him finally. Maverick gasped into my mouth and I took full advantage bending him where I could take the kiss deeper. His hands found my thighs and picked me up and put me onto his lap straddling him. I moaned and he moaned back before I released him lips and rested my forehead to his. Our breathing laboured with need.

Maverick POV

The kiss was everything I wanted and equally never enough. I wanted to never stop, she felt like salvation. My knees ached, but I didn't rise until she made me and gods help me, if this turns into a habit, I'm going to need better padding. Or at least a dramatic cape to fall back on. Dignity doesn't come cheap. Not because I was hers to command but because I wanted to stay there. At her feet. In the one place I had dreamed of for centuries.

And now I stood, tethered to her not just by memory, but by magic so ancient it made the air around us taste like ozone and honeyed ash. I didn't realise I was shaking until she looked away. When she turned from me, head held high, shoulders squared, the goddess and the weapon both; I felt the bond stretch between us like a drawn bowstring. Ready to snap. Or sing. The Hollow Vein trembled in my blood, as if it too had been waiting for this moment. For the balance to shift. Caspian was moonlight and gentleness. His bond wove like silk around her heart.

But mine? Mine was forged of fire and forged *for her*. Not to soothe. Not to temper. But to *match*. And gods, I had *missed* her. Across lifetimes. Across losses. Across blood and bone. And now..... My knees buckled and I caught myself on the edge of the altar where she had just lain. The stone was still warm from her body. My body ached in places it shouldn't. My magic stirred, raw and chaotic, glyphs crawling over my skin, flickering silver and violet and gold. That's when I felt it. Not just the bond.

Him. Caspian. I swore softly. "Well. Fuck." Not that I minded being part of a cosmic ménage à trois, but someone really should've given us a manual. Or at least a safe word. Guess the wolf's starting to realise he's not the only one with a leash. Mine just comes with better manners and more tongue. The Triskelion. Of course. I'd felt it before, subtly, distantly. But now that her side had accepted me, the third tether surged into place. And it *knew*. It *wanted*. It *demanded* balance. I leaned my head back and stared at the ceiling of the Hollow Vein, muttering, "Couldn't just be a normal warlock, could you? Just had to be all powerful and agree to a deal with the goddess's themselves."

My magic was reacting to Caspian's even from afar. His emotions thrummed along the link, low, smouldering, unwilling. Jealousy, yes. Possessiveness. But also... a reluctant *pull.* He was starting to feel it too. And he hated that. Good. I grinned, slow and sharp, and then promptly winced as the glyph flared hotter than before. "Alright, alright, I'm not gloating. Much."

Chapter Thirty: The Night of Hunger

"Delay is the deadliest form of denial." -British historian C. Northcote Parkinson

Maverick POV

Weeks have passed since Allyssa accepted our bond. The Vein runs as it always does. Contracts negotiated. Secrets traded. Power balanced on knife edges and silk threads. I preside. I listen. I gather. And I watch.

I have learned more about her origins in the last month than in the three years I have been tracking her since she stepped into Veyloris. Threads that should not exist. Reports that contradict themselves. Names scratched from archives.

I have not told her. I tell myself it is strategy. That I am verifying before I disturb her. That she carries enough prophecy without adding ghosts. The truth is uglier. She has been leashing herself. Training. Learning restraint instead of drowning in blood. Navigating the weight of Caspian and I without breaking. And selfishly... I wanted the time we have — those fleeting training sessions where she allows me close — to be about us. Not about another threat. Not about another war forming in the dark.

I know she will be furious when she finds out I kept this from her. She will be right. Tonight is Lilith's celebration. And my hunger is already beginning to sharpen beneath my skin. Desire.

It is always desire for me. It coils low and patient, waiting for the Rite to strip away civility and reveal what the body has known all year.

The problem is simple. I will not take another to bed. Not when I have knelt for her. Not when I have sworn myself. Even if it means defying Lilith. Even if it means pain. And the pain has already begun. Because Allyssa is close. I feel it when she lets her guard down. The way her pulse shifts when I step into her space.

The way her dominance sharpens instead of recoils. She wants me. She just hasn't decided what that means yet. Lilith's night does not allow indecision. I am running out of time to tell her the truth before hunger makes decisions for us.

By noon, the Hollow Vein had already started to thirst. Not for blood, not for bodies, not for coin. For *release*. The building itself knew the calendar better than most of the creatures who crawled through its doors bringing with them the smell of the last cycle of the year. The contracts in the foundation shifted like tendons under stone. Wards sharpened, then softened, then sharpened again. The Vein didn't prepare for Lilith's night the way a venue prepared for celebration.

It prepared the way a throat prepares for a scream. I walked its corridors with my hands in my pockets and my appetite chained behind my ribs. Staff bowed as I passed. Performers paused mid-laughter, suddenly aware they were in the presence of someone who could rewrite their recollections with a word. "Eastern gallery," I told the floor manager without slowing. "Keep it open. No closed rooms until the abstinence bell breaks."

He blinked once. "Even for—"

"Especially for," I said, and he swallowed the rest of the question. Desire on Lilith's night wasn't a suggestion. It was a truth drawn up out of your marrow and paraded through the halls like a confession. Private hungers became public smoke. Public restraint became a joke.

People always assumed the Vein was indulgence. They never understood it was *containment*. Cathbad waited for me at the base of the spiral stairs that overlooked the main floor. He was dressed like he belonged to the forest instead of velvet and vice: black trousers, boots that could cross mud silently, a dark coat with the faint green stitchwork of druidic warding hidden along the seams. His hair was pulled back in a tie that made his face look even sharper, as if time had carved him and then grown bored halfway through.

He watched me approach with that expression he wore when he already knew what I was going to do and hated that he couldn't stop it. "You're leaving," he said. Not a question. I rested my hand on the railing, looking down at the lounge below where the first guests had begun to gather, pretending they were sober enough to be innocent. "I am." Cath's jaw tightened. "On *this* night." "Especially on this night."

He gave a short laugh that didn't contain humour. "You're supposed to host." I could feel it already, the way the Vein's hunger tugged at my skin like a hook. Lilith's Rite wasn't just cultural. It wasn't just tradition. It was magic, and magic had rules. In Veyloris, gods didn't ask.

They *took account*. "I'm leaving you in charge," I said.

Cath stared at me as if I'd offered him a blade and asked him to cut his own throat. "I'm a druid, Maverick. Not your polished warlock staff." "You're the only person in this building who can tell a room full of hungry monsters to sit down and make them believe it was their idea."

His eyes narrowed. "Flattery."

"Accuracy."

He took a step closer. Close enough that if anyone had been watching, they might have mistaken the tension for intimacy. It wasn't. It was older than that. "You're doing this for her," he said quietly. I didn't pretend not to understand. "Cath," I said, mild as moonlight, "I do a great many things for a great many reasons." He leaned in just slightly, voice dropping. "And you'll leave me with your Vein and your contracts and your night of devotion, so you can go play faithful at the Academy?"

Faithful. He said it like a slur. My lips twitched, not with amusement but with recognition. Cathbad had never cared who warmed my bed. Not when it was casual. Not when it was controlled. Not when it was sex and nothing else. But the moment it stopped being entertainment and started being *orientation*...

He noticed. Everyone did. I looked at him then, truly looked. "Keep the rite contained," I said instead of answering. "No blood on the main floor. No coercion. No glamouring the students. If a Tribunal-linked guest so much as breathes wrong, you throw them out." Cath held my gaze like he wanted to say something sharp enough to draw blood from me without touching a weapon. Then he exhaled through his nose and nodded once.

"Fine," he said. "Go." A beat. "And Mazzer," he added, voice rougher now. "If Lilith punishes you for denying your hunger... don't pretend you're too proud to come home." I smiled. Soft. Real. "I'm never too proud," I lied. Cath's expression twisted like he'd heard the lie as clearly as I had. Then he turned away, already moving into command. The Vein accepted him. The contracts flexed and settled. The building didn't love Cathbad, but it respected him. As I left, the hunger inside the Vein pressed against my back like a palm, reluctant to let go.

And the hunger inside *me* answered.

By sunset, the Academy had become something else. The day of abstinence sat on the campus like a held breath. Students moved quieter, sharper. Even laughter sounded careful, as if everyone knew that anything indulgent before nightfall was an insult to Lilith. It wasn't just food and drink they abstained from. It was unnecessary pleasure. No casual kisses. No flirtation for sport. No games. You arrived at the night hollowed out. So, your hunger could echo louder.

Lanterns ringed the courtyard in black-glass globes filled with slow-burning violet flame. The banners hanging from the upper balconies had been changed to deep crimson and ink, their sigils stitched in metallic thread that caught the light like fresh cuts. At the centre stood the Ritual Dais. A circle of dark stone surrounded by shallow channels etched into the ground, designed to carry offerings back into the ley lines.

They called it a celebration. But the shape of it was a mouth. I moved through the edge of the crowd, unnoticed in the way I preferred. Not because I couldn't be seen. Because I chose not to be. My body already knew what night it was. My mouth felt too dry, as if every swallow was rationed. My skin prickled with heat and cold at once, nerves vibrating like they'd been plucked. The chastity beneath my clothes felt like a brand pulled tight, my own magic turned inward like a blade pressed to flesh.

Desire was not a thought. It was an animal. And mine was pacing. Tonight, Lilith would draw out whatever you hungered for most. Not what you wanted to hunger for. Not what you wished looked noble. Your truest appetite. The one you lived your life orbiting. I knew what mine was.

I had known it for years. I just hadn't expected it to become a person. It had never been so specific before, in the past I had taken all manner of naturals to my bed, male, female, both, a handful. Tonight, it was slightly different, that is something I couldn't explain to Cath.

I spotted Allyssa before I saw anyone else. The crowd parted without meaning to. Not from fear, exactly, though fear was present. From something instinctive. The way bodies moved around storms. The way prey moved around apex predators. She stood near the dais with her arms folded, posture deceptively loose, eyes scanning as if she expected an attack at any moment. She despised events. She was dressed in black, of course. Not ceremonial, not delicate. Practical. Dangerous.

A black crop covered her top half and over that was a lattice of leather straps at first they looked decorational and then I snorted to myself as she turned and a blade was sheathed at the centre of her shoulder blades inverted ready for her to drag it down and slice into anyone that tried to get on her nerves. My gaze went down her body, her stomach was bare, a rarity, her tiny silver scars on clear display over taunt muscle and I began to salivate. She was wearing a floor length skirt, never have I seen this woman out in public wearing anything but leather pants. And oh, gods there is a slit that travels up the left leg all the way to her pelvis, all that toned, shapely moon kissed skin waiting for me to run my tongue up. I groaned out loud, I need to look away, but before I do a slight glint of something catches my eye as Allyssa moves and Lilith kill me now, she is holstering three daggers in that slit of fabric tucked against her thigh.

My cock goes hard in an instant at the thought of that blade traveling along my skin while she rides me, nicking my skin so that the blood runs through our bodies and turns everything a slick sensory overload. I avert my gaze and it takes a monumental effort to gain an assemblage of control on my hunger.

I look out at the adornments of the celebration to give me something, anything else to think about. The black night wasn't empty tonight. Lilith's banners and flames painted her in crimson edges, turning her silhouette into something that looked carved from blood and night. Caspian was nearby, white wolf restlessness in fae skin. His gaze tracked her more than the ceremony. The bond between them hummed faintly, a tension line you could pluck. And there, on the edge of the Frostpine delegation, stood a woman, the same one from the bloom celebration. From my sources that includes my own eavesdropping to know the woman's name is Trinity and she is the mate to Caspian's sister Emily.

She was smaller than the Frostpine warriors around her, but she wore her presence the way an experienced wolf wore teeth. No obvious aggression. Just certainty. She stood half a step behind Caspian, close enough to speak privately, far enough to show him respect. She wasn't here for ritual. She was here for *him*. I wonder why she is not with her mate tonight, perhaps her hunger is something else. Perhaps she has ulterior motives as I follow her gaze back to Allyssa. Once my gaze was on her, the world narrowed until she was the only object in focus. I had to bite down physically, jaw tightening, because I wanted to move toward her like gravity.

No one chose their hunger. But Lilith had a sense of humour. Because tonight my hunger was not abstract. It was her mouth. Her hands. Her voice commanding me down to the marrow. And I was denying it. The denial wasn't noble. It was agony. Every breath felt like I was inhaling fire and refusing to exhale. Lilith's bell rang. One deep note that rolled across the Academy like a wave. The abstinence broke. The hunger woke. The crowd shifted as if the entire courtyard had been given permission to become honest. Magic flared, subtle and then less subtle. Pupils dilated. Scents sharpened. People leaned closer to strangers like they were about to drink them.

The dais pulsed with crimson light. And the goddess arrived. Not physically, not wholly. Gods didn't step into the world like mortals did. But Lilith's presence touched the courtyard like a tongue across a wound. Hunger made the air heavier. It made every heartbeat audible if you listened. It made *denial* into pain. I felt it immediately. A twist low in my body that wasn't arousal and wasn't not. A need that wanted to turn into action, and when I refused it, it punished me by tightening. The chastity burned against my cock. My breath hitched. I kept my face composed. Warlock of Secrets. Collector of power. A male who could make kings forget their own names. And tonight, I was a creature with his appetite chained, and the chain was cutting.

Allyssa stepped toward the dais. Of course she did. Where hunger was strongest, she went. Not to indulge. To confront. To control. If that look of determination on her face is anything to go by. The darkness in her shadow pulled closer, curling around her ankles like it wanted to hide under her skin. I need to tell her; tell her about the secrets I have been keeping from her before it's too late.

Lilith's voice didn't echo. It simply appeared, inside the bones. **"Black Wolf."** A hint of amusement in her tone. The crowd went still enough to listen without realizing they were listening. Never has a goddess spoken to one of us. Everyone seemed to be about to loose their collective minds. Allyssa didn't kneel. She didn't bow. She lifted her chin. "I want my hunger bound tonight," she said, voice carrying like steel. A ripple went through the courtyard. No one dared say a word. No one asked Lilith for restraint, less the favour her wrath. People begged for permission to indulge, instead. Lilith's presence pressed closer. **"You do not choose."** A little disappointment cutting through her words. "I'm not asking to choose," Allyssa said. "I'm asking to not... destroy."

Her jaw ticked. Not fear. Frustration. The kind that came from having to speak a need aloud.

Her shadow trembled. The goddess tasted that tremor. **"You hunger for blood my child. Not like that of my Vampire children but the blood of Violence."** Allyssa didn't deny it. She didn't pretend it was anything poetic. "I have attachments," she said, and that single word held more vulnerability than anything I'd heard from her mouth in months. "I won't... hurt them." Lilith's amusement was dark. **"If I bind one hunger, another will take its place."** Allyssa's shoulders squared. "Fine." A pause. Lilith's voice slid like a knife between ribs. **"Then I mark you. And before Autumn's end, you will feed what I hold back."**

The courtyard shivered. Caspian went rigid. I felt the bond tremor between him and Allyssa like a snapped string. His inability to hold back what he is feeling to give her reprieve is infuriating. Allyssa's block on our bond, cracks and a slither of uncertainty make its way down before she clamps the block down again. Allyssa's eyes flashed. "What mark." The goddess answered by touching her. A flare of crimson on Allyssa's throat, just below the jawline, intricate swirls of scarlet streak across her throat, it looked almost like blood splatter. It sank into skin and vanished, only visible when the flames flickered just right.

A promise. A debt. Allyssa didn't flinch. But her shadow curled tight, like it wanted to bite the goddess itself. Oh fuck. I really don't want to fight Lilith, but Allyssa keeps her emotions controlled and Lilith smiled a touch of disappointment in her gaze. Almost as if she was sad to not have a fight on her hands tonight. Lilith's presence eased back, satisfied for now. And suddenly Allyssa's posture changed. Not relaxed. But... different. As if something inside her had been leashed temporarily. She exhaled, slow. Then her gaze swept the courtyard. And landed on me.

The moment she looked at me, her eyes travelling down my body, my magic responded warming through my veins, creating a warmth all over me. My body reacted like it didn't care about chivalry or patience or prophecy. It wanted. And Lilith's night demanded truth. Allyssa's eyes narrowed. Not anger. Calculation. I could feel her probing the bond. She stepped toward me through the crowd like she was moving toward a target. Caspian followed, instantly, a white wolf shadow at her shoulder. Trinity held her position near Frostpine, watching with the kind of stillness that meant she was memorizing every detail to report back.

Trinity's eyes met mine briefly, my warning glare not masked and she stiffened, quickly averted her gaze. Looks like Trinity has some secrets she does not want me knowing, interesting. Allyssa stopped a few feet from me. Close enough that her scent hit like a hit of smoke and frost. Close enough that I could see the faint glow of Lilith's mark under her skin. "What's wrong with you," she said flatly. Not a question. An accusation. I smiled, because if I didn't, I might have groaned. "Hello to you too gorgeous."

Her eyes flicked briefly, as if the humour annoyed her but didn't have the energy to kill it. "You're tense," she said. "You're... fighting something." Caspian's gaze sharpened, reading me like a battlefield. He understood faster than she did. Of course he did. Caspian was hunger with a conscience. He could recognize restraint as suffering. I kept my hands in my pockets. Kept my posture easy. Kept myself from stepping closer. Because if I stepped closer, I wasn't sure I would stop. "Lilith's night isn't polite," I said lightly. "It bites."

Allyssa's eyes narrowed further. "Is it biting you," she said, "or are you biting yourself." Caspian's mouth twitched once. He knew. I didn't answer. That was answer enough. I felt blood trickle from my nose, a clear warning from Lilith, that she does not take kindly to those that deny hunger tonight. I lifted my hand to wipe the blood away. Allyssa's hand whipped out as fast as a snake and stopped me. Stepping closer she wiped the blood over my lips, slowly her eyes fixated on them. As I froze in place, my hunger burning me from the inside, I looked into those eyes and saw them flitting from one colour to another, just like I have seen so many times before now. She was arguing internally with herselves about something. It was obvious she was struggling with something.

I was about to ask her to let me in, to tell me what is happening in there when she pulled herself away from me. Her jaw tightened. "If you want someone else tonight," she said, voice carefully controlled, "take them." The words were level. But the bond tremored. Not jealousy exactly.

Something deeper. Something that sounded like three versions of her all speaking at once, overlapping. One cold and furious. One frightened. One almost... starving.

My laugh came out low, startled, genuinely amused. She blinked like she hadn't expected that reaction. "You think," I said, voice roughening despite myself, "that I would be with anyone else." Allyssa's eyes flashed. "I'm telling you; you can, someone with experience" she said, as if the offer was a challenge. Caspian stepped closer, voice quiet but firm. "Lys." She didn't look at him. Still staring at me, daring me to admit truth.

Caspian's tone shifted, gentler. "He's denying it." Her gaze flicked finally to Caspian. "Why."

Caspian's throat worked. He looked at me, then back to her, and the bond between them tightened. "Because he won't push you," Caspian said simply. "And he won't betray you." Allyssa's breath caught. Just once. Then she masked it. "Betray," she repeated, like the word tasted wrong. My hunger surged so hard my vision went briefly sharp at the edges, like the world wanted to tunnel toward her and nothing else. I had to get the chastity off, I needed....

I inhaled carefully. "You're not ready," I said, voice quieter now. "And I am not going to make Lilith's rites your first time giving me something you'll regret." Allyssa's eyes went dangerously still. "You're being chivalrous," she said. "Don't sound so insulted," I murmured. "Chivalry is a mask," she snapped. "It's what males wear when they want something and don't want to admit they want it. Using it as a lure to those vulnerable enough to believe in fairy tales."

I smiled again, because she wasn't wrong. Caspian made a soft sound beside her. Not laughter. Recognition. Allyssa's gaze cut to him. "Don't." "I didn't say anything." He defended, hands raised and the most innocent look he could muster on his face, he fails miserably at it. "You thought it." He didn't deny it. A smile ghosting his lips. I am definitely going to return the favour of his time with Allyssa, he forgets I have been alive a lot longer and have had more bonds than him. I know how to navigate them, and I know that we are connected through Allyssa, payback is a bitch.

The bond hummed, Allyssa responding to my devious emotions even if she doesn't know exactly what my thoughts are. Allyssa turned back to me. "You're in pain." The words were blunt. Not sympathy. Observation. I didn't answer. Because if I admitted it, it became real in a way I couldn't control. Allyssa tilted her head, eyes scanning my face, my posture, the way my hands stayed in my pockets like I was afraid of what they would do if freed.

Then, slowly, she straightened. Her shoulders rolled back. Her chin lifted. Something in her shifted. Not hunger. Control. Lilith had bound bloodlust, and what rose in its place wasn't softness. It was *authority*. Allyssa's voice dropped, quiet enough that only the bond and our proximity could carry it. "If you take someone else," she said, "I will rip the memory out of you and feed it to a cu-sith." Caspian made a sound that might have been a cough and might have been a laugh.

My hunger flared so violently it felt like laughter could become a groan. Allyssa's eyes burned. There. That truth. That possession. That revolt in her psyche she didn't even name, but I could feel it, layered. One part of her furious at the idea of my hands on anyone else. One part of her terrified she wasn't enough. One part of her quietly, desperately wanting to be in control of what happened next. It wasn't pretty. It was honest. And honesty on Lilith's night was sacred.

I leaned in a fraction, just enough to let her feel how carefully I was holding myself back. "I'm not chivalrous," I admitted softly. "I'm obedient to my own limits. And my limit is you." Allyssa's pupils dilated. Her shadow tightened close, as if it wanted to wrap itself around my throat and pull me down. Caspian watched her closely, something shifting in him too. Not jealousy. Not anger.

Understanding. Perhaps a little aroused, tucking that away for later use. His hunger tonight, I could feel it: not flesh, not blood. Honor.

The need to stand straight in the storm and not break. To be worthy of the role he'd been shoved into. It was burning in him the way my desire burned in me. His jaw flexed like it hurt.

And then he exhaled, slow. "Trinity's here," he said, voice low to Allyssa, like he needed to anchor himself in something practical. "I think Emily sent her, to get me to talk to her." Allyssa's gaze flicked past him toward the Frostpine line. She saw Trinity watching, steady as a blade.

"Good," Allyssa said, surprising all of us. Then, after a beat, quieter: "You should talk to her."

Caspian blinked, as if he hadn't expected permission. She looks at him and rolls her eyes at his dazed expression. "Don't think I have not noticed you have been avoiding her. I assumed things have been strained because of me." Caspian looked like he might argue but she cut him off. "Don't try to insult my intelligence and lie besides, you also need to get into that ring, to feed your hunger. Don't think I haven't noticed your pain in waiting beside me now." She looks over to the circle made from werewolves all seeking the same hunger Caspian is, Honor of battle and to prove themselves worthy in whatever why they need. She gives him a pointed stare and he huffs in acknowledgement.

He looks at me. I nod once. Not because I was in command. Because I understood. If Caspian didn't feed his hunger for honour, it would eat him alive. He needed to do something that belonged to *him*, not prophecy, not bond, not us. He stepped back, reluctant, eyes flicking to Allyssa like leaving her alone with me was a risk. Allyssa's gaze didn't soften. But the bond pulsed. A reassurance. Caspian turned and moved toward Trinity, his posture adjusting as he approached Frostpine's edge, slipping into pack discipline like armour. Allyssa watched him go. Then she looked back at me.

"You're still in pain," she said flatly. The ache in my body was no longer subtle. It had become a pulse behind my eyes, a heat in my spine, a tightness low and brutal that made breathing feel like defiance. Denying hunger on Lilith's night wasn't just discomfort. It was punishment. The goddess didn't tolerate abstinence once the bell broke. "Let it," I said. Allyssa's mouth curved, sharp. "You're insufferable." "Noted." But I could see the gleam in her eye. She stepped closer. Not all the way. Just enough that the heat of her body made my skin react.

Then she spoke, voice low, controlled. "You don't get to suffer quietly and call it noble." My laugh came out rough. "Since when do you care if I suffer, if memory serves correctly and I can guarantee it does beautiful, your fierceness with a whip has given me such delicious suffering along with the near constant edging you put me through." Her eyes flickered. And heated with the memory. For a second, something softer tried to appear. It failed. She replaced it with steel. And a devious smirk.

"Since you became mine, and that suffering isn't of my own making of course" she said, like the statement annoyed her but refused to be denied. My hunger surged so hard my hands curled in my pockets, nails digging into my palms, my toes curled in my boots. Allyssa watched the movement. And in her eyes, I saw the decision forming. Not hunger-driven. Not coerced. Chosen. Control, not compulsion. She inhaled once, steadying herself like someone stepping into a fight. Then she spoke like a dominant issuing a command.

"Come with me," she said. My body reacted before my mind could. A vicious rush of relief that almost dropped me to my knees with gratitude. My chest tightened. I didn't move. Not yet.

Chivalry tried one last time to pretend. “You don’t have to do this,” I said quietly. “Not to save me from a goddess’s tantrum.” Allyssa’s gaze sharpened to a blade. “I’m not saving you,” she said. “I’m taking what I want for myself and my hunger.”

There it was. I felt it like a lock clicking open. My hunger didn’t calm. It *bowed.* Not because it was satisfied. Because it recognized command. And that realization hit me with brutal clarity.

I hadn’t been chivalrous. I’d been afraid. Afraid of pushing. Afraid of wanting too much. Afraid that if I let myself admit how deep this went, it would swallow the last of my restraint.

But restraint was not morality. Restraint was fear wearing a polite face. Allyssa stepped closer again, eyes dark, voice lower. “You’re going to keep your chastity,” she said, and my body jolted at the words, pain spiking in protest. “Until I decide otherwise.”

I swallowed hard. “Yes,” I managed. Her mouth curved, satisfied in a way that wasn’t cruel.

It was *right.* She turned, starting to move toward the darker corridor that led away from the courtyard festivities, away from Lilith’s watching flame. Then she paused, glancing back at me.

“And Maverick,” she said softly, like an afterthought. I stilled. Her gaze slid over my face, almost gentle. “Don’t ever try to make decisions for me again, I decide what I am ready for,” she said.

I smiled to myself, thoroughly entranced and chastised for forgetting it is my darkness that compliments her own, that she is drawn to, and my mind goes completely blank of everything else but following her commands. “Yes, my goddess” I said, and followed.

Allyssa closed the door behind us with deliberate calm. The latch settled into place with a soft, final sound. Not dramatic. Not violent. Certain. The corridor beyond dissolved into muffled celebration. Music. Laughter. The pulse of Lilith's rite carried faintly through stone. Inside the chamber, it was quiet. I didn't even know where she had taken me only that I followed.

I stood where she had left me, hands still in my pockets as if they were the only thing keeping me upright. My breathing was controlled. Too controlled. The chastity was so tight, I'm still surprised I'm standing. Allyssa watched me. Hungrily. Assessing. "You're shaking," she said a smirk playing on her lips.

"I'm containing," I corrected softly. Her eyes darkened. She stepped forward slowly, boots whispering across stone. The space between us tightened with every inch she closed. My magic responded instinctively, silver threading faintly beneath my skin, but I did not move toward her. I was waiting for her command.

She stopped close enough that I could feel the heat of her seep through my clothes. Close enough that my breath ghosted against her forehead. "Look at me," she commanded. I did. No mockery. No flirtation. No cleverness. Just want. Raw. Unhidden. And restraint wrapped tight around it.

"Denying yourself so I don't have to decide isn't noble Maverick." She chastised. My jaw flexed. "I would rather burn," I said, voice roughened by honesty, "than make you choose before you're ready." She reached up. I thought to kiss me. Instead she touched my throat. Lightly. My breath caught.

My hunger flared and the chasity cage around my cock had me griding my teeth in pain reminding me it was still there. But I didn't pull away. "You don't get to decide what I can handle," she said. Her thumb traced slowly along my jaw, down the column of my neck. Testing. Feeling the tension coiled there. My hands remained in my pockets.

"Take them out," she commanded softly. I did. Immediately. My fingers flexed once at my sides, as if reacquainting themselves with air. She circled me then, slow, measured. Like a predator assessing a worthy opponent. Or a queen inspecting a knight before granting favour. I turned only enough to keep her in my sightline. The anticipation was killing me. She was absolutely doing this on purpose and enjoying every second of it. She was so fucking sexy in command.

"You are in pain," she observed.

"Yes."

"You could make it stop."

"Yes."

"With anyone."

His lips curved faintly. "No."

Allyssa stepped closer until there was no space left at all. A satisfied smile on her face. She placed her palm flat against my chest. Over my heart. The bond answered instantly — a low, resonant hum threading between them. Blue and silver intertwined. Not explosive. Not consuming.

Balanced. My eyes fluttered briefly at the contact. "You are not starving," she said. My brow creased. "You are waiting." She leaned in, lips brushing just beside my ear. Not a kiss. Again. A whisper against skin. "You do not get to suffer quietly I want to hear your suffering, Maverick."

The chastity burned hotter, reacting to proximity, to denial, to divine pressure. I inhaled sharply through my teeth. "Then what would you have me do?" I asked. Her smile was slow. Dangerous. "Obey." I shuddered. Not from fear. From relief. Allyssa stepped back just enough to look at me fully. "Strip to your base layer," she said. "Nadu pose. You will take what I allow. And give me every sound of pleasure and pain I demand.

My head dipped instinctively. Not submission born of weakness. Alignment. "Yes, my Goddess." I stripped out of my clothes as fast as I could manage while keeping my composure as best I could. I dropped into the pose and kept my head down awaiting her next command.

She reached for my wrist then, pulling my palm towards her. Her fingers traced the lines there slowly, deliberately, grounding rather than igniting. "Your desire does not control you," she said quietly. "I do." The words settled into me like gravity finding centre. I exhaled. And she stood. Turned around and snapped her fingers in quick succession then pointed down to her boots. The message clear. I was to kiss my way from the bottom of her boots to her ass where her finger had travelled showing me my path.

I obeyed immediately; elation isn't a strong enough word for what I am feeling at submitting to this female. I took my time kissing up her ankle high boot before I reached the skin above them. I kissed up the path she had directed me, every second kiss was infused with my tongue, tasting her skin as I went. Her skin was so smooth and decadent as I continued up her calf to the back of her thigh. The slit in the skirt giving me the perfect space to work.

Her moan was so delicious I could feel it through the bond, and I opened the pathway to Caspian best I could. I could feel his answering need and chuckled internally. Focusing back on the goddess in front of me. A quick turn and tight fingers under my chin as my face was forced upwards had me gasping. Allyssa's eyes were alight with need and arousal, but also humour. "Tsk tsk tsk, did you just open the bond to Caspian? Naughty boy." My answering grin was enough of an answer and when I saw her face shift to calculated smugness, I knew what happened next would-be torture.

Allyssa flicked her fingers and I felt a heavy weight settle down on me keeping me on my knees. She walked away and grabbed a chair from a nearby table I hadn't even noticed and placed it in front of me. What she didn't do however was ask me to close the link to Caspian. I took that as permission to torture Caspian with what we were doing. You know what her breathing came in faster when I acknowledged her accusation. It's turning her on more knowing the link to Capsian is open.

She locked eyes with me and smirked. She reached around and removed the short blade from her back, then took away the leather harness over her crop top. Dropping them in front of me. Realisation dawned and I strained against the chains and weights she had conjured to keep me still. I looked down at them now shaking my head at them knowing I wouldn't be able to touch her now. I was not above begging however so I looked back with the most pleading look I could come up with and begged her "Allyssa please, let me take them off, let me touch you." She just smiled triumphantly and took the thigh dagger holster off her and let it drop with the others.

I struggled against the chains again. My cock straining in it's cage. I stopped struggling resigned and stare at the beautiful creature in front of me as she strips herself. The skirt comes off next, but she leaves the boots on and oh fuck she is wearing a completely lace panties that are soaking wet at her centre. The crop top comes off and gets dropped to the floor but I can't tear my gaze from her glistening tight pussy. I moan out loud and feel myself leaking onto the floor from my cage.

Allyssa takes a seat and I watch her use her still booted left foot to push my cock from left to right in its cage, the pain is white hot intense, and I leak even more for her, all over her boot. She looks at me then using that same boot to lift my chin, so we come face to face and I catch sight of a matching bra and the swell of generous breasts that I want to instantly burry my face into. My cum on the toe of her boot is smeared under my chin as she raises it.

"Look what you just did to my favourite boots Maverick" Disappointment lancing her tone. "Sorry my goddess, I can clean them for you" I quickly add, wanting to please her.

She looked down into my face and sighed. "Next time, I have not finished punishing you for earlier. I want your eyes fixed to my pussy Maverick and you will watch until I let you out of those chains." My eyes darted straight to where she wanted and I waited. She cleared her throat and I groaned. "Yes, my goddess, as you wish." Satisfied she pushed her legs apart and started trailing her fingers down her throat over the top of her breast, over her nipple moaning as she went further down. Over the toned abdomen then to the strip of lace covering my new favourite place in the world.

Her fingers glided slowly across the flimsy material before they slip underneath. She slowly strokes herself but I cant see as she keeps her panties strategically over her fingers. I start panting and pushing at the chains. I need to see her more than I need anything. I was starting to go feral when the sweet sound of her chuckle at my discomfort reached me, I didn't dare look away from where she commanded me. Afraid she would stop. She rubbed circles over her clit and she started to writhe on the chair. My muscles were locking and I could feel myself leaking at an alarming rate, that I swear I was about to cum through my cage just watching her.

She dipped her fingers inside her core and the sounds it made with how wet she was had my orgasm pushing through without my control. I cried out "Oh, fuck, shit". I came on the floor in front of her and I panicked looking up to meet her eyes, eyes that were on the spot where I knew there would be a puddle of my seed.

She took her time meeting my gaze and I thought I would find wrath there waiting for me. And I did but I found something that had me straining hard again in seconds, raw, carnal desire. I swore under my breath at the pain from the cage and her wrist flicked and before I knew it a tendril of my own shadow was stripping the cage from my cock releasing me.

I breathed out a sigh of relief, but before I could settle with that feeling. Claws were at my throat as I was pushed to the floor on my back. Next my underwear was torn off. I still couldn't move my body as Allyssa straddled my face ripped her own panties off and commanded "No more teasing, I'm going to ride your face until I cum and you are going to lick every inch clean. I panted "Yes please my goddess anything you wish." I opened my mouth and used my tongue to spread her open as I sucked her clit into my mouth.

I licked and sucked, nipped and flicked over and over as she rode my face. She tasted like every indulgence and every sin. I could feel her getting closer as her hip bucked and rolled. I flattened my tongue and stiffened it slightly letting her control the pace and where she needed me most. It didn't take long for her to scream my name as she came and I drank her in, licking her through the after shocks and making sure I didn't miss a drop.

I need to be inside her, apparently, she was of the same mindset because in the next instant she had me positioned as she kissed me and lowered herself on my cock. Pleasure pulsed behind my eyes and my hips bucked searching for home. Then she was fully seated and I found home. Deep inside her. The chains that were holding me vanished and she grabbed my hands put them over her ass as she started riding me. I took my time squeezing and helping her keep rhythm as she tore her bra off and started pulling and twisting her nipple moaning. Small wisps of her black hair framed her face, and she looked so devastating that I almost broke rhythm. "Faster Maverick, push harder" I obliged as soon as the words finished forming.

"Yes, that's it your mine" The possessiveness in her tone had me begging. "Please, I'm so close". Desperation at keeping my orgasm at bay was a struggle. Which never in my life has that ever been the case.

She moaned at my plea, basking in my desperation for her. "You will not cum until you feel my pussy squeeze your cock, Maverick." The command in her tone was final, and I gritted my teeth trying to think of anything except how tight her pussy latched onto me. How warm and wet she was for me. How I had never felt anything as good as her in my very long life. Finally, her walls started to quiver, and I reached to roll circles on her clit, that is when she detonated. My shadow had pushed my arse up burying me as deep as possible as she rode through her orgasm. I couldn't move even if I wanted to. My toes strained to points when I called out "Fuck Allyssa baby, yes" as I came so deep inside her, there was no getting me out. Our skin light up with the runes again, all over our bodies, strength, protection, wisdom, then they faded again.

We both collapsed panting still joined, her forehead rested on mine, I stroked her hair from that gorgeous face and kissed her slow and thoroughly. Wanting to memorise this moment. My hunger dissipated magic seeming from the both of us into the floor back to the ley lines. Allyssa steadied herself and started to stand, I let her go watching as her body came into full view. Appreciating every inch of her when I noticed her boots still on. I smiled and looked up at her returning my smile with a shrug.

We got cleaned up and dressed preparing to go find Caspian I could feel her wanting to check on him after allowing him a back seat into the night. I couldn't tell if she was excited or worried about how he was going to react. Now that I could focus on more than just Allyssa I checked internally. Caspian was so turned on and so angry I couldn't wait to see him again. Then reality set in. I still haven't told her about the information I found on her origins. I'm absolutely fucked. She is going to be so angry.

When we returned to the courtyard, the world looked different. Not softer. Not safer. Just... aligned. Caspian stood with Trinity near the Frostpine line, shoulders squared, expression steadier than it had been earlier. Trinity was speaking quietly, her hand resting briefly at his forearm in that pack way that wasn't romance and wasn't not: reassurance through contact, connection through proximity.

Caspian's hunger for honour had been fed, at least enough to keep him from breaking. He took a wet cloth from Trinity to wipe away the dried blood on his face and hands. But I could still see the cost of restraint in the tension of his jaw, the way his eyes kept flicking toward Allyssa like he needed to be sure she was still real. When Allyssa stepped back into view, Lilith's flames caught her throat and lit the goddess's mark like a secret smile.

I watched Caspian see it. Watched him go still. Then his gaze met mine. For a moment, no rivalry lived there. Just understanding. He gave me the smallest nod. Not permission. Acknowledgment. This was what we were now. Not two males fighting over a storm.

Two anchors holding the same sky. Then he glared at me and I knew exactly what that glare was for. The smile that split my face was pure smug satisfaction. Just because we weren't enemies doesn't mean I wouldn't make things entertaining. The music rose. The crowd indulged. Hunger poured into the ley lines like wine into soil. And somewhere far away, in the Hollow Vein, I knew Cathbad was holding the other rite in his hands like a knife he refused to drop.

Tonight was about the truth Lilith had branded into the air: Master hunger, or hunger masters you. And tonight, for the first time, I understood something I hadn't wanted to admit. Allyssa's hunger was not blood. Not really. Blood was just what it looked like when she lost control.

Her truest appetite... was sovereignty. And if Lilith had marked her to reclaim bloodlust by Autumn's end, then this night was not mercy. It was warning. A promise. A deadline. And gods do not mark what they do not intend to test.

I watched Allyssa's shadow shift at her feet, calmer than usual, as if the goddess's temporary binding had given her a sliver of quiet. But quiet never lasted around wolves. And prophecy didn't care about patience. I felt the mark on her throat like a countdown. And I knew, with cold certainty, that whatever debt Lilith had demanded would come due before the year ended. Whether we were ready... or not.

I beckoned Caspian closer and turned to Allyssa. "We really need to talk now, sweetheart." The words came out wrong. Too sharp. Too weighted with the knowledge of what I was about to detonate. She turned toward me, eyes bright with the afterglow of satisfaction, calm and content in a way that made what I carried feel obscene. She raised a brow in question just as Caspian stepped in beside her, his arm sliding naturally around her waist, pressing a kiss to her temple in easy greeting.

I went still. She didn't pull away. She leaned into him. It was subtle. Almost unconscious. But it was trust. And the realization stunned me long enough that I forgot what I was about to say.

Caspian cleared his throat. When I looked at him, he was already watching me with that knowing half-smirk, the bond between them humming with quiet elation. He understood what had just happened too. And he was giving me back what I gave him. Now this could be fun. I turned back to look at Allyssa.

Growth. Without fear. Without recoil. Allyssa's gaze sharpened as my silence stretched too long. "What is it?" she asked. I forced myself to move before the moment slipped. "I need to tell you both something," I said, voice tighter than I intended. "Since we've all fed our hungers tonight... perhaps we could return to the

Hollow Vein. There are a few secrets I've been keeping." It came out too forceful. Too urgent.

The shift in her was immediate. Her body went still. Caspian reacted on instinct, curling closer around her, angling himself slightly between us. Wrong move. The moment he crowded her, the air snapped. Allyssa stepped out of his hold so fast it looked like a strike. Her eyes flooded black. Not shadow. Not wolf. Something layered. Chin raised. Her voice came out lower. Rougher. Threaded with more than one tone beneath it. "What secrets, Maverick?" I flinched.

Not from fear. From recognition. That name coming from her, was so sweet if the tone wasn't tinged with expected betrayal.

I opened my mouth to suggest somewhere private. Somewhere warded. The communication orb in my pocket trilled. Sharp. Urgent. Emergency. I pulled it free. Cath had triggered the silent alarm. I looked up at them both. "There's been a breach at the Vein," I said. "I have to go."

I swallowed what I'd been about to confess. "I'll come to you after. We'll finish this. I'm sorry for keeping things from you. But you deserve to know."

I was already gathering magic to portal when her hand clamped around my arm.

I almost argued. Cath would not have triggered the alarm unless it was serious. He was important to me. He— "We're coming," Allyssa said. No hesitation. No debate. Whatever fury had been building was gone. Replaced with something colder. Focused. Caspian didn't argue either. He was already moving. There was no time left to negotiate. I tore open a portal to Draethen. And stepped through.

Chapter Thirty-One: Ruptures and Refuge

"What lies behind us and what lies before us are tiny matters compared to what lies within us." — Ralph Waldo Emerson

Allyssa POV

The portal tore open with a scream of warped air. We stepped into chaos. The Hollow Vein was no longer a cathedral of velvet shadows and whispered contracts. It was a wound. Obsidian pillars were cracked down their cores, glowing fissures bleeding dull red light. Smoke rolled thick and greasy along the ceiling, laced with crushed rosemary, burnt bone, and iron-heavy blood.

Cath was mid-roar when we arrived. Not a dignified druid chant. A battlefield bellow.

He had shifted partially — bark crawling over his forearms, veins lit moss-green beneath skin. A cultist hung impaled on a spear of living wood that had erupted from the floor through his spine. Cath twisted his wrist and the wood splintered outward, shredding the body like a broken puppet.

To the left, three druids moved in formation, chanting in low, guttural cadence. The ground beneath their boots liquefied into root and stone. Vines burst upward, ensnaring robed figures whose masks cracked as they struggled. But the Severed Flame had come prepared. These weren't frantic zealots. They were layered.

The first wave wore bone-threaded armour, ritual knives etched with mirrored runes designed to reflect shadow magic back at its source. The second wave — thinner, pale, eyes rimmed in kohl — whispered synchronised incantations that hummed like flies around an open wound. And at the centre—

Caspian. The glyph ignited beneath him with a sound like a heart splitting. Crimson lines spiralled upward around his legs before he could step clear. He snarled, Royal Seelie healing magic from his palms as he slammed it into the sigil. It didn't shatter. It constricted. The bond between us screamed. Not pain. Violation. Caspian's pulse spiked — a thunderclap inside my skull. They weren't binding muscle. They were threading into his heartbeat.

Maverick was already moving. He didn't charge. He cut. Silver sigils flicked from his fingers in precise, surgical arcs as he muttered spells faster than anyone I have ever seen. A cultist lunged at Cath's blind side — Maverick snapped his wrist and the man froze mid-stride, memories unraveling behind his eyes. He collapsed sobbing, unable to remember why he'd raised his blade.

"Anchor formation!" Maverick barked. "They're binding to his pulse!" Laya stepped into view from behind a fractured pillar, robes untouched by the carnage. Her eyes found mine. "Step back," she said calmly. "Or we remove him piece by piece." Caspian tried to step out of the circle. It tightened. His breath hitched violently — ribs constricting. I felt it. Every strain. Every forced inhale. He was trying not to panic for my sake. That made something ancient and feral in me sit up.

A blade came at Maverick's neck. Cath intercepted, bark-arm catching steel. He twisted, ripped the cultist's arm free at the shoulder with a wet crack. Blood hit the obsidian like spilled wine. "Don't touch the circle!" Maverick barked at me without looking.

The monster stirred. Not shadow. Instinct. They are touching what is ours my wolf growled pushing to shift. The first cultist rushed me; blade aimed for my throat. I didn't reach for magic. I reached for steel. Muscle memory taking over. My hand found the dagger at my thigh before thought caught up. I stepped into his swing instead of away from it, letting the blade glance past my shoulder, then drove my dagger up beneath his ribs.

He gasped. I twisted. Hot blood coated my hand. I let him fall. My monster sang. I could feel Lilith's mark pulsating at my neck absorbing the blood spray. The smile I had on my face was pure terrible joy. This is our dance my commander responded.

Two more came from opposite sides. I drew the second dagger. Close quarters. Fast. The monster leaned forward inside me — not possession, not frenzy. Permission. I moved low, slicing hamstring before either could complete their incantation. One screamed as he fell; I ended it cleanly with my claws through his throat. A dark chuckle tore out of me, unrecognisable and entirely mine.

The other tried to grapple me. I drove my knee into his sternum and shoved him backward into a druid's waiting spear. Using my wolf's strength, I grabbed his head and twisted until my combined strength with the spear ripped the natural in half. The Vein rang with steel against stone. I saw it — a shallow cut across his ribs, silk darkening. I snarled so low and vicious that even the druids gave me space. He ignored the wound. That only fed the monster more.

He was severing ritual threads mid-air, dismantling spellwork before it could fully form.

Cath fought like the earth had decided to devour trespassers. He grabbed a cultist by the mask and slammed his skull into the obsidian floor hard enough to crack both. Caspian forced his magic into the heart-bind again, trying to break it's hold. The crimson lines flared brighter in retaliation.

I moved like this was choreography I'd practiced since birth. Through the bond, Caspian's fear began to bleed through. Not fear of death. Fear of me. It wasn't screaming terror. It was the visceral recognition of what I looked like in that moment. Cold. Efficient. Unhesitating. Calculating. He had not seen me without the brakes. And I felt the moment it hit him—

She doesn't even hesitate. It wasn't condemnation. It was awe edged in something darker.

And beneath that— A flicker of terror. The monster heard it. It did not retreat. It moved faster. Laya wasn't fighting. She watched

Caspian watching me. And she smiled. I could feel the precision of the spell — surgical, deliberate. They weren't killing him. They were preparing to take him.

I could break it. Not delicately. Not cleanly. If I ripped the entire foundation apart, it would tear him free. It would also shatter half the Vein. The commander calculated collateral. The sovereign calculated contingencies. Collateral acceptable. The monster approved.

Another cultist lunged at Maverick. I moved without thinking. Short sword from my back. The steel sang as it cleared the sheath. I intercepted the strike meant for his spine and drove my blade through the attacker's chest. The impact jarred up my arm. I didn't hesitate I twisted as I ripped the sword free — her heart came with it. I plucked it off the blade and kicked it across the floor toward Laya. Then I pivoted into the next threat.

Bodies were falling faster now. But so were druids. A masked female hurled a vial that exploded into black ash, poisoning one of Cath's men. He died gasping, clawing at his own throat. A ritualist began reinforcing the circle around Caspian with a thread of blood drawn from his own palm. I crossed the distance in three strides and severed his wrist before the blood could complete the pattern.

He screamed. The monster approved. I could feel Caspian watching me again. Not just fighting. Watching. Through the bond, Caspian felt it all. Not just the kills. The enjoyment. The way I crossed from necessary violence into something sharper. Sport. Ownership. The way I stepped through male and female alike as if they were obstacles, not Naturals.

He had seen the commander. He had not seen this. This— This was colder. I drove my sword down through a fallen cultist's sternum without breaking eye contact with the next attacker. And through the bond— Another flash of fear. She would destroy everything for me. And that terrifies him. The monster stilled. The child inside me shrank. Of course. Of course he's afraid.

Fuck it. I sheathed one dagger, gripped my sword in both hands, and brought it down on the sigil itself. Steel met blood-etched light. The chamber detonated. The circle shattered in a violent spray of red sparks. The backlash threw me backward a step, but I held.

Caspian staggered free, breath tearing into his lungs. Silence fell in violent chunks. The Severed Flame lay broken around us. Laya stood alone across the wreckage, a thin line of blood at her temple where debris had grazed her. She watched me. "You see?" she murmured softly. "This is what you are." She dissolved into a warlock portal before I could reach her. Coward.

The Vein groaned. My sword dripped. I turned to Caspian. His chest was heaving. Hands trembling. Eyes on me. And through the bond— It hit me. Not disgust. Not rejection. But he was shaken. Deeply. Because he had felt it. How easily I stepped into brutality. How cleanly I chose annihilation. He swallowed. "I said I could handle you," he said quietly. No accusation. But there was distance now. A half-step he hadn't meant to take. A flicker of uncertainty before he crushed it.

His guilt followed immediately. I didn't mean it like that. I'm not afraid of you. But he was. A little. And that was enough. The child went very still. The monster went rigid. The sovereign hardened. Too much. You are too much. "You're better off without me," I said. Flat. Certain.

"Lys—"

But I was already stepping back. Not shadow. Not power. Instinct. I took one last look at Maverick. He was crouched beside one of his druids, silver light threading through his fingers as he conjured medical supplies for a torn flank. His movements were precise. Efficient. Focused entirely on stabilizing the Vein.

His block was up on our bond. Thick. Controlled. Deliberate. Not distance. Discipline. He had raised it the moment we stepped through the portal — to keep emotion from flooding the connection, to keep Caspian's panic from bleeding into me, to keep my own fury from destabilizing him mid-cast.

He would not add to my mental load. He trusted me to handle myself. He always had. As if he felt the shift in me — the retreat — his head snapped up. Not to me. To Caspian. His eyes swept the scene in a single, sharp calculation: the broken circle, the tremor in the Vein, the silence after carnage. Then his gaze locked onto mine. And he lowered the block.

The bond slammed open. Not rejection. Not doubt. Anger. Sharp. Focused. Controlled fury. Not at me. At Caspian. At the emotional bleed he hadn't contained. At the way I had felt it. At the fracture forming in real time. I felt Maverick piece it together in an instant — the recoil, my reaction, the decision crystallizing behind my eyes.

His anger spiked. *You let her feel that.* It was directed at Caspian. But in my vulnerable, splintered state— It landed wrong. It felt like condemnation. His eyes widened for half a heartbeat as he understood what I was about to do. *Allyssa—*

I gave him a weak smile. An apology without words. The Veil tore open behind me like fabric ripped by unseen hands. Cold air rushed through. And I stepped into it.

Cold swallowed me whole. Not wind. Not air. Absence. The Veil is not a tunnel. It is a tearing. A thinning between places where reality forgets its shape. My body didn't move through it — it *unravelled* and reassembled in pulses. My stomach lurched. My ears rang. For a split second I was nowhere — suspended between dominions, between selves.

Then gravity remembered me. My boots hit cracked stone. The world slammed back into place. Ireland. Mortal realm My original home. Or is it my second now? I've been in Veyloris almost four years. Four. I forgot my birthday. Twenty-one. The thought landed strangely. Hollow. Irrelevant. The air here tasted different. Damp. Salt-heavy. Real in a way Veyloris never is. No hum of ley lines. No pulse beneath the ground. Just wind through hedges and the distant cry of gulls somewhere beyond the grey horizon.

I stood at the end of a narrow lane I hadn't walked in almost a year. I had purpose for going back into that house last time. Green paint peeling from the house ahead. Rust blooming around the hinges. The same sag in the roofline. My childhood home. My breath shortened immediately. Not because of magic. Because of memory.

The house didn't glow. It didn't thrum with dark energy. It looked small. Pathetic. Ordinary.

And that made it worse. This was where silence saved lives. Where floorboards creaked warnings. Where closets were safer than beds. Where I learned how to fracture to save myself.

I took a step forward. My hands were shaking. Not the tremor of battle adrenaline. The tremor of a seven-year-old bracing. The monster inside me didn't surge. It didn't snarl. It simply watched. You wanted normal. Here it is.

I approached the front door slowly. The paint was chipped around the handle where fists had once struck it. I could still see the faint dent in the lower panel — where Fionn had kicked when I lashed out at him for following me home. I wouldn't tell him. Wouldn't tell any of them. I refused to let them see what lived here. I lifted my hand to the handle. It hovered there. The wood was so close I could see splinters beneath the varnish.

Just open it. Just walk in. Prove it doesn't own you. My lungs tightened. The air thickened. Suddenly I was too big for my own body. Too aware of every scar beneath my skin. Too aware of what I had just done in the Vein. The blood. The efficiency. The look in Caspian's eyes. You stepped over them like obstacles. You smiled. I swallowed hard. Maybe he was right to hesitate. Maybe I am something that doesn't fit inside love.

My fingers curled against the door. Push. I couldn't. My wrist locked. My chest constricted. The house didn't need magic to defeat me. It only needed memory. Tears blurred my vision. You killed a room full of trained cultists without blinking. And you can't open a wooden door. Pathetic.

The child inside me stirred. Small. Ashamed. I wanted to tear the house apart. Burn it. Rip it from the earth. Instead, I stepped back. The gravel crunched beneath my heel. My throat burned. I came here to prove I wasn't broken. All I proved was that I still am. My knees buckled. Not from injury. From collapse. I dropped onto the cold step, breath hitching, forehead pressing to my fists. Loosing the battle on this panic attack.

The monster didn't mock me. It didn't disappear either. It stood behind me like a shadow cast by something larger. You survived this place. But survival is not healing. The wind picked up. The sky darkened. The edges of the world flickered. Not because I summoned it. Because something inside me finally stopped fighting for control. The fracture widened. Not violent. Not explosive. A quiet surrender. The ground beneath my palms felt less solid.

The air shimmered. My glyphs flickered faintly across my skin — not in attack. In instability. I had held too much for too long. Caspian's fear. Maverick's anger. My own self-loathing. The monster. The sovereign. The child. They were no longer arguing. They were overlapping. And the overlap was tearing me open. The alleyway blurred. The house warped. The edges of Ireland dissolved into something bone-white and silver-veined. The world tilted. Cracked. Split. And I fell inward.

Stone met my knees. Not dirt. Not bone-white forest. Stone. Cold. Circular. Echoing. When I lifted my head, I was no longer in Ireland. I stood in a round chamber carved from black basalt veined with silver light. The ceiling arched high above like the inside of a cathedral ribcage. No doors. No windows. Just five thrones spaced evenly along the curved wall. Five.

The chamber breathed. Not hostile. Waiting. The first throne was small. Not ornate. Not carved. Just stone softened by time. A child sat there, knees drawn up, bare feet dusty, hair tangled around a face too young for the things it had seen. Eyes a dull blue hue. She looked at me.

"You left me."

The words did not echo. They settled. The second throne was taller, sharp-edged. The Commander sat straight-backed, dark coat immaculate, eyes sharp green calculating even here. Hands folded. Observing. "You had to leave," she said calmly. "Survival required distance."

The third throne was darker, wrought in shadowed iron that pulsed faintly. The Monster leaned forward in it, elbows on knees, eyes blacked and feral. "She didn't leave," the Monster snarled. "I stayed. I stayed and took it. I bit it back. I swallowed it whole."

The fourth throne gleamed. Silver filigree, black velvet, thorns curling up its spine. The Sovereign reclined there, posture effortless, expression amused and distant. Eyes a bright silver. "All of you speak as if survival was the goal," she murmured. "Survival is the floor. Rule is the ceiling."

And then—

The fifth space was not a throne. It was stone worn smooth. My Wolf sat there. Massive. Midnight black fur just as glimmering as my hair. Watching. Turquoise eyes bright with her strength moved between them. Waiting.

I pushed myself to standing. "I didn't leave you," I said to the child, but the words felt weak. "You did," she whispered. "You got big. You got scary. You stopped crying." The Monster growled low. "Crying gets you killed." The Commander's jaw tightened. "Emotional expression without leverage is inefficient." The Sovereign tilted her head. "Pain is useful. Weakness is optional."

The Wolf's tail thumped once against stone. A warning. The child's lip trembled. "I needed someone to fight for me." Silence. The Monster stood. "I fought," she snapped. "I tore throats. I sharpened us. I made sure no one ever touched us again."

The Commander rose as well. "You acted without discipline. Excess creates collateral. Collateral creates vulnerability."

The Monster turned on her. "You would have calculated while he—"

"Enough."

The word didn't come from any of them. It came from me. The chamber vibrated. The Sovereign's gaze sharpened. Interesting. I stepped toward the child. "I didn't leave you," I said again, softer. "I became what you needed."

"You became what I was afraid of," she whispered. That landed. The Monster went still. The Commander's posture shifted. Even the Sovereign's expression cooled. The Wolf rose to her full height. She padded forward, enormous paws silent on stone. She stopped between the child and the Monster.

She did not growl. She simply looked at the Monster. The Monster's shoulders lowered a fraction. "I protected her," she muttered. "You did," I said. The Monster blinked. Raw. Uncertain. The Commander exhaled slowly. "And I ensured we never depended on anyone again."

"You did," I said to her too. The Sovereign's smile faded into something sharper. "And I reminded you that you are not prey."

"I know."

I turned to her fully. "You think small," the Sovereign said to the Commander. The Commander's chin lifted. "I think in achievable outcomes."

"You think in rooms," the Sovereign replied coolly. "I think in kingdoms."

The Wolf growled softly. Truth bending toward pride. The Sovereign stilled. "Yes," she admitted quietly. "Pride is my flaw."

The chamber shifted. The child slid off her throne and stepped into the centre. "You left me," she said again. And this time it broke something open. I knelt in front of her. "I'm sorry," I whispered. The Monster stiffened. The Commander frowned. The Sovereign watched, unreadable.

"You were seven," I told the child. "You were not supposed to fight. You were not supposed to win. You were supposed to survive." Tears spilled down her cheeks.

"I couldn't stop him."

"I know."

I took her small hands in mine. "And it was never your job." The Monster stepped closer.

"I would have killed him." The child looked at her—not afraid. "I know."

The Commander moved too. "We learned."

The Sovereign descended from her throne, black velvet trailing. "We became inevitable."

The Wolf pressed her head gently against the child's shoulder. And the child straightened. Not because she grew. Because she understood. "You're not so scary," she said softly to me. "You're strong."

The Monster inhaled sharply. The Commander looked away. The Sovereign's lips curved faintly. The chamber's silver veins began to glow brighter. I stood. "I am not fractured," I said, voice steady. "I am layered."

The Monster stepped to my left. The Commander to my right. The Sovereign behind me. The Wolf in front. The child moved last. She placed her hand over my heart. "I forgive you," she whispered. "And I forgave you".

The thrones began to dissolve. Not shattering. Merging. Stone liquefied into light. The Monster's shadow folded into my spine. The Commander's sharp angles settled into my posture. The Sovereign's crown did not rest on my head. It fused into my bones. The child stepped forward and simply— Walked into me.

Warmth spread through my chest. The Wolf's eyes held mine one last time. Then she, too, stepped forward. Not disappearing. Becoming breath. The chamber did not collapse. It remained. Empty thrones. Council complete. Harmony, not silence. Their voices did not vanish. They aligned. And for the first time in my life— There was no argument in my skull. Only consensus.

I inhaled. When I exhaled, the dreamscape began to thin. Not because I was falling. Because I was ready.

Chapter Thirty-Two: The Watcher in the Mist

"We do not break the rules to save them. We break the rules because they deserve to be saved." — Unknown Watcher

Indigo POV

The mist was thicker tonight. Mist was not magic to me. It was birthright. Born Shadowfen, my very blood carried the *Umbrasil Veil* a hereditary shroud woven from the marshes of Shadefen, where light bent away and shadows moved like instinct. Only Shadowfen could summon that living mist, a trait the Tribunal coveted and weaponised. Veilwalker.

It curled around me now, soft as breath and cold as oath-water, allowing me to slip unseen through any dominion of Veyloris and through dozens of realms surrounding ours. Not because the Tribunal had taught us to vanish — but because our people had always been ghosts long before the Tribunal learned to name them.

I stood motionless staring at her from the side of the sad looking human house, cloaked in dusk and enchantment. My body blended with the shadows, my deep blue-black skin aiding me, keeping the pulse of my bioluminescence under control, my breath a whisper against the veil of silence.

My fingers twitched at my sides. Not from fear. But from the deep, bone-hewn tension of hesitation. I had seen many things through the veil of the Watcher's scrying pool. Assassinations. Lovers torn apart. Magic too ancient to name unleashed in bursts of cataclysmic hunger. I had never intervened. Not once. Not until now. And yet... here she was. Out in the open, alone, and vibrating with barely-contained wild power.

The bond mark were bright and restless. Not sealed. Not complete. Two bonds rooted, the third pattern only beginning to *move* The faded glyphs pulsed erratically unreadable to most, but not to me. I had studied her so long they were etched into my mind like sacred runes. Calyxion, the City of Glass, would have demanded I watch from afar. In that city's mirrored halls, mercy was considered a flaw, not a virtue..

I clenched my jaw. *No one at the Tribunal predicted this would happen so soon.* Let alone that the prophecy's fulcrum would *choose* her. I should walk away. Should turn and let fate do as it willed. That was the law. The Tribunal's First Principle: *A Watcher does not touch or intervene. They only record rise or ruin.*

And yet... I moved. A single step toward her. Then another. My boots clicked softly on stone, magic cushioning the sound, but she didn't stir. My breath caught, and the memory came: A tribunal courtyard. Stone columns. A lectern of bone. "You will observe, not guide. Watch, not warn," intoned Instructor Thaelan. His robes were blue that day, the colour of detachment. I had memorised the way his voice carved through the crowd, cool and clean like an executioner's blade.

"If the subject falls, they fall. If they rise, they rise. We are not gods. We are archivists of fate."

That had been my first lesson. And his last warning. Complete bullshit. None of us understood what they were buying with our oaths. They promised independence from unstable kings. What they delivered was servitude to evil with better manners.

And still my hand hovered above her the training and years under the Tribunal given more power over me than I realised. She twitched, murmured something. A name? A plea? I couldn't tell. The glyphs on her wrist flared bright for half a second, reacting to the bond.

Another memory followed, unbidden: A room lit by blue flame. Scrying pool reflections rippling. Allyssa at twelve, holding a broken stick like a blade. A foster father screaming in the distance.

She didn't cry. Didn't flinch. Just gritted her teeth and whispered something that made his heart ache, even through the mirror:

"You'll never break me."

I had watched that scene a dozen times.

"I should not be here," I murmured. Her cheek pressed against her arm. Her mouth moved again. This time I heard it clearly. "...I forgive you..." I exhaled. For a horrifying half-second, I thought she meant me. Then I felt it. The forgiveness wasn't for a Watcher. It was for a little girl who'd been left behind inside her own ribs. Then broke the Code. I scooped her into my arms, effortlessly light despite the power pulsing under her skin. Her head lolled against my shoulder.

I expected her magic to lash out, the way most Black Wolves did when unconscious. Instead, the glyphs beneath her skin flickered in patterns only recorded in Tribunal prophecy vaults. My cloaking spells shifted, hiding both of us beneath layered mist and illusion. A warlock couldn't have traced them now if they tried. I closed my eyes and summoned the mist. "Back to the batcave."

The first thing that unsettled me was not the integration. It was the mist. When I lifted her from the house porch, the Veil had not responded to me alone. It had responded to her. "That's impossible," I told myself. "And yet," I replied, because I am nothing if not annoyingly consistent. The Umbrasil Veil is not learned. It is inherited. Shadowfen blood carries it like marrow.

And yet when she tore through dominion boundaries, the mist curled around her like an old friend greeting someone who had simply been gone too long. Not clumsy. Not accidental. Instinctive. I stopped pacing. "Well," I muttered to the ancient tree roots threading through the bunker ceiling, "that is deeply inconvenient."

The roots did not respond. They rarely do, though I remain hopeful about future conversational developments. I resumed pacing. Shadowfen blood does not wander. It does not dilute easily. Entire political alliances have collapsed over less than the possibility of that lineage resurfacing unexpectedly. And yet—

She had summoned my birthright like breath. I clasped my hands behind my back and studied her sleeping form. "Somewhere," I said thoughtfully, "someone made a very dramatic romantic decision." Pause. "Possibly several." The roots creaked faintly. "I know," I said back, offended. "Romance is not dead. It's just... excessively theatrical."

But the mist was only the beginning. Because then I felt the second change. When I first began observing Allyssa years ago, her aura had resembled a storm system colliding with a battlefield. Violence. Trauma. Instinct. Restraint. Everything competing for dominance. It was fascinating. Dangerous. Messy. Now?

It was structured. Layered. Ordered. Not smaller. Just... aligned. The shadow beneath her skin no longer flared unpredictably. It waited. Patient. Controlled. Royal. Ah. There it is. I crouched beside the cot, studying the subtle dark currents threading through her magic. I wonder which Royal you belong to.

"It was never just an unseelie political play," I murmured.

That had always been the Tribunal's mistake. They saw the potential for more power wielded by their own hands. They catalogued the rage. They ignored the possibility of her being chosen by the black wolf spirit. Classic oversight. It happens frequently when powerful institutions believe they understand prophecy better than prophecy understands them.

There were other manifestations beneath the shadow too. Not active. Not yet. But present. Bloodlines stacked upon bloodlines.

Shadowfen. Unseelie. Fae. Wolf. And something else. Something buried deeper. I leaned slightly closer. "...interesting."

Then I felt it. The well. I have stood near ancient magi whose reservoirs felt like deep lakes.

I have watched warlocks whose power hummed like lightning trying very hard to behave. This was neither. This felt— Infinite. Not explosive. Not unstable. Just... vast. Like standing at the edge of an ocean that had no shoreline. I reached out with the smallest thread of perception. It did not hit bottom. It did not echo back. It simply continued. I withdrew immediately.

"Ah," I said. Silence stretched. "Well." I stood again and began pacing, because pacing is an excellent coping mechanism when reality begins bending in politically inconvenient ways.

"With great power comes great—" I stopped. "Responsibility." Pause. "No. Wait." I frowned. "Destruction?" Another pause. "I should really write these things down."

The roots creaked again. "Don't be so judgy" I retorted. "That particular realm produces an alarming number of philosophical statements from individuals wearing brightly coloured costumes," I continued to tell the roots defensively. "It is hard to keep track, okay."

I glanced back at Allyssa. Still asleep. Still terrifyingly stable. "Regardless," I concluded, clasping my hands behind my back again, "the message appears to be that immense power creates... complications." I tilted my head slightly. "Although in this case the complication may be the entire Tribunal." The roots creaked louder this time. "Yes," I nodded. "I agree. We rebel"

Then I looked back at the Black Wolf. Shadowfen mist. Unseelie crown. Wolf instinct. Unknown bloodlines layered beneath it all. And a magical reservoir that appeared to have no discernible limit. "Well," I sighed quietly. "That explains several things." I paused. "No." Another pause. "That explains absolutely nothing." I say exasperated.

A Tribunal briefing room. Indigo assigned Subject #37. Codename: The Black Wolf.

"She is not to be pitied. Do not anthropomorphise her. Do not look for empathy. Watch the bond. Record the divergence. That is all." I had nodded. Sworn the Oath. But the first time I saw her truly saw her was not through orders. It was through a crack in her mask . Allyssa, age twenty after a fight, sitting under a broken tree. Caspian asleep beside her. Blood on her knuckles. She whispered to herself, eyes cast to the stars: *"What if the only way to survive is to become the thing that broke you?"*

I hadn't reported that memory. I should have. But something in me knew that truth wasn't for the Tribunal. It was for her. And now here I was, violating every principle I'd been raised to obey. Because she'd said *I forgive you.* Because I'd *seen her.*

Back to the Present she stirred again. Her glyphs flared. Her hand twitched, searching the air like she could feel the bond even here. I reached toward her just to steady her fingers. And she gripped my hand. Eyes flew open. Black and silver. Steady and assessing. "You," she rasped. I didn't let go. "You're not supposed to—" she started to say. "I know." I interrupted. She blinked. Confusion warred with exhaustion. "You're one of them." She said as she stared into my eyes like she could see right into my soul. "Yes." I breathed out, totally transfixed by her eyes. "So why...?" she asked. I hesitated.

And for the first time, told the truth. "Because I think they're wrong about you." She stared. And something in the bunker shifted. Not magic. Hope. Mine. For she could be the end of our servitude.

Chapter Thirty-Three: The Cost of the Flame

"A flame that burns across lifetimes will always leave ash behind" – Unknown Author

Maverick POV

The Veil closed behind her. One second the Shadowfen mist tore the air apart. The next— Nothing. Silence rushed in like a vacuum. Allyssa was gone. My beautiful goddess left believing the lies she had been told since she was a child. For half a heartbeat the entire battlefield froze.

Then the Hollow Vein erupted again. Vampire mercenaries shrieked from the lower arches. Druids barked commands as roots slammed upward through the stone floor. Warlock fire split the cavern in jagged arcs of violet and white.

But all I could see was the place where she had vanished. Mist. Shadowfen mist. Not wild. Not accidental. Instinctive. The Veil had answered her like she belonged to it. Caspian staggered beside me. "She—"

"I saw it," I snapped. My voice came out sharper than the warlock blades clashing against my shields. "She veilwalked." Caspian stared at the empty air where the tear in reality had sealed. "The mist," he whispered. "Yes," I growled. "The mist." Because that wasn't supposed to be possible. Shadowfen mist answered blood. Only blood.

Which meant somewhere buried beneath the chaos of Allyssa's lineage was another secret the Tribunal hadn't catalogued. I let out a short, incredulous laugh as I blasted a vampire off the cavern wall. "Unseelie royalty." A second vampire exploded under a hex. "Black Wolf." A third crumpled beneath a druid spear. "And now Shadowfen blood apparently." I shook my head.

"She is always going to surprise us." Another vampire lunged. I snapped its neck with one word and a flick of arcane force. "And gods help me," I muttered darkly, "I love her even more for it." Caspian didn't respond. He was staring at the Vein floor like something had hollowed him out.

And suddenly my patience snapped. "You idiot." His head jerked up. "What?"

"You pushed her." The accusation came out like a blade. I was so close to pinning him a making sure his nose never healed properly again.

"You recoiled from her."

"I did not—"

"You flinched," I cut him off. My wards slammed another cultist back. "She felt it through the bond." Caspian's face went pale. "I—"

"Congratulations," I said coldly.

"You just convinced the most powerful female in at least three realms that she's exactly the monster she has been told she will become, you just destroyed the progress we have been doing for the last year."

Another explosion rocked the chamber. Caspian didn't respond. Because he knew. Then the air shifted. Wrong. Magic twisted across the eastern archway. Another portal. My head snapped toward the disturbance. "Oh for—"

The second wave arrived. Give me a break. Warlocks spilled through the arch in coordinated formation. More vampire mercenaries followed. Behind them walked Laya. Her midnight robes flowed around her like ink spreading through water. Her eyes locked onto Caspian. And something inside my chest went very still.

"Take the White Wolf alive," she ordered calmly. The warlocks moved instantly. Caspian lifted his blade. "Oh that's just fantastic,"

I muttered. The battle exploded. Warlock fire slammed against my shields. Vampires crashed into the druid perimeter. Caspian fought beside me, blade flashing silver through the chaos.

But something was wrong. I felt it in the rhythm of the fight. Too controlled. Too deliberate. The warlocks weren't pressing forward. They were adjusting. Circling. Guiding. Herding. My eyes flicked across the battlefield. Druids pushed one direction. Vampires forced the other. And Caspian—

Caspian was being pushed toward the centre of the cavern. Toward a ring of warlocks already weaving a spell. Teleportation. Not a portal. "Oh you sneaky little—"

"Caspian!"

He turned just as the spell circle ignited beneath his boots. Six cultists stood around him, their hands raised in synchronized casting. I saw the binding sigils forming. I saw Laya watching. And I understood the plan. They wanted the White Wolf. Not the warlock. Not the druids. Him. "Druids!" I roared. Root-vines erupted from the Vein floor, coiling around Caspian's arms and chest.

"Maverick—!"

"Hold him!"

The druids tightened the bindings instantly. Caspian struggled. "What are you doing?!"

Saving your dumb arse so you can get our goddess back. I thought bitterly. The teleport circle flared brighter. Caspian's eyes widened as the realization hit. "Maverick—"

The bond exploded. Pain ripped through my chest like lightning. Allyssa. My love. Both of us felt it. Her panic. Her grief. Her mind collapsing inward. Caspian gasped.

"She's falling—"

"I know."

And just before the spell completed—

I stepped forward. Caspian saw it. His eyes went wide. Both he and Cath yelled at the same moment. "No!"

Too late. I stepped into the circle. The cultists' magic snapped around me like iron chains. Caspian roared behind the druid vines. "MAVERICK!"

I met his gaze as the teleport spell ignited. "Find her," I said quietly. His breathing hitched. "Fix the bond." The magic surged. The Hollow Vein vanished. And darkness swallowed me.

Caspian POV

The Hollow Vein had gone quiet. Not peaceful. Just... empty. Smoke drifted through the broken arches. The last of Maverick's spellfire still crackled along the stone walls, fading slowly like embers refusing to die.

I stood in the centre of it. The bond pulsed weakly beneath my ribs. Allyssa. Distant. Somewhere far beyond the Vein's reach. And Maverick... Cold. Not dead. Just gone. But Laya's face pushed into the darkness behind them. Her voice. *Take the White Wolf alive.* I should have seen it. All the signs had been there. The way she lingered in the training halls. The way her gaze tracked me like I was a prize she believed she deserved. The bitterness when Allyssa entered the room.

I had dismissed it. Told myself it was rivalry. Competition. Something that could be reasoned with. Everyone deserved a chance at mercy. That was what I believed. Still believed. My stomach twisted. Because that belief had just cost Maverick his freedom. Maybe more. I knelt slowly, pressing my palm against the Vein floor. "Find her," Maverick had said.

I closed my eyes. The bond stretched outward. Searching. But the connection slid through my mind like water through open fingers. Too far. Too fractured. Too incomplete. I exhaled sharply. "Come on," I muttered. "Come on, Allyssa..."

A heavy boot scraped across stone behind me. I turned about to lunge at the new threat. Cath stood across the chamber. At least that is what the other druids called him. Blood streaked down one side of the druid's face. His armour was cracked, his breathing heavy, but his eyes burned with something far hotter than exhaustion.

Fury. Two other druids stood behind him. Watching. Judging. Cath walked forward slowly. "You're the White Wolf," he said flatly. I straightened. "Yes." Cath studied me for a long moment. Then he punched me in the face. My eyes teared up at the unexpected assault. The blow landed like a falling tree. I staggered backward, barely catching myself before hitting the stone floor. "What the—"

"You arrogant little shit," Cath snapped. The druids behind him didn't move. Didn't intervene. Which told me everything I needed to know. Cath stepped forward again. "Mazzer just got himself taken by a cult because you couldn't keep your emotions under control long enough to not destroy the bond between you and the Black Wolf." I wiped blood from my lip.

"I didn't—"

"You flinched," Cath cut me off. "You recoiled from her." The words hit harder than the punch. Cath's jaw tightened. "I don't particularly like the female," he continued bluntly. "She's dangerous. Unpredictable. And half the time I'm fairly certain she'd burn this entire club down if someone looked at her wrong." I said nothing. Cath's voice dropped. "But tonight?"

He gestured toward the battlefield around them. "She was magnificent." The words carried grudging respect. "And you," Cath continued, eyes narrowing, "managed to make her think she was the monster she's always feared becoming." I looked down, feeling the gravity of what I had done. The bond flickered painfully in my chest, the reminder clear. "I know," I said quietly.

Cath blinked. The anger didn't disappear. But it shifted. "You know?"

"I felt it." My voice came out rough. "The moment she broke." Silence stretched between them. Cath studied him again. Then he exhaled slowly. "Well," he muttered. "That's inconvenient." I lifted my head. Hope kindling that Cath might know a way to track her down. Maybe even get to the mortal realm, I think that is where she would have gone in her state of mind.

"We need to find her." Cath snorted. "Yes, obviously." Then he gestured vaguely at the Vein. "Problem is, the Black Wolf just veilwalked across realms." I froze. This is the sort of information if leaked could be a death sentence for Allyssa. "You saw that?"

"Hard not to notice when someone tears a hole through reality using Shadowfen mist." Cath rubbed his jaw thoughtfully. "Still not sure how that works, by the way."

A voice spoke from the shadows. "Neither am I." Everyone turned. Mist rolled quietly through the broken archway. It moved wrong. Too deliberate. Too alive. Then the mist parted. And a tall figure stepped forward. Blue-black skin. Bioluminescent shadowfen markings glowing faintly beneath the shadows.

Silver eyes studying them with unsettling calm. Cath blinked. "Right," he said slowly. "And who in all dominions are you supposed to be?" The stranger clasped his hands behind his back. "I was hoping we could postpone introductions," he said mildly. "But since you asked..."

His gaze shifted to me. "You're looking for Allyssa." It wasn't a question. I stepped forward. "Where is she?" The male tilted his head. "In my bunker." Cath blinked again. "You kidnapped the Black Wolf?" He looked like he might actually feel sorry for this male. The stranger looked mildly offended. "I rescued her." Cath pointed at him and scoffed. "That sounds suspiciously like kidnapping."

The male sighed. "Yes, well. Your species tends to struggle with nuance." I stepped forward again. "Take us to her." The stranger studied him. Then nodded once. "Yes." He gestured toward the mist gathering behind him. "You should come quickly." His expression shifted slightly. Because somewhere far beyond the Vein... something had just changed. "And preferably," he added dryly, "before she wakes up again."

Chapter Thirty-Four: The Depths of Consequence

"Every myth begins with a wound too deep to name. And some wounds learn to whisper back." — Scrolls of the Hollow Vein, Fragment VIII

Maverick POV

They didn't bother with doors.

The earth opened stone turning wet and yielding, like flesh parting for a blade and the Severed Flame dragged me through. The tunnels were carved through the Broken Spine, once Dryad homeland before greed wars gutted it. The Severed Flame had claimed these ruins as sanctum, weaving their grief into bone-altars and salt-circles that defied every map of Veyloris. This was not just a hideout. It was a wound. The Hollow Vein's chaos vanished above, its final echoes swallowed by dirt and darkness.

Roots scraped my shoulders. Cold earth pressed against my ribs. I tasted iron and the faint sweetness of death-magic. But none of it mattered. Because halfway down, the bond flared.

Not gently. Not as a whisper. A rupture. Allyssa's agony tore through my ribs like lightning catching bone, and the gag caught the sound I tried to make. Her fear. Her shame. Her old wounds tearing open. The feel of her falling inward into the dreamscape.

Not there, I thought, helpless as the stone throat swallowed me deeper. *Not alone.* My body shuddered once, violently. Caspian better do as he is told. I swear I will chain him up and edge him to within an inch of his life if he doesn't fix this. Then gravity spat us out. The cavern was enormous, carved like a cathedral by hands that worshipped grief. Milky pillars rose like rib bones. Salt-veins glowed through white stone like trapped starlight. Faces were carved in the walls children, soldiers, elders all frozen in screams, as if trying to warn me.

Toys littered an altar beside torches of blue flame: A wooden wolf. A scorched ribbon. A child's bracelet. Loss was layered in every stone. Cultists surrounded me witches with hollow expressions, fae with ash-caked skin, dryads with bark-scorched scars, warlocks with hatred held together by ritual ink. Each one had the same look in their eyes. Grief sharpened into faith.

"The Warlock of Secrets," someone whispered.

My title spread like a contagion. I was hauled to the centre of a ritual circle carved from ash, bone-thread, and iron. Chains snapped around my wrists, hoisting them above my head. My ankles locked apart. A collar sealed around my throat.

Then....... the audience parted. The ember-robed priestess stepped through. Ash-streaked lips.

Eyes blackened by old magic. Scars from feral bites held tight along her jaw. "Let him speak," she murmured when someone moved to gag me again. "We have waited centuries to hear what the Wolf-Keeper sounds like when he hangs." "And here I thought you just missed me," I rasped. A few cultists nearly smiled. Most didn't.

Instead of beginning the rituals immediately, the priestess pulled a chain. Stone groaned. A mural unfurled from the ceiling. The Wolves. Not as I remembered them. As the Severed Flame remembered them.

The First Wolf, drenched in the blood of rebels. The Second cleansing a grove with soulfire. The Third tearing a tribunal apart. The Fourth kneeling alone in a circle of her own magic. And the Fifth Allyssa drawn in dark charcoal, incomplete, surrounded by spirals of unfinished prophecy. And beside each Wolf.........me.

My face rendered again and again. Always kneeling. Always watching. Always their shadow. It hit harder than any ritual could. The priestess turned to me, expression soft with violence. "You see it now?" "I see your propaganda needs a better editor." The slap cracked my head sideways. The ritual circle flared. "Begin," she said. And the poisoning started.

RITUAL I — THE REVERSAL VEIL

A high fae approached older than she looked, glyphs spiraled in ash across her veins. Her palm pressed to the bond mark that had started to transform. My entire body went still. "You carved this in devotion," she murmured. "We will turn it into absence." Cold magic pierced the mark.

Her magic brushed mine for a heartbeat—cold moonfire braided with wolf-instinct. And beneath that instinct, I felt it again: the faint, impossible echo of royal Unseelie blood, the kind that once bent shadows into obedience. The shadowfen mist. Something more but I can't place it. No Black Wolf had ever carried so many lineages. No realm should have allowed it. Yet she did. For one breathless heartbeat.....I felt Allyssa's hand. Her claim. Her warmth. Her whisper of my name Maverick half a threat, half a vow. Then the bond inverted. And silence filled its place like a grave. I didn't cry out. My jaw locked. But tears burned behind my eyes, traitorous. The fae tilted her head. "She still lives. It will hurt more this way." She wasn't wrong.

RITUAL II — THE BLOOD ECHO

A male with antler-glyph tattoos stepped forward. Without looking at me, he slit the inside of my elbow and poured black ichor into my blood Ichor distilled from the marrow of Naturals who died cursing Wolves. It slid into me cold and intimate, dragging memories behind it like thorns.

A child crying under a collapsed roof. A woman begging her son to live. A man whispering, *Let me haunt him.* Each memory hit like a lash. The ichor wrapped around my heart. "This is mercy," he said. "You need to work on your bedside manner." He didn't smile.

RITUAL III — THE REFLECTION SHARD

The Echo Shard wasn't just a mirror. It was a graveyard with a surface. The priest held it up, chanting. Light flickered. Then...Adrian. His ash-streaked smile. His shake of the head before battle. His last breath curling frost-white. Except the shard twisted it showed him slaughtering the White Wolf, showed children burning behind him.

"That's not what happened," I growled. The shard shimmered. Then the Fourth Wolf. Her screams replayed. Her suffering warped. Then..... Allyssa. Wrong. Her glyphs black. Her laughter broken glass. Caspian kneeling beneath her heel, dying.

"Do you think she loves you?" the priest whispered. "She will be worse than any Wolf you've ever served." My ribs tightened. "She is *not* them," I hissed. "She will be." The shard pressed to my sternum. Pain tore through me, white-hot, fractured. Then darkness swallowed the world.

When consciousness returned, there was no sound except my own heartbeat and the ghosts. My Wolves whispered in the dark again. "You always knew it would end like this," Adrian sighed. "You love power more than people," the Fourth murmured. "You think devotion is redemption," Selene laughed. I clenched my jaw hard enough to bleed. "You are old lies," I whispered. "Not truth." They didn't stop.

The ichor turned my veins into funeral bells. My wrists bled down my arms. My throat tasted of rust. My lungs trembled with every breath. Allyssa was distant. Muted. Silent. I had never been so terrified of quiet.

Footsteps. Soft. Uneven. A youngling barely sixteen appeared, carrying a bowl of salted water trembling in his hands. He stared at me as if I were a ghost that could bite. "It's to... to keep your lips from cracking," he whispered. "The shard burns... sometimes."

"How thoughtful," I rasped. "Your hospitality is impeccable." He flushed with shame and fear both. He dabbed water on my mouth carefully. His hand shook. A drop landed on my chest hissing against the inverted glyph. "How old were you?" I asked softly. His throat bobbed.

"Nine." He looked away. "My sister. She burned when the Wolf came."

"That wasn't my lifetime, the black wolf had not even re-surfaced at that point" I said. "I am many things. A liar is not one." His eyes glistened. "That doesn't matter," he whispered. "The elders know and someone must pay." "Maybe," I said. "But killing me won't resurrect her." He flinched. "Why did you save him?" he asked suddenly. "The White Wolf." Caspian.

Because I love him too, I realized. I went to edging instead of killing him for hurting our bonded. I don't love him the way I love Allyssa. But something just as dangerous. "Because he is hers," I said. "And that makes him mine." The youngling fled.

Footsteps thundered from the upper balconies dozens of them. A crowd formed. A storm gathering. The ember-robed priestess returned, flanked by two leaders: A warrior-priest with paint streaked down her jaw. A Rootborn male with sap-scarred cheekbones, the youngling hid behind a pillar again.

"You told us you'd kill him quickly," the warrior hissed. "We are not torturers. We do not become what the Wolves were."

"We become what we must," the priestess snapped. The chamber erupted in whispers. "We cannot follow a zealot," the warrior spat. "You want the Black Wolf not justice."

A gasp rippled. The Rootborn raised his voice. "The children are confused. The novices ask why we prolong his death. Some want him dead. Some want him alive." "He is the key," the priestess hissed. "To what?" the warrior demanded. "Revenge? A myth? Her?" Silence. The accusation hung like a blade. "I invoke the Council," the Rootborn said. "A vote tonight. On whether he lives or dies."

Shouts erupted. Robes swirled. Arguments clashed like blades. The priestess leaned close to me. "You've infected us," she whispered. "I'm very contagious," I murmured smirking. She stormed off.

As the factions divided, voices drifted across the sanctum. "the White Wolf's bonded male, Caspian", "a threat", "too soft", "no, too loyal", "kill him first". My blood chilled. "He is not her weakness," someone argued. "He is her anchor." "That is *worse*," another snapped.

"He steadies her. He tempers her. He gives her humanity."

"If we kill him," a third voice whispered, "she will come feral." The Rootborn growled, "Touch the male and the Wolf will burn the sky." "And if we let him live?" a female hissed. "He will come for the Warlock. They both will." A long silence.

Then the priestess's voice cut through the chamber like a blade: "We kill the White Wolf." My blood went to ice. If I could have torn free right then, I would have ripped the sanctum apart stone by stone. But the coil held. And for the first time, true panic hit me. *Caspian. Allyssa. Gods,* I bit my tongue until blood filled my mouth. "You touch him," I whispered to no one and everyone, "and no one will be able to save you." The walls did not answer. But the magic shuddered.

When the chamber finally emptied, the silence pressed in like a tomb. The ichor burned. The Coil throbbed. My arms shook with the strain. Then..... Under all the poison and absence....her mark within the bond mark pulsed. Quiet. Small. But alive. My breath hitched. She was still there.

I raised my head, blood dripping from my jaw, and whispered into the dark: "I will not let them use me against you. I will not forget you. I will not stop choosing you." A beat of silence. Then.....

so faint I almost imagined it..... the silence whispered back. And the myth began.

Chapter Thirty-Five: The Spark That Wakes the Storm

"To watch is to witness without changing. But love... love changes everything."

—The Watcher's Codex, Rule #1

Indigo POV

The mist shifted with every breath I took.

My people had walked unseen between realms long before the Tribunal learned how to weaponize silence. That was why Watchers were Shadowfen. Only our blood could carry the Veil without losing ourselves inside it.

Which made the female lying in my sanctuary... deeply concerning. Her blood was wrong. Royal Unseelie. Shadowfen. That union had been forbidden since the first shadow wielder.

She did not twitch. Did not stir. Did not breath in a satisfying, reassuring way that living bodies usually did. Allyssa lay on the carved tree cot like a fallen statue, and the worst part was: statues sometimes moved more than she currently did. I studied her face. Still. Pale. Lips cracked. Fingers twitching only when the bond mark sparked.

Not ideal. Definitely concerning. Potentially catastrophic. "Fantastic," I muttered to the empty room. "She's either becoming a god or she's dead-adjacent. Those are the only two settings she seems to come with." The silence didn't disagree.

I paced once....twice.....hands behind my back. The bunker hummed in the way places only hum when they're holding a miracle or a disaster. I wasn't yet sure which she would choose to be. I had watched her slip into this state. Watched her fall inward. Watched the dreamscape swallow her whole like a creature expecting a meal.

I couldn't follow her. Couldn't help her. So I *waited.* Because that is what Watchers do. Technically.....*Usually.* "'I'll be back,'" I quoted under my breath. "Yes, thank you, Terminator. That would be helpful." I sighed into the empty room. A Watcher does not touch the flame. They only record its rise or ruin. Right. Except apparently I now carried flames around like lost kittens.

The scrying crystal pulsed and my stomach tightened. The crystal attuned to Caspian flickered violently, his aura spiking like someone had lit a match inside his ribs. "Oh good," I said flatly. "He's having a breakdown...... Again."

The image finally came into view. Cathbad punching Caspian in the jaw. The crack made me wince in sympathy, but also "take that! Float like a butterfly, sting like a bee". I really like that human movie. The scrap of roots against the stone was loud and I took that as a cheer on for Cathbad.

"Fine," I told no one. "Go to him. Break protocol. Again. Why not. The Code is really more of a... suggestion." The mist parted as I opened the veil. And I stepped out to meet the wolf who had no idea how to stop loving someone even if it killed him.

The Hollow Vein still smelled like smoke and broken magic. Caspian stood in the centre of it, breathing like a male who had forgotten how lungs worked. The druid beside him, Cath, looked marginally more stable, though the way his eyes tracked every shadow suggested he was expecting the cavern itself to attack.

Reasonable. Tonight, had been very dramatic. I folded my hands behind my back and regarded them both. "You're looking for Allyssa," I said. Caspian's head snapped up. "Yes."

Cath didn't speak. He simply watched me the way soldiers watch unfamiliar weapons. Suspicious. Evaluating. Possibly planning to break it. Good instincts. Sound like a good time. "Convenient," I said mildly. "Because I happen to know where she is." Caspian took a step toward me. "Where." Not a question. A demand.

I gestured toward the Shadowfen mist gathering behind me. "In my bunker." Cath blinked once. "You kidnapped the Black Wolf?" That is just offensive or perhaps it's flattery. Kidnapping someone so powerful makes me like a ninja doesn't it. I smiled to myself. "I rescued her." I said honestly. "That sounds suspiciously like kidnapping." He retorts.

I considered that. "Yes," I admitted. "Your species does struggle with nuance." Caspian was already moving. "Take us." The mist parted. The Veil opened. Shadowfen magic curled around the stone like living fog. Cath stared at it. "That stuff safe?"

I scoffed at him "No," I said. Then I stepped into it. They followed anyway. Which was encouraging. Or deeply concerning. Hard to say.

The bunker reassembled around us as the Veil closed. Stone. Wards. Shadowfen mist clinging to the ceiling like patient ghosts. Caspian barely noticed. The moment the room resolved he saw her. Allyssa lay on the tree carved cot exactly where I had left her. Still. Silent. Very inconveniently unconscious. Caspian crossed the room in three strides and dropped beside her.

Cath stopped halfway, arms folding across his chest as he assessed the chamber. "Interesting hideout," he muttered. "Thank you," I beamed. I was very proud of the bunker, I made all the furniture myself, from all my favourite movies from the mortal realm.

"Several people have tried to kill me here. I consider that a strong architectural endorsement." I said. He huffed something that might have been a laugh. But Caspian didn't hear any of it. "Allyssa." His hand trembled as it touched her cheek. "I don't know if that is a great idea actually". For a moment nothing happened. Then the bond shifted. And everything went very wrong.

Caspian POV

Indigo led me through the twisting roots as if he were guiding a condemned man to the last place he would ever kneel. Part of me wondered if he was. The bunker smelled like old stone and secrets, and the air thrummed with the kind of magic that made my wolf pace restlessly beneath my skin.

Indigo walked like he belonged in this place. I walked like I was trespassing in my own life. His cloak rustled softly as he glanced at me over his shoulder. "Try not to touch anything," he said. "Some of these sigils bite."

...Was that a joke? I couldn't tell. His tone never changed. I muttered, "You're a very strange male." He didn't deny it. "Yes. I've noticed." Then we entered the chamber. And I forgot he existed. Allyssa. My wolf howled her name before my mouth could. She lay so still the world felt wrong around her. Too quiet. Too cold. Too fragile.

"Allyssa." My voice came out quieter than I meant it to. Her skin was colder than I expected when my fingers brushed her cheek. Not lifeless. Not dead. Just... distant. Like the warmth inside her had retreated somewhere far beyond the reach of my hands.

The bond between us pulsed faintly beneath my ribs. Frayed. Uneven. Incomplete. Behind me I could hear Indigo moving quietly around the chamber, muttering to himself in that unsettlingly calm tone of his. Cath said nothing at all. The druid stood near the entrance of the bunker with his arms folded, watching everything like a soldier standing guard over a battlefield he didn't quite trust.

But none of it mattered. All I could see was her. "You're still here," I whispered. My thumb brushed the edge of her knuckles. The bond stirred. Not gently. Something deeper answered. For a heartbeat the world went silent. Then pain detonated through the bond. Not mine. Maverick.

The sensation tore through my chest like a blade being driven between my ribs. Agony, sharp and immediate, laced with something darker—ritual magic, restraint, the cold echo of chains. My breath seized. Behind me Indigo went very still. "Oh, that's not good" he said softly.

Allyssa's body convulsed. Her back arched violently off the obsidian cot as power erupted from her like a storm breaking open the sky. The bunker detonated. Darkness burst across the floor like liquid night. Wards screamed as raw magic slammed into the stone walls hard enough to crack the outer sigils.

Cath swore sharply. "Fuck" he covered his head out of instinct. Indigo stepped back with impressive calm for someone who had just narrowly avoided being vaporised. "...Right," he murmured. " stronger protection glyphs next time".

Allyssa's eyes snapped open. Black, with a silver ring around her iris. The turquoise shinning through as her eyes moved around. Not wild. Not feral. Controlled. The darkness in her gaze swallowed the light of the chamber as if it belonged there. For the first time since I'd met her, my wolf didn't surge forward. He dropped low inside my chest. Watching. Recognizing something older than instinct. Something that had nothing to do with fear and everything to do with hierarchy.

Cath broke the silence first. "...Well," he muttered slowly. "That's new." Allyssa inhaled once. The movement was small. Deliberate. The storm in the bunker settled immediately, like a battlefield going silent the moment its commander stepped onto the field.

Her gaze moved across the room. First Indigo. He inclined his head slightly, studying her like an astronomer who had just discovered a new star and wasn't entirely sure whether it might explode. Then Cath. The druid's posture stiffened. For several seconds they simply looked at one another. Allyssa raised just one eyebrow at him. Cath's expression didn't change. But the careful way he shifted his stance told me everything.

He no longer saw her as unstable. He saw her as dangerous. Finally her eyes settled on me. The bond between us tightened. Heavy. Complicated. "You came," she said. Her voice was quiet. Calm. Completely unlike the Allyssa who had collapsed into the dreamscape hours ago. "Of course I came," I said. Her gaze held mine for a long moment.

"I know." The silence stretched between us. I swallowed. "Allyssa—"

"I understand why you reacted the way you did." The words stopped me. Cath's eyebrows rose slightly. Indigo muttered something under his breath that sounded suspiciously like *this should be interesting.*

"I was afraid," I admitted.

"Yes."

Her expression didn't soften.

"You saw a monster."

My chest tightened.

"I saw someone I care about losing control."

"You saw someone you care about become something you couldn't control. You thought I would change. That I would eventually see things your way."

The distinction landed like a knife sliding between my ribs. She sat up slowly. Every movement was precise. Measured. Power hummed quietly around her like a predator breathing. "I did what was necessary," she said.

"You would have arrested them, that is your line in the sand." I didn't answer. Because she was right. "Yes," I said finally. "I would have."

"I killed them." No apology. No hesitation. "I protected what was mine." Behind me Cath exhaled slowly. "Well," he muttered.

"Hard to argue with efficiency." Indigo tilted his head. "From a purely observational standpoint," he added thoughtfully, "most people would find that statement mildly alarming."

Neither of us looked at him. Allyssa's gaze never left mine, but there was a slight upward twitch in her lips. "Understanding your reaction," she continued calmly, "does not mean I forgive it." The words were quiet. But they struck harder than anything she could have done with magic. "I know," I said.

The bond between us pulsed again. Different this time. Not anger. Not rejection. Just distance. And something else. Something deeper. Pain flickered across her expression. For the first time since she woke. Her head tilted slightly. Listening. The bond flared. Maverick.

The agony rolling through it was impossible to miss now. Her eyes darkened. The black taking away the other colours before returning to what they had been. The silver coming through just a little more. Cold. Focused. "They've taken him." Cath straightened instantly. "Where?"

Allyssa swung her legs off the cot and stood. The room seemed to adjust around her without her even noticing. Not because she demanded it. Because the world understood what she was now. Sovereign. A Queen. "The Severed Flame," she said. Her voice carried absolute certainty.

Indigo blinked slowly. "Well," he murmured. "That's inconvenient. We don't know where they hide. Only that they are somewhere in the ashes of The Grove, I don't know if you know this, but that place is huge and dense and most of their structures are underground."

Cath cracked his knuckles. "Maverick's going to be extremely annoyed if we take too long getting him back." Allyssa's gaze moved toward the far wall of the bunker. Toward where the Grove would be, if direction meant anything in a place like this.

There was no hesitation in her posture now. No doubt. No fear. "We're going to get him back. Whatever it takes, no one takes what is mine. I just wished that we had completed the bond so I could use it to fine him."

She turned toward the door. The decision was already made. Behind her Indigo sighed quietly. "...I really should start charging for nights like this." Cath glanced at him. "You funny or just weird?" Indigo considered that. "Both," he said, nodding along with his words.

I didn't move. I was still watching Allyssa. Because the female standing in front of us wasn't the same one who had fallen into the dreamscape. The monster was still there. I could see it in her eyes. But it wasn't loose. It wasn't feral. Wasn't even trying to take over. It was patient. Controlled.

And somehow that was far more terrifying. Indigo watched her too. "...Well," he murmured quietly. "And now the storm wakes."

Indigo POV

When Allyssa's eyes snapped open, black void spilling from iris to sclera, a perfect silver ring circled the darkness. I took one involuntary half-step back. That wasn't only Wolf. The silver ring was the colour of Umbrakyn royalty. Shadowfen knew that hue. It belonged to bloodlines who once commanded obedience from shadows themselves.

"Well," I muttered. "That's... not ideal." Cath's horrified whisper echoed beside me. "Oh fuck." I nodded along thoughtfully. "Accurate summary." The air detonated. Power slammed into the bunker walls hard enough to set every ward screaming. Darkness sheeted across the floor. I stumbled back, cloak snapping violently as a blast of raw magic tore through the space I had been standing in a split second earlier.

The stone wall behind me exploded. Roots charred. Sigils cracked. A smoking crater yawned where my torso had almost been. I stared at it for a long, quiet moment. Then, in the driest voice imaginable, I muttered, "...Right. Noted. Don't stand there again."

Another surge of power tore across the ceiling. Dust rained down. I brushed a pebble from my shoulder and sighed. "'You can't handle the truth,'" I added under my breath. "Apparently the Wolf can."

Caspian didn't hear me. Or pretended not to. He was too busy reaching for her. Brave, reckless idiot that he was. I took another cautious step backward, raising my hands in a gesture of calm surrender directed entirely at the universe. "Excellent," I murmured to myself, eyes flicking between the void in Allyssa's gaze and the cracking wards overhead.

"She's awake. She's terrifying. And apparently capable of spontaneous structural demolition." A spark ricocheted off the wall beside me. I did not flinch. "I am in hell," I whispered politely. Then, quieter. Almost fond. "...She really is magnificent, though."

Her aura exploded outward, shadow tendrils crawling across the stone as if they were searching and cataloguing on her behalf. Power slammed against the wards so violently they sparked, hissed, and began debating early retirement.

"This is fine," I muttered. "This is absolutely fine."

"'I've seen things you people wouldn't believe.'"

Blade Runner. Appropriate. Her feet lifted from the stone for a fraction of a second before she settled again. The bunker trembled. Caspian stepped toward her like a male voluntarily walking into the jaws of a dragon and daring it to love him back. Brave. Stupid. Predictable. "And this," I murmured quietly to myself, "is why I don't date."

Cathbad turned his head slowly and stared at me as if I had finally lost what remained of my mind. Apparently he had been listening. When Allyssa rose, when Maverick's pain ripped through the bond like prophecy, when the void inside her screamed— I braced against the wall and whispered. "And now the storm wakes."

Power cracked through the bunker again. I began weaving counter-wards automatically. "'We're gonna need a bigger boat,'" I muttered. Because apparently quoting Jaws was the only thing keeping me sane. Then the storm stopped. Allyssa drew the chaos back into herself with terrifying precision, coiling her power like a blade sliding back into its sheath.

Fascinating. I had never seen an Unseelie royal control that much shadow. Most of them simply drowned in it. "Thank the gods," I whispered, "she didn't vaporise us." Caspian shot me a glare over her shoulder. I raised both hands innocently. "What? I'm being supportive." He looked unconvinced. I summoned the mist. "Come on," I said, opening the Veil again. "Let's go rescue the Warlock of Secrets before she decides to level the continent."

Maverick POV

Pain had shape. Not the kind the body understands cuts, burns, broken bone, but the kind carved directly into the soul. The kind that rewrites the edges of a man. The Severed Flame wanted to unmake me. Ritual poison crawled through my veins like icebound insects. My wrists throbbed against the cultweave restraints. My heartbeat stuttered, wrong, a fractured rhythm echoing off the bone-chamber walls. I hung there, suspended in shadow and salt-light, feeling myself pulled apart one memory at a time.

Until; The bond hit. Not a thread. Not a whisper. A detonation. Raw power slammed into me so violently my body arched against the chains. Magic sparked from my fingertips, burning through the ichor-stained air. A sound left me somewhere between a sob and a gasp.

Allyssa.

She was awake. Not waking. Not rising. Awake. Her power not fractured anymore and potent. And gods... her rage. It tore through the flickering triad bond like wildfire finding dry grass. It seared down my spine, flooded my ribs, sank claws into every part of me the cult hadn't broken yet. I felt her power pour outward like a night-howl across the realms. Cold. Black. Beautiful. Inevitable. A predator unchained. A goddess remembering her teeth. I feel my body tighten desire somehow runs through me reaching for our regal monster.

For a moment, I couldn't breathe. Then, I laughed. At first, it was soft a broken exhale, a sound scraped raw by pain. But it grew. Deepened. Twisted into something hysterical and wild. I threw my head back and laughed. The priest nearest me froze. The acolytes stepped back. Even the ritual flames guttered. Because through the bond, through the agony, through the haze of poison, I felt her move.

Death. Not metaphorical. Not poetic. A tidal wave of absolute, merciless, bone-splitting death rolling out from wherever she stood and all of it aimed in one direction. Toward me. Toward them. Toward anyone who had dared put a hand on her Mate. "Oh," I whispered, voice shaking with amusement and delirium and devotion, "you poor, stupid bastards."

I lifted my head, blood running from my temple, eyes burning through the haze. "She's coming." I sing-song. The cult members hissed, recoiling like I'd spoken a curse. I smiled, cracked, ruined, ecstatic. "You hurt me," I murmured, letting the laughter bubble up again, unstoppable. "You touched what's hers. You *took* me."

I leaned forward as far as the chains allowed, voice dropping to a reverent whisper: "And now you have more to fear than just her Black Wolf, the queen is awake." The bond thrummed, violent and holy. Her darkness brushed my consciousness a promise, a vow, a roar, I shivered in response the desire for her flaring again.

My laughter broke again, ragged, breathless, impossible to contain. "You don't understand," I choked out between hysterical gasps. "You didn't steal a hostage." My vision blurred. Ritual ichor burned through my veins. But gods, I had never felt so alive. "You just declared war on her sovereignty." The chamber trembled.

My chained and bleeding body was barely clinging to consciousness, but I grinned like a male already saved. "She's coming," I whispered, letting the truth steady what the rituals tried to unravel. And this time, my voice wasn't laughter. It was prophecy. "She will kill you all."

Chapter Thirty-Six: Threading the Inferno

"The fire that burns within her could unmake empires. And I am the fool who would gladly stand in its path, just to feel the heat."

— Unknown Seelie Love Letter, sealed and unsent

Caspian POV

The Hollow Vein had been turned into a war room. That alone should have terrified me. Usually the cavern hummed with pleasure, reckless wagers between naturals, and the low roar of magical experiments with sex that occasionally set someone's sleeves on fire.

Tonight it was quiet. Too quiet. Indigo had claimed the central table and transformed it into something that looked suspiciously like a battlefield map.

Runes hovered above the stone surface, weaving together threads of light into a projection of the western forests. Ley-lines glowed faintly beneath the terrain like veins beneath skin. And at the centre of the projection—

The Grove. Cath leaned over the table, arms folded, eyes scanning the illusion with the steady patience of a male that has planned plenty of raids. "You're sure that's him?" he asked. Indigo nodded once, his eyes briefly flicked toward Allyssa. "Yes."

"How?" Cath pressed. Indigo lifted the small shard of crystal sitting at the map's centre. "Maverick is the Warlock of Secrets," he said calmly. "His magic leaves impressions in the fabric of the realm." The shard pulsed weakly. Silver. Unmistakable. "As long as I charge this crystal by placing it where his magic has been to absorbe the overflow it will track him. The closer to the source the longer it lasts.

I was able to charge it a little more while Allyssa was out his voice dragged out "collecting herself".

Curiousity had me asking. "Where you able to charge it through our bond with Maverick?" Indigo paused and looked back at Allyssa, who was still in deep thought. "Ah, yes lets go with that option." He said his face blushing a baby blue into his cheeks.

Cath burst out laughing at the sight and seemed to understand Indigo's unusual answer. Cath then looked at me and saw my confusion and laughed even harder. My wolf growled at him in warning and he wiped at his eyes finally settling down. Cath said "He was able to generate enough of a connection to Maverick's magic not through the bond but because Maverick and Allyssa had come straight to the battle zone from being *together* their sexual essence along with the magical kind was still clinging to her, you idiot"

My face and neck burned, I can't believe I had forgotten about that. It feels like it was a lifetime ago but it has only been 24 hours. I looked at the crystal again. It had an etching on it, my eyes narrowing on it, Emily's signature is on it, must be from her company.

"Anyway, I was also able to charge it further when we came back here, his magic is everywhere. When the Severed Flame abducted him," Indigo continued, "they carried him through two ley intersections. That created a resonance." The light flickered. Weak. But alive. "He's here," Indigo said.

Cath studied the map again. "That forest is half a kingdom wide."

"Yes."

"And the cult has tunnels."

"Almost certainly."

I dragged a hand through my hair. "So we're looking for one hidden sanctum inside miles of underground caves." Indigo tilted his head. "Correct."

"That's not a plan." I stated flatly. "It is a starting point." He countered. Behind us, Allyssa sat cross-legged on the stone floor. She hadn't moved in nearly ten minutes. Magic rippled around her like heat above a battlefield. Not uncontrolled. Contained. That might have been more frightening.

Her breathing was slow, deliberate, each inhale like she was forcing the storm inside her to kneel. Cath glanced toward her. "She been like that long?"

"Since we got here," I said. The truth sat heavier in my chest than I wanted to admit. Because the moment we left Indigo's bunker, we'd had the conversation I'd been dreading. What happens when we find them. I looked at the map again. "She plans to kill them."

Cath didn't even blink. "Reasonable."

"They're Naturals," I said sharply.

"So?"

"So they deserve trial."

Indigo's voice was carefully neutral. "You believe they should be arrested."

"Yes."

"For kidnapping and ritual torture."

"Yes."

Behind us Allyssa spoke. "They will not surrender." Her voice was quiet. But the cavern seemed to bend toward it. I turned. She opened her eyes slowly. Black still stained the whites of them like spilled ink. "They took Maverick," she continued. "They will not surrender."

"That's not how justice works," I said. Her gaze settled on me. "Justice requires mercy." I responded immediately "And mercy requires restraint." Her eyes darkened slightly. "You saw what they did."

"I saw enough."

"No."

Her voice sharpened. "You felt a whisper." Silence fell. The bond pulsed faintly between us. Muted. Distant. I could feel Maverick's pain. But it was like hearing thunder miles away. Allyssa felt the lightning. She stood slowly. Magic rolled off her in controlled waves. "You want mercy," she said.

"Yes."

"You want arrests."

"Yes."

Her head tilted slightly. "And if they refuse?" My jaw tightened. "Then we stop them." The Monster flickered behind her eyes. Lilith's mark flared at her throat. Both hungry. But she held it back. "Stop," she repeated quietly. "That is a gentle word for war."

Allyssa POV

The world sharpened around me like the edge of a blade being honed. Breath in. Breath out. Heat beneath my skin. Maverick's suffering burned behind my ribs like runes carved into bone. Caspian's warmth still lingered on my face even after he lit his fingers drop away.

His steadiness. His fear. His devotion. So bright it almost made the Monster snarl in resentment. We do not need him, the Commander whispered. We do, said the Queen calmly. We want him, the Wolf added. We break him, purred the Monster. I exhaled slowly.

The voices did not fight anymore. They advised. The council chamber formed around me inside the bond. Stone walls. A circular table. Four figures waiting. The Queen sat at the head. The Commander stood beside her studying invisible maps. The Wolf paced territorial instinct roaring. The Monster leaned against the wall smiling like blood was already on her hands.

Maverick's pain rippled through the chamber. The Wolf whimpered. Mate. Maverick is our mate I asked her. She nodded her big black head. Both of them are, it is why the triskelion bond is ours and was never the prophecy for my previous hosts.

The Commander leaned forward. "They're weakening him." The Monster's smile widened. "Then we destroy them, perhaps Lilith was predicting something holding of the bloodlust." The Queen raised one hand. "Control."

The chamber quieted. The bond between us three flickered into view. Not threads anymore. A braid. Incomplete. Alive. Searching. Blocked. "They're dampening it," I said aloud. The Commander nodded. "Salt and bone rituals."

"They don't have the power to sever it," the Queen said. "But distance weakens it." Which meant one thing. We needed proximity. Or—

I could force the bond wider. Outside the council chamber, Caspian's presence flickered against the connection. Warm. Steady. Muted. He felt Maverick's pain. But barely. I opened my eyes. Caspian was watching me carefully. "You can't feel him properly," I said. "I feel enough."

"No." Before he could react, I grabbed his wrist. The bond exploded open. Pain slammed into him like lightning. Chains cutting skin. Salt burning wounds. Maverick screaming through clenched teeth. Caspian staggered. "Gods—"

"That's what I feel," I whispered. His knees nearly buckled. Cath swore quietly. "...shit." Indigo looked fascinated. "Educational." The connection eased slowly. Caspian dragged in a breath. "How long?"

"Hours." I replied. Silence filled the Vein. Finally he looked up at me. "We find them."

"Yes."

"And when we do?" The Monster stirred. Patient. Waiting. "We take Maverick back."

"And the cult?" I held his gaze. "They will have a choice." Caspian exhaled slowly.

"Surrender."

"Yes."

"And if they don't?" The Monster smiled. "Then it looks like Lilith's mark will be fulfilled after all."

The bond pulsed faintly. Far away— deep beneath the Grove— Maverick heard me. Hold on. Just a little longer, mo scáth. I'm coming. And this time— I wasn't running from the storm. I was bringing it with me.

Maverick's POV

Pain had become a landscape. A geography I could map by nerve and breath and memory. But even landscapes evolve. This one had teeth.

I hung suspended from ritual-forged cuffs bolted into an altar wall made of obsidian and grave-bone. My arms burned. My wrists bled. My heart stuttered like it was trying to remember how to beat under the weight of so many poisons. Sweat mingled with blood, dripping onto the carved floor sigils that writhed like worms hungry for offerings.

The Severed Flame did not believe in mercy. They believed in symmetry. They believed suffering should be measured in equal weight: one grief for another. And they had so very many griefs.

The chamber around me pulsed with sickened magic. A desecrated shrine, old Seelie architecture gutted and rebuilt with Druidic death-runes and Shade-born bone wards. Stolen faith. Violated purpose. A sanctum built entirely for one thing:

Unmaking.

My unmaking.

But the worst part? They thought it was righteous. They thought they were saving the world from me. From the Wolves I'd served. From the fate Allyssa embodied. Irony tasted metallic on my tongue.

A Druid acolyte entered first robes stitched with root-veins that pulsed like living arteries. Behind him, a Seelie woman in ceremonial war paint carried the Reflection Shard with reverence, as though it were a holy relic instead of a blade meant to flay truth from spirit.

The Druid circled me, studying the bond mark burned into my chest. "The mark dims," he said. "It flickers," the Seelie corrected. "It resists." They said *it* like the bond was an artifact. A curse.

Not a promise I had carved willingly into myself and had transformed into the most intimate bond of my long life.

The Shard gleamed, and the Seelie's fingers stroked its surface almost tenderly. "He's strong," she whispered. "Warlock of Secrets indeed. But all secrets break." She tilted her head. "Especially when the Wolf that forged him is fractured."

I smiled with bloody teeth. "If you think she's fractured, you haven't been paying attention." They didn't like that. Good. Ritual I: The Reversal Veil had clouded my magic. Ritual II: The Blood Echo had poisoned my veins. Ritual III: The Reflection Shard had repeated every sin I'd ever witnessed, every death I'd ever survived, every Wolf I'd ever failed. Adrian. The Fourth. The missing ones. The ones I'd buried in silence. The ones who trusted me too much. The ones who needed saving. The ones I couldn't save

They tried to make me believe I had loved wrong. Served wrong. Chosen wrong. But they had forgotten something fundamental: I do not break cleanly. And Allyssa— Allyssa was no fracture.

She was a convergence. A pulse ripped through the bond then, violent, opalescent, cold, divine. Her power tore into the sanctum again—this time unmistakable. Not just Wolf. Not just glyphfire. The shadows obeyed her. Shadows never obeyed Wolves. They obeyed only the royal line of Umbrakyn.

My head snapped back against the wall. My breath hitched, not from agony but from recognition. Allyssa. Close. Strong. Unrestrained. Her fury washed through me like heaven set on fire. A flood of cold flames, burning intent, and the sharpened clarity of a predator with purpose. The Seelie woman froze. "Did you feel that?" The Druid stiffened. "Something crossed the perimeter wards."

"No," I rasped, letting a laugh unfurl from my cracked lips. "Not something." The bond flared again, this time with the force of a spell that hit bone-deep. "She's coming." The Druid backhanded me; my head snapped sideways, blood dripping from my lip. But I kept laughing. Soft. Breathless. Unhinged. "You think you know the prophecy," I whispered. "You think you know the Black Wolf." The walls vibrated under the next pulse, her connection with Caspian. Their alignment still strained but intact. Their choice. "But you don't know *her*." The Shard trembled in the Seelie's hands.

"She will fall," she insisted, though her voice wavered. "Just like the others." "Others?" I repeated. "You mean the Wolves you butchered in your grief? The ones you claim to honour by desecrating the very magic they died to protect?" My smile widened, feral and wild. "Yes. Very noble." The Druid snarled and lifted his staff. Vines erupted from the ground, twisting around my ribs, tightening. Wait not normal vines, shadow vines. I gasped, the pain exquisite, sharp, precise. I savoured it.

Because beneath the pain... through the bond... I felt her smile. Predatory. Beautiful. Terrifying. "You stole a Warlock," I murmured. "You chained a mate." "And now the Wolf is here." The Seelie stepped closer, voice trembling. "She won't reach this sanctum. We are prepared." "You are prepared for a weapon," I corrected quietly. "Not a Queen." That stopped them. The Druid's grip faltered. His pupils contracted. "What do you mean?" he demanded.

I lifted my head, blood dripping from my chin, eyes burning through the haze. "Your history is wrong," I whispered. "Your prophecy, flawed. Black Wolves don't destroy because they lose control." I exhaled, slow. Intentional. Letting the truth slide like a dagger between their ribs. "They destroy because they choose to." Silence. Thick. Smothering. Terrified.

From the fracture, a vine erupted through the stone, black-green and glistening with shadow-magic. It lashed upward in three sharp strikes against my chest.

I looked down. Across my skin, carved in fresh blood and living thorns, was a single letter.

A.

A brand. A promise. I smiled. The vine curled upward, brushing my cheek like a lover's hand, and I whispered to it, to the magic threaded through it, to the bond that ran deeper than blood. "I missed you too, my Queen." The cultists recoiled. They felt it now.

The runes flickered. Salt veins in the walls screamed. Wards shuddered under the pressure of a power they had not accounted for. And I... I laughed. Not broken. Not hysterical. Exultant. "Do you hear that?" I crooned softly. "That's not fury."

They backed away. I leaned forward as far as the chains allowed, voice dropping into something reverent. "That's inevitability." Light ruptured across the sanctum ceiling. A ward detonated somewhere above. The ground trembled like something ancient and furious had placed a hand upon the world and begun to push.

The Druid scrambled, shouting for reinforcements. The Seelie dropped the Reflection Shard. It shattered across the floor, splintering memory-light across the stone. I closed my eyes.

Through the pain. Through the ruin. Through the bond. I felt her. Cold. Precise. Hunting. Across the tether, her voice brushed my mind like velvet wrapped around a blade.

I'm coming, mo scáth.

A shiver tore through me. Desire burned through the agony in a sharp, glorious surge. Gods, I loved when she called me that. "Good," I breathed. "Let them run." I lifted my head, shoulders shaking with a laugh that tasted of blood and devotion.

"You didn't steal a hostage," I told the trembling cultists. They stared at me, pale, sweating. "You declared war." My voice dropped to a whisper. "And your reckoning walks on two legs." The bond roared. The triskelion bond flared white. Her power slammed into the sanctum like a storm breaking across a battlefield. I tilted my head back and smiled like a man watching dawn devour the night. "She's here."

Chapter Thirty-Seven: The Reckoning is Mercy

"They thought the fire meant destruction.

They never asked who lit it—or why she smiled watching it burn."

— Unknown

Allyssa POV

The mist had already begun to form. Shimmering vapour crept across the obsidian-stained timber floor of the Hollow Vein like living breath, gathering around Indigo's feet and stretching outward in delicate threads. The Veil between realms shivered where it touched the air, thin as spider silk and twice as dangerous. It whispered to me. Indigo's head snapped to mine. The mist curled closer. I let it.

Maverick screamed. The sound tore through the bond like lightning splitting a tree. My vision blurred. Not from weakness. From rage. I stepped toward the mist. "Wait." Caspian's voice cut across the chamber. I stopped. Not because I wanted to. Because the bond between us tightened when he spoke, his presence pressing against mine like a steady hand against a blade.

"I don't have time for hesitation," I said without turning. "You don't have time for mistakes either." That made me look at him. His crystal blue eyes were sharp, burning with fear and determination in equal measure. Behind him, Cath leaned against one of the Vein's pillars, arms crossed, expression carved from suspicion and stone.

Indigo was already calculating "If it helps," he said, "charging headlong into a cult fortress without preparation statistically results in death 94% of the time." "My gaze flicked to him, unimpressed. Caspian stepped closer. "Lys," he said quietly. The name cracked something in my chest. Not Wolf. Not weapon. Me.

But it's going to take a lot more than a nick name to earn back my affection.

"You feel him," he continued. The bond pulsed again. Agony. Chains biting flesh. Blood. Maverick trying not to scream and failing. "Yes," I said.

"Then listen to me." My patience thinned dangerously. "I am listening white wolf." I snapped at him. He flinched back as if I had stabbed him straight through the heart. He shook it off. "You're about to walk into the Severed Flame sanctum alone, blind, and furious."

"Correct." I said, while the commander within offered you know *we need a plan*. I know, I just really hate that he caught us rushing through because of the bond. We are really not impartial when it comes to our mates it seems.

"That's not a strategy." Caspian continued.

"It's a rescue." I said, sweet as poison that Maverick would be proud of, I'm sure. Cath barked a laugh behind him. "Well that's one way to phrase it." Caspian didn't look away from me. "If you want Maverick alive," he said quietly, "we take five minutes to plan." His name had slipped into Caspian's mouth the way it lived in the bond now: unavoidable. The fractures stirred.

Wolf – go now

Commander – strategy first, he is right

Monster – kill everything

Queen – listen, before we commit.

Child – please hurry

My hands trembled. The storm inside me clawed for release. But Caspian was right. And gods help me, I hated that. "Five minutes," I said. Caspian exhaled slowly. "Thank you." I scoffed at him in response. Still thinks I'm unreasonable it seems.

Behind us Indigo clapped his hands together once. "Wonderful," he said. "I adore when rational thought prevails over homicidal impulse." I chuckle at him; it was so random I couldn't help it.

The Hollow Vein shifted. Indigo flicked his fingers through the air and the mist collapsed back into the stone floor. The Vein's central table erupted into light, ancient roots and ley lines blooming across its surface.

The Grove appeared. Even in illusion the place looked diseased. Cath stepped forward immediately. "That used to be the Dryad capital," he said. His voice carried the rough authority of someone who had studied battlefields most of his life. "Before one of your Wolves burned it down." The words weren't cruel. Just factual. I didn't flinch. The guilt belonged to history, not me. Cath traced a line through the projection.

"There are roots everywhere. Old ones. Deep ones." His finger tapped a hollow beneath the terrain. "And tunnels, most of the city was underground. They only build structures above ground for Entry and exit points to their underground city."

Indigo nodded. "It was extensive." He pulled a pouch from his belt and scattered several thin green tokens across the table. Runes burned faintly across their surfaces. "Temporary ward breakers." Caspian frowned. "You can do that?"

"Of course." Indigo crouched beside me and took my wrist without asking permission. His fingers were cool. Precise. Magic flared as he began carving glowing sigils along the inside of my skin. The runes sank into me like ink into parchment. "Shadowkin craft?" Cath asked.

"Partially," Indigo replied. "The manipulation of mist, veil-space, and temporary wards is traditionally a generational skill among my people." His eyes flicked briefly to the shadows curling at my feet. Interesting. He didn't comment. He finished the final rune and leaned back.

"These will unravel outer sanctum wards long enough for us to pass they will vanish once you have used them once." Caspian folded his arms. "And if they have inner wards?" Indigo shrugged. "Then we improvise." Cath grinned. "That's my favourite kind of plan."

As Indigo stood, he studied me again. Not my face. My shadow. It stretched across the floor like living ink. Too fluid. Too obedient. Royal Unseelie magic. But stronger. Layered. I can feel it. "If I may clarify something," he said mildly. "I am assisting purely for contractual reasons." Caspian raised an eyebrow.

"Contractual." I said. Intrigued. "Yes." Indigo dusted his hands. "If I survive this, the contract with the Tribunal that has basically enslaved the shadowkin and our veilwalkers becomes void."

I blinked. "You're helping us so you can quit your job."

"Correct." He simply said. "That might be the most relatable motivation I've heard all year." I said. Cath laughed. "Alright. I like this one."

Indigo summoned the mist and I ran my fingers at the vapers fanning up to greet me. This time when I stepped into it, Caspian followed without hesitation. Cath cursed softly and stepped in behind us. Indigo closed the Veil. The world folded.

Cold air struck my face like a slap. Autum was in full swing, the wind was howling and made it seem all eerie. The Grove smelled of rot. Not fresh decay. Old rot. The kind that soaked into soil centuries ago and never quite left.

Broken pillars jutted from the ground like the ribs of a dead town. Blackened trees twisted toward a sky that seemed permanently bruised. Cath inhaled sharply. "This place used to be beautiful." The roots beneath the earth stirred uneasily beneath my feet. They remembered. What my wolf spirit had to do in her previous life. And what I was becoming now.

Something rustled in the brush to Cath's left. A blur of fur and teeth launched toward his throat. Pooka. The creature moved like a nightmare. I moved faster. Shadow snapped upward from the Pooka halting it mid-air. I walked up to it. It was snapping at me looking for a meal. I clicked my tongue once. I mapped its shadow, the power as easy as breathing now I laid my palm to its skull. Command, not comfort. It made guttural noises, trying to communicate with me.

I held its shadow keeping it in place and called over my shoulder for the dry meat I know Caspian packed. He handed it over begrudgingly and I fed it to the Pooka while bargaining with it, they are tricksters after all. "You will not attack this group again. Understand?" It nodded its head in understanding accepting the bargain and ran off as soon as I let go of its shadow.

Cath stared at me in bewilderment. Then at the retreating Pooka. "...I take back several things I said about you." I chuckled a little. "Only several?" He smirked at me. "Let's not rush it. That Unseelie bloodline of yours comes in handy doesn't it."

The entrance to the underground tunnels was half-hidden beneath collapsed stone and creeping roots. Caspian pushed aside the debris. The air that spilled out smelled like blood and wet bone. We descended. The tunnels twisted downward through ancient Dryad architecture, stone corridors carved with runes so old even Indigo had to pause to study them.

Caspian walked beside Cath. The two of them argued quietly about battle formations. "You can't flank in a tunnel," Cath muttered. "You can if the tunnel forks," Caspian replied. "That's not flanking, that's getting lost." He scoffed.

Behind them Indigo hummed softly. A melody. Familiar. I glanced back. "You listen to human music."

"Of course." He looked faintly offended. "Humans produce remarkable art." Cath snorted. "They also produce reality television." Indigo looked at him now, a mix of excitement and understanding. "Every culture has its flaws." He announced. "You know mortal realm things" Cath looked at him and I swear I could see a deep shade of brown covering his cheeks. Shy or embarrassed. How interesting. Apparently, a nod was all Indigo was going to get. It didn't seem to faze him, however.

It felt like we had been walking for hours and not getting anywhere. I kept a close eye on the bond to Maverick. While I practiced controlling the shadows around me and those attached to me. I had already pulled Caspian's shadow at least a dozen times, making him trip over his feet, sadly he always caught himself before face planting. Damn werewolf balance.

He looked toward me each time but didn't call me out on it. Just looked away without meeting my gaze, and even though I wanted to keep being petty, my heart was aching at the sight of his expression of acceptance. Like this was a punishment he deserved. I mean he absolutely did but really, he didn't. I was terrifying and he can't help his instincts on a reflex. He was still here and still wanting to be close to me. I could feel it through the bond. He was punishing himself by denying his need to have skin to skin contact.

Indigo walked beside me for several minutes before finally speaking. "May I ask something?"

"You already are." I said amused. His eyes were thoughtful. "You're allowing me close."

"Yes." I said even though it was not framed as a question but observation. "But my kin let you suffer or is it our kin either way, why?." The words weren't cruel. Just curious. "Shadowkin observe mortal realms," he continued. "They rarely interfere." A memory flickered behind my ribs. No sound. Blood. A locked door. "I know," I said quietly. "Then why?" he asks again.

I looked at Caspian. He was arguing with Cath about something ridiculous. I looked back to him and sighed. "Because you did interfere. I know about the contract with the Tribunal. I was doing some reading in Maverick's study after one of our training sessions and he left the information out on his desk. That male should be more careful with who he invites to his bedroom/ office. He chuckled at my joke and as it was. "Anyways I couldn't image being put in that position and having to do the horrible job because you are bound by magic.

At least in the mortal realm you just quit when you get sick of a place or don't have the same values. It's different here. Even still you broke protocol which you are still doing just by coming along with us when the contract is still in effect. I don't know how you have managed to do this while avoiding consequence, but you will have to tell me sometime. You also have the advantage of knowing me better than anyone else in this realm because of your stalking." He laughed again.

Indigo considered all that I said. Then nodded. "Fair." That was it. Another reason I don't mind having him around. Feels nice to laugh and smile.

The tunnels finally widened. The air changed. Salt. Blood. Ritual magic. Maverick's agony slammed into me so hard my knees nearly buckled. He was close. Very close. "There," I whispered. Ahead of us stood a set of stone doors carved with ancient wards. Layers of magic pulsed across their surface. Indigo swore softly. "That is... impressive wardcraft." Caspian looked at me.

"Can you break them?" The shadows around my feet stirred. They rose slowly. Bow-like. The wards trembled. But held. I tried again this time summoning the mist to work with the shadows and pushed the runes that Indigo sketched toward the ward. Cracks spread across the glowing sigils.

Indigo's breath hitched. "How did you do that." Caspian felt it too through the bond. Something older. Something royal but also something more. "...Umbrakyn, and shadowfin together," Indigo whispered. The final ward shattered. The doors groaned open. The sanctum waited beyond. I smiled. Cold. Patient. "Found them."

The air tasted acidic. The bond stabbed through me. Maverick screamed again, through the rituals, through the runes, through whatever hell they'd bound him into. My vision went black completely black. The fractures rose as one: *No mercy*. The air changed first. Then the roots recoiled from my steps. They remembered what I was... and what I wasn't. And beneath that, deeper, older—the shadows stirred. Responding to my command. The bloodline I understand is unseelie royal but have had no time to examine to figure out yet.

The first breath inside the sanctum tasted like Maverick's blood. My claws burst through my palms. "Stay close," I said, voice fractured and resonant. Caspian nodded. Indigo murmured, "This is the worst idea we've ever had." I smiled. Mercy died the moment they touched my mate. The sanctum corridor unfurled ahead of us like a throat carved into the earth, ribbed with bone, lined with Dryadic root-veins, pulsing faintly with a heartbeat that wasn't mine. Caspian exhaled a shaky breath beside me. Indigo muttered something about "perfectly fine places never having walls that breathe." Cath was at my other side, the picture perfect warrior, looking for his charge.

But my focus was singular. Maverick. The bond mark on my shoulder blade thrummed in synchrony, pulsing brighter every time his heart stuttered through the bond. We turned a corner. A hooded acolyte was there. He froze mid-step, a clay bowl of ink and bone dust in his hands. His mouth opened to shout. I didn't let him.

My power snapped outward—

a whip of shadow wrapped around his throat.

He didn't even drop the bowl before I yanked him off his feet and slammed him into the wall with such force the stone cracked like ice on a lake. The snap of his neck echoed down the corridor. Caspian swallowed. "That was—" "Merciful," I said, stepping over the body. Behind me, Indigo whispered, "If that is mercy, I am deeply afraid to see your wrath." Cath just nodded and started scanning the tunnel looking for a way through to Maverick.

I closed my eyes and searched for the bond pushing the limit of its power while it was still incomplete. I used all my senses and found his blood pooling further across the sanctum. Lilith's mark at my throat flared crimson and began to pulsate. Cath called out next wave.

Three acolytes rushing from a side passage, robes billowing, glyphs glowing, chanting in clipped, frantic syllables. Death rituals. Bindings. Memory flaying. I let them chant. It didn't matter. Their spells hung in the air like smoke as I thrust out my hand. Magic obeyed instantly, no hesitation, no restraint and the shadow under my feet rose like a living creature.

It struck the first acolyte in the chest. Not piercing. Engulfing. He shrieked as the shadow- wolf wrapped around his ribcage and dragged...... yanking bone from muscle like peeling bark from a tree. My wolf preening satisfied in her work and looking for acknowledgement, which I give her, smiling. Caspian flinched. Indigo whispered, "Oh gods," and took a step to the side.

The second acolyte tried to run. I flicked my finger. A sliver of magic, thin, silver-black, shot forward and cut his Achilles tendons cleanly. He collapsed, screaming, crawling backward on blood-slick hands. I stalked toward him. Not rushed. Not frenzied. Not monstrous. Regal. Every fracture in me aligned with a single thought: You hurt what is mine.

He lifted his hands in surrender. "Please—" I placed my foot gently on his chest. His breath hitched. Then I pushed. Just a little. As I stared into his eyes. The ribs caved in with a sound like collapsing timber. He went still. I watched the light leave his eyes wanting to make sure his was not coming back.

Caspian reached me then, fingers brushing my elbow a grounding touch, or maybe a plea. "Allyssa... Lys... slow down." "I can't," I whispered. "If I slow down, I'll feel everything they're doing to him." He closed his eyes for a heartbeat, pain tightening his jaw. "Then don't slow down. Just don't lose yourself. I'll take as many that are willing to surrender, and you do what you must." Another scream echoed deeper in the sanctum Maverick's. Raw. Choked. Dragged from somewhere soul-deep. My vision went starless-black. Cath roared a battle cry, Caspian swore under his breath chasing after him and Indigo stayed at my side.

The third acolyte, the one who had realized too late he should've run, threw up a shield. A shimmering barrier of pale green light. I didn't break it. I smiled as I summoned the mist and stepped back into it. The mist curled around me opening back up behind the acolyte. I pulled on his shadows pinning his arms behind his back and smiling at him. "Where is my warlock" I snarled in his face. He paled but swallowed hard before replying "Fuck you." My smile grew, Indigo mumbled something about trapping souls here and he telling everyone he can see dead people. I focused back to the acolyte. "I was hoping you were going to say that". He frowned at me confused then one of my tendrils of shadows crawled up his neck and into his ear canal. "I wonder what I am going to find in here." My shadows found his brain, and I infused some intent with it. It was Maverick's technique, the one he'd warned me never to use unless it was life or death. I had told him where he can shove his rules and he just smiled at me.

I get fragments of his thoughts, which way to go next. A map of the sanctum and where on that map Maverick is. Magic streamed off my skin in ribbons of shadow-light, curling around the acolyte like hungry mist, tasting it, unravelling him, pulling it apart thread by bloody thread. The acolyte stared, mouth open, terror leaking from every pore. "What—are you—?" I didn't answer. A thousand cuts across his body from my shadows like little blades. He bled out by the time that I dropped him. I closed my eyes until my shadows found him, I concentrated on creating vines with my shadow and wrapping them around him. Branding him and stroking his cheek. *I'm coming mo scáth*. His desire was answer enough.

Indigo blinked once. Twice. "Note to self," he muttered. "Never, ever, use a barrier spell near her." Caspian and Cath raced back to us, chest heaving, blood splattered here and there. Lilith's mark absorbed all the blood from them and me. Caspian froze and stared at the mark. He took a step toward me, but I took a step back, he hung his head and nodded to the mark. "Are you okay?" I nodded "I am fine, Lilith is just taking what is owed."

"We were able to restrain a few of them and Cath will go back later to take them to the Academy. We left a message with Lakemond. The children here have been escorted by an older kid to the exit it was her job when the black wolf showed up to take all the children to a safe place in The Grove and wait for an elder." Caspian looked around and took in the bloodshed I had created but didn't say anything just looked back to me making sure I had no injuries.

"Lys," he murmured, stepping close more determined this time, cupping my jaw lightly with trembling fingers. "We're going to get him. But we do this together. All of us."

The fractures hummed at that:

Wolf – *mate*

Commander – *anchor*

Queen – *claim*

Monster – *yes… together… more power*

Child – *please don't leave me*

I leaned into his touch for the briefest heartbeat. Then Maverick's agony surged through the bond again, sharp, hot, broken. I hissed, baring my teeth. "They've started another ritual." Caspian gripped his blade so tightly the leather creaked. "Then we move." Indigo flicked a knife the hilt obsidian glass and the blade made of shadow into his palm. "I am regretting this entire profession." I stepped forward— blood on my cheek, magic swirling at my heels, rage sharp enough to cut the realm in half.

"We go," I said. "And gods help anyone between us and our warlock." We descended deeper. Where the screams were louder. And the walls began to bleed. The corridor narrowed into a throat of carved bone and dripping stone, every surface vibrating with chanting, ragged, discordant, frantic. They knew we were here. They knew *I* was here. Good.

Let them prepare their rituals.

Let them sharpen their knives.

Let them pray to their broken gods.

None of it would save them. A deeper surge of agony ripped across the triad bond, so violently my knees nearly buckled. Maverick wasn't just hurting now, he was fading.

The fractures inside me snarled in unison.

Wolf: *MATE. MATE. MATE.*

Warrior: *Cut through them.*

Queen: *Spare only those who kneel.*

Monster: *No survivors.*

Child: *Save him. Please save him.*

I surged forward. Following the path I had seen in that acolytes' mind. The next chamber opened like a diseased heart, massive, circular, lined with root-veins dripping dark ichor into ritual basins. Torches burned green-blue. Glyphs carved through bone and blood lit the walls with pulses that matched Maverick's weakening heartbeat. And there, in the centre, a dozen acolytes knelt around a ritual circle. Not just voicing spells.

Feeding them. With their own blood. With their own memories. With Maverick's agony. One acolyte looked up. His chant broke. "Black Wolf," he whispered. I smiled. It was not a kind smile. Caspian stepped beside me, blade raised. Indigo stayed back, shadows clenched at his ankles as if afraid of what I would do next.

I didn't make them wait long. A roar, not just fae, ripped from my chest as I dove into the circle. The first acolyte raised a glyphstone. I tore his arm off at the elbow. Blood sprayed in a perfect arc, warm on my cheek. My wolf howled in delight. The Monster purred. Lilith absorbed my bloodlust and fed it back to the ley lines.

Another acolyte tried to bind me with a chain of light. I let it wrap around my torso, then grabbed the chain and pulled him forward until the light cut his own throat. He fell at my feet, clutching the ruin of his neck. Caspian didn't look away this time. Didn't flinch. Just muttered, breathless, "Gods, Lys..."

A third acolyte shoved his hands into the dirt, summoning a mass of roots to ensnare me, ancient Druidic magic that could immobilize a Guardian. Roots wrapped around my ankles. Then my calves. Then my waist, I inhaled. And let my power bleed out. Shadowfire erupted along my skin, black-blue flames licking down my body like molten night. The roots recoiled, then shrivelled, then turned to ash. The acolyte who cast them screamed. I silenced him by driving my shifted hand straight through his sternum. My claws closed around his heart. I pulled blood streaming down my arm as I watched in fascination. It beat twice in my palm before the magic seared it into smoke, I licked one of the streaks of blood as I looked at the rest of the acolytes.

Indigo made a small noise. Something between awe and existential despair. "Remind me," he said faintly, "never to get on your bad side." "You're already on her good side," Caspian replied.

"You should hope it stays that way." Maverick's pain slammed into me again, sharper, weaker

more distant. No. No no no...... I moved faster.

Five acolytes remained. They scattered like insects, shouting for reinforcements, glyphs blazing, some clutching daggers, others holy relics twisted by their cause. I cut through them like rot through silk. A dagger met my side; I didn't feel it. A spell hit my shoulder; I took it.

A spear of light pierced my ribs; I snapped it in half and shoved the broken shaft into its wielder's stomach. Cath joined me then, blade flashing silver-gold, cutting down those who got too close to my back. Caspian's wolf howled through the bond, fear, fury, devotion all tangled into something raw and overwhelming. "Let me heal you, your bleeding and wounded" I growled at him. "Caspian if you come near me instead of fighting I am going to chain you up myself for slowing me down". I felt his love through the bond and acceptance and a little lust. I shook my head and continued.

Indigo moved like a blade that didn't reflect light. He was silent. Precise. Every kill he made was surgical. Mine were not. The last acolyte tried to flee. I let him run. Let him think he had hope. Then I snapped my fingers and the shadows on the floor pooled upward, catching his legs, dragging him screaming across the stone toward me. He clawed uselessly at the floor. His fingers scraped bone. Skin tore. Blood smeared in streaks behind him. I crouched as he reached me, gripping his hair, lifting his face to mine.

"Where is your shrine master?" I whispered. "I—I can't—he'll kill me—" I laughed "I will," I said simply, "but slower." He screamed as the bond surged again; Maverick's voice, hoarse, broken: *Allyssa—don't—come—* My heart cracked. I threw the male to Caspian "deal with him however I need to keep going.". Silence followed. Heavy. Absolute. Caspian exhaled hard, Cath's voice was hoarse he took a few good hits. "We need to move." Indigo wiped blood from his cheek. "They know she's inside. The inner sanctum will be warded. Heavily."

"Good," I said. I stepped over the bodies. My shadow stretched long behind me, longer than it should have. Alive. Hungry. Crawling like a beast unleashed. My wolf standing tall proud of our shadow ability. The shadow flame was new, not sure where that comes from, be curious later the queen reminded me. The triskelion bond mark on my shoulder blade burned molten-gold through my skin. Maverick was calling. Faint. Frayed. Desperate. I raised my face toward the deepest tunnel of the shrine.

Chapter Thirty-Eight: Cathedral of Obsession

"He who fights with monsters should look to it that he himself does not become a monster.

And when you gaze long into an abyss, the abyss also gazes into you."

— Friedrich Nietzsche, Beyond Good and Evil

Allyssa POV

The doors didn't open so much as... give up. The last ward cracked under my palm and Indigo's temporary sigils, and the stone split with a low groan that sounded like an animal conceding defeat. Salt-light flickered. Bone-runes trembled. Then the seam widened and the sanctum exhaled.

The first breath inside tasted like blood soaked into prayer. Maverick's pain hit the bond at the same time. Not a spike. A *constant.* Like someone had taken a hot wire to my ribs and decided to leave it there.

My fractures surged.

Wolf: *Mate.*

Monster: *Make them pay.*

Commander: *Assess before you strike.*

Queen: *Walk in like you own it.*

Child: *Please... please...*

I stepped through. The space beyond wasn't a chamber. It was a cathedral built by grief that had rotted into obsession. Ash grey columns rose in a wide ring, tall enough to vanish into shadow. Between them, the walls were layered with bone and salt-veins, lightning-bright seams of white cutting through the dark stone like a frozen storm. Skulls were set into the masonry in careful patterns, each one carved with a sigil, each one turned outward as if the dead had been recruited to watch their own shrine.

And the floor... The floor was a mosaic of obsidian and bone slivers arranged into a vast triskillian spiral. They'd taken my symbol, our prophecy's symbol, and made it something to walk across. To bleed on. The Monster in me purred approval at the insult. The Queen in me noted it like a ledger entry.

To my left, Cath stopped dead for half a heartbeat. He didn't flinch, didn't swear, just stared at the spiral like it offended something deep in his bones. "Dryad craft," he muttered, voice rough. "Old. Sacred." Indigo's breath came thin behind me. "And desecrated. I'm adding this to the list of places I'd like to never return to."

Caspian moved to my right, blade half-raised, aura bright enough I could feel it through my spine. His fear brushed the bond... restrained, disciplined, but present. Not fear of the sanctum. Fear of what I would do in it. That didn't soften the bond. It tightened it into a bruise.

"Eyes up," Cath said, stepping slightly forward like he'd decided, for now, that standing near me was safer than standing anywhere else. The pull in my sternum yanked hard.

Centre. Altar. Now. We walked. Every step made the mosaic shudder. Not from my weight. From my presence. Runes flared and recalibrated, trying to categorize me. Trying to decide whether I was threat or a goddess or mistake.

They chose wrong.

At the centre of the triskelion stood a translucent altar backed by a jag of raw stone. Blood channels ran from it in delicate grooves, branching outward like roots. Names. Dates. Places. The dead written in living red. And there, suspended in ritual-forged cuffs, arms stretched, head bowed, was Maverick.

His chest was a map of damage. Old scars under new burns. Fresh cuts laid over the letter he'd branded into himself for me. Ritual vines and iron chains coiled around his torso, embedding where his glyphs flared faint and stubborn.

His aura flickered on the edge of dying. My throat tightened around something that wanted to be a sound. The child in me made one small broken noise and the Monster swallowed it before it escaped. Maverick's head lifted, slow as dawn in a ruined world. His eyes found mine. For a heartbeat, the pain haze dulled him. Then recognition cut through like a blade.

He smiled. Bloody. Wrecked. Beautiful. "You're here," he rasped, voice shredded. The bond flared white-hot. My knees didn't buckle. Not because it didn't hurt. Because the Queen held my spine steady and the Wolf refused to fall. I moved one step closer. The air resisted.

A translucent veil of magic stretched between altar and outer ring, pulsing like a second heartbeat. Veil-ward. Blood-tuned. Indigo lifted a hand slightly. "It reads soul first."

"Let it," I said. Caspian's voice came tight. "Allyssa..." Not a command. Not even a warning. A plea. A reminder that I still had options besides slaughter. Mercy. Arrest. Chains that weren't made of bone. I didn't answer him. I didn't look away from Maverick.

I stepped into the veil. It met my skin like cold honey and teeth. It tried to taste me. Measure me. Weigh me against every Black Wolf before me. It found the monster, the commander, the queen. It found the prophecy. It found my Unseelie blood, shadowkin blood. And then it found something it hadn't been built to understand.

Shadows inside the ward... bowed. Indigo sucked in a sharp breath. Cath's posture stiffened. Even Caspian's wolf went silent, listening. I placed my palm against the veil and felt its structure. The layered intent. The rules. The fear. I instinctively knew the feel and that I could destroy it. Then I curled my fingers and pulled. The ward tore open with a sound like wet skin ripping. Light threads snapped and fell in glittering strips, dissolving into smoke that smelled of burnt prayers.

Indigo made a pained noise. "I hate when magic does that." Caspian swore softly under his breath. Cath's gaze flicked from the torn ward to me, unreadable. Less suspicion now. More calculation.

A figure stepped from behind the altar. Older. Seelie, or something that had started that way and been hollowed out by devotion. Hair silver, braided in ritual cords. Eyes like burnt glass. Robes bone-white and charcoal, layered with crawling glyphs that looked alive if you stared too long.

His aura stank of conviction and loss and the kind of hatred that wore a saint's face. The Shrine Master. "Black Wolf," he said, voice amplified by the cathedral's cruel acoustics. "At last."

I tilted my head. "At last."

He smiled thinly. "You know me."

"I know your work," I said, flicking my gaze across the altar bindings, the blood channels, the stolen artifacts hanging from the columns like trophies. "It's... sentimental."

That drew a murmur from the kneeling figures around the outer ring. Acolytes. Druids. Warlocks. Shade-born. Seelie. A mix of factions that should have hated each other on principle. Indigo's voice went quiet, clinical. "They're feeding the wards with memory and blood." Cath's jaw clenched. "Grief cult," he muttered. "Makes them brave and stupid."

The Shrine Master's eyes slid to Maverick. "And the Warlock," he said, voice smooth. "The enabler. The keeper of Wolves. The one who turned massacre into myth." Maverick's laugh came out torn and low. "He's wordy," he rasped. "You bring me a drink or a sermon, mo bhanríon?"

The Irish hit my ribs like a hand on a wound. My Queen. He learnt my language for me. I took another step. Caspian shifted with me, close enough that the warmth of his aura brushed my shoulder blade. Protective. Steady. Afraid. Cath moved on the other side, blade loose in his grip, scanning the outer ring for a formation break. He didn't like being trapped in open space. He liked tunnels. He liked edges.

"Allyssa," Caspian murmured, "the blood channels. If we cut the right ones, we might disrupt the—"

"I know," I said, because I did. I could see the pattern. I could *taste* it. The sanctum was a machine and Maverick's blood was the fuel. The Shrine Master lifted his staff. "Every stone here is built from the dead your kind left behind," he said. "Every rune etched by a hand that lost a child, a lover, a home to Wolves who called it balance."

His gaze flicked to me, sharp. "And you stand here like you are choice. Like you are love." He spat the last word like a curse. I smiled, small and cold. "You built a cathedral out of pain and expected it to make you holy." He stiffened. "We built this to correct the mistake of your existence." And then the air changed.

Sweet as poison. Sharp as broken glass. A presence I'd learned to loathe. A soft clap echoed from the left side of the cathedral. "Well," Laya drawled, stepping out from behind an Ash grey column like she belonged to the place. No Academy uniform. No mask. A fitted dark mantle marked with the Severed Flame's sigil over her heart. Ritual paint across her cheek in a jagged black streak, as if she'd tried to make herself look like a wound.

She didn't look at me first. She looked at Caspian. He went still. Not the stillness of longing. The stillness of a man seeing a ghost walk in wearing the skin of his past. "Laya," he breathed. Her smile sharpened. "Hello, Caspian." The bond between us twitched.

I felt his shock, his grief, his old instinct to protect something familiar even when it was wrong. I hated the feeling.

The Shrine Master's eyes glinted. He wanted this. Divide. Split. Fracture. Indigo muttered quietly, almost cheerful in the way only he could manage. "Ah. Emotional sabotage. Classic." Cath's voice went flat. "She's bait." Laya stepped closer, voice too soft to be kind. "You came," she said to Caspian. "Even after you knew."

"I know what you are," Caspian said, and his voice steadied. "And I know what you've done." Her expression flickered, something like pain flashing through the cracks. Then it hardened into conviction. "You don't understand," she whispered. "He doesn't deserve this. You don't deserve to be chained to her. To prophecy. To rage."

Caspian's jaw flexed. "Maverick is dying."

"And she's going to turn the world into ash to stop it," Laya replied, finally glancing at me. Her gaze was hunger dressed as righteousness. "Tell me, Black Wolf. When you break, do you even notice who burns?"

The Monster surged at my ribs. The Queen lifted her chin. The Commander tracked the room: the kneeling acolytes, the angles, the blood channels, the staff in the Shrine Master's hands. Caspian took one step forward, putting himself between Laya and me without meaning to.

It was not betrayal. It was instinct. I was the biggest threat and he still wanted a chance to try and save her. He whispered through the bond, let me try please. And it still tasted like a blade sliding under my sternum. "Don't," he said, low, to Laya. "Don't do this." Laya's smile widened like she'd been waiting for that one vulnerable note. She moved fast.

A glyph ignited in her palm, blood-red and jagged, older than Druidic spirals and dirtier than Seelie light. She slammed it into

Caspian's chest. His body seized. He choked, collapsing to his knees as the magic detonated through his nervous system.

"CASPIAN!" Cath roared, lunging forward, but Indigo grabbed him hard by the shoulder. "Don't," Indigo hissed. "That's a trigger glyph. You touch him wrong and you'll complete the circuit." Cath froze, teeth bared. My vision went sharp and starless. The Shrine Master raised his staff.

Cultists rose in a coordinated wave around the outer ring. Dozens of glyphs flared. Spells crackled. Memory magic hissed through the air like a swarm. Laya stepped back beside the Shrine Master, eyes bright with triumph that didn't reach her hands. She was shaking. She hated this. She did it anyway. "Now," she whispered, and the cathedral listened. "Let's see if your bond breaks as easily as the cult believes."

My fractures roared.

Wolf: *KILL.*

Warrior: *PROTECT.*

Monster: *LET ME OUT.*

Queen: *TAKE THE FIELD.*

Child: *Please don't lose him—*

From the altar, Maverick's voice, ragged and furious and alive, tore through the bond like a command. "ALLYSSA... RUN THROUGH THEM." I smiled. And the storm inside me finally stopped asking.

The storm broke the moment I let go. Not outwardly... not yet, but inside me, the fractures stopped arguing and aligned like blades placed edge-to-edge. Maverick's bond burned white-hot, his pain rising like a tide about to swallow shore and sky. Caspian's gasp echoed behind me, the aftershock of the glyph Laya had driven into his spine.

But what shattered something inside me wasn't the attack. It was his hand on my arm. And the hesitation under it. Not *wait.*

Not *think*. Not *be safe*. Just... don't hurt her. My chest went hollow. Not broken. Emptied. A coldness slid through me like midnight water, a wall rising from spine to sternum and setting into granite ice. Not rage. Not anymore.

A Queen's distance. A Wolf's retreat. A Monster learning that tenderness was just another way to bleed. I didn't shake his hand off. I simply stepped out of it, and the contact withered on its own. The Shrine Master lifted his staff. The ring of cultists surged. Laya smiled through her ritual paint like she'd been waiting her entire life for this moment.

And I stopped looking at Caspian. Something in him cracked when I did. I felt it faintly, from a distance, like hearing someone scream underwater.

Good, the Monster whispered.

Distance keeps you alive, the Queen agreed.

Don't feel it, the Child begged.

He didn't choose us, the Wolf growled.

I didn't answer them. I just moved. The first wave of acolytes reached me with staves dripping blood-ink and memory magic. Their chants tore at the air like claws. I tore back. A shadow-ribbon burst from my shoulder, slicing the nearest cultist's throat before he could lift his hand. Blood sprayed warm across my cheek, familiar, grounding. The bond surged in response.

Maverick felt it. Felt me. Recognized the violence as mine. Come to me, he whispered raggedly through the tether. I'm trying *mo scáth*.

Another acolyte lunged from my right. I caught his arm mid-swing, twisted, and felt bone snap through skin. He screamed. I didn't. I drove my knee into his solar plexus hard enough to collapse cartilage and drop him like wet grain. A binding net whipped toward my face, woven from stolen memories like silk made of grief.

I stepped into it. Exhaled. And let the Monster rise. My aura expanded in a jagged bloom. The net dissolved against my skin like cobwebs meeting flame. The cultists hesitated. I didn't. I tore a spine free from the nearest body and drove curved bone into the throat of the next acolyte who dared lift a hand toward me.

They fell back, chanting louder, frantic, terrified. Good. Behind me, Caspian coughed, clawing at the corrupted glyph burning under his shoulder blades. Cath was over him in a heartbeat, blade out, stance wide, daring anyone to try finishing what Laya started. Indigo dragged Caspian farther from the centre line of fire with the efficiency of someone moving a chess piece out of check.

"Allyssa—" Caspian choked.

I didn't turn.

His voice slid off the wall inside me like water off crystal. A spear of memory-blood shot toward me. I let it pierce my shoulder, not because I had to, but because pain gave me something clean to hold onto. I gripped the shaft, ripped it out, and hurled it back. It seared through three bodies before burning to dust.

The Shrine Master snarled, lifting his staff again, fear beginning to bleed through his conviction. "That bond should never have existed."

"You say that," I murmured, stepping through the blood pooling under my boots, "as if your opinion matters to me." Laya stiffened. She had expected fury. What she got was indifference. She stepped forward anyway, eyes glass-bright, voice shaking with conviction she didn't have the strength to hold.

"You're losing control," she whispered. "He'll see it eventually. Caspian always sees the truth sooner or later and when he does—"

I raised my hand. She froze mid-sentence, breath catching as my magic brushed her throat. Not choking. Not crushing. Just... touching. Cold as a blade laid flat across skin. Caspian struggled upright, pain and panic tangling in his aura. "Lys—don't—please."

That hurt. His voice hurt. I let the hurt fall somewhere deep, where it couldn't cut deeper.

"I'm not doing this for him," I whispered to Laya. Her lips parted. "Your choices decide your fate tonight. Not his. Not mine." I leaned closer, voice soft. Soft like snow. Soft like a lullaby. Soft like a blade sliding between ribs. "I hope you find peace," I said, "even if you never gave me any." And then I killed her. Quick. Precise. Merciful. A pulse of shadow slipped through her chest, severing heart from spellwork, severing fear from flesh.

She died instantly. I lowered her gently to the stone as if she were something that had once been human to someone I couldn't afford to hate anymore. Behind me, Caspian made a broken sound, half gasp, half plea, and reached out as if to touch me. I stepped back. The bond didn't sever. It just... muted, as if I'd drawn heavy curtains across a window and refused to look through it.

He froze. And I felt nothing. Or I let myself feel nothing, which is not the same thing. The Shrine Master was still standing, shock whitening his face. I didn't waste time on speeches. Shadow seized his legs, fused them to the floor, and ripped the staff from his hands. I snapped it and let my fire eat the remains.

"Stay," I told him, as if speaking to a dog. "Like a good boy. While I tend to my mate." Mate. Not mates. The distinction was a knife I chose to twist. I didn't look at Caspian. Not anymore. Whatever happened next would happen without hesitation. Without softness. Without mercy shaped like hope. I would save the one who never hesitated for me.

Caspian POV

The moment Allyssa stepped out of my reach, something quiet and catastrophic split open inside me. Not the bond. Not the magic. Me. It felt like someone slid a blade under my sternum and turned it slow, carving a hollow I didn't know how to fill. I'd known pain. I'd lived through terror. Through fire. Through the moment the bond claimed me.

But I had never felt her walk away from me. Not like that. Not with ice in her spine and silence thick enough to choke on. Laya's body lay on the stone, blood spreading in a thin dark halo beneath her. Allyssa had lowered her gently. Gently. That did something worse to me than brutality would have. It wasn't forgiveness. It was distance. It was finality. It was Allyssa deciding that even her mercy would never reach me again.

"Lys..." My voice broke. She didn't look. Her eyes were black. Empty. Closed. My wolf whined, wounded and furious. You hurt our mate. Indigo gripped my arm hard. "Don't," he hissed. "You'll make it worse." He was right. Agreeing with him tasted like ash.

I forced myself away from Laya. Forced my eyes past the blood and the altar and the cultists that still moved like a storm around us. And then I saw Maverick properly. He sagged in the chains, barely conscious, breath shallow, body marked with cuts and glyphs and burns. His blood soaked the spiral beneath him. His aura flickered like a dying ember.

"Maverick," I whispered. The triad bond shuddered. Weak. Present. Then... faltering. A pulse of horror slammed into me so hard I staggered. The bond between him and Allyssa flickered like a candle guttering in wind. Allyssa's body went rigid. She inhaled sharp, like she'd been stabbed from the inside. "Maverick?" she whispered. No answer. Just a heartbeat that didn't land right.

Her shadows snapped outward, jagged and wild. "Caspian," she said, voice like ice cracking under strain. "I told you to stay back." But this wasn't about her wall or my guilt or Laya's corpse. This was Maverick dying. So I stepped forward anyway. "I'm not staying behind," I breathed. "Not this time."

For the first time since she killed Laya, Allyssa looked at me. A hairline crack appeared in the wall. Barely there. But there. Because he needed me. Because she needed me, whether she wanted to admit it or not. Indigo exhaled softly, deadpan as ever. "Oh good. Emotional resolution via warlock crisis. My favourite genre."

I ignored him. We moved toward Maverick together, Allyssa with the precision of a war-goddess, Cath flanking like a shield, Indigo drifting like shadow given purpose, and me with the desperate determination of a man who had already failed too much.

And deep inside the bond, frayed and fading, Maverick stirred. About time, he whispered. "I was starting to think you two forgot about me". A broken laugh punched out of me. Allyssa's jaw clenched around a sound that might have been a sob or a snarl.

And both of us reached for him. My Seelie light rose in my palms, trembling, ready to pour into his failing aura. Allyssa lifted her hands toward the cuffs. The sanctum answered. The stone groaned. The bones in the walls lit. The salt-veins screamed. And the cathedral's remaining wards snapped awake like a beast opening its eyes. The last battle began.

Chapter Thirty-Nine: The Fracture

"I am rooted, but I flow."

— Virginia Woolf, The Waves

Maverick POV

Pain had shape.

For hours, maybe days, it had been the only reliable architecture in my world: cuffs biting bone, ritual vines burrowing under skin, the steady drip of my blood into channels carved with names the cult wanted me to remember as guilt.

But when Allyssa crossed the threshold of the circle, pain gained purpose. The sanctum reacted like a living thing recognizing its predator. Runes contracted. Glyphs rippled like muscle around a wound. The translucent altar beneath me thrummed with a low, almost pleading note, as if the stone itself wanted to warn her away.

It didn't want her here. The magic in these chains knew exactly what she was. And what she was about to do.

She cut through the dark like a blade forged from prophecy and restraint. Not the raging storm I'd felt earlier through the bond, not the wild fury that would have scorched everything to ash. This Allyssa moved with a quiet that frightened even the bones in the walls. Calm. Deliberate. Deadly.

Caspian was at her side, light flaring in unsteady pulses, his aura trying to remain steady while the sanctum pressed back like a tide. A shadowkin veilwalker followed, his form shadowing at his ankles, muttering a curse that sounded like it had learned to pray out of spite.

And Cath. Cath wasn't trailing. He was flanking.

Blade loose in his grip, shoulders squared, scanning the outer ring where cultists shifted in coordinated silence. He placed himself half a step behind Caspian like a shield that had decided it didn't trust anyone else to do the job properly. When a glyph sparked near the far column, Cath moved without asking permission, intercepting it with a hard swing that shattered the rune in the air before it could form.

Practical. Efficient. He glanced at Allyssa once, quick and wary, then refocused on the threat. Not devotion. Not trust. But... respect, beginning to happen against his will. My breath scraped out of me. "Mo bhanríon..." The words were torn raw, dragged from a throat that had screamed too much.

Allyssa didn't look at me. A colder pain went through me than any ritual blade. She lifted her hand toward the first cuff. And that's when I saw it. Not on the altar. Not on me. On her. Blood, dark and sticky, had soaked the seam of her ribs where someone's blade or spell had kissed her on the way down here. It wasn't dramatic. It didn't gush. It was worse than that.

It was ignored. My voice sharpened instinctively. "Why is my Queen bleeding." Allyssa's hand paused a fraction. Caspian flinched like I'd struck him. His light flickered, then surged as if he was about to redirect it.

I let my gaze cut to him, merciless. "You have healing in your hands, White Wolf," I rasped. "Did it occur to you to use it on her." Caspian's jaw clenched. Guilt rolled off him in a wave.

Cath made a low sound that might have been agreement or warning. The shadowkin muttered, "I would like to file a complaint with fate," and shifted closer to Caspian's blind side, mist gathering like poison fog.

Allyssa's voice came quiet. Controlled. "Maverick. Focus." I laughed, breathless and broken. "I am focused. On the fact that my Queen is bleeding and her bonded healer is standing right there." Caspian's light flared brighter. "I—"

"Don't," I cut in, because the sanctum was listening and the cult loved cracks. "Save the confession for later. Heal her. Now." For a heartbeat, Caspian hesitated. Not because he didn't want to.

Because he didn't know if he still had the right I narrowed my eyes, finally seeing the fear on him. Or perhaps he was afraid of what she would do if he tried to touch her. And gods, that told me everything.

My gaze flicked to Allyssa again. She didn't turn toward Caspian. She didn't soften. She didn't reassure him. That cold calm on her face wasn't mercy. It was distance. I groaned inwardly at the rift that was still there and somehow even larger than before.

Something had changed in her while I was chained here. Something had... aligned. It made the bond hum in a different key. It also made my blood run hot with questions I didn't have time to ask. Yet. And damn if it didn't make her even more irresistible.

Allyssa's fingers lowered to the cuff. The enchantments didn't melt. They recoiled. Geometric spellwork twisted away from her touch like it was trying to avoid being seen. The glyph-serpents hissed and writhed, attempting to repulse her essence.

"Blood-linked triple-lock," Caspian whispered, forcing steadiness into his voice. "Druidic, Seelie, and Warlock layers. I don't know if—"

"She knows," I said, because she did. Her eyes weren't void-black now. No monstrous glow. No storm-lash. Just an ancient, sharpened calm that made my stomach clench with something dangerously close to devotion. She saw the braids of magic the way I did: threads, knots, intersections of intent and memory. She was using the memories of the black wolves who came before her. Four lifetimes of magic now lived inside her mind.

And she didn't fight the braids. She unwove them. Her shadows thinned to hairline strands, sliding between the layers like silk needles through tapestry. She touched the first thread, teased it loose, and the entire structure shuddered like it had just realized it was about to be unmade by something that didn't believe in its authority.

I felt the moment the lock faltered under her impossible identity.

Unseelie.

Black Wolf.

Monster.

Queen.

Alpha...... and more......

A contradiction so complete the ward couldn't categorize it. Perfect. Allyssa whispered, soft as a kiss and cruel as a verdict. "Unmake." The cuff disintegrated like sugar under flame. The moment it released, white-hot agony shot through my wrist as blood returned and nerves screamed. I bit down on a sound that wanted to become a howl.

Then something else slammed into place. The Triskillian bond surged. Not like connection. Like hunger. Like the triad itself inhaled sharply and decided it was done waiting. My vision blurred. Not from pain. From need. The pull wasn't only toward Allyssa. It was toward both of them. Toward completion. Toward touch. Toward merging in a way we'd circled for lifetimes and refused to name until now. Finish this. Seal us. Now. Translucent glyphs flickered in and out over all three of our bodies.

Caspian staggered like the bond had hooked him by the spine. His light flared too bright, then wavered, his control slipping under the pressure of prophecy screaming in his blood. Cath swore under his breath and shifted closer to him instantly, one hand half-raised like he'd catch Caspian if he fell, the other keeping his blade trained on the outer ring.

"Stay upright," Cath muttered. "You collapse; she goes nuclear." He cat a quick wary glance in Allyssa's direction before resuming the protector pose. The shadowkin male, somehow, found time to mutter, "Wonderful. I adore when destiny becomes physically unbearable." Allyssa's breath hitched once. Then she swallowed it. Queen, always.

She tore her gaze away from the bond's call and moved to the second cuff. This one wasn't metal. It was memory. Warlock glyphwork carved from fragments of my past, faces and failures braided into a shackle meant to flay me with my own ghosts until I begged to forget. My throat tightened. "Allyssa—don't—" Not because I wanted to hide anything from her.

Because she was already bleeding, already strained, already balancing a storm behind her teeth. And the cult had seeded this cuff with every soft spot I'd ever had. Including the ones that looked like lovers. She didn't listen. Of course she didn't. Her hand hovered inches above the glowing knot of timelines braided through the shackle. Her voice dropped to a whisper I felt more than heard. "You're mine, mo scáth."

Desire slammed through me hard enough I almost laughed. My body, traitor that it was, remembered devotion before it remembered pain. The glyphs ruptured. My memories spilled into the air in jagged shards: Wolves long dead, blood on snow, fire in temples, hands reaching for me and dying before they could hold.

The cult wanted her to drown in it. They wanted her to see every bruise on my soul and decide I wasn't worth it. Allyssa watched the shards without flinching. Then she closed her fist. Shadow swallowed the fragments like a mouth closing around a scream. "Mine," she said again, and the cuff unravelled like a lie exposed.

The bond bared its teeth. All three or none. Now, now, now. Caspian's breath came ragged. His light shook as if it wanted to become something else entirely, something primal and bright and owned. I turned my head just enough to look at him through the pain. And I let my voice go sharp. "Caspian."

He met my gaze, eyes wide, guilty, burning. "What did I tell you." He swallowed. "To find her." "And fix what you fucked up," I rasped. "Not find her and fuck it up further." Cath's mouth twitched, barely. Like he wanted to laugh and knew it would get him killed.

The shadowkin male murmured, "I would enjoy this argument much more if we weren't about to die." Caspian flinched, like my words had landed exactly where they were supposed to. Good. Because Allyssa didn't have room to carry his guilt right now. She moved to the third cuff embedded into my ribs.

This one was old. Older than the cult. Older than me. Shadowkin ritual work knotted with something stolen from the dawn of Druid magic. It pulsed like a second heart, feeding on my breath. The artifact was absolutely beautiful and if it wasn't currently trying to kill me, I would be collecting it and taking it home and displaying it like the artwork it was.

Allyssa's fingers hovered over it. "This might burn," she murmured. "It already does," I whispered back. She placed both hands on the shackle. Not tearing. Not ripping. Unweaving.

Strand by strand, she teased apart the framework, shadows guiding threads while her magic held the collapsing structure in suspension. It was artistry. Violent, sacred artistry. And with every thread she pulled, the bond swelled. Expanded. Demanded. Caspian inhaled sharply and nearly dropped to one knee. Cath caught him by the forearm before he hit the floor. "Hold it," Cath snarled. "She's doing surgery. Don't you dare faint."

Caspian's voice came strained. "It's... loud."

Loud.

Yes.

That was one way to describe prophecy screaming for completion like it had teeth. Allyssa froze, a flicker of panic trying to slip through her control. "Caspian—?" He shook his head violently. "Keep going. I'm fine. I've got you." She didn't say thank you. She didn't say anything. But her shoulders eased one millimetre, like that was all she could afford to give.

The third cuff cracked. And the Triskillian bond snapped wide open. A shockwave of need and power and belonging detonated through the chamber. Allyssa gasped, deep and primal. Caspian's light flared so bright it painted the cathedral bones gold. I threw my head back and choked on a sound that was half moan, half prayer. Our souls weren't just touching.

They were trying to fuse. One heartbeat away from irrevocable completion. Allyssa's eyes widened a fraction, and in that tiny slip of control I saw it. The change. The sharpened edge. The fractures... quieter, but not gone. Not subdued. Aligned like a council that had finally agreed on the verdict. It was... exquisite. It was also terrifying.

"Later," I rasped to her, breath shaking. "You're going to tell me what happened to you."

Her jaw clenched. "Maverick—"

"Promise," I insisted, because I needed it like air. "Your mind," I breathed, voice wrecked and reverent, "that dangerous edge... that's what drew me in. You were so damn beautiful with all that restrained power I could taste it across lifetimes. Now you're magnificently breathtaking."

Her gaze flicked to mine. For the first time since she stepped in, her calm cracked. Not much. Just enough that I knew the words landed. "I promise," she said, like it hurt her to admit she could still be reached. Good. Because the Shrine Master chose that moment to ruin everything.

A mutter under his breath. A failsafe triggered. The floor split. Stone screamed. Roots cracked open like ribs. The ceiling shook loose ancient dust. The sanctum wasn't collapsing from wear. It was collapsing by design. A last-ditch execution. "NO!" Allyssa roared, catching me as the altar lurched.

Caspian lunged forward, hands blazing with light, anchoring us all with sheer stubborn will. Cath shoved the shadowkin back with one violent motion, putting his body between the falling debris and the Watcher like he'd decided, without ceremony, that the male was now his problem to keep alive. The watcher screamed, "OH GODS WE ARE GOING TO DIE—"

Stone fell. Bone shattered. Wards detonated. And through the chaos, through the ruin, through the bond stretched tight as a noose, the triad whispered a single truth like a vow carved into the world:

Together. Or not at all.

Chapter Forty: Truth through fire

"The soul becomes dyed with the colour of its thoughts." - Marcus Aurelius

Maverick POV

The sanctum didn't collapse. It confessed. The moment the final shackle disintegrated beneath Allyssa's hands, the chamber convulsed like a living organism finally forced to admit the lie it had been built to protect. The Triskillian mosaic beneath us spun violently, spirals grinding against one another as ancient wards tore free from the stone.

Obsidian columns cracked open. Salt veins burst along the ceiling like lightning trapped in bone. And through it all—

The Shrine Master laughed. A wet, broken sound. He was still pinned exactly where Allyssa had left him, shadows wrapped around his limbs like iron chains, driving his body into the stone floor. Black tendrils crawled across his chest and throat, tightening whenever he struggled.

He struggled often. "Look at it!" he rasped, blood bubbling from his lips. "Look at what you've done, Wolf!" The sanctum groaned again. "You think this place was built to hold you?" he snarled. "It was built to bury you!" His eyes glittered with fanatic triumph. "The failsafe is already awake." A deep grinding noise echoed through the chamber.

"No Black Wolf leaves this mountain alive," he hissed. "No warlock bonded to her survives." His grin widened. "And no prophecy completes itself." The ceiling cracked. Allyssa caught me before the altar could drop. Her arms locked around my torso instinctively, hauling me upright against her as the floor shifted beneath us. Pain ripped through my ribs where the final cuff had been embedded, but the bond flared hotter than the agony.

Alive. She had me. Caspian appeared at my side immediately, hands blazing with white-blue Seelie light as he forced healing magic into my shattered ribs. Bone began knitting. Slowly. Painfully. I turned my head toward him.

"Have you lost your senses?" He blinked. "What?" "You're healing me," I rasped, " While she's bleeding." His jaw tightened instantly. "I already tried." The answer came sharp. "She won't let me touch her." That landed harder than any spell in the room.

Above us a massive root-vein snapped loose from the ceiling. "DOWN!" Cath moved before anyone else could react. The druid slammed the ironwood staff he carried into the floor, runes carved along its length igniting in a burst of green-gold light. The staff focused his magic instantly, the energy surging outward in a protective arc.

Stone shattered against the barrier. Most of it deflected. One jagged piece didn't. The shard punched through the edge of the shield and slammed into Cath's shoulder, throwing him violently to the ground. His staff clattered across the Triskillian.

"Cath!" I yelled for my best friend. The shadowkin male was moving before the name finished leaving my mouth. The veilwalker dropped beside him, grabbing his collar as blood spread rapidly through the torn fabric of his coat. "You suicidal oak-headed idiot," The shadowkin snapped.

Cath tried to push himself upright. Failed. Allyssa turned sharply. "Indigo." The single word cut through the chaos like a blade. At least I now had a name to go with the slightly eclectic veilwalker. "Use the mist." She commanded. He froze. "What?"

"Take him back through the veil," she said coldly. "Now." Indigo stared at her. "My well is nearly empty." The words came out tight. "I burned most of it following you through the mist the last few days and fighting through this damned sanctum. I saved what's left to get all of us out once Maverick can travel."

Cath coughed weakly beside him. Blood hit the stone and it disappeared. Allyssa didn't hesitate. "There isn't time."

"He'll die in the mist if I force it," Indigo snapped. "And you are injured." He gestured sharply toward her side. "That will make summoning the mist difficult enough." His voice dropped lower. "But carrying someone else through it? That's something veilwalkers train years to do."

Another piece of the ceiling collapsed nearby. "And even if you could manage it," he continued, "you still haven't been trained to shield others from the mist itself." Caspian frowned. "Why would we need to be shielded from the mist?"

"It's poisonous," Indigo said sharply. "To anyone who doesn't summon it." He pointed at the swirling shadow and mist already beginning to gather around Allyssa's feet. "The veilwalker has to actively shape the mist to *carry* the others, not infect them. It takes control. Focus."

The word snapped my attention toward her. Mist. Veilwalking. I knew the magic well enough. Shadowkin used it to cross the seams between realms. But Allyssa shouldn't have been able to command it. When I'd first felt the layers in her bloodline I had sensed Shadowkin in the mix, buried beneath wolf and Unseelie... but that had been theory. Possibility. Not proof. The mist gathering around her boots suggested otherwise.

I felt something colder than the collapsing sanctum settle in my stomach. If Allyssa could summon the mist... Then the Shadowkin blood in her veins wasn't dormant. It was awake. And judging by the way the vapor curled toward her like something recognizing its master— It had been waiting for her.

His eyes flicked toward her wound again. "You're injured. Furious. Half-feral." He shook his head. "That combination historically ends badly." Allyssa's gaze hardened. "Take him." Indigo hesitated. Her shadows tightened around the Shrine Master instinctively. The cultist wheezed as the tendrils constricted. "If you let Cath die," she said quietly, "there is nowhere in this world you will be able to hide that I will not find you."

Indigo closed his eyes. "Wonderful." He sighed heavily. "Threatened by a mythical wolf goddess while standing in a collapsing death temple." He looked down at Cath. "Just another Thursday." Then he hauled the druid upright. "If we die in the mist," he muttered, "I am haunting you personally." Allyssa let out a little smirk "looking forward to it" Then the air behind him warped. Mist flooded the chamber as Indigo tore open the veil between realms. He dragged Cath through the breach—

—and both vanished. The sanctum shook harder. The failsafe was accelerating. Stone began falling in earnest now.

Allyssa still held the Shrine Master pinned in shadow. The Shrine Master's head snapped toward where Indigo as the veilwalker had left as their words started to process. His cracked lips split into a horrified grin. "Mist?" he rasped. His eyes dragged slowly back to Allyssa. "No... no, that can't be—" "Shadowkin," he breathed. "NO!"

Allyssa didn't even turn her head. Her shadows reacted before she did. They surged across the chamber like living blades. The Shrine Master's scream cut off mid-breath as the shadows slammed him into the stone wall. Bone cracked. Flesh tore. Blood exploded across the sanctum floor. The impact didn't kill him instantly. The second strike did.

The blood hit the floor. And the mark on Allyssa's skin ignited. The sigil burned crimson against her throat, drinking in the violence around it like a starving thing finally fed. Then the absorption. Every drop of spilled blood began to slide toward her boots. Not flowing. Pulling. As if the earth itself had opened a vein beneath her.

I stared at the spreading crimson as it crawled across the stone toward Allyssa's feet. Then slowly looked at Caspian. The expression on my face said only one thing: *What the actual hell is that.* Caspian's mouth thinned. He didn't look surprised. Just... tired. "It has been doing that since we arrived."

The crimson light surged. Allyssa's body went rigid. Her back arched as if invisible hands had seized every vein in her body and pulled. The bloodlust she had carried through the battle tore free from her in a violent rush. The magic slammed downward. Straight into the ground. The sanctum floor shuddered.

For a heartbeat nothing happened. Then the cracked earth began to glow faintly green beneath the stone. Roots pushed upward through the fractures. Thin. Fragile. Alive. A whisper brushed through the chamber, soft and ancient and amused. "Well done, Black Wolf." The crimson sigil on Allyssa's skin flickered. Then vanished. Gone as if it had never existed.

The force of the magic dropped Allyssa to her hands and knees. For a moment she stayed there, breathing hard, fingers pressed into the cracked stone. Something brushed her hand. She looked down. Through one of the thin fractures in the floor, a small green stem pushed upward. It unfolded slowly. Deliberately. Four delicate leaves spreading open in the dim light. A single four-leaf clover. It brushed softly against Allyssa's fingers as if in thanks. Or affection.

I exhaled a slow breath. "Well," I muttered. "That's new." Caspian didn't answer. His posture was rigid, half in a crouch turned toward Allyssa ready to go to her but holding himself back. Then, beneath their feet the Triskillian begun to glow. Once. Twice. Then the first spiral ignited.

The bond between them was still twisted tight with hurt. Still raw. Still unresolved. Caspian and Allyssa still weren't breathing as one. Still weren't looking at each other. The Triskillian bond strained like a creature trying to be born. A pulse, deep, hungry, booming through my ribs, tore through me. Not a request. Not a whisper. A command. Complete the triad. Unify. Truth through truth through truth. NOW. I exhaled, bloody and shaking and furious that I had waited this long.

This strain meant the prophecy couldn't stabilize. Which meant— We were about to die. Stone began to fall. Allyssa's shadows lashed upward instantly, catching several chunks mid-air. Caspian's light flared outward, reinforcing the barrier. My sigils flickered weakly beneath my skin. Not enough. Not alone. But together... The bond shifted. Not completion. Alignment.

Temporary. Instinctive. Three forces reaching for each other like magnets suddenly remembering how they were meant to sit. Caspian's hand caught my shoulder as the floor lurched beneath us. Allyssa's grip tightened around my ribs at the same moment. For the first time since the altar chains shattered, the three of us were touching at once.

The mosaic beneath our feet flickered. Once. A thin line of light tracing one spiral before dying again. "Don't fight it," I murmured to Allyssa. Caspian swallowed. Allyssa's gaze snapped toward me. The old instinct to resist flickered in her expression.

So, I did the only thing left. I reached into the bond. Not gently. Not carefully. I pulled. Secrets tore free first. Caspian's truth burst through the bond like white fire. He loved Allyssa. He feared losing himself in her. He feared failing her. But beneath all of that— His feelings toward me. Not rivalry. Not resentment. Brotherhood. Affection. Trust. The desire to stand beside me protecting her. To be chosen. To be enough for both of us. He gasped as the truth ripped free of him.

Allyssa froze. Her glare promised a creative murder in the future but I just smiled at my beautiful terror. I knew she was going to hate this part. Then her truth followed suit. Dark. Wild. Beautiful. She needs me. Not want, need. On a primal level. The wolf in her latches to me the way it latches to blood, to battle, to destiny. I am her shadow, her sin, her sanctuary. Her hunger. Her mirror. A shiver of anticipation at the devouring emotions was intoxicating. Then Caspian—

Caspian was something else. He was breath. Morning light. The one thing that made her hesitate before killing the world. Her anchor. Her tether to humanity. Her reminder that she was more than a weapon. She loved us. Just not gently. Not safely. I have never known love to feel so endless. Like she would burn the realm down and not feel a sliver of guilt for it, as long as we were safe and unharmed.

Both truths collided in the bond like opposing tides. Her breath stuttered. Her eyes widened. Her shadows flared. Caspian inhaled sharply as her truth hit him through the bond. Then I released mine. My devotion to Allyssa. Ancient. Unapologetic. I need Allyssa. Just as primally as she needed me. Like marrow. Like breath. Like fate carved into bone. She is my queen. My crime. My cathedral. My destruction. My devotion to her body, mind and soul. Predates the last five Black Wolves. Predates the wars that created hunters in the first place.

And Caspian— I choose him. Not as a lover at least not at this stage. Not as a rival. As my brother. My partner in protecting her. The man I would kneel beside in battle. Or die beside when prophecy finally demanded its due. The only man I would trust to stand beside me loving her. My partner.

Beneath us the second spiral ignited. This time it didn't fade. Caspian reached for Allyssa. This time she didn't pull away. I placed my hand over theirs. The third spiral blazed to life. The symbol beneath us erupted in gold, white, and shadow-black light. Not exploding outward. Rising. As if something ancient had finally remembered how to breathe. Shadow curled from Allyssa's skin like living ink. Caspian's light hardened around it like starfire. My sigils threaded through both currents, binding them before the power could tear itself apart.

The Triskillian awakened. Their thoughts brushed mine. Not merging. Interlocking. Three separate currents of magic collided and twisted together like braided flame. Darkness. Light. Balance. The sanctum paused. Just for a heartbeat.

Allyssa turned toward us. Caspian turned too. For the first time since the battle began— They looked at each other. Not healed. Not whole. But honest. Allyssa staggered. "What did we just do?" I smiled through blood. "Exactly what the prophecy wanted."

Stone exploded overhead. The sanctum began to collapse inward. Allyssa's breathing went ragged, like she was struggling to breath. She was still bleeding. Her shadows flared violently. Then she made the decision. "I'm getting us out."

"You're injured," I rasped. "I don't care." She responded with her don't argue with me voice. I ignored the tone. "You've never been trained for that," I continued. She didn't look at me. "I'll figure it out." The bond surged again. Mist erupted around us. Caspian grabbed my shoulder. Allyssa grabbed both of us. The Triskillian flared—

—and reality tore sideways. Mist swallowed the sanctum. Stone. Dust. Magic. All of it vanished. The world slammed back into place inside her dormitory. My knees nearly buckled as the mist collapsed around us. I stared at her. "You just veilwalked without killing us." She wiped blood from her lip. "Apparently." Silence filled the room.

Caspian's healing magic surged instantly into her wound before she could stop him. This time— She let him. I leaned against the wall, exhausted. I shook my head slowly. "You're going to kill Indigo."

"Why?" She asked sounding so adorably confused at what she just pulled off. "Because when he realizes you did that without training, he's going to have an aneurysm." I joked. Allyssa's gaze shifted toward me slowly ignoring the joke, as if she just remembered something vitally important.

"You pulled secrets from the bond." Not a question. A warning. I smiled faintly. "Necessary." Her eyes narrowed. "You still have secrets of your own." She accused. "Always." I agreed, knowing it would infuriate her just a little. Her wolf stirred inside the bond. "Do not mistake my acceptance of this bond for forgiveness Maverick." My smile was so bright that I couldn't stop it even if I tried. "I wouldn't dream of it Mo bhanríon."

Her gaze flicked toward Caspian. Then back to me. The air between the three of us tightened. Expectation. No more delay. No more barriers. Her voice dropped low. "We need to finish this." The Triskillian pulsed between us. Not complete. But unstoppable. And this time—

None of us looked away. My world, however, narrowed to two figures: Allyssa — my Queen, my poison, my purpose. Caspian — our anchor, our light, our beloved idiot.

Chapter Forty-One: On Her Terms

"To dare is to lose one's footing momentarily. Not to dare is to lose oneself."

— Søren Kierkegaard

Caspian POV

The veilwalk ended like the world had been folded in half and snapped back into place. Mist collapsed around us, dissolving into nothing as the three of us stumbled into Allyssa's dormitory. The familiar room felt strangely small after the collapsing sanctum. Quiet. Safe. Too quiet.

For a moment none of us moved. Then the bond surged. Not violently. Hungrily. Not just sexual. Something deeper. Older. A resonance humming through my bones like a second heartbeat. Complete. Merge. Seal the Triskillian. Choose to remove all barriers.

My breath shook as I looked at her.

Allyssa stood between us, shoulders tight, shadows curling around her ankles like restless wolves. Her black-silver eyes flicked between Maverick and me, calculating, wary. Her hand was still in mine. She hadn't pulled away. But I could feel the tension through the bond like a wire drawn too tight.

That the last step to secure the Triskillian bond required proximity, too close, too intimate, too vulnerable. It wasn't just sex, but the magic demanded a kind of merging that mimicked it in intensity. Bodies close. Hearts aligned. Souls open. Trust not just with the physical, but the emotional. She'd been hurt before. Used. Trapped. Claimed without consent. This was... different. But the resemblance alone, the feeling of being trapped was enough to make her pulse spike with panic.

Her thoughts tumbled down the bond thread, the mental barrier she'd been holding had crumbled at Maverick's secrets reveal earlier. *One of them we could fight. Both of them far more difficult— Two of them meant the possibility of surrender.* The voice sounded like her but not at the same time. Her pulse spiked. I squeezed her hand gently. "Lys," I murmured. Her eyes snapped to mine. "You don't have to fear us." The words trembled as they left me, but they were true down to the marrow. A shiver ran through her. Not rejection. Recognition.

Maverick had gone still beside her, watching her the way he watched unstable magic—patient, focused, waiting for the moment to intervene. He had heard her as well. "Mo bhanríon," he murmured, voice rough with affection and reverence. "It isn't force. It's choice."

Allyssa swallowed hard. "I know," she whispered. "But the bond... it feels like pressure, like I'm being trapped. Like......like something is pushing me toward—"

"Toward us," I finished softly. Her jaw clenched. She looked away. Her shadows twitched in warning, like wolves pacing behind a door. Maverick stepped forward slowly, deliberately letting her see every movement. Not approaching like a predator. Like a man offering a hand to someone standing at the edge of a cliff. "Not toward anything you don't want," he said.

"The Triskillian only stabilizes if the three of us choose it." He paused. "Together." The bond pulsed harder. "Mutual claim."

My pulse hammered at the word claim. Because gods help me, I wanted that. Her shadows curling around me again. Reaching for me subconsciously. Maverick's magic humming under my skin. The three of us aligned so fully that for one moment we were something more than ourselves. The bond pulsed again, hard enough that my knees buckled.

Allyssa inhaled sharply, pain and desire tangled together. "I can't—" she whispered. "I don't trust my reaction, I could lash out, you didn't see what I was when I lost control when they picked me up mo scáth."

"You don't distrust us," Maverick said softly. "You distrust being vulnerable." She flinched. He didn't touch her, not yet, but his voice dropped to something low and intimate:

"You trust us enough to save you. Enough to fight with you. Enough to bleed with you. Trusting us to hold you..." His eyes softened. "...that's the part that scares you." My throat tightened. Because he was right. And because the bond *agreed.* A low, resonant hum spread through the air, brushing against the inside of my ribs. Allyssa felt it too. Her eyes snapped to mine. Black swallowing silver. Fear and desire and want braided so tightly I couldn't tell them apart.

I stepped closer. Slow. Careful. "Lys," I said softly. "If you say stop, everything stops." Her breath hitched. I could feel the truth of the promise settle into her bones. "You decide how this goes." Maverick nodded. "Control isn't the opposite of surrender." His voice dropped lower. "It's choosing when it happens." The tension in her shoulders loosened slightly. Just a fraction. Then she said the words that changed the air in the room.

Allyssa POV

The bond wasn't quiet. It was a living, breathing thing. A creature made of hunger, destiny, and need that prowled beneath my ribs.

Complete.

Merge.

Seal the triad.

Choose.

When I still hadn't responded to them. Caspian's eyes flicked to me, then down, then up again shy and overwhelmed, but steady, always steady. "Lys... if you want to stop—" I huffed in frustration

"Don't say that." My voice cracked sharper than I meant. His wolf whimpered behind his eyes. My chest tightened.

"Lys... what do you need from us?" There it was. The only question that mattered. What did I need? My breath shuddered. Shadows curled around my ankles like restless wolves. The bond pulsed against my spine, urging, craving, pulling. "I need..." The word scraped out like glass.

"...to stay in control." Maverick exhaled softly, like my confession was a blessing. "Then you will." Caspian nodded without hesitation. "At your command."

Something in my chest loosened at that. Just a little. I stepped back from them, only a step, but it changed the air completely. Their bodies straightened as if responding to a silent command. Maverick's shoulders lowered. Caspian's breath caught. My shadows rose behind me, tall and slow and powerful. I held out my hand. "Come here," I said. They came instantly.

My pulse jumped, fear, want, memory, power, braided too tightly to separate. I forced myself to breathe, to stand tall, to meet their eyes. Caspian looked at me like I was the dawn after a long winter cycle. Maverick looked at me like I was the altar he would willingly bleed on. Both reactions lit fire low in my belly. "The bond needs touch," Maverick murmured. "Intention," Caspian added. "And choice," I finished. I stepped close enough that their breaths mingled with mine. Close enough that our shadows and light tangled on the floor. Close enough that the bond thrummed with impatient hunger.

Maverick's hand found my waist and let his forehead rest on my temple breathing me in. Caspian's hand found my lower back, hesitant but wanting. His forehead brushed mine from the other side. "Lys..." he breathed, voice trembling. "Tell us what you need." What I needed was terrifying. And real. And mine. "I need," I whispered, "to choose you both. My way. My pace. In control."

Maverick closed his eyes. Caspian nodded against my skin. The bond coiled, tight, hot, urgent. "And I need," I continued softly, "for both of you to surrender to me." Caspian's breath caught, a gasp of want and fear and devotion. Maverick shuddered, hands fisting at his sides. "As you command," he whispered. The bond roared with approval.

I stepped back, my shadows rose slowly behind me like a dark crown. My gaze sharpened. Predatory. Powerful. Commanding. My voice steady now. "Kneel." They did. Without hesitation. Without question. Without fear. Not submission to weakness. Submission to trust.

To me. The bond surged so hard my vision blurred. Heat pooled low and deep. Power hummed over my skin. Their eyes, lifting, waiting, wanting, pulled something fierce and hungry from inside me.

I cupped Caspian's chin. Ran a hand through Maverick's hair. Let them feel my choice. "This," I whispered, voice low and dangerous and soft "is how we begin, eyes down." The bond snapped tight, hungry. The room dimmed. My shadows moved around me like living silk as I stripped away the torn remnants of battle-ruined clothing. Darkness wrapped itself around my body, forming a gown of living shadow that clung to my form before falling in soft waves to the floor. A long slit up the side that reached my hip. Power was radiating from me. Fierce. Controlled.

Caspian trembled. Maverick bowed his head. And then, I closed my eyes, taking a deep breath before I smiled ready to take what was mine and complete this bond.

Chapter Forty-Two: Worship the Queen

"Eroticism is assenting to life up to the point of death."

— Georges Bataille

Allyssa POV

Power settled into my bones like a throne I had been born to claim. The room was quiet except for the sound of breathing. Mine. Theirs. And the bond. It pulsed through the three of us like a living thing, restless and hungry. Not simply desire. Something deeper than that. Something older than language.

Completion. The Triskillian waited.

Caspian knelt before me, white-blue light flickering faintly along the edges of his skin as if his magic could not quite decide whether to hide or celebrate. His eyes were fixed on me with that same fierce devotion that had anchored me through every battle since we met.

Maverick knelt beside him, head bowed slightly, dark hair falling forward as if he had already chosen his place at my side long before this moment arrived.

Both of them waited. Not because the bond demanded it. Because I did. The monster within me purred. The queen stood tall. And for once the two of them agreed. I moved slowly around them, the soft whisper of shadow magic trailing behind my steps like silk dragged across stone. Every instinct in my body was heightened. Every emotion sharpened.

Desire.

Trust.

Fear.

Choice.

The bond vibrated under my skin. Not pushing. Waiting. I brushed my fingers lightly across the back of Maverick's neck as I passed behind him. He inhaled sharply but did not move. Perfect obedience.

Caspian shivered beneath my touch when my hand followed the same path across his shoulders. Both of them felt it. The power. The connection. The unspoken promise of what we were about to become. I stepped away and sat at the edge of the bed, crossing one leg slowly over the other. They watched me. Hungry. Reverent. Mine.

With the voice of a queen and commander "Both of you, crawl to me". Without hesitation they both crawled to me, one hand in front of the other. I could feel their anticipation with every breath bathing in it. The bond flared in approval. Not dominance. Trust. When they reached me, I tilted my head slightly, studying them as if committing every detail to memory. Caspian's breath trembled. Maverick's hands rested open against his thighs, palms upward in silent offering. I smiled faintly. Once they were at my feet, I lowered my voice to a seductive whisper; "now worship your queen".

Maverick answered immediately "yes Mo bhanríon", Caspian answered straight after "yes mistress". The words rippled through the bond like sparks striking dry tinder. But even as the heat between us grew, something else stirred beneath it. The magic. The Triskillian. Waiting. Watching. Testing.

They started kissing up my leg one on each side all the way up to my thigh. My shadows shifted instinctively when Caspian moved too quickly, curling around his wrist in gentle warning. He froze. I see Maverick's eyes go wide and I make a "tsk, tsk tsk" sound.

Maverick scrambled back on his hunches, head bowed, palms facing up, resting on his thighs. I let the moment stretch. Then I rewarded the obedience with a soft laugh. "well done mo scáth".

The bond warmed in response. Control. That was the key. Control meant safety. Control meant trust.

I focus my gaze onto Caspian and smirked; his eyes widen a little fear mixed with anticipation and damn if that wasn't the sexiest thing I have seen so far. My eyes heated in response and my shadows curl around him, snaking up to his throat, tightening, lifting him from his knees. I stand and start to circle him. "It seems someone needs to learn the rules" I say with a smug satisfaction. His body is unable to hide his response the scent of his arousal is intoxicating. I look down and Caspian was straining against his pants. I look over to Maverick and sure enough his length is clearly defined. Taking a deep breath. A deep growl of approval comes out of my throat, and a new saturation of arousal comes from my mates.

I find the winged armchair in the corner and take a seat while watching Caspian standing their throat bared to me. I looked over to Maverick and clicked my fingers in his direction, "you are both wearing too many clothes" I said in a low seductive voice and waited. Maverick started to undress himself, but I clicked my fingers at him and he stilled. Maverick locked eyes with me and my eyes went to Caspian still there with my shadows around his neck keeping him upright. Caspian spoke up in that moment "Please Mistress" but I ignored his plea and arched an eyebrow at Maverick.

Maverick's eyes widened in shock when he realised what I was commanding. He walked over to Caspian and I smiled. Caspian started to protest although I'm sure he was not aware what he was protesting about, "Lys.... Mistress...." As Maverick started to take Caspian's shirt off, I got rather impatient to get my men naked. I let Maverick keep undressing Caspian as I let loose shadows from my hands ripping through Maverick clothes so that it tattered and hung loose as my shadows pull them off. I was engrossed in pulling off each piece of fabric like a present I conjured for myself and didn't quite notice that both men had gone quiet staring at me with open hunger in their gaze.

I looked up into their faces as soon as I was done and gasped at the pure need in their faces. Heat pooled low and my wolf purred in my mind heating my skin. My patience was gone. I directed my shadows to grasp their wrists forcing them back to their knees. I locked eyes with them both and commanded crawl to me again. I lifted my leg, so it opened my thighs resting it on the arm rest. My shadows drew back as they crawled Maverick's long crawling strides to get in front of Caspian, had me grinning at the little competition.

I smiled at Maverick and as he reached an arm's length away with a look of victory in his eyes. I was about to rip that victory away; the thought made my blood sing with the power of it and heat continued to pool between my legs. I quickly lifted my leg and snapped it out my foot landing on his forehead as Caspian overtook him. Mavericks' eyes cut to mine and he smiled, I could feel his disappointment and anticipation through the bond, he loved being tortured by me, all his emotions were pouring in, and I smiled back at him.

Caspian stopped just before he was about to dive to my opening, realising he was not given permission to do anything but crawl to me. I sent him my pride he is learning fast, He shivered in response. Satisfaction roared through me. I looked back to Maverick and I commanded "watch" another saturation of arousal from them both. Voyeurism and Exhibitionism this will be fun. Maverick responded "yes Mo bhanríon".

I looked to Caspian and commanded "your going to kiss up my inner thigh and take your time slowly licking and sucking every inch of my pussy mo sholas" Caspian replied looking into my eyes sending excitement and hunger through the bond, "yes mistress". Maverick was panting, jealousy still trickling down the bond as we both watched. My clit pulsed and throbbed in need, as Caspian was doing exactly as I told him. Caspian felt my need through the bond and started stroking his tongue faster and flicking it over my clit.

I moaned out at the sensation, and I could feel Maverick shaking with his restraint. His eyes were trained on my pussy; his submission and intensity almost had me going over the edge already. I was pouring into Caspian's mouth causing him to growl in satisfaction licking up the leaking juices. His growl vibrated through my body making me gasp and moan out louder and longer. I looked towards Maverick and clicked to gain his attention, his eyes snapped to me a look of longing and hope in his eyes, I commanded "from the bottom-up mo scáth" he was quick to respond with "yes Mo bhanríon".

He dived in holding my foot gently while kissing up my legs and thighs. I looked to Caspian and tapped on his head to gain his attention. I couldn't help rolling my hips to drag his tongue over my clit one more time groaning at the sensation. I could feel the smile against my skin, but he looked up at me.

I continued to command him "you can bring those lips *Mo sholas* up to my breasts". He was already nodding before I had even finished talking "yes Mistress" he said. I looked down to Maverick his lips burning into my skin so deliciously. My core throbbing in anticipation, and then he was there licking me up from core to clit, bringing his tongue back down to my entrance. I moan out using one hand to hold Maverick at my clit. Then the next thing I know my shadow's part from my breasts, allowing for Caspian to kiss the underside of my right breast, moving his tongue from the underside to the nipple that was begging for attention.

My back arches into Caspian looking for more. Caspian takes the hint and his fingers start to twist and flick my left nipple and I growl my approval. I feel Maverick slide a finger inside and I gasp my juices flooding onto his hand. Both my mates inhale and

Caspian growls as Maverick groans, need pulses through the bond from them both. Maverick pushes a second finger inside of me and I moan out "yes" and start rolling my hips while Maverick's tongue works on my clit, Caspian is already moving his mouth to my left breast and fingers over to my wet right nipple.

I can't focus however when I start to ride Mavericks fingers chasing my first release. "Do not stop either of you, I am so close" I command. Moaning and riding Maverick fingers as he circles my clit with his tongue. The pressure is so sweet that I am falling off that edge with a cry "don't leave any behind mo scáth." I come down from my orgasm my shadows whip out and collar them both, a tendril of my shadow working as a lead as I take them to the bed.

Impatient is far to mild of a word for this driving feeling, I feel our bond pulsing fasting as if urging me forward. With a speed I didn't know I possessed I grabbed Maverick by the neck and threw him onto the bed. His back hit the mattress a burst of air left his lungs at the impact. I sent him a look that told him to stay. The look he gave me was one I couldn't put into words, the exhilaration and impatience to be inside me was all I felt through our bond. Caspian was just as impatient to feel me around his cock.

I crawl up Mavericks body dragging Caspian behind me. Apparently, that did not help him if his cursing as he watched me crawl was any indication. I dragged my hand up Maverick's leg making him close his eyes in bliss. Both Caspian and I gasped at the feeling, I smirked at Maverick's evil little smile. Maverick's cock was standing proud long and thick my mouth watered. His cock a beautiful tan like the rest of him with a pink head almost a consistent flow of pre-cum leaking. I couldn't help myself I leaned in licking him from base to head, tasting my mate and a purr of victory from his hiss of pleasure had me taking him into my mouth.

I slowly circled my tongue around the head dragging me teeth over the head, Maverick and Caspian groaned. "Mo bhanríon, please, it's too much" Maverick gasped out. All of my fractures gleamed with satisfaction from the pained begging coming from our mate. I felt a vibrating coming from behind me, Caspian had moved into a position behind me, and I moaned at the feeling of his cock against my folds. He was struggling to hold himself back but was submitting still, waiting for instruction. I took Maverick a few inches further into my mouth and hollowed out my cheeks before sucking him in deeply while dragging my mouth back to the tip. "Holy fuck, yes, your mouth is a gift from the goddess herself" Maverick yelled into the room.

Caspian's jealousy came down the bond, and I smiled with Maverick still in my mouth clutching the sheets. Caspian's hips jerked in response to Maverick's pleasure and a deep moan left me, as his cock slipped through my folds coating his cock in my juices. I popped Mavericks cock out of my mouth, "You are not to cum mo scáth, I am going to torture you to the brink and then you and Caspian will swap positions so I have the taste of both my mates on my tongue". Maverick nodded in response while Caspian quickly responded with "yes mistress", with barely restrained excitement in his voice.

I arched my back into Caspian hearing him curse "fuck me dead" his cock pushing in just a little further into my folds. I take Maverick back into my mouth, my tongue swirling, my teeth dragging, my head bobbing up and down fasting while sucking him strongly. Mavericks' moans, panting and begging were like kindling to the fire building inside me. I could feel the moment he was losing the fight with his control, his hips slightly jerking to hit the back of my throat. I immediately pulled back and kneeled straight to give him a moment. "No, no please Mo bhanríon, I need you" Maverick begged.

I just smiled down at him my shadow collar squeezing just a little and he gasped and his cock throbbed so hard I thought he might cum just from that extra pressure alone. I loosened and he calmed but I wasn't done with my torture yet. I flicked my wrists to twist their leads using more shadows to force them to change positions. Caspian laying back flat and Maverick positioned behind me.

Maverick cured "oh fucking hell", Caspian laughed "what you thought I had it easier back there". I smiled at him and bent my head licking his inner thigh to the base of his cock, all his laughing stopped. He moaned loud as did Maverick as he felt his cock slide into my folds without penetrating. Caspians cock was different from Maverick a little thinner but just as long, his skin smooth and glistening with his pre-cum and my juices. I held eye contact with him and commanded "you will not cum, you will keep your eyes open, Maverick will watch you take pleasure and when I am done, I will take both of you and you will fill me up". The panting and arousal coming from them while nodding their heads unable to form speech was deeply entertaining.

I started on Caspians cock as I did Mavericks, and he was cursing, begging faster than Maverick with his inexperience. His hips started jerking so I fasted a shadow band over his hips to keep him still. I could feel Maverick dragging the head of his cock between my folds his control back on the edges. Caspian was struggling to keep his orgasm at bay and I used my shadows to squeeze both of their necks cutting their air supply. Both their backs arched in pleasure, I knew I needed to feel them inside me, although I was getting a little nervous...... I didn't want to lash out. But as the bond pulsed through me their reassurances and my own driving desire was all I needed.

I start to move then stop, I need to change them back, so without warning I use my shadows to change their positions again. I look into Mavericks eyes with intent, and he looks at me with understanding and determination. I look back to Caspian behind me, and I see and feel his determination and understanding of my need as well. I climb into Maverick's lap with Caspian close behind me, Maverick takes a hold of my hips gentle but firm a low hum of his power flowing over my skin, making me moan. "You are the most beautiful creature that has ever walked existence Mo bhanríon".

I line Maverick at my entrance and slowly slide down inch by inch. My body is on fire in the most delicious way, moaning my pleasure. Caspian trails kisses down my spine making me shiver in delight at the sensation. I work Maverick inside me until I am fully seated into his lap, "Mo bhanríon you feel so fucking good" Maverick breaths out in awe and reverence. I roll my hips testing the feel of him and moaning my whole body vibrating with need. I balance my hands on Maverick's chest and start to move myself up and down his shaft stretching myself and making my pussy flow, I am so turned on it feel almost overwhelming.

Maverick helps me move a little faster holding onto my hips as he moans and repeats "fuck yes" repeatedly. I look over my shoulder catching Caspian watching as Mavericks cock slides in and out of my pussy, he feels me watching his eyes snap to mine and I gasp. His wolf has completely come to the surface, a snarl of need rumbles from him. I smile at my fierce wolf mate, and I command him "come to me *Mo sholas*". He doesn't hesitate, he starts to kiss me hungrily as I ride Maverick and then I turn lean over Maverick kiss him passionately as Caspian lines himself to my entrance first adding one finger and thrusting in time with Maverick, then two fingers and I gasp at the stretch but soon I moan and push down into them seeking more. Caspians wolf growls his approval, and I feel the head of his cock, as he slowly removes his fingers, and pushes the head of his cock inside "fuck you feel like heaven". I tense and Maverick brings me back to his lips "we will go slow Mo bhanríon, relax for us" he kisses me deep and I start to relax.

Caspian starts to move in time with Maverick as inch by inch he slowly seats himself inside me and I feel so full I can't speak. They both stop moving to allow me to adjust as Caspian reaches around me rubbing circles on my clit as I moan. Maverick flicks his thumb over my nipple as he continues his deep kisses. I start to move thrusting myself back into my mates as I get more and more wet. The feelings are becoming overwhelming now I feel mine and theirs mixing and conversing. The shared bond is a constant pulse now almost like it is on the verge of exploding like a C4 charge. Caspian growls close to my ear "mine", Maverick moans out at the same time "mine", my voice drops in tone my fractions coming through the moment "ours", that seemed to be the catalyst for all three of us to start chasing the impending orgasm.

My voice taking on otherworldly tone I command my mates one more time " you both need to bite me. I look over my shoulder and Caspians body is gleaming with sweat making me moan again fuck he is gorgeous. He smirks and replies in his gravelly wolf voice "yes my love". I look to Maverick and nod to him, and he looks pleased to be claiming me in this way as well, he nods "of course my love". His tone holds such sincerity that I blink emotion welling up inside.

The bond feels like raw power inside waiting it seems as if holding it's breath. Caspian circles his fingers faster over my clit. Maverick rolls my nipples within his. Their pace increases a fever that couldn't be stopped if we tried. All our panting and the sound of skin slapping along with our cursing about how close we are until finally I break apart. My orgasm so strong, I scream, causing Caspian to let out a roar as he floods my insides with his cum, Maverick shouting out "fuck" as his orgasm rips through him filling me up in the most delicious way.

Caspian pushed my hair out of the way and he sinks his teeth into my left shoulder. Fast as lightning Maverick was sitting up sinking his teeth into me, both drawing blood and a euphoric feeling filled me up sending us into a second orgasm. Every dominion would feel this.The Queen was claiming her mates. And the realms listened.

That is when the bond explodes just as predicted. A power so strong I thought was going to force us apart and fling us across the room. However, it did the opposite, Maverick clung to my front while Caspian clung to the back of me both sets of arms wrapped around me when a burst of golden light flared from the three of us like a shock wave earth quake the walls shuddered, the windows blasted out and then we aligned completely. I could feel them both as if they were apart of me and we spoke in our minds collectively each of us hearing the other;

"When the blood of kings and the fury of the Black Wolf merge,

When the White Wolf's light steadies the storm's edge,

When the Warlock of Secrets binds them in shadow and truth,

The Triskelion shall awaken—three souls woven in one fate.

From the ruin of empires and the ashes of kings,

Their bond will forge a throne unclaimed by mortal hand.

Through them, the Hunt shall rise and the old orders shall tremble,

For the Black Wolf is not just fury, but the promise of reckoning.

The White Wolf is not just mercy, but the quiet strength of night.

The Warlock is not just cunning, but the keeper of all that was lost.

The Academy shall stand as silent witness, its halls bound by ancient pacts,

Vowed to nurture the Black Wolf's rise, yet shackled by duty to the shadows.

In secret they watch, their loyalty woven into the walls themselves,

Guardians of the prophecy's breath, awaiting the Queen's call.

Together they stand—wolf, fae, warlock,

Three threads of the world's last hope and final ruin.

In their union, the fractured realms shall find peace or perish.

And in the shadow of their love and rage, a crown will be claimed."

The inked runes that had been fading in and out were now present. All our bodies were covered in them, for Maverick it replaced ones he had put on himself over his long life. We were covered from the neck down. Caspian gasped in awe at the runes our internal wells reacting to these ancient language shifting over their skin. He asked, "what are they for". I shrugged having no idea. Maverick though with all the "These aren't just prophecy markings," Maverick said quietly. "They're God Trial champion runes."

We all looked at each other and mix of emotions, "Of fucking course they are" I said deadpan.

Chapter Forty-Three: The Day Power Chose a Side

"Everyone sees what you appear to be; few know what you truly are."
- Niccolò Machiavelli

Indigo POV

The sanctum should have been rubble. The last time I stood here the mountain itself had been splitting apart, stone collapsing under the fury of battle. Now the place was... breathing. I stepped cautiously through the broken archway and stared.

The ruins of the Severed Flame cult lay scattered across the cavern floor like discarded bones. Bodies twisted in impossible shapes. Some had been crushed into the stone as though the earth itself had clenched a fist. Others were carved cleanly in two. Shadows still clung to the wounds like hungry serpents refusing to release their meal.

One man's skull had collapsed inward. Another had no eyes left at all. His sockets still smoked faintly. The cult had not died cleanly. They had died afraid. And yet... Beneath the carnage something else stirred. Power. Not destructive power. Living power. I stepped further into the cavern and felt it pulse through the ground beneath my boots.

The Dryad homeland. It was waking. The underground city beyond the sanctum was no longer a graveyard of roots and broken stone. Green light flickered along the cavern walls. Thin shoots of silver bark pushed through cracks in the rock.

Life was returning. "She restored it," I murmured. Of course she had. Allyssa did not simply destroy things. She rewrote them. My gaze drifted across the battlefield again. The Tribunal hadn't come. Which meant they had chosen not to. Convenient. Either the Black Wolf died here, solving their prophecy problem...

Or the cult died instead, eliminating an inconvenient rebellion. Either outcome would have suited them perfectly. Hands clean. No witnesses. No blame. I scraped ash from a melted altar rune and shook my head. "The perfect outcome for them," I muttered.

But the perfect outcome hadn't happened. She had survived. All three of them had. And that meant the Tribunal's carefully balanced future had just collapsed. A tremor rippled through the cavern. Not from the earth. From the realm itself. I froze. Then it came again. A pulse of power so immense my bones recognised it before my mind could.

The Triskillian. My Shadowfen blood surged in response. Old blood. Royal blood. Recognition slammed through my body like lightning. Not merely power. Not merely prophecy. Royal lineage. His Line. Older than the Tribunal. My knees nearly buckled.

"She's not just the Black Wolf..." I whispered. "She's the Queen, his heir." The second pulse struck harder. Gold. White. Black. Three powers braided together. The bond had completed. The prophecy had awakened. And the realms had just felt it. I didn't wait for the third pulse. "Cath!" I shouted.

The druid stepped forward from the tunnel behind me. "Take us back to the Academy." Because whatever happened next... The Tribunal would not be ready.

The Tribunal

They arrived in silence. Seven Elders. Thirteen Wardens. Masks carved in the cold geometry of ancient authority. The sanctum needed no explanation. The stench of blood and prophecy hung thick in the air. One Warden gagged. Another pointed toward scorch marks carved into stone like enormous claws. A third knelt beside a corpse whose ribcage had been opened like the pages of a book.

No one spoke. Not until the eldest Elder stepped forward. "Efficient," they said. The word carried no admiration. Only calculation. Another Elder crouched beside the shattered ritual altar. "The Severed Flame is annihilated," she observed. "Every ringleader. Every acolyte."

"Their entire network," another finished. A pause followed. Then one of the Elders spoke quietly. "If the Black Wolf had died here, the prophecy problem would have vanished."

"And if she lived," another replied, "the cult would be erased." A faint ripple of approval passed through the group. Two threats removed. No Tribunal involvement. A perfect outcome. Except—

"She lived," the eldest Elder said softly. The silence that followed was colder. "And worse," the Warden Commander added, "the Academy stood with her."

Mutters spread. "The Academy grows arrogant."

"They believe themselves guardians of prophecy."

"They believe they can choose the fate of the realms."

The eldest Elder studied the devastation carefully.

"And now their Black Wolf is no longer alone."

"They have bound the White Wolf."

"And the Warlock of Secrets."

A hiss rippled through the Wardens.

"The triad..."

"Impossible."

"No triad has succeeded in centuries." The eldest Elder opened their mouth to respond—

When the world shuddered. A pulse of magic rolled across the cavern. Gold. White. Black. The Triskillian. Several Wardens collapsed instantly. Masks cracked under the strain of power. Even the Elders staggered. "The bond..." someone gasped. "...has completed." Silence fell again. But this time it was not calculation.

It was fear. Real fear. Because they all understood what came next. The prophecy had begun. Another tremor rippled through the sanctum. Ash lifted from the ground in spiralling currents.

The shape it formed was unmistakable. The Triskelion. Three arms. Three powers. One fate. The eldest Elder steadied themselves against a broken pillar.

"It seems," they said slowly, "our experiment has failed." A Warden turned sharply. "What experiment?" The Elder ignored the question. Instead, they looked toward the distant direction of the Academy. "Prepare the Tribunal chambers."

"Summon the Oathkeepers."

"Gather the faction leaders."

The Wardens stiffened. "For what purpose?" one asked. The Elder's mask tilted toward the distant pulse of power still echoing through the world. "For the trials and possibly war." Another tremor cracked through the stone beneath their feet. Because somewhere far away...

The Black Wolf had claimed her mates. The Warlock had sealed the bond. The White Wolf had anchored the storm. And the realms had felt the moment power chose its side. Nothing would ever be the same again.

Chapter Forty-Four: Before the First Arrow Falls

"Victorious warriors win first and then go to war."

– Sun Tzu

Lance Lakemond POV

The Academy had stood for eight thousand years. Empires had risen and crumbled into dust during that time. Factions had burned cities, redrawn borders, and rewritten histories to suit their ambitions. But the Academy endured. Because it had never truly belonged to any of them.

I stood at the tall windows of my office overlooking the oldest courtyard of the Academy. Beneath the moonlight, the ancient wards carved into the stone were beginning to glow faintly. The wards were stirring. That alone would have been enough to trouble any Director.

But the first warning was not magic. It was instinct. A tightening beneath the ribs. A prickle along the spine. I had only felt it twice before. Once when the last Black Wolf died when I was a boy living in Greenhollow. And once the day Allyssa stepped onto Academy grounds and the old stones held their breath. Tonight, the sensation returned like thunder on the horizon.

Something ancient had awakened. The communication orb in my hand vibrated. "Hawthorne," I answered. Static crackled across the line before the Hunter spoke. "Director... you'll want to hear this firsthand." I stepped closer to the window overlooking the courtyard. "Report."

"The Severed Flame is gone, sir." His voice trembled. "Gone how?"

"Erased." He exhaled slowly. "We expected the sanctum to be rubble. It was collapsing during the battle. But when we returned..."

He paused. "It isn't dead anymore." That caught my attention. I'll ask why he left soon. "Explain."

"The land," Hawthorne said quietly. "The Dryad homeland... it's alive." Silence filled my office.

"The roots are growing again," he continued. "Green shoots pushing through the stone. The underground groves are breathing. The city is waking up like something just poured life back into it." Of course. Only one force in the realm could accomplish something like that.

"What happened during the battle?" I asked. "We pieced together what we could from survivors. There was only one left in the last chamber and watched the last of what happened. The Black Wolf killed the Shrine Master herself. It was messy... shadows everywhere. But then something else happened."

His voice lowered. "The mark on her neck—Lilith's mark—it started absorbing the blood from the shrine master. Every drop of it, according to the witness, the white wolf confirmed that it has been doing that throughout the entire battle."

I closed my eyes briefly. So that was the price. "She released it," Hawthorne whispered. "All of it. The bloodlust magic. The oath. She forced it into the ground, or it had reached some unknown fulfilment and surged from her body and she directed it to the land."

Into the dying land. Healing what the factions of Veyloris had broken generations ago. The Dryads had lost more than territory when their homeland burned. They lost their culture. Their roots. Their living memory. And the Black Wolf had just given it back. I exhaled slowly.

"That," I murmured, "is why the Dryads agreed to the alliance to stand with her." Hawthorne continued. "Cath and his Grove were there. They said the land responded instantly. The moment the magic drained from her, the soil started healing." A pause. "Director... the Dryads are calling it a miracle."

No. Not a miracle. A reckoning. The factions of Veyloris had taken that land. The Black Wolf had returned it. "And Allyssa?" I asked. "Alive."

"Confirmed?"

"Yes, sir. She summoned the Mist during the battle."

Interesting.

"She isn't a Shadowfin veilwalker, are you sure?" I said quietly.

"Yes, sir." Bloodline instinct. This just got more complicated. Where did the Shadowkin bloodline come from, what else should we expect. "And the White Wolf?" I asked. "With her."

"And the Warlock?"

"Also present." Good. The triad held. Then Hawthorne's voice dropped. "The Tribunal arrived after the fighting." Of course they did. "And?"

"They're circling the ruins now. Talking quietly. I caught fragments."

"What fragments?"

"They think letting the Black Wolf live may have been their mistake."

A humourless smile tugged at my mouth. "It was." The orb trembled suddenly. Then the first pulse struck the Academy. Gold. White. Black. Three powers braided together like strands of a crown. Across the grounds students staggered. Professors froze mid-stride. The ancient wards buried beneath the Academy flared to life. Hawthorne gasped. "Director... what is that?"

I watched the sky fracture with lines of light like an awakening constellation. "The Triskillian bond," I said quietly. "It has completed." Silence followed. Then Hawthorne whispered, "Gods... she actually did it." The second pulse rolled outward. This one carried weight. Authority. It struck every Natural in the realm.

Wolf.

Fae.

Warlock.

Druid.

Shade.

The world itself felt it. Because somewhere in Veyloris, prophecy had just chosen its champions. The God Trials had begun. The Academy responded instantly. Silver wards carved into the stone buildings ignited. Statues turned slowly toward the east. Toward the source of the power. Then the ground cracked.

At the centre of the courtyard the Huntstone split open with a sound like the earth exhaling. The volcanic glass shell fractured apart. Inside, a sphere of shifting violet magic pulsed slowly. Ancient. Alive. The true heart of the Academy. The Huntstone. It pulsed again. Not magic. A summons. Across the realm every Hunter tied to the Academy would feel it. Every Lodge. Every bloodline. Every warrior who had ever sworn to protect the balance. The Huntstone was calling them home.

Soon they would gather here. Soon they would kneel before the stone. And they would swear fealty to the Black Wolf as their ancestors once had. The Tribunal believed the Academy belonged to them. They had always been wrong. "Director," Hawthorne whispered.

"The Tribunal felt the pulses too. Some of their Wardens collapsed. Their Elders are already summoning Oathkeepers." Good. Let them panic. "They believe the Academy will move first."

"They're not wrong," I said. The Hunter hesitated. "What happens now?" I looked across the Academy. Across the towers that had quietly prepared for this moment for centuries. War between factions was coming. Every court of Veyloris would soon choose a side. But another storm loomed beyond that. The God Trials.

Now that the prophecy had awakened and the champions had been chosen, the ancient trials would begin again. Trials that had not been attempted in centuries. And the Black Wolf would face them with two souls bound to hers. "Hawthorne," I said calmly.

"Yes, Director?"

"Return to the Academy."

"Yes, sir."

"And prepare your Lodge."

"For war?" he asked quietly.

"For reality," I replied. "War will follow soon enough." I ended the call. Outside, the Academy continued to awaken. Then the communication orb vibrated again. Another channel. Older. Colder. Unseelie magic pulsed through the glass. Finally. I answered the call and leaned back in my chair.

"So his Highness finally graces me with a call," I said dryly. "Where the fuck have you been, Caelrith?" "I have been leaving messages with your court since the start of the winter cycle."

Chapter Forty-Five: The Heir of Night and Ruin

"It is better to be feared than loved, if one cannot be both."

- Machiavelli

Unseelie King POV

Far beneath the mortal realm, in the palace carved into the marrow of night itself, the Unseelie King slept beneath a canopy of living shadow. He had not dreamed in centuries. Dreams were for creatures who still carried hope in their bones. But tonight the darkness fractured.

A tremor tore through the world, shaking the roots of the Underground Court. The obsidian pillars groaned. The throne chamber keened in a voice older than kingdoms. Even the Hollow River paused its eternal flow, rippling backward for a single heartbeat.

Then—

A pulse.

Gold.

White.

Black.

Power so ancient it predated language slammed into his chest. The King bolted upright, shadows exploding outward like startled ravens. Frost-silk sheets slid from his body as his heart—silent for centuries—lurched painfully into motion.

"No..." he whispered. Not disbelief. Recognition. Blood calls to blood.

The palace of Dubh'Linn, carved into the spine of the Hollow Night itself, trembled. The obsidian walls sweated shadow. The great pillars—veined with starless luminescence—arched inward, sensing their blood-heir's awakening across the realm.

He felt the Triskillian bond ignite like a new star carved into an eternal sky. Felt the magic spill across ley lines and shadow paths. Felt prophecy unfurl. And beneath it—

His blood. The King pressed a trembling hand to his sternum. "Impossible." He had lived millennia. He had tried—gods, he had tried—to produce an heir worthy of the Night Throne. None had survived. None had carried the correct power. But this...

This power carried him. The Black Wolf. His daughter. A ragged breath escaped him, frosting the air silver. Emotion he had not felt in centuries crashed through him all at once. Exhilaration. Fear. Pride. And jealousy sharp enough to taste like iron. A laugh tore from him—half delighted, half horrified. "After all these empty centuries..."

A princess. A future queen. A blood-heir to the Unseelie throne. But his laughter faded quickly. Because the magic he felt through her bond was not purely Unseelie. It was storm. Shadow. Wolf. Warlock. It was prophecy incarnate. It was more. More than him. More than any king.

Her power surged through the shadow-paths of the realm, igniting ancient markers of Umbrakyn sovereignty. Forgotten towers flared awake. Rivers of night reversed their flow. A chill crept down his spine. "Should I celebrate you," he murmured into the dim chamber, "or fear you?" The shadows did not answer.

He rose slowly, bare feet touching the cold stone. The palace shifted around him, walls leaning inward as if bowing. Acknowledging. The Black Wolf had awakened. And Unseelie blood answered her. "A daughter," he whispered. "A queen."

"A threat." He moved toward the throne as shadows fled his path. "I have an heir," he breathed. "The Court has a princess." His eyes gleamed crimson-gold. "And fate has forged a weapon sharper than anything in my halls." Then another realization struck him. The bond he felt through her magic was unmistakable. Shadow.

Wolf. So many layers. Bloodlines converging. Someone had taken his lineage and bound it with a wolf Alpha.

His expression darkened. "I have never lain with a wolf." Who had done this? Who had stolen that choice from him? Ancient enemies flickered through his mind. Seelie splinter courts capable of weaving bloodline illusions. Warlock enclaves skilled in memory-forging. Druidic rites powerful enough to twist heritage itself. Someone had stolen from the Night Throne. And lived. For now.

But when he felt his daughter's power again, the rage cooled—set aside rather than extinguished. There would be time for vengeance later. For now... He looked toward the ceiling of the cavern palace, toward the source of the power. "Will you take my throne, little wolf?" he murmured. Far above, the shadows bent toward her.

Across the Unseelie dominion every creature of Umbrakyn blood felt the shift. The Princess of Night and Ruin had awakened. Another tremor rippled through the realm as the Triskillian bond pulsed again. The King smiled slowly. "Or will you simply burn the world?" The palace shuddered. The age of prophecy had begun. And suddenly, the King turned sharply.

Because one final truth struck him. There was only one man in all the realms who could have hidden something like this. Only one man cunning enough to raise the daughter of the Night Throne in secret. His hand closed around the obsidian communication orb on the arm of his throne.

The orb flared with Unseelie magic. Across the realm, in the Academy at Verdfall, another orb began to glow. The King did not hear what his friend said, rage coursing through his veins:

"Shut up, Lance."

His voice trembled with fury and something dangerously close to awe.

"I have a daughter."

And after a beat of seething silence, he added:

"You hid my daughter from me."

www.ingramcontent.com/pod-product-compliance
Lightning Source LLC
LaVergne TN
LVHW050911080826
845145LV00001B/46